SILVER LINE

Jill C. Baker

SUDBURY
Publishing
Group

Published worldwide by Sudbury Publishing Group.

Editor, Interior Design, and Production: Jonathan W. Baker
Cover Design: Jill C. Baker

ISBN 978-1-949283-02-0 (paperback)
ISBN 978-1-949283-03-7 (e-book)

Manufactured in the United States of America

10 9 8 7 6 5 4 3 2

First Edition

Acknowledgments

Many people have inspired me and encouraged me to write: parents, teachers, family, friends, colleagues, and creative collaborators. I especially thank these authors, who generously shared their personal experience, insight, and resources: Daniel Blum, Connie Johnson Hambley, Jeff Miller, Satin Russell, and Ric Wasley. I deeply appreciate the enthusiasm, vigilance, and constructive feedback offered by my *Silver Line* beta readers, Dagny Goldberg Baker, Gail Gamble, and Cimarron Buser. To my husband, Jon, I say thank you for giving me the time and space to write, for tolerating my endless musings, and for providing professional expertise in making my content presentable. Lastly, I am sincerely indebted to Michael Gordon for his friendship, representation, guidance, and industry connections. For *Silver Line* especially, I want to give a nod to our National Park Service and the dedicated rangers, who preserve and recount our history, to the generous campground owners in Flagstaff, AZ, who, ages ago, loaned us their car when ours broke down and to Cruise America, which allowed us to retrace our original cross-country journey many years later, from the comforts of an RV.

"To see a world in a grain of sand...
and eternity in an hour..."

– William Blake

1
TRAILS

"Let me be perfectly clear. I was never a soiled dove, a lady of the night. I was a dance hall girl, an entertainer—there's a distinction. I didn't work on the line but drew the line when it came to favoring men. I came to the town of Buckskin Joe in 1861 to use my God-given talents of song and dance, not to be mistaken for some rouge-cheeked painted cat. That error in perception still galls me.

Sure, I hung around saloons—something a respectable, East-Coast woman might not do—but I was a 'good girl' by Western standards and was treated as such by patrons.

Those who didn't know me might confuse my flirtatious nature and flashy shoes with offering something else, but I can assure you, a dance with me required hands where I could see them. On a good night at Bill Buck's dance hall, I'd twirl the floor with 50 gents, pulling in as much as a dollar a turn. But they were customers, nothing more. And thanks to them, I made a damn good living. Better than some of the sporting women down the street.

I was never one of those scarlet women who would bosom-up to the first cowboy who came to town. That's not to say I didn't have a few special beaus in my life, but only one man holds my heart.

I had a soft spot for miners. They were industrious, dedicated, and patient. Maybe that's because they spent long hours working in the dark. But rest assured, they knew how to have a good time. A couple placer nuggets or a find in the Phillips lode would mean drinks all around.

I do have a story to tell about life and death and doing what's right, but I'm not quite ready to commit it to paper. It seems that my friends and neighbors have woven a tale that's far more intriguing and I'm inclined to let it be. See, I was just living my life when two sheepherders from the San Luis Valley brought smallpox into town. I did what any good-hearted woman would do. I had to do it, because most everyone else left.

So, I'm going to think some more about rectifying my story. Right now, I'd rather contemplate the mountain outside my window. The evening air is filled with sagebrush and pine, and the aspens are setting up a rustle that starts at their core and travels up their branches into a splendid frenzy. Really, what more could a woman want?"

✦✦✦

Jared Sutherland had never heard the legend of Silver Heels, nor did he—or most people for that matter—know of the diary that lay hidden in a small metal box in a quiet corner of Colorado. All Jared knew was that he was 18 years old and this was his last hurrah before starting college. Armed with a backpack and camping gear, he had flown cross-country to meet his friends at a trailhead near Scott Gulch.

Seven years had lapsed since his family moved from New England to D.C., following what could only be described as his mother's weird encounter with a presence from the past—a Revolutionary War agitator, who had previously posed as a Tory. Despite the dramatic upheaval in her life, she had parlayed her unique abilities into a job with the FBI. At the same time, his father, an unassuming science teacher at the local high school, had gained prominence through an academic paper he co-authored. As a result, he found himself invited to join a prestigious think tank near the nation's capital. With the family's relocation, Jared and his younger sister, Abby, went through the painful process of evolving from new kids to cool kids.

Abby, now 16 years-old, had no trouble being accepted. She was funny, outgoing and precocious. It didn't hurt, either, that she was downright adorable. She had long, straight, strawberry-blond hair that made other girls jealous and made boys her age, want to run their fingers through it.

As for himself, Jared underestimated his appeal—partly because he was inherently shy and partly because he was selective. Sure, there was that summer fling at the shore, some stolen nights away from camp, and those angst-ridden weeks before and after the prom, but mostly he had girlfriends who were just friends and gorgeous female classmates he was too afraid to approach.

But Jared was wrong to be so modest. He was a fit, handsome young man with a shock of dark hair that fell across his brow, giving him a rock star attitude, whether he wanted it or not. He bore a striking similarity to his father in personality—artsy, cerebral and elusive, with a dry sense of humor that could be easily missed if someone were inattentive. Jared was not an easy guy to get to know without investing some time, but according to a few young ladies, who tried, he was worth the effort.

✦✦✦

Ever since Jared was 9, he knew that he was like his mother—'gifted' as they say—with talents some call 'precognitive' and others call 'extrasensory.' He had an uncanny way of anticipating events, slipping into history, and relating to his environment with a heightened awareness that others lacked. This was not something he particularly enjoyed or employed. In fact, these skills proved more of a burden than a blessing for most of his young life.

Once, when his class took a field trip to the zoo, he was overwhelmed by the experience, having become immersed in it. He found himself crouching in the tall grass of the Savannah, warned by the sibilant voice of the dry reeds, as a young lion prowled nearby on paws the size of platters. From his vantage point, he could see giraffe and zebra moving among the flat-topped acacia trees. He could hear the plaintive trumpet of elephants caught in ropes and the loud, ominous purr of a cheetah, draped in camouflage across an overhead branch. His nose was filled with the smell of dung and musk. Cowering in place, he was gripped by fear as a Cape buffalo snorted and kicked up dust just inches from his face. None of his classmates seemed to notice these things or the fact that he had separated himself from the group.

When he was 11, Jared saw a love note and flowers on the grave of Sarah Hawthorne Covington at the same time his mother stepped into this Colonial woman's shoes; but according to his father, there was no note and, certainly, no flowers—just a cemetery as stark and deserted as one would expect on a late winter's day.

Thinking it best not to muck around in the past, Jared purposely set his ability aside, repressing it and letting it lay dormant, suspecting he could summon it someday if needed. Occasionally, this skill would surface on its own accord and imbue him with insight he didn't like. He regarded this added intelligence as an unfair advantage, an edge he felt he didn't deserve—and he did his best to ignore it. Jared just wanted to be a 'regular guy,' and he worked hard at fitting in.

✦✦✦

Hundreds of trail boots—maybe thousands—had traipsed across the remains of old Hoosier Pass before continuing along Scott Creek up to the mountain that loomed ahead, so the idea of Jared doing what others had done—scouring the ground and scanning the stream for a glint of gold—was not unusual. Within the hour, Eric and Andy had arrived as planned—flying in from California and Michigan, respectively, and driving together to the site. After a few slaps on the back and "Hey, dudes," the trio eagerly began their trek.

They had barely started toward the 13,000-foot summit, when Jared noticed a shimmer in the shallow water that ran along the trail. Bending over, he extracted a small square buckle—silver, it seemed—not big enough for a belt, but maybe for a shoe. It was surprisingly shiny, and it sparkled handsomely, when held up to the light. That's when he heard the plinking sound of a piano in the recesses of his brain and the banter of barroom conversation.

"Hey, Sutherland, get moving," his buddies called, prompting Jared to pocket his find.

+++

Not far away, in Breckenridge, Alexa St. Clair was with her family on a pre-college road trip. She hadn't really wanted to go, let alone spend time with her kid brother, Will, but it was hard to resist the lure of wide-open spaces, dazzling mountains, and the promise of a horseback ride through the aspens. That evening, with sore bottoms and aching muscles, they had all eased into the warm pool at their RV campground, so when Alexa finally emerged, she was relaxed and happy.

While her parents made dinner, she and Will walked out to the tailings along the river bank. They moved slowly, hunched over, eyes to the ground, scanning the smooth stones and lumpy slag, in hopes of finding a meteorite. No luck uncovering sky rock, but Alexa found something else that was old and interesting—the rusty cup from a miner's lunch box.

As she held the cup in her hand, she wondered who might have owned it and how it came to rest on this riverbed. But hearing her mother call to say food was ready, she wedged the little cup into her backpack and joined her family.

In a matter of weeks, both she and Jared started their freshman year at the same university.

+++

College orientation was exciting and offered an opportunity for reinvention. Like the thousands of students who descended on Boston at this time of year, Jared and Alexa were consumed with academic and social activities. There were books to buy, devices to purchase, software to upgrade, parties to attend…items needed for dorms and labs…access cards and permits to acquire…and, of course, a class schedule to finalize that would allow for the most sleep possible.

Standing in line for his student ID, Jared quickly learned that unlike in high school, college kids talked to each other. They were interesting, diverse, helpful, and not afraid to be themselves. Most importantly, they were accepting. He discovered that he was surprisingly popular among his new-found friends and that gave him confidence.

Alexa lucked into some well-matched dorm mates and, shortly after settling into their rooms, a group of them headed to Harvard Square. While living in rural Pennsylvania, she had heard tales of this funky, intellectual intersection and she soon marveled at the fact that she was standing there in person. Those well-heeled preppy boys were not hard to look at and the street performers were remarkably good. She also learned that it was never too late in the day for a cup of coffee.

✦✦✦

When Jared and Alexa finally met, it was well after the semester began. As it turns out, they were in the same English class and, one day, when Jared looked around the tiered lecture hall, he couldn't help but notice the jet- haired girl in the burgundy sweater sitting a few rows below him. When she turned to talk to a friend, he caught a glimpse of her translucent complexion and instantly knew what the word 'porcelain' meant.

He'd probably claim it were an accident, but when he saw her later that day sitting on the edge of a concrete street planter, he walked unusually close and his foot caught the strap of her backpack. Out tumbled an apple, white ear buds, a couple of pens, a bottle of water, a book, and a small rusty object that took flight as it rolled down the sidewalk. "I'm so sorry," Jared said, hurrying to stop the object with his foot. "Here you go," he said, bending over and handing it to her. He thought he would drown in the depth of her dark eyes.

"No problem, thank you," she said, taking it from him. "Shouldn't have left my backpack so far out in the street. Kind of forgot this was in there."

"What is that anyway?" Jared asked, tilting his head, and peering out from under the hair that fell over his right eye.

"Oh, something I found out West—near a river," she said as she looked at him, sizing him up.

"Where out West?"

"Colorado. Breckenridge, to be exact."

"That's funny. I was just out near Alma and Fairplay."

"Small world, I guess," she said, glancing back at the smartphone in her hand.

Of course, Jared should have taken this move as a cue to end the conversation, but something prompted him to continue. He reached into the planter and picked a marigold, presenting it to her with a flourish. "For you, m'lady," he postured. She couldn't help but smile as she glanced up again.

"Want to talk some more where it's quiet?" he asked, nodding at the steady stream of cars moving along Comm Ave.

"Sure. But I just want you to know up front that I'm not looking to get involved in anything. No time for a relationship right now," she said, making her intentions perfectly clear. He liked her honesty.

"No problem, me neither," Jared confirmed. "Just trying to meet a few people."

They swapped phones and typed their respective information into Contacts before handing back the devices.

"I'll text you later," Jared said, as he headed to his next class. "I'm Jared Sutherland, by the way," he called over his shoulder.

"Alexa St. Clair," she called back, watching him disappear into the sidewalk crowd.

✦✦✦

Several days went by—Jared didn't want to appear too eager—but on Saturday he sent Alexa a message. "Want to meet up for coffee?"

"Sure, when?" she texted back.

"About an hour?" They decided on a hangout mid-campus as she lived on the west side and he, on the east.

Jared spotted her easily—her hair shone like a crow's wing in the morning light—and he quickly ushered her in toward a table. Jared had never been much of a coffee drinker, but after working as a summer intern at a newspaper company, he learned that caffeine was a way of life. He and Alexa placed their orders, welcoming the cozy setting and aroma that enveloped them.

"So, you never told me what that rusty thing was," Jared reminded her as they waited to be served.

"It's the top of an old miner's lunch box that doubled as a cup," Alexa said, reaching into her backpack and setting the tin cylinder on the table.

"That's cool," Jared commented. "A flash from the past."

"Yeah, it was really interesting out there. Lots of history," Alexa acknowledged, trying to read his face.

"I found something, too," Jared said, pushing his hand into his pocket. He pulled out the buckle and held it up.

Alexa leaned in. "I can't see it from here," she said, squinting at the delicate object. He pressed it into her palm and immediately felt a jolt.

"Pretty," she said. "Where do you think it came from?"

"Maybe a clothing store or one of those old theaters? Looks fancy, like it was part of a costume."

She dropped the small buckle into the cup and that's when it happened.

✦✦✦

Jared found himself leaning on the polished bar of an 1860s saloon waiting for the show to begin. He was 10 years older, about 28, and possessed what some would call 'smoldering good looks.

"Hey, Red, don't hog all the space. We can't see back here," one of his buddies ribbed.

Red turned around and raised his glass in recognition. He was wearing a faded blue plaid shirt and San Francisco denim pants that hung low on his hips. His boots were dusty, his belt wide, and his face showed a couple days' growth. His fingers were long and his hands, strong, accented by veins that ran up his forearms to where his shirt cuffs rolled back. His hair resembled the charcoal left by campfires. Despite hours of time spent underground, his skin was tight and tanned, giving him a healthy, rugged appearance.

"Hold your horses," Red replied, stepping back to join his friends. They called him 'Red' not for red hair—but for the red Lisk lunch pail he carried to work at the Phillips mine. Some, however, could swear the nickname came from the way he blushed around women. "So, who do you think she is?" he asked, looking at the lady at the side of the stage. He sat down with the men at the table, his dark eyes hinting at mischief.

"No idea," one of them said. "All I know is that she came in on the stage from Denver decked out in a long black dress and veil."

Another man whistled. "I like the way she walks," he added, swallowing his beer as he watched her pace along the sidelines.

"We could sure use a looker around here," a third fellow commented.

Just then, two shots rang out and ricocheted off the ceiling. Bill Buck stepped up on a chair as the area around him cleared.

Bill was a squat, burly sort of man, proprietor of the dance hall and accompanying saloon. He had a full peppered beard, an unruly moustache that wreaked havoc under a small upturned nose, and a gravelly voice that made him sound tougher than he really was. His piercing blue eyes could spot BS a mile away, and he'd have none of it. He adjusted his string tie—a bolo threaded through a ring of silver—and cleared his throat.

"Gentlemen, friends, neighbors. Now is the moment you've been waiting for. The fair lady who came to our humble town to delight us with song and dance is about to be revealed." He turned toward the stage.

A dance hall girl about Red's age stepped out into the center. She was wearing a long burgundy gown slit up the side, her dark hair swept up by a sterling barrette. On her feet were silvery satin pumps with low heels—and at the arches, small square buckles that sparkled in the glow of the kerosene lamps. A hush fell over the room as the men audibly gasped. There stood a petite woman of perfect proportion with a face that rivaled a classic painting.

"Hey, Silver Heels," one of the men shouted out, christening her with a name that would last forever. Despite her calm demeanor, her heart was pounding.

"Lydia? Are you, all right?" her friend, Sadie, whispered from the sidelines.

Silver Heels nodded yes, took a deep breath, and moved forward. "Welcome, gentlemen, to the best dance hall in the West," she purred, offering a smile that could melt ice. Hoots and hollers rose around the room.

Red stood up, fixed on the vision that greeted him. He thought she may have noticed him, because her gaze seemed to stop where he was anchored. That's when the smile that played around her lips moved up into her dark eyes.

"Don't let me interrupt you, fellas," she teased, knowing full well that she had revved their testosterone into high gear. "Let's do a little song first, and then we'll dance," she promised, moving to expose the ruffles halfway up her thigh. Cat calls and cheers followed. She cued the piano player—Lou—and began to sing.

✦✦✦

Her performance was disrupted by a modern voice and the din of a busy café. "Here you go guys. One French Roast and one Chai Latte." Jared and Alexa snapped to attention.

"Sorry, Lexa, I seemed to have zoned out. Something really weird just happened," Jared started to explain, holding his temples. He didn't want to reveal his ability to 'travel' so early in their acquaintance and he wasn't sure this sensation was the same thing. "I just got an incredibly vivid image of being in a bar in an old Western town. What were you saying?" Jared asked, trying to regain his composure.

"That's crazy. Me, too. It seems like I just zoomed back in time, but forward in age. Does that make any sense?" Alexa replied, not expecting an answer. "I feel kind of out of it," she said, shaking her head and exhaling, hand on chest, as if to dispel the sensation.

"Hopefully your tea will help," Jared said, nodding toward the tall mug. At least he wasn't the only one experiencing this odd occurrence.

Alexa blew the foam around the top of her drink to expose the spicy liquid. "Ahh, much better," she said after taking a sip. The warmth felt good on this cool autumn day. "I wonder what that was."

Jared noticed that she ran her tongue across her upper lip to remove the tell-tale signs of froth and thought how nice it would be to do that for her. "I have no idea, but my head is spinning," he admitted, reaching for a small chrome pitcher of milk.

"Maybe we walked through a cloud of weed or something," she joked as she sipped her tea. That broke the ice. Slowly their stilted conversation evolved into a relaxed exchange. They talked about summer jobs, family, school, music and movies, ending with a "See you in English."

✦✦✦

Jared did see Alexa at the end of English class the following week, but she was engrossed talking with the professor. She looked visibly distraught, using both hands for emphasis. Jared waited in hopes of intercepting her. "Hey, Lexa, are you OK? Looks like you were in a pretty deep discussion."

"I'm bummed, that's all. I got a B on my first paper, because of some stupid phrases in it. Thing is, I don't even use those words." She held up the paper for him to see.

Jared glanced at the page and noticed comments in the margins. "Too colloquial." "Slang." "Regional."

Jared looked more closely. The first sentence referred to a wine imbibing character being "as full as a tick." When the character survived a duel, she wrote that he was "still above snakes." And at the conclusion, upon the dude's death, Alexa had him heading off to the "bone orchard".

"Sounds like a great film title," Jared said, pointing to the last line, trying to make her feel better.

"Yeah, it does," she admitted, giving him a weak smile as she slipped the paper into her backpack. "But I have no idea where those words came from. I don't really talk like that. Guess I'll have to edit more closely next time." They waved good-bye and went their separate ways.

+++

A few days later, Jared turned to his roommate and complained, "This coffee is strong enough to float a colt."

"That's a good one," Doug laughed. "You a cowboy?"

Jared shrugged. "I don't think so." Those words were unfamiliar.

Armed with his backpack, Jared headed toward Bay State Road for a scenic walk to the main campus. Sunlit brownstones stood in a pristine row just as they had done for a hundred years. Hydrangea bushes, morphing from summer white to late season pink, were crammed into small gardens pressed behind wrought iron railings. A trim woman in fluorescent green yoga pants ran by with her dog in tow. In the shadows, he could see another woman, too—a figure dressed in a high-necked, cream-colored Victorian gown, standing on the stoop, sipping tea.

"Hey, Jared, wait up!" he heard as Alexa slammed into him from behind.

"What are you doing way over here?" he asked, slowing so she could fall in step.

"Errand in Kenmore Square," she said, holding up the tablet she had purchased.

"Looks like a good size," he commented as they walked together. "I'm going to the library to force myself to study. What are you up to?"

"I'm headed that way, too. Need to listen to some stuff for Music Comp."

"Want to catch a bite afterward?" Jared asked. "Around noon. My treat. Meet at the entrance?"

"Now that's an offer I can't refuse," Alexa answered, giving him a thumbs-up and taking off in a sprint down the street.

When Jared got to the library, Alexa was nowhere to be seen, but they later met up as planned and went to a convenient cafeteria. The place reminded Jared of going to the lake with his parents, where food was prepared in great quantities and laid out in a central dining hall under a high, beamed ceiling. He made a beeline for the salad bar and loaded his plate with greenery and protein. He balanced that off with a large chocolate-chip cookie and a bottle of lemonade. Alexa chose a tuna sandwich, fruit, and iced tea. They found an out-of-the-way table and picked up their conversation.

"You know those weird phrases in your paper?" Jared mentioned.

"Don't remind me," Alexa groaned.

"Well, I said something this morning that was pretty bizarre, too."

"What did you say?" Alexa asked, mouth full, looking up from her sandwich.

"I said 'this coffee is strong enough to float a colt.'"

Alexa burst out laughing. "Sounds like you just came in off the prairie."

Jared chuckled and shook his head. "Crazy thing is—I don't talk like that either."

"Wonder if it's because we were both out west," Alexa suggested. "Maybe we subliminally picked up some slang."

"Old-fashioned slang, I'd say." Jared paused to chew. "And speaking of old," he continued, "do you still have that old cup with you?"

Alexa reached into her backpack and extracted the low rusty cylinder. "Here you go," she said, setting it into Jared's hand. He immediately smelled a whiff of gun smoke.

"Do you smell that?" he asked Alexa.

"You mean those French fries?" she asked.

"No, something smokier."

"Not really," she said, sniffing. "Now let me see your treasure again, if you still have it."

"It's right here. I'm keeping it as a lucky charm."

Jared reached into his pocket and retrieved the little square buckle, plopping it into her palm. Alexa examined it and felt her pulse quicken. "Whew, is it warm in here or is it me?"

Jared reached over to feel her forehead. He liked the touch of her skin. "Must be you. Do you have a fever?"

"I don't think so," Alexa said, patting her own cheeks. She had enjoyed the gentleness coolness of his hand on her brow.

"You do look a little flushed," Jared said, as he speared a piece of grilled chicken and dipped it into salad dressing. "Drink some fluid," he suggested, pointing to her iced tea.

Sarah put the buckle into the miner's cup and picked up her drink. Without missing a beat, she and Jared were in the town of Buckskin Joe, Colorado, 1861, in its Gold Rush heyday.

+++

"Lydia, you've been out on the floor all night. Take a breather." She looked up into the weathered face and clear eyes of Bill Buck, her boss and dance hall owner. "You've already brought in a payload of money. Want another tea?"

Lydia shook her head. "No thanks. I've had a gallon already."

Bill Buck knew that his patrons liked buying drinks for the new dance hall girl, but he purposely substituted tea for liquor when he served her. That kept her steady on her feet and made him a tidy profit.

"I'm stepping out for some air," Lydia said, dabbing the perspiration from her décolletage and tucking a lace hanky into the space between her breasts.

"Oh, what lovely mounds," Bill Buck sighed to himself as his eyes followed her hand—but he simply nodded to acknowledge.

The evening brought with it a coolness that replaced the dry heat of the day. Lydia leaned against the dance hall wall and let the air wash over her. "Evening, ma'am," several men said, tipping their hats as they walked by her. "Nice night out," a few others mumbled as they stole a look at her pretty face.

Red stood at the other side of the building behind a split rail fence where patrons tied their horses. He was gazing up at the sky, his lean form silhouetted in the yellow window light. He had the heel of one boot hooked on the crossbar, hands in his pockets. He wore a flat felt cap as most miners did—gray or tan, hard to tell—and a loose-fitting striped shirt over Henley-necked underwear that peeked out where the collar opened. Cloth suspenders held up his flap-front canvas pants, crudely reinforced with burlap patches at the knees. Lydia couldn't help but admire his broad shoulders, slim hips, and long legs. His dark hair, despite his otherwise dusty look, was appealingly clean. Mostly, she liked the way he seemed comfortable in his own skin.

"Guess you don't get to see much of that," she said, nodding toward the moon as she approached the attractive man.

He turned his head quickly as if interrupted from deep thoughts, retracted his heel to stand and touched the brim of his hat. "No, ma'am. Get to see a lot of rock, though," he said, smiling.

"Be still my heart," Lydia thought as she reacted to his wide grin. "That man is a thoroughbred." She moved closer and noticed that her head barely reached his shoulders.

"Red Suter," he said, extending his hand to introduce himself. "Jim, actually, but they call me 'Red'."

"Lydia Calhoon," she said, offering her hand. "Nice to meet you."

"I liked your song," the man said, scuffing the toe of his boot in the dirt. Conversation was not his strong suit.

"Glad you enjoyed it," she smiled. "One of my favorites, too."

"Where did you learn to sing like that?" Red asked, trying to extend the conversation.

"From my mother," Lydia said. He noticed a bit of sadness flit across her face. "She used to sing all the time, when we lived in Missouri."

"Where in Missouri?" was all he could think to say.

"Outside Independence. We had a dairy farm there," Lydia answered, recalling the many hours she had spent milking.

"Are you all booked up for dancin' tonight?" Red asked, mustering the courage he didn't think he had.

"Not quite," she said, adjusting the ribbon and cameo at her throat. "I'll save the last dance for you." Lydia winked as she turned to leave. A slight breeze followed her. Red had never smelled anything so good.

As the night wore on, Red waited patiently, watching man after man steer Silver Heels around the room. Her lilting laughter rose above the smoky haze and dispersed into the heavy air, teasing each patron with an alternative to the scrappy life they knew. Her dazzling shoes left a trail of stardust, so it seemed, on the wooden floor, evaporating when each number ended. Finally, the piano player announced the last tune. She motioned Red forward. He slipped his arms around her tiny waist and pulled her toward him. He was sure she let out a little gasp.

Red could feel the warmth of her body as they moved to the music. A tendril of her hair brushed against his face. She followed easily, appreciating the strength in his arms and sureness of step as he guided her across the floor. This was one dance neither of them wanted to end.

✦✦✦

"Mind if I borrow this chair?" a young voice interrupted, jarring Jared and Alexa out of their reverie.

"Sure, take it," Jared offered, pushing the chair toward the fellow student.

"We're not using it," Alexa added, wanting to seem attentive. She and Jared looked at each other in a peculiar way.

"It happened again, didn't it?" Jared tentatively asked. "That zoning out?"

"Yup. I wonder what's going on. I've never experienced anything like this before," she said. "The person I saw looked a lot like you, but older."

"That's funny. The person I saw could have been you 160 years ago, but 10 years later." Neither admitted the attraction.

"This would be creepy if it weren't so cool," Alexa said, her eyes dancing at the delight of adventure.

"I know. It's weird but fun. Wonder how it happens."

"And why," Alexa added, arching her eyebrows.

"We'll have to pay more attention next time," Jared said, hoping there would be a next time. They continued to make small talk, simply enjoying each other's company.

"Well, I've gotta go," Alexa announced once her sandwich had been reduced to crumbs. She stood up and put on her backpack.

"Want a piece for the road?" Jared asked, breaking his cookie in two.

"Thanks. You're sweet," Alexa said. Jared didn't need to hear anything else. That comment had made his day.

✦✦✦

Later that week, somewhere near midnight, Jared sat hunched over his desk trying to focus on homework. As his fingers subconsciously ran around the edges of the buckle in his pocket, he thought about the alluring woman in the dance hall and wanted to see her again. He wasn't sure what it all meant, but he knew it had something to do with Alexa.

✦✦✦

"Hey, Lexa, you there?" he texted, hoping she had not gone to sleep.

"Yeah, unfortunately. Still working on a paper. Why u up?"

"Studying for an exam. Besides, can't sleep."

"???"

"Keep thinking about the Wild West," he wrote and added a horse emoji.

"Me, too. Wanna go back?"

"You bet. After class tomorrow?"

"I'm done at 3," she wrote.

"I'm done at 2. I'll wait for you in front of the chapel." They signed off with some zzzzzz's and eventually called it a night.

✦✦✦

Friday was a beautiful day, unseasonably warm and filled with autumn color. They found a place by the river where they could watch the rowing team's practice. Jared and Alexa sat in silence, hypnotized by the oars that rhythmically sliced the water, propelling the slim craft forward and rippling the reflection of orange trees that floated in it.

"Clearly, we've got something going on here," Jared finally said. Not wanting to imply a relationship, he clarified: "I mean, between the buckle and the cup. It seems that alone, neither one is very special, but together—Boom!"

"Yeah, I tried holding the cup in my hand and thinking back to that fellow I saw—but nothing happened," Alexa admitted.

"For me either. I tried conjuring up the woman I met there, but no luck."

"So, do you want to try this again?" Alexa asked.

"Got nothin' to lose."

"As long as we can come back," she half-joked.

Jared thought for a moment. He hadn't really considered that. "Maybe we should set our phone alarms just in case. Say, in a couple hours?" he suggested as he reached for his device. Alexa did the same.

"Ready?" Jared asked, pulling the buckle from his pocket.

"Ready," Alexa confirmed, setting the cup on her thigh.

Jared gently placed the buckle into the cup and they both reeled back. This time, their transition was immediate.

✦✦✦

It was a mid-summer's night in Buckskin Joe —seasons here seemed to run three months earlier than in present time—and Red was coming off his late shift at the mine when he heard a commotion up ahead.

"Leave me alone," Lydia shouted, pushing the unshaven cattle drover back, trying to twist away from his grip. "All I do is dance," she said, giving the grizzly man an icy stare.

"Well, I had something else in mind, pretty lady," the man slobbered, pawing at her with the hand that didn't hold a whiskey bottle. His pants were baggy and stained; his shirt, ripe with sweat. Lydia tried to call Bill Buck for help, but he couldn't hear her.

"Get away from me," Lydia yelled. "You're not my type." She kicked his shin, but her foot hardly made a dent through his thick leather boots.

"I've got something in my pocket that says otherwise," the man insisted, lewdly adjusting himself.

"I don't want what's in your pocket," Lydia snarled, struggling to wrench her arm away. She felt the barrel of a Colt press against her side.

"You're coming with me," the man insisted as he pushed Lydia ahead of him out into the street.

"Where are you taking me?" Lydia demanded, trashing, hoping a passerby would come to her rescue.

"Someplace quiet and romantic." He laughed at his own sarcasm.

Fear was racing through Lydia's mind as she stumbled across the dirt road. She thought of the blade hidden in her garter but knew she couldn't reach it. Besides, this man was twice her size and probably five times as strong.

As she dragged her feet in the dust, her shoes left two thin lines—a trail that could have been mistaken for the hoofprints of deer. "Keep moving, or I'll do you right here," he growled. Lydia tried to stall. She could see the mine on Buckskin Creek looming ahead and noticed the circle of the arrastra in the moonlight. She knew that was the place where they crushed ore but had never really paid attention to it.

"In there!" the man commanded, forcing her into the ring of stones. "On the ground," he ordered. She knelt on the hard-packed soil near the flat grinding surface at the center. Looking up, she could see a large stone suspended from a pole that reached across the diameter. This stone was typically lowered, and the bar rotated by a horse or mule hitched to the beam. The results were extremely effective in pulverizing the ore-laden rock. It would be equally effective in crushing her bones.

"Please don't hurt me," she begged, scared of what was to come. "There are plenty of girls who do this sort of thing."

"But they're not you," the man retorted. "You're pretty." She could smell his foul breath and hear the buckle of his belt unhook.

Lydia cowered under the pole that was positioned above her head. She tried to bargain. "Leave me alone now and I'll be extra nice to you at the dance hall." The man stepped in front of the pole and swayed over her. Suddenly, there was a thwack as the massive beam moved and slammed into the back of his head. The man fell forward, and Lydia rolled away.

"Not so fast," Lydia heard a familiar voice say as a fist connected with the man's face. More punches followed.

As the man laid there groaning, a lean figure in a faded blue shirt and suspenders stepped out of the shadows. "Red!" Lydia cried, standing up and brushing herself off.

"You OK, ma'am?" Red asked, sweeping a shock of hair out of his eyes as he picked up his cap. She thought her hero was dashing and nodded yes as he helped her up. "I'll walk you back," Red offered.

"How did you find me? Why are you even here? Don't you need a mule to run one of these things?" Her questions spilled out.

"Heard the scuffle. Night shift at the mine. And no, you can move it by hand," Red said, not wasting words.

Lydia leaned on his arm, trying to steady herself. "Thank you so much," she said, straightening her ruffled skirt and centering the cameo at her throat. She studied his profile and admired his jaw, clean and strong, not obscured by a beard like the ones so many miners wore. He looked straight ahead as they walked, resisting the urge to put his arm around her shoulder.

When they got back to the dance hall, Lydia motioned him closer. He thought she was going to whisper something, but instead, she planted a kiss on his cheek. Soft as velvet. Lucky for Red, no one was around to see him blush. He tipped his cap and watched Lydia disappear through the batwing doors.

✦✦✦

Suddenly, the chapel bells chimed, and Jared and Alexa bolted back to reality. Jared was afraid he was still flushed.

"I wonder if we're having the same experience," he said, looking at Alexa who seemed visibly shaken.

"I was attacked," Alexa continued, shutting off the alarm on her phone, face solemn.

"I rescued someone who was attacked," Jared said, disabling his alarm as well.

"My rescuer was ruggedly handsome," Alexa noted, angling her head to look at Jared in the late day light.

"Guess that leaves me out!" he joked, then added, "The woman I rescued was quite beautiful."

Alexa looked down, not comfortable with the compliment. She put away the tin cup and Jared pocketed the buckle.

"Crazy stuff," he said as they stared across the water watching the Cambridge skyline change in the fading light. "Like virtual reality without the head gear."

Alexa smiled although she was still rattled. "It's been an interesting afternoon, but I should get back."

"Me, too," Jared said. "A bunch of us are going clubbing tonight." He stood up and stretched his lean form.

"Don't run off with any dance hall girls," Alexa teased, resisting the urge to hug him. Jared grinned. Now he knew for certain they were having the same dream—or whatever it was.

That night slightly after 1 a.m., Alexa's phone vibrated. She could hear it hitting the hard surface of her bedside table. "Hello," she said when she saw Jared's number. She had just fallen asleep. Groggy, she mumbled, "A little late, isn't it?"

"I didn't know who to call. I'm in pretty tough shape," a raspy voice at the other end said.

"Jared? Is this really you or does someone have your phone?"

"It's me, I promise."

"Give me a clue," Alexa insisted. She had grown suspicious after reading an article about phone scams.

"The buckle and the cup," Jared said, figuring they were the only two who knew about the random objects.

"OK. What happened? Too much to drink?" Alexa sassed.

"No. I got beat up—but I'm not sure why."

"Where are you?"

"They left me at the T station in Kenmore Square."

"Who's they?"

"Two guys. I didn't see them. Sorry, I can't really think straight."

"Stay there. I'm coming to you."

Alexa grabbed her pocketbook and caught a late-night trolley from the west side of campus. When she got out, she saw Jared sitting on a bench, legs spread, elbows on his thighs, head lowered into his hands. There were droplets of blood on the cement below.

He looked up at her, attempting to focus. She could see bruises swelling up around his head and jaw. His nose was puffy and bloodied. His bottom lip, split.

"Oh, my God!" she said, rushing over to him. "What on earth happened?"

"I have no idea. I was with my buddies and stepped away to use the men's room. Then two guys jumped me and started beating me up. I told them I thought they had the wrong person, but they kept saying, 'You're that kid. Stop poking around.'"

"Poking around what?" Alexa asked.

Jared shook his head. "Don't know. I pretty much keep to myself."

"Can you stand?" Alexa asked, putting her arm around Jared's torso to support his weight. He grimaced as they made their way to the outbound platform. Once on the T, he slumped against her shoulder.

"Are you sure you didn't tangle with anyone? Bump someone carrying a beer?" she asked.

"Nope. The club wasn't even crowded, and I've had my nose to the grindstone all week," Jared said as he touched his misshapen face. He added in an attempt at humor: "Or what's left of it."

"Maybe you should see a doctor," Alexa suggested, as they got off the trolley and hobbled to her dorm lobby.

"I just want to sit for a while. Could really use some water, though." Alexa went to a vending machine and returned with a cold bottle. Jared laid it across his forehead before twisting off the cap and gulping down the contents. "Ahh, that's better," he exhaled, his voice nearly restored.

"Did your friends just leave you there?" Alexa asked, appalled at the idea.

"No, no. It was cool. They had just hooked up, so I told them to go ahead. Said I would hang out a while longer." Jared shivered.

"I'll go up and get a blanket. Be right back," she said. Jared nodded in appreciation, trying not to groan as he shifted his position. When Alexa returned with the fleece throw, Jared was lolled back, half asleep.

"I don't think you're supposed to sleep after a head injury," Alexa said, putting the blanket around his shoulders and shaking him awake. "Let's just sit and talk. Then we can decide if you should go to the infirmary."

"I don't want to go anywhere," Jared said, showing the signs of exhaustion. "So, sure, let's talk."

Alexa attempted to make conversation, trying to keep him awake. "So, what was it like interning this summer?" she asked, hoping to get Jared's mind off the assault.

"Did a bunch of research for a reporter. And a lot of grunt work," Jared said. He attempted to smile, but he was quickly reminded of his split lip. His hand went to his mouth.

"So not much glory, eh?"

"Well, I did get credit in the paper."

"That's cool. You want to be a journalist, right?" she asked.

"Hope so. I love the investigative stuff, and I have a great assignment for class," he volunteered. His color was returning, and he was sitting upright. "We have to find a news story—ideally one that's ongoing—and tell it from a different angle. Need to identify details that could be turned into leads. Extra credit if we do the legwork."

Alexa listened as she searched "Head Injuries" on her smartphone. "So, what did you pick?" she asked, looking up from the device.

"The Gardner Museum heist," Jared answered. "It's what I researched last summer. Took place in 1990. Thirteen pieces of art worth $500 million were stolen and never recovered."

"I heard about that," Alexa said.

"The robbers were disguised as cops and they lured the guard away from the alarm station," Jared explained, wincing as he moved. He seemed eager to talk now and was energized by it, so Alexa didn't interrupt. "The story surfaces every year around St. Patty's Day to commemorate the anniversary. I've always been fascinated by it. Read just about everything Kurkjian has written for the *Globe*, but I want to know more."

"Who's that and like what?" Alexa prompted, wanting to make sure he was coherent.

"He's an authority on the heist. Been covering it from the start."

"But there's still more to learn?" Alexa asked.

"A lot. Like, why did the regular guard call in sick? What happened to the red hatchback the burglars supposedly drove? Who is the man in the AP video that turned up 25 years later? And of course, where are the paintings and that rare Chinese vase?"

"Really does sound like an unsolved mystery," she remarked, happy to see Jared more alert.

"It is. And I want to solve it. Not to catch the crooks but to find the artwork. Supposedly, the FBI knows who took it—mob connections they say—and in 2016, for a third time, they raided the same house in Connecticut, but nothing turned up. The paintings are too hot to sell: Rembrandt, Vermeer, Degas…so there's still a $5 million reward for the recovery."

"Now that would pay for tuition!" Alexa joked. She let her hand rest on Jared's forearm.

"If you go to the museum website, you'll see they're still asking for tips. I sent their Security Director an email to see if I could get a comment for my assignment, but I haven't heard back yet. I did swing by the building the other day to look around, hoping for an inspiration. Even with a virtual exhibit, it's sad to see the empty spaces on the walls."

Alexa sat up straight. "Maybe that has something to do with the assault."

"I doubt it. I didn't talk to anyone," he said as he wrapped himself tighter in the blanket, although her comment made him wonder if someone had been watching him. He had certainly been visible when researching the story before. Maybe someone recognized him. Maybe someone wanted to stop him. That had never really crossed his mind. Eventually, he closed his eyes and Alexa dozed off on his shoulder.

When she awoke, Jared was still asleep next to her. "Hey, sleepy head," she said, gently jostling him.

"What? Who?" Jared started to say as he opened his eyes. He quickly realized the lights were too bright and the sounds, too loud. He held his head, squinted at her, and then looked at his surroundings, trying to process how he got there.

"Coffee?" Alexa suggested as she stood up, folding the blanket. "There's some in the caf," she said, motioning toward the dining hall. Jared wobbled to his feet and shuffled to the men's room. She, to the ladies' room. Still bleary-eyed, they walked into the cafeteria together, savoring the smell of toast and eggs that greeted them. They were ravenous.

"You look at lot better than you did last night," Alexa said, glancing up from her tray.

"Only thing is, I feel like my head is in a vice," he said, cupping his forehead.

"I'll walk back to your dorm with you," Alexa offered, inviting herself to join.

"If you want," Jared said. He was too tired to protest.

"You wait here. I just want to freshen up first," Alexa said as she cleared away their trays. Jared nodded as he watched Alexa pick up the blanket and exit into the corridor. He wondered how she could possibly look so good with so little sleep.

"Hey, dude. What happened to you?" he heard a familiar voice say. He looked up to see Eric, one of the friends, who had hiked with him that summer.

"Walked into a wall," Jared mumbled, not sure he really wanted to talk about it.

"Some wall, I'd say. Did you break it?" Eric jabbed.

"No. Man. It was more like two guys came out of nowhere and tried to break me."

"What did they want?"

"Close as I can figure, they want me to keep quiet. I just don't know about what."

"You got me there."

"I'm beginning to think it has to do with the story I investigated this past summer...the museum heist."

"I remember that one. But why now?"

"Not sure...though I am researching it again for an assignment." They talked a bit more about classes and reminisced about the summer.

Just then Alexa appeared in a clean change of clothes. She smelled of soap, and her hair was wet. "I'm ready if you are," she said and then she noticed Eric sitting there.

Jared made introductions after which Eric indicated he had to go. "Take good care of him," Eric called as he left the duo standing in the cafeteria. Alexa and Jared cautiously stepped onto the sidewalk for a slow stroll across campus. Anyone who didn't know them would assume they were a couple. This time Alexa waited in the lounge as Jared went up to his floor to shower. The hot water felt good on his sore muscles and the steam cleared his head, but after checking his bruises in the mirror, he knew that shaving was out of the question. His lip looked awful, but at least he still had his teeth.

When Jared returned, Alexa was surprised how well he had cleaned up. Given a few more years, he just might be as handsome as that man in the saloon. Without saying a word, she reached into her backpack and took out the rusty cup, setting it on the glass top of a low table in front of her. She and Jared programmed their phone alarms for two hours ahead, after which he ceremoniously produced the silver buckle. He placed the shiny rectangle into the miner's cup and sat back.

✦✦✦

In an instant, they were in Colorado on a late summer's day, walking through an aspen grove out to a clearing that offered a dramatic view of the mountains and dry landscape. Their horses, tied to two young trees, nickered from a distance. "Watch the gravel," Red said, taking Lydia's arm as they maneuvered down a slope. They both had the day off and were bent on enjoying it. "See that arroyo over there?" he asked, pointing to a narrow gulley that cut through the rocks and into the hills. Lydia peered out from beneath her small-brimmed bonnet, untied at the chin to stay cool. She looked past the yucca spikes that poked into the sky where the day's heat was already rising, creating the illusion of waves above the flat stone surfaces.

"It's down there. Or shall I say, up there. That's where I staked a claim when I was a kid. I registered it in my mother's maiden name, so no one knows it belongs to me."

"Is it worth anything?" Lydia asked, more interested in the man than the money.

"Not a plugged nickel as far as I can tell," Red laughed. "Guess I got fooled by some pyrite when I was too young to know better." He had an easy way about him that made her relax.

Red found a stick and began drawing a rough map in the dirt. "See, this is the spot—between two boulders. The entrance is hidden by a small shack," he said, marking an X near an outcropping of rock. As he squatted on his haunches, Lydia rested her hands on his shoulders and looked out across the horizon. She could feel the warmth of his skin beneath the fabric of his shirt and it quickened her pulse.

"What a glorious sight!" she said, soaking in the view.

Getting to his feet, Red knew this was the moment he had anticipated. He turned to face her and became lost in her dark eyes. Leaning over, he brought his lips close to hers and saw those dark eyes close behind a veil of lashes. Ah, the sweetness of that first kiss. So tentative. So pure. Lydia felt the same way. The scenery that she had just admired paled in comparison to the small, safe world created by Red's arms. She felt his strength surround her and inhaled his scent. Consumed by the experience, she didn't notice the slight breeze kicking up at her back.

"Let's go down," Red said, willing himself to step away. His lips still tingled from where they had touched hers. He took Lydia's hand and guided her sideways down the hill. Stones rolled in their path and dust was cast off by their boots as the couple made their way to the base of the arroyo. They followed the dry stream bed up into the rocks, where a long-ago river had left its mark. Now, only sagebrush and Mormon tea clung to the caked soil caught in the crevices.

Lydia noticed a green collared lizard scuttle across a rock. "Look," she said, excitedly pointing to the unexpected visitor. Red delighted at the joy she took in even the simplest things. He already knew that she awakened in him a vitality he has previously lacked.

"We're almost there," he said, steering her to an incline that led to the mine entrance. "Hop up," he said, extending his hand to help her over a small ledge. Soon they were on a landing beneath a tower of cliffs and above the arroyo, near a small cabin built into the side of the mountain.

By this time, the sky had grown dark, and they could see a bank of clouds rolling in. "Don't worry about rain," Red said, sensing her concern. "Those are a long way off." He pulled a small crowbar from his pocket and pried away the piece of wood that had been nailed across the door.

"Aren't you the prepared one," Lydia teased as she heard the slat break free.

"I try to be," Red said, flashing a smile at her. He went in first and looked around, blinking to adjust his eyes to the dim light. An old lantern, pickaxe, shovel, and rope were exactly where he had left them. A pair of work boots was tucked under a small cot, and a change of clothes hung on a hook. Just then, a gust of wind sent Lydia's hat over the ledge into a downward spiral where it snagged on a branch. She let out an "Oh dear" and inched toward it. Red stepped out of the cabin in response and watched her retrace her steps. She heard him say, "Let it be. We'll get it later." One look at the sky had told him he had underestimated the cold front that was driving rain into the hills above them.

Lydia turned to go back, but without warning, there was a streak of lightning and a clap of thunder. A surge of water came rushing down the cliffs and caught her off-guard. Wind howled like a coyote caught in a trap, and torrents of rain began to fall. Within seconds, the gorge below was seething. "Quick! Inside!" was all Lydia could hear above the roar. She knew about flash floods, but had never been caught in one, let alone anticipated the speed and power that came with it. She tried to climb up, but her boots slipped on the wet rocks. She slid backward and lost ground. Water was quickly rising and pooling around her. Her long skirts, now wet and heavy, weighted her down. She felt herself being sucked into the roiling current, away from Red's outstretched arms.

Panic set in. "I'm going to drown," was all she could think as she tried to grab onto anything within reach. Water churned around her, swallowing stones, uprooting plants and pulling debris into its path. "Red!" she screamed as a tide of silt washed over her, loosening her hold. Just as she felt herself about to go under, she was jerked above the flow by a length of rope that lassoed her torso and settled under her arms.

Holding on for dear life, she wedged herself between the rocks, propping her feet against the wall of the ravine. "Don't move," Red was calling. "Wait 'til the rain passes." Lydia clung desperately to the rope, twisting her right hand through it for a better grip. Rain continued to pummel her, and water tugged at her from below. Searing pain shot up her arm as if her tendons had been torn from the bone. Her muscles went weak and her hand released. She felt her body begin to slide, but the rope under her shoulders held her fast. Her heart was pounding, and she started to cry.

A few minutes later—though it seemed like hours—the roar subsided, and the pellets of rain turned into a steady downpour. She watched as a slow river of mud replaced the teeming rapids that had swirled in the arroyo below. When she finally looked up, she saw Red, drenched and lashed to one of the boulders, held by the rope that had previously hung in the shed. She was tethered to him. A softer rain was falling now as thunder rumbled into the distance. "I'm coming to get you," he said, loosening his ties and edging down toward her, using the rope as a guide. His years as a ranch hand were proving useful.

Lydia was too shaken to move. The sudden drop in temperature had made her cold and the pain in her forearm was excruciating. Shivering, she clung to Red as he helped her over the ledge and up to the mine entrance. His hands were raw where the rope had cut into them, and his blood left a spreading pink stain on her sleeve.

"Come inside where it's protected," he said, guiding her through the narrow doorway of the cabin. She could hear him rummage around and then saw a spark ignite the wick of a lantern. Rain pattered steadily on the roof as she tried to get her bearings. He offered her a flask of whiskey and instructed her to drink. She took a gulp and felt the welcome heat of alcohol sting her throat.

"As I said, I try to be prepared," he joked, bringing the lantern closer, attempting to create a sense of levity where none existed. He pointed her to the cot. She sat down and instinctively huddled to protect her injured arm. As her eyes adjusted to the dim light, she noticed a row of canned goods lined up on a crude shelf. There was a book wedged into a chink in the wall and a piece of flint on a small table. "Slip these on," Red said, tossing a pair of woolen long johns toward her. She looked at him, doubtful. "They're clean, just dusty," he assured.

"I don't think I can move my arm," she said, grimacing as she tried to retract it from her wet sleeve. By this time, she was trembling.

"I'll help you," Red said as he carefully undid the back of her dress and gently rolled the drenched fabric over her shoulders and down to her elbows, easing her arms out. He couldn't help but notice the lace-trimmed corset she wore and how her skin glistened where the rain had soaked through.

Lydia groaned in pain, but once her injured arm was free from the cloth, she felt better. Red braced her arm with a small board and tied it with a bandana. "That'll hold you for a while. It's probably only a strain," he consoled. For an outwardly rugged man, Red possessed an endearing quality. "Now you need to get dry," he said, picking up the long underwear again. "I know, not the prettiest thing you ever saw, but they're warm." Lydia stared at him as if he should know what she was thinking. "Oh, of course," he said, remembering his manners. "I promise I won't look." As he turned his back on her, he could only imagine what was taking place behind him. "Too bad I'm such a damned nice guy," he thought to himself, wanting nothing more than to take her then and there.

He could hear her skirts dropping to the floor, her corset being undone, and the rustle of petticoats being stripped away. He imagined boots being unlaced along the inside of her firm calves and stockings being unhooked from garters, rolled down to expose perfectly pale legs. He wondered if she wore the split drawers that women often did to accommodate bathroom needs or solid ones cinched at the waist. He toyed with the idea of whether they ended at her knees or hovered at her well-toned thighs. He could feel himself getting aroused and tried to think of other things. When he could hear nothing else, he called over his shoulder. "Are you all right?" That's when he felt her slim arms slip around his chest from behind and her body press against his back. He smiled when he saw her right forearm emerge sporting the red paisley cloth he had tied to the splint. Not quite the image of seduction he had envisioned, but, oh so nice.

"We need to get those wet clothes off you, too," Lydia said in her best flirtatious tone, quickly adding, "and I promise, I will look."

Red turned around and saw Lydia discretely holding the long johns to obscure his view. Her dark hair tumbled down behind them and concealed her breasts, but he could see the curve of her hips where the cloth didn't cover. "Well, if you insist, ma'am," he nodded as he slowly looked her up and down. She could feel her breathing catch under his gaze.

With her right hand immobilized, she used her left hand to awkwardly unbutton his shirt. His chest was smooth except for a soft tuft of hair in the middle, and she wanted to rest her head there. The wet shirt stuck to him like a second skin, rippling over his muscles, clinging to his rib cage.

Just as he had done for her, she peeled him out of the confining cloth. He used the toe of one boot to pry off the heel of the other, not wanting to bend over and risk losing sight of her. Standing close, he stepped out his trousers and skivvies, tossing them aside. His belt buckle clinked against a chair. She attempted to dry him off with the long johns, and only then did he see the all of her. In turn, she greedily devoured him with her eyes before yielding her body.

In the glow of the lantern they explored what had previously been forbidden, finally retreating to the cot and sliding under the covers. They laughed as the bed creaked with each movement, but they soon became oblivious to the sound.

This was not at all what he had planned for their first encounter. Red had envisioned a long bath in a deep tub and a canopy bed with smooth satin sheets. Nor was this what she had imagined in her perfect fantasies—a white blanket laid out in a field of flowers and an endless afternoon in which to linger—but surroundings were unimportant now that they had found each other. Lydia didn't recall exactly when the rain stopped or when she dozed off in his arms, but she remembered hearing Red say, when he thought she was fully asleep, "Thank God, I didn't lose you," at which point she knew their attraction was more than a passing fling.

+++

The sound of electronic music jarred Jared and Alexa into present time, as they reached for their phones and reclaimed their artifacts. Neither of them said a word because they were both turned on and terribly embarrassed. "I think we need to stop for a while," Alexa said, not looking Jared in the eye. He was, after all, only a casual acquaintance.

"I agree," Jared managed to say. "Not that I don't like what's happening back there, but it's going way too fast." Although he was attracted to Alexa, the last thing he wanted at this free-wheeling stage in his life was commitment. They both sat there for an awkward moment. "You don't have to stay," Jared said, eager to sort out his thoughts. "I'm fine. I'll let you know if anything turns up about the assault."

Alexa nodded, mumbled a good-bye, and hurried out the door. She was uncomfortable with this forced connection to Jared—she hadn't planned on getting involved—and she wanted nothing more to do with that rusty cup. Once she got back to her dorm, she took the small cylinder out of her backpack and shoved it behind some books on a shelf above her desk, trying to forget the power it held. During the following days, she focused on schoolwork, avoided Jared on campus, and only occasionally let herself think about the dark-haired man from long ago who had rescued her twice.

2
SEPARATION

When Alexa's mother called, the news from home was not good. Her father had had a heart attack and was in intensive care at the hospital. With little more than a change of clothes, Alexa caught the next flight to Pennsylvania. Her brother, Will, 14, was too young to drive, so she took a cab from the airport. The cost strained her already tight budget, but it saved time.

Alexa notified her professors about her family emergency, in hopes of getting an extension on her assignments. She knew she might have to drop out of class if she missed too much work. She thought of calling Jared since he had become her closest friend, but their last encounter was so awkward, she let it slide.

Jared noticed that Alexa wasn't around in the beginning of October, but he busied himself with other things. He spent increasingly long hours developing the museum story, reading police reports, requesting public information, and retracing his steps to the club where he was jumped. He got an 'A' on his paper and was asked to present it in front of the class. He did that to a receptive audience, who later surrounded him with compliments and back-slapping praise. Nothing like props from your peers to make a guy feel good.

With Alexa out of the picture, Jared concentrated on getting in shape. Each morning he'd run with his roommate, Doug. When they weren't talking about sports, music, or girls, his thoughts drifted to the dark-haired woman from the dance hall. As he replayed their intimate moments in the mining shack and he longed to go back.

While Alexa was away, her roommate, Gail, thoroughly cleaned their dorm room, discarding old magazines and recycling used water bottles. She straightened piles of books, polished furniture surfaces, and lifted their throw rug to wash the linoleum floor. She had no idea the rusty object that rolled out from under the desk was anything more than a remnant from previous occupants. "Yuk!" Gail said, as she chased after the cylinder. She tossed it into their wastebasket and threw the contents into a rolling bin tucked away at the end of the hall. Custodians removed this cart twice a week, adding its collection to the dumpster behind the building. Gail didn't know—nor would Alexa—that a homeless man picked through the trash that day, found the cup, and decided to use it for panhandling. In fact, Alexa had no idea the cup was missing until weeks later, when out of the blue, Jared texted.

+++

By this time, she was back on campus with her father resting comfortably at home. Other than receiving incompletes in a couple of projects, which she quickly finished, she was on track for the semester.

"Hey, Lexa. How you doing? Been a while," Jared texted.

"Didn't think I'd hear from you again," she replied.

"Yeah, got a little hot and heavy, didn't it?" he admitted.

"Just wasn't ready for anything that intense," Alexa replied, equally blunt.

"Me neither," he wrote, then interpreting her concern, added, "But remember, you and I never did anything."

Alexa paused not quite sure how to respond. "True, but it feels like we did."

"That's what we get for having lusty alter-egos," he typed, adding a winking icon. If nothing else, humor usually diffused tension.

Alexa smiled. Truth is, she *had* missed him. "Want to meet up?" she asked.

At this point, Jared was smiling, too, and entertaining thoughts of a playful escape. "I've got to go over to the Gardner to check on a few details. Want to meet me there?"

"Sure, but wasn't your paper due already?"

"It was. I got an 'A,' but my adviser said that if I continued to work on it, even after deadline, he'd give me extra credit and might help me get it published."

"Cool," she said, liking the idea of hanging around with a writer; it appealed to her intellect.

When they saw each other this time, they hugged as friends do. Jared thought he detected in Alexa a slight change. She seemed subdued, but not distant.

"What have you been up to?" he asked as they walked toward the Dutch Room of the museum—a second-floor sanctum encased in celery-green wallpaper and warm brown trim. Time seemed to stop here, sandwiched between the dark beamed ceiling and polished brick floor—a mosaic of small squares that reflected the natural light pouring in through tall arched windows. Candelabras glowed from atop ornate pedestals and spindly sconces protruded from the walls, creating a mellow, vintage mood that offset the subtle track lighting. The room was anchored by massive carved furniture, long draped tables, and straight-backed chairs, most in matching green and gold tones, some in a soft apricot hue. Jared and Alexa could feel the hush of history surround them as they strolled through the room, staring at dark portraits in heavy, gilt frames and gazing at the empty spaces, where priceless masterpieces had been stolen.

"My father nearly died," she said, eyes misting over as she recounted the recent events.

"I'm so sorry to hear that. Didn't realize you were away. I thought you were just mad at me," Jared said, resting his hand on her forearm in a gesture of comfort.

"I was mad at you, mostly because I was afraid of what was happening—back there, I mean—but I wouldn't have disappeared without saying anything."

Jared felt the same way. "Guess we just got ahead of ourselves," he said, pausing to look out the windows. In his mind, he saw pieces of artwork being carried off in the dark of night to a nondescript van and he heard the low voices of two men wearing masks. He made a few notes and asked Alexa to pace the distance between points. She wasn't sure what he was trying to prove, but she was happy to help.

"Since you're being so honest with me, I need to tell you something, too," Jared said, not sure how to begin. He guided her into a public seating area under a row of modern red ceiling fixtures.

"What is it?" Alexa asked, expecting some sort of confession about a true love back home.

"Well," he said, pausing to collect his thoughts. "Sometimes I see or sense things that others can't detect. I don't mean to freak you out—it's not all heebie-jeebies—but, every so often, I get a very vivid impression of a person, place, or event. It can be from the past, present, or future."

"Like being clairvoyant?"

"I wouldn't go that far. I don't usually predict things, but I seem to have inherited from my mother a heightened sense of awareness that transcends time.

"What do you mean? Like going to Buckskin Joe?" Alexa pulled back ever so slightly.

"Not exactly. It's hard to describe. I'm not always part of the story, but I feel like I'm there." Alexa stared at him, wide-eyed.

"For example, when we were in the Dutch Room, I could sense palette knives applying paint to canvas. I could smell Gouda cheese from a street vendor and hear the clop of wooden shoes. I felt warm light coming into Rembrandt's studio along the Old Rhine in Leiden. I saw windmills and fields of tulips in the distance. I even sipped from a jigger of Cognac that Dutch merchants had learned to distill."

"Wow. That's incredible!" she said in a near whisper, moving closer. "Can you do it whenever you want? Do they see you?"

"I'm not sure about either," Jared said. "Mostly I try to suppress it."

"But why?" Alexa asked. "It seems like a gift you'd want to use."

"I don't know. It almost feels like I'm cheating," Jared said. "And if I'm going to be a journalist, it might not be ethical."

"How is this any different from having an 'in' at City Hall?"

"Maybe it isn't. Maybe it's just another tool."

"I think you should be more open to it. I mean, if a guy's good at running and he becomes an Olympic sprinter, no one says anything about it. He's just using his natural talents."

Jared shrugged. "I don't know? I'll give it some thought. I just didn't want you to worry if I ever drift off a bit."

"I'm glad you told me," Alexa said, putting her hand over his. "It makes you even more interesting."

Jared felt his cheeks flush. "Not sure about that…."

"I wonder if your ability is helping us go back to Buckskin Joe together?" Alexa pondered out loud.

"I'm not sure it's transferable."

"Well, maybe your talents are letting me tag along," Alexa suggested, her face bright at the possibility. "You know, like holding open a door."

"In which case, I should be asking why? Why now? Why you and me? Why Buckskin Joe?"

"Maybe you'll discover the reason if you're more receptive."

"Could be," Jared said, but he made no promises. He was glad to have gotten this off his chest and was relieved to hear Alexa's next remark.

"Well, you can't scare me away," she said, firm in her conviction. "If anything, now I'm really intrigued."

"Intrigued enough to take a spin?" Jared asked, reaching into his pocket for the buckle.

Alexa picked up her backpack from the floor and fumbled around for the rusty cup but with no luck. "It's not here!" she exclaimed, forgetting she had taken it out.

"Did you lose it?" Jared asked, trying not to accuse, but feeling crushed.

"I remember, now," Alexa said. "I didn't want to look at that thing for a while, so I stuck it behind some books in my room. I'll bring it with me tomorrow."

"Not to worry," Jared said. "It's nice seeing you, even if we don't trip down memory lane." They took a long walk back to campus and this time their conversation was more fluid. Alexa liked the new-found complexity in his character and Jared liked her open-mindedness.

+++

The next morning Alexa texted. "It's not here! Looked everywhere." Jared responded with "???"

"Don't know what happened to it. Will ask my roommate if she's seen it."

Gail didn't return until early afternoon, but when she arrived, she said she had done some house cleaning and might have thrown it out. Not wanting to make her roommate feel bad, Alexa minimized the importance of the cup.

"It's gone, baby, gone," Alexa texted to Jared, paraphrasing the movie by the same name.

"Bummer," Jared replied as he felt for the buckle in his pocket. "Want to come over anyway? Maybe we can figure something out."

Alexa slipped into a clean pair of skinny jeans, high boots, fleece windbreak jacket, knit hat, plaid scarf and lined gloves. Boston could be cold this time of year and she knew she'd have a long walk across campus. She buzzed into Jared's dorm, swiped her student card, and went upstairs.

"Not bad for a guy's room," she thought as he opened the door. The space was relatively neat, except for a pile of printouts and articles at the foot of his desk chair. She plunked onto his bed, which bounced on the risers.

"So, lady, we're stuck in time it seems," he said, folding his arms as he leaned against his desk. His roommate, Doug, was gone, and Jared couldn't help but entertain less platonic thoughts.

"Guess so," Alexa said, getting up to leaf through a book that was near his computer. She noticed he was tossing the silver buckle from hand to hand. "I'm so sorry I lost the cup," she said, "Should have put it in a safer place."

"You didn't know," he said, letting her off the hook. "But I've been thinking...it seems that the buckle and the cup set up some sort of link between past and present...between Red and Lydia."

Alexa was surprised he had used their names.

"That is who you're seeing...err, being...right?" he asked.

Alexa shook her head yes. "Yup, you got it," she said, admitting something she hadn't quite been able to acknowledge before.

"It seems that the objects complete a circuit..." his voice trailed off. "I just wondered if you and I connected...maybe with the buckle between us...if we could replicate what the cup does."

To Alexa, this seemed logical and, certainly, holding hands was rather benign. She set the alarm on her phone and extended an upturned palm. "Give it to me."

✦✦✦

Jared placed the buckle into Alexa's hand and covered it with his. He held on tightly, as did she.

Within moments, Lydia was leaning over a bent back chair charming a customer. She stood on her tip toes, letting the ruffles of her skirt rise above the back of her knees and allowing the neckline of her gown to dip just a bit lower than it should. She giggled at the patron's attempt at humor and affectionately tousled his hair. The man reached up to pat her arm, but she graciously deflected him, wagging her finger and advising that he could touch her only if they danced. But that would cost fifty cents.

Red watched from across the room, not really liking this exchange, but realizing it was just an act. He hoped that someday he could support Lydia, so she didn't have to do this kind of work.

Red and Lydia kept their relationship quiet, aware that her being attached wouldn't be good for business. She had learned early on that a successful dance hall girl promised the allure of possession while practicing the discipline of denial. "Sexual tension" is how that might be described today, but in her world, it was just a way of life. There were only a handful of women to hundreds of men in these mining towns—towns that sprung up with the discovery of gold and vanished just as fast. "The Fifty-Niners," as they were called, were lucky to see a woman, let alone have one.

During those hot days of summer, after the dance hall had closed and his night shift ended, Red visited Lydia at her cabin which was off-limits to most. In fact, he started spending more time at her place than at his. There she would step out of her ruffles and garish gowns into a simple cotton camisole and chemise to fend off the heat. To him, she looked even better that way. The next morning, they would linger in bed, and only after an infusion of coffee and sweet rolls, would they put on clothes and walk through the quiet countryside. They'd stroll over the flats and into the foothills, holding hands, breathing in the scent of sage brush and pine as they explored the dry ground beneath their feet. They'd pick up odd-shaped stones and items dropped by those who had passed that way: a hinge, a pin, a tin box.

Without a man around the house, home repairs had been neglected until Red entered the scene. From then on, fences were built, leaks plugged, and floorboards fixed. By working at night, they had daylight hours to spare. Red hoed a garden plot, which Lydia planted with beans and potatoes. She started to pay attention to details that would make her cabin attractive. She made curtains from muslin and hung a tintype of local miners on her kitchen wall. She put wildflowers in a jar and set a sachet under her pillow. She bought fragrant soap from a traveling vendor. Red arrived like clockwork, often with household supplies or treats from the general store.

Lydia felt a sense of peacefulness and stability she had never experienced. She could count on Red to come around several times a week, so she was surprised when he didn't show up at all the third week of July. She rationalized that he, like everyone else, was busy preparing for the first territorial election in August. Daniel Witter, brother-in-law of future Vice-President Schuyler Colfax, was coming to town to campaign for a seat on the Legislature. Saloon keepers, bankers, and merchants were tidying up for the occasion. Steps were swept clean, counters polished, and horse droppings shoveled from the street. A sign was painted to mark the Dan McLaughlin stage stop that put Buckskin Joe on the map.

Lydia looked for Red in the usual places but didn't see him. Maybe he had to go into Denver, she thought, or maybe he just needed to get away. She couldn't begrudge him that—after all, she didn't own him—but something didn't feel right, and it gnawed at her throughout the day. That evening, as she stepped on stage, she was distracted with worry. She forgot a few words of a song and missed several steps of her favorite routine. Afterward, she was unusually thirsty.

Once the dance hall closed for the night, she walked out toward the mine, hoping to catch a glimpse of Red leaving work. The place was deserted, but that's when she noticed his red lunchbox sitting on a rock. He had to have been there. Lydia called his name as she walked by the arrastra where rail cars were laden with ore. "Red, you here?" she yelled across the open space. "You here?" came echoing back from the hills.

Just as she was about to leave, she heard the faint clanging of a bell. It rang seven times, then nothing. She paused to listen more closely. After seven more chimes, the night went still.

Lydia knew it wasn't a church bell—that had an entirely different sound—and this seemed far away and muffled. She thought back to the last time she had heard a bell and recalled Red using a small hand bell to demonstrate the miner's signal code: 1, 2, and 3 chimes meant 'hoist,' 'lower,' and 'men on' respectively…but 7 bells meant 'shaft accident' and that was a warning. With 7 bells, the cage or any shaft conveyance was not to be moved, because it was likely that someone was caught there.

A sense of dread spread over Lydia. She imagined Red engulfed in darkness, struggling for air, pinned by a boulder, with no food, light, or water. In her mind, she saw him injured and bleeding, with crushed ribs and a broken leg. She ran back to dance hall, frantic and breathless, and pounded on the side door. "Bill, come quick! I think Red's trapped in the mine." It seemed like ages before she saw a lantern ignite in his room. He emerged bleary-eyed. "What is it?" he asked as if he hadn't completely heard what she said.

"I think Red's hurt—in the mine. I haven't seen him for days. No one's around, but I can hear the bell."

Bill pulled loose pants over his long johns and threw on his boots. As he stepped out into the street, he called to a stranger, who was watering a horse. "Get help down to the mine."

Lydia lifted her skirts, so she could run faster, and soon, a rescue team followed. The foreman arrived carrying keys. He opened the office door and hollered into the darkness, "Anyone here?" There wasn't a sound. Several miners moved toward the main shaft using hammers to bang on the walls, hoping the noise would rally anyone below.

Just when they were about to try a different location, they heard the faint clink of a miner's pick and then 7 bells. Quickly, they bent the end of a spike, jabbed it into a beam, and set a candle into the makeshift holder. In the wan light, they could see a layer of dust that had risen from the shaft. When they held a lantern above the opening, they could discern the cage hanging askew from a broken chain. Part of the scaffolding had been ripped from the wall. They called down to say help was coming but weren't sure if their voices carried far enough.

Not knowing where Red was trapped, they tied a canteen to a length of rope and lowered it into the shaft, hoping to accomplish two things: test the drop distance and provide Red with life-saving water. Red could see the rope dangling above his head but was too weak to move. Hunger he could manage, but dehydration was something else. "Red, we're here," Lydia called from above. "Try to reach the rope."

Red attempted to stand but his legs buckled. His voice was inaudible. His head swam with hallucinations. "Red, the rope," the foreman called, knowing there was still some scaffolding intact that could support Red's weight. "We've sent down water."

"Red, please try," Lydia appealed.

The thought of water and the voice of Lydia tapped a reserve of energy Red didn't know he possessed. He forced himself to stand

and threw himself against the wall. He hooked his pick into the nearest beam and pulled himself up to the first rung of scaffolding. He did that again and again.

"Just a little more," Lydia called, trying her best to sound optimistic. "We're all here, waiting for you." The crowd at the surface cheered him on.

Eventually, Red reached for the canteen, and he gulped the water without stopping. "Thank you," he muttered in an imperceptible voice.

"Climb up, brother," someone called down.

"I'm trying, but I can't put pressure on my leg," Red said louder.

He harnessed himself with the rope and tested the rigging. "Pull me up if you can," he instructed and, moments later, squeezing alongside the dislocated cage, he was hauled to the surface. Stepping onto solid ground, he was greeted with a blast of fresh air. He filled his lungs with oxygen and shook the gravel off his back.

Two men put their weight under his arms and helped him away from the building. Once Red could stand on his own, one boot firmly planted, one touching the ground with just the toe, he looked around for Lydia. Everyone else seemed to disappear as Lydia floated forward, a statue of ethereal perfection, alabaster in the moonlight. She had become his savior, just as he had been hers.

Wanting nothing more than to kiss her and pull her close, he stood gazing at her, practicing their agreed-upon restraint. She, on the other hand, put formalities aside and ran into his arms. Realizing how this might appear to the others, she quickly hugged the rest of the men standing there, conveying a sense of joy all around. Her bond with the miners was cemented that night. Bill Buck re-opened the saloon and poured free drinks for all. This time Lydia drank heartily with the rest of them.

3
SPIRITS

Jared and Alexa were jolted back to the present when Doug entered the room.

"Oh, sorry, guys. Didn't know you had company," he said, looking at Jared. It was clear that Doug wanted to be introduced to the pretty girl.

"Doug, Alexa. Alexa, Doug." Jared made the introductions brief, still reeling from the rescue in the mine.

"You guys going up to Salem for Halloween?" Doug asked, knowing that was the place to be on All Saints Eve. "A bunch of us are heading up there."

"Hadn't really thought about it," Jared said, trying to assess whether Alexa would want to join. He thought she might defer in view of her recent family problems, but she surprised him by saying she needed a change of pace.

"Gotta be in costume," Doug reminded, "or at least, masked."

+++

Three days later, at 2:00 in the afternoon, Doug, Jared, Alexa and a few of Doug's friends were standing in line at Long Wharf waiting for the Salem Ferry. They had been told to go early to avoid the crowds that descended upon this quaint North Shore town. Doug wore a purple cape and gold crown, depicting a king of unknown origin. Jared sported a handlebar moustache, ten-gallon hat, leather vest, and chaps for a stereotypical Western look; and Alexa—as one might expect—transformed into a wickedly naughty dance hall girl with a short, ruffled skirt and black fishnet stockings. For warmth, she wore a tight leotard top that had long black sleeves and a scooped neck. A red satin ribbon was threaded through an ivory cameo at her throat. Jared couldn't take his eyes off her.

As he looked around his surroundings, he remembered his mother describing Long Wharf as it had appeared more than 250 years ago, when she, in a past life, had witnessed a Sons of Liberty meeting in the North End. A sense of history washed over him, flooding him with a rush of impressions. He heard a gavel coming down to call a gathering of rabble-rousers to order, he smelled firewood burning in massive hearths, and he saw a tall man in knickers sitting in an armchair, smoking a white clay pipe. He felt the heft of a tankard of ale in his hand, and he tasted the dry salt of smoked cod in his mouth. In the distance, he heard a group of men belting out a sailor's song and found his foot tapping to the rhythm of "Heave Away, Heave Away."

"Are you OK?" Alexa asked, noticing the far-off look in his eyes. He didn't respond until she asked him again.

"Fine," Jared said. "Just thinking." Alexa suspected it was something more but didn't want to pry.

Soon the ferry arrived, and they were on their way to Witch City, a reputation that Salem fiercely downplays, but nonetheless celebrates, to great economic benefit, every October.

When Jared and his friends arrived in Salem, the streets were already teeming with revelers: teenagers who had cut out of school early, thirty-somethings with young children, senior citizens who morphed into marvelous wizards, and of course, an influx of college students who would party all night.

Some had come for the magicians and drummers; others for the Witches' Ball; many were strolling the streets in search of an amulet or elixir that would bring love or riches; and a few had managed to score tickets to a documentary film about the resident witch, Laurie Cabot.

What happened next to Alexa and Jared had nothing to do with planned activities. Doug and his friends had gone into the Witches' Museum and agreed to meet the couple an hour later at the Witch Trials Memorial near the Old Burying Point.

This small park consisted of 20 granite benches, staggered in height, to commemorate the 14 men and 6 women executed for witchcraft in 1692. Each seat displayed the name of the accused and the date of death. Jared and Alexa dawdled on their way to the landmark, strolling into shops and sampling refreshments. As Jared approached the monument, he could feel the hair on the back of his neck stand up.

They took a seat, side-by-side, on a cold surface, saying very little. They not only sensed the presence of the name-bearers but of others who had died. Jared nervously ran his fingers around the buckle in his pocket as Alexa slipped her arm through his for warmth.

"I've got to do this!" he said, producing the buckle. "The pull is just too strong. I feel like there are people here who need to talk to us, and we need to talk to them." She nodded OK, at which point he laid the buckle on her forearm and covered it with his hand.

+++

Within moments, they were in Colorado, on an 1861 August night, rambling through the small cemetery in Buckskin Joe.

The town was still new and, as expected, the burial ground, sparsely populated. Graves were marked mostly by handmade crosses and boulders painted with the names of the deceased. There were also plots staked for the still-living.

"What are you two doing out here?" a voice with a British accent asked. Red and Lydia turned around.

"Why, Giles, how are you?" Lydia replied, not really answering his question.

Giles Ilett was a fixture in Buckskin Joe, having been one of the first to arrive in the fledgling community. He was a master storyteller who, years later, would still delight in describing the ambiance of the place he loved, poetically recounting “arrastras grinding out their yellow grist from rich surface quartz in the old Phillips mine.” Red nodded hello.

Giles was about 44 at the time and had married late in life. His wife, Jennie, was in declining health, so one could assume he was in the graveyard making plans.

“We’re just taking a walk,” Red finally answered. “Nice quiet place to think.”

“One of these days I’m going to vacation here,” Giles stated, pointing to a plot in the middle of the cemetery. He was known for his wry sense of humor. “But I can’t kick the bucket for at least 30 years. Got too much work to do first.”

Red chuckled. One thing about life on the frontier—it made men practical.

Although the night was warm, Lydia felt a chill as Giles headed down the path. “It’s going to get very crowded here soon,” she said to Red. That seemed to be a strange comment, but he didn’t press for an explanation. “Yes, a lot of people—young and old—we’ll need to carry them,” Lydia said, her eyes fixed on something in the distance.

“Are you OK?” Red asked, deciding that maybe this wasn’t the best place to walk after all.

“Oh, I’m fine,” Lydia laughed, shaking off her premonition. “Come, let’s go over to the saloon and get some food. I’m starved.”

They turned their back on the cemetery and walked into the night, following the sound of Lou playing *Sister Carrie* on the piano. The mood in the dance hall was boisterous and bawdy. Red and Lydia fit right in as they ordered beers and toasted loudly. They purposely mingled with others as not to appear as a couple. The distance they kept in public only added to their desire in private.

Lydia excused herself and stepped into her dressing room, emerging in a short, ruffled skirt and silver shoes. But just as she finished her first number, there was a ruckus at the faro table.

Someone she didn't know—a tall fellow wearing spurs and armed with a Starr Double-Action Army .44—drew it on Tom Shaw, one of Bill Buck's men. The stranger accused Tom of tampering with the cue box that tracked cards pulled from the deck. Tom, proud of his fair and decent reputation, kept a pistol stashed in a pitcher and was quick to counter-draw.

"Take it outside," Bill Buck called from across the room, not wanting to disrupt the show that fueled his robust liquor sales. He figured it was none of his business what these cowboys did on their own time. Usually, once the men got outside, they'd lose their bravado and resolve their differences.

This night, however, the scene didn't play out like that. The two men pushed their way into the street and began swinging at each other. Tom's integrity had been challenged and he wasn't about to accept that. He lunged at his accuser, swearing. The accuser responded in kind and wrestled Tom to the ground. The scuffle was loud and dusty. Suddenly, a shot rang out. Men from the dance hall ran outside, and women screamed from behind lace curtains. There lay Tom, bleeding from a wound in his chest, as his assailant galloped away.

Lydia flew to Tom's side, pressing her hand on the wound. She issued orders to anyone within hearing distance. Cloth. Water. Scissors. Doc Jones. It looked as if the bullet had lodged above Tom's right lung, a few inches below his shoulder. Doc came running, and together they moved Tom to the porch of the closest shop.

Someone plied Tom with liquor; somebody else wedged a dowel between his teeth, and two beefy men positioned themselves to hold him down. Applying pressure with her left hand, Lydia cut away Tom's bloody shirt with her right, lifting her palm only when Doc was ready to operate. In one swift move, he splashed the remaining liquor over Tom's bare skin, reached into his medical pouch for a pair of pliers, and prodded the torn flesh. Red cringed.

The guttural cry that rose from Tom's throat was that of a wounded animal. He violently wrenched his body—clenching his teeth around the wooden rod as Doc fished for the bullet. Once the slug came into view, Doc grabbed it and quickly extracted it, dropping the bloody metal into a bowl that Lydia held.

Tom released the dowel, letting it roll into the street. That's when Doc Jones pulled a flask from his own pocket, took a long draw and poured the rest of the contents over the open wound. Tom's blood-curdling scream pierced the night, startling the horses, and sending a flock of birds off the rooftop. After that, he passed out.

Lydia covered his wound with strips of muslin and waited for him to rally. She changed his dressings several times, speaking softly, and laying a cool cloth on his forehead. She stayed with Tom until he regained consciousness, ignoring the blood on her hands and the dark streak across her dress.

Red stood back, trying to be out of the way. He admired Lydia's ability to take command and was impressed with her innate understanding of medical care. That moment, he fell in love with her all over again, marveling at her kind and generous nature.

By this time, the dance hall had emptied, and Bill Buck was shutting the doors. "I'll stay with her," Red said to Bill, who waved good night as he headed around the building to his living quarters.

"Glad we're not gonna have that man for breakfast," Bill called over his shoulder.

Lydia looked up at Red with appreciation. "Thank you for being here," she said, exhausted.

"Happy to help, but you really did it all," Red said as he gathered up the bloody cloths. "You know, you could be a nurse." Lydia smiled but said nothing.

They remained with Tom throughout the night, taking turns sleeping. By morning, Tom managed to sit up. Bill Buck brought out some strong coffee and sourdough biscuits. The four of them sat on the porch enjoying the food. "I won't forget this," Tom said, looking at Lydia with gratitude. "My entire family is in your debt."

Lydia shook her head and made as small hand gesture as if to dismiss the praise, but Tom's kind words resonated and filled her with purpose. "I'll just rest here a bit longer, but you can leave," Tom said, reaching out to pat her hand.

"Ma'am, I'll walk you back," Red offered in his best attempt at propriety in the presence of Bill.

"No need," Lydia replied.

"I insist," Red said as he escorted her from the porch. Once out of sight, he put his arm around her shoulder and brought her close to his side.

Sun was lighting up the hills by the time they got back to Lydia's cabin. In the stillness of the morning, they stepped out of their dirty street clothes and ran to the creek at the edge of the woods. Half sliding, they made their way down the steep incline to the clear water below.

Recent rains had filled the previously dry gulch and turned it into a neighborhood watering hole. Leaving their undergarments on a branch, they carefully inched across the rocks and eased into the cold water. The temperature was brutal, but the result was refreshing. An Arapaho family was downstream, playing. Lydia could hear the happy squeals of children and the barking of a dog. She looked at Red as if to say "Someday," but he was already thinking the same thing.

The water felt like an ice bath as they submerged and came up gasping, dark hair dripping wet, a rosy glow on their cheeks. They splashed each other in jest and dove in again. When they were no longer able to tolerate the temperature, they hurried to shore, and ducked behind a stand of choke cherry trees, using their undergarments to dry off. The day was new and just beginning to warm. Lydia relished the feel of sun on her skin as she watched droplets of river water evaporate.

Red wrapped his arms around her and pushed her long hair away from her cheeks. Without lipstick and rouge, she looked innocent and clean, as if her toes had never touched the floor of a saloon. A pattern of light played across Red's face, accentuating his features. He reminded her of a mountain lion, sinewy and lean, poised to pounce.

His lips were cool as were his fingertips when they first touched her skin. She could feel him pressing against her, sharing his heat and his intentions. The voices of the Indian family fell away, as did the sound of their yapping dog. Only the rustling trees were witness to this pairing—passionate and primal. Red and Lydia clung to each other long after their needs had been met, reluctantly pulling apart.

+++

The Salem night, in present time, was brisk by comparison. When Doug and his buddies returned to Alexa and Jared, the twosome were still mentally miles away. "What have you been up to?" Doug asked, not really expecting an answer. He was now sporting face paint and a silly grin.

"Not much. Just talkin', waiting for you," Jared answered, thankful that the encroaching darkness and brim of his hat concealed his flushed face. Alexa became suddenly busy adjusting her skirt and checking her cell phone which, in keeping with her costume, she had tucked into a small string purse tied around her wrist.

"Listen, guys. You don't have to keep hanging with us," Alexa said. "We'll be up most of the night, so we'll catch the first ferry back in the morning. Besides, I might want to get this cowboy alone," she winked.

Doug and his friends could take a hint and were quick to leave. This was the first time Jared had ever gotten that kind of message from Alexa and he liked it. As his friend ambled off with his buddies, Jared turned to her. "Did you mean what you just said?"

"Maybe," she said, seeming shy and vulnerable. "Agree to go slow?"

Jared took off his hat and removed his fake moustache. "Yes, ma'am," he said in his best Western accent as he edged closer and leaned in for a kiss. As his mouth hovered above hers, she could feel his hair sweep across her forehead, blocking the ambient light and creating a cocoon of sorts. She closed her eyes and savored the moment. His lips were soft and warm on that cool autumn night, and the contrast was startling. She could taste the salt from chips he had recently eaten, and he could detect the flavor of cherry candy that had melted on her tongue.

The experience was new and delicious, and he didn't want to break the spell. Jared promised himself not to rush her into anything they would later regret. Undeniably, he was becoming as attracted to Alexa as Red was to Lydia. Yet this whole scenario was so strange, so out of order, in that they already knew each other in many ways.

+++

By the time Alexa and Jared got back to Boston, they were exhausted. When they finally hit their respective pillows, they saw behind their eyelids a mélange of ghoulish faces from the night before. Somewhere between Goth zombies and gossamer ghosts, they dreamed of each other and the kiss that promised more.

Alexa awoke well into the afternoon, got dressed and checked her cell, surprised to see an email from her brother, Will. With puberty upon him, he was usually more moody than chatty. When she read the subject line "Need to talk," she immediately opened it, but knew quite quickly that it was not from him. The message read: "You looked lovely in Salem."

Alexa dropped her phone on the bed as if it were on fire. She glanced over her shoulder and pulled her sweater tight, feeling suddenly cold and afraid. Walking to her dorm window, she looked out on the street and scanned the adjacent apartments, trying to spot anyone who might be watching her. She saw nothing but closed the blinds anyway. Sitting on the edge of her bed, she texted Jared.

"Get any weird emails lately?

"No, why?"

"I just got one. Made to look like it came from my brother. Seems like someone's been following me—or wants me to think so."

"Don't delete it. I want to see it."

"Sure. Here goes." She hit Forward.

"Get any sleep?" Jared texted as he waited for the email to arrive.

"Out like a light."

"Me, too. I'd meet up with you, but I'm heading out to a press conference for class."

"Can you even get into those things?"

"I've got credentials from the school paper and I still have my intern ID from last summer. You up to anything exciting?"

"Nope. Just gonna chill. Maybe stream a movie tonight."

"Good. Keep your eyes open and your door locked. I'll look at the email later and call you in the morning."

+++

Jared put on a sports jacket and headed to City Hall. The Mayor's Office was announcing a new safety initiative for the city and the Communications staff was fielding questions from the press. One matronly reporter asked about improvements in schoolyard security; Jared assumed she had children or grandchildren. A fit young man, whom Jared took for a runner, asked about better lighting on public walkways. In the back of the room, a scholarly gentleman in a tweed overcoat raised his hand and inquired about protection for art and antiquities. He pointed out that Boston and State Police had been excluded from solving crimes like the legendary Gardner Museum heist, which to him, seemed like a waste of resources. Jared's ears perked up.

The Mayor knew it best to avoid politically charged questions, so he danced around it—commending local authorities for their willingness to help, while praising the FBI for doing an excellent job. Of course, everyone in the room knew that the priceless artwork had never been recovered.

The topic shifted to graffiti and gangs, at which point Jared lost interest. He glanced around the room and noticed the man in the tweed coat looking his way. Jared wondered if they knew each other. Without further acknowledgment, the man turned back and adjusted his tortoise shell glasses. He ran his fingers over his moustache and resumed writing in a small, top-hinged note pad. Jared put a few memos into his own phone and took several photos of the Mayor. He picked up a press kit on the way out and left feeling confident that he could produce a solid paper about the press conference experience.

Deep in thought, Jared took his time walking to a trolley stop. Cold air was coming in off the ocean, briny and damp, and as it mingled with the smell of roasting chestnuts lifting from a vendor's cart in Downtown Crossing, Jared was hit with an image of Boston at the turn of the century—gas lights, top hats, Victorian frocks, and restrained elegance.

He shook off the vision and made his way to the corner of the Commons, welcoming the underground warmth as he descended the stairs to Park Street Station. He swiped his Charlie Card and pushed through a turnstile. As he stood on the subway platform waiting for an outbound train, he noticed the man in the tweed coat leaning against a pillar. When the trolley pulled in, Jared hopped on, happy to get a seat. He settled in and aimlessly looked out the window. The Tweed Man was still standing there. He nodded in Jared's direction and gave him a thumbs-up.

Preoccupied with this gesture, Jared did not notice the young fellow in a red and white leather baseball jacket sitting a few seats behind. Nor did Jared see the baseball jacket guy get off the trolley and tail him to his dorm. Once upstairs, Jared powered up his laptop and started writing.

✦✦✦

The next morning, as promised, Jared called Alexa and they met on campus for brunch. This time, they were both eager to talk—partly because their kiss had brought their relationship to a new level and partly because of the mysterious message Alexa had received. Now relaxed and decidedly more comfortable with each other, neither pulled away when their knees touched. The anticipation was palpable. Jared watched as Alexa slowly ate a strawberry, an act far more seductive than she probably realized. She stared at Jared's long fingers wrapped around his coffee mug and wondered how they would feel on her bare back. "Tell me about this email," he said, swirling a piece of pancake around in the remaining syrup. "Did you ever get one like it before?"

"Nope. I only opened it 'cause I thought it came from my brother."

"That's what they count on," Jared said between bites. "Easy enough to pick up a family name from Facebook and then set up a fake email account. Your address is probably out there in a million places."

"True," Alexa admitted, thinking of the school directories and her online profiles. She lathered grape jelly onto a triangle of toast. "But this would mean someone knew I was in Salem."

"Did you tell anyone we were going?" Jared asked.

"Only my roommate, Gail, and she would never do anything like this."

"Did you notice anyone strange when we were up there?"

"Sure—everyone!" They both laughed at the truth of it.

"Wonder if the email came from one of Doug's friends?" Alexa pondered, looking for a logical explanation.

"I doubt it, but I can ask."

Alexa polished off her eggs and paused. "Well, I'm just going to ignore it for now." Jared was concerned but didn't want to scare her. This seemed like a lot of effort for a one-time prank.

After finishing their coffee, they stepped onto the sidewalk and joined the bustle of Sunday churchgoers coming out of the university chapel. Their conversation took a serious turn, starting with college credits and ending with talk of careers. Alexa was on a poli-sci track and planned to sign up for classes that others found too tough. She had participated in a conflict-resolution program in high school and realized she enjoyed the art of negotiation. Jared made it clear he was determined to become an investigative reporter and that his immediate goal was to break new ground on the museum story.

When they got back to Jared's dorm room, they were both pleasantly surprised that Doug was out. They sat on the bed looking through the course catalog, trying to concentrate on next semester's offerings. Being so close and conveniently alone, it became obvious that there were other ways to occupy their time.

Jared turned to Alexa and let his fingers trail through her hair, moving a strand behind her left ear. His thumb ran across her cheek and landed at her chin where he outlined her lips as if to memorize the arc. Alexa responded with the slightest exhale that left his thumb feeling warm and damp. He continued to trace down her throat, across the softness of her neck, to that velvety spot above her collarbone. He moved his thumb along her jaw, while his palm sat securely at the juncture of her neck and back. Trapezius muscle, his human anatomy book would say. Her loose tee shirt made for easy access to her perfectly smooth skin, warm and inviting below the neckline.

As if exploring an unknown object, Alexa reached up to touch his face, following his cheekbones before resting her forefinger on his lips. His tongue moved across the pad so slowly, she suspected he could feel her fingerprint. She removed her finger and substituted lips, then they both rolled back onto the soft pillows to enjoy each other.

There's no telling how far this interlude might have gone had Doug not bounded in, talking on his phone. Upon seeing the twosome, Doug did an about face, mumbled an apology, and said he'd be back later. Alexa and Jared jumped to their feet, straightened their clothes, and chased after him.

"Doug, no need to go," Jared insisted. "We're not doing anything you haven't seen before."

"Really, Doug. Come back. We have to ask you something," Alexa reiterated.

"What is it?" Doug responded as he returned to the room.

"Just curious, did you see anyone following us up in Salem?" Alexa asked.

"No. Why?"

"I got a strange email from someone suggesting they saw me there. One of your friends wouldn't have sent it, would they?"

"Not likely. They would have just asked me how serious you two were and whether they'd stand a chance." Alexa laughed at his bluntness. "You gonna answer it?" he asked.

"Doubt it. I don't want to encourage anything."

+++

The following week, Jared and Alexa were busy with classes and only able to see each other in passing. Three days later, she received a second message from the fake Will—by text instead of email. She felt even more violated.

"You didn't get back to me. Did you make it to Civics on time?" the text read.

Alexa was rattled. She had in fact made a mad dash to Civics class after oversleeping the day before. Clearly someone was watching her. She closed out the message and texted Jared.

"He's at it again. This time I got a text. He seems to know my class schedule. Wonder if he's a student."

"You probably should let Security know. They might have him on tape."

"Good idea. I have some free time tomorrow morning."

"I'll go with you," Jared added in a way that left no room for discussion.

The next day Alexa and Jared met mid-campus and headed for the Security Office. The officer on duty asked them several questions, then opened a case file. He entered some pertinent information on a job ticket, and said he'd pull up the video footage later. Almost as an afterthought, he called as they turned to leave. "You don't have one of those stalker apps on your phone, do you?"

"What do you mean?" Alexa asked, walking back to him. "I didn't download anything like that."

"No, this would be something someone else would have put on your phone. Like MSpy. It lets them into everything—your email, phone calls, text messages. Overrides the security settings."

"I don't see anything like that," she said, opening the apps screen. "Besides, I keep my phone in my bag when I'm not using it."

"You wouldn't even know it's there," the security officer said. "Only takes a few seconds to install. Could be done right in front of you, if you loaned your phone to someone."

A look of alarm crossed Alexa's face. "I let some guy use my phone for about two seconds a few weeks ago. He was headed to a Red Sox game and said he needed to call his girlfriend to tell her where to meet. Claimed his phone had died."

"Bet that was it," the officer said. "Sit tight. I'll call my technician—nice guy, real geek. He can remove it. Do you remember what that baseball guy looked like?"

"Average height, weight, sandy hair. Maybe 30. Red and white leather jacket, I think."

While the security officer added this information to the file and buzzed his colleague, Jared and Alexa paced. Jared feared that he had unintentionally involved Alexa in something sinister by way of his Gardner Museum investigation. Alexa wondered why her whereabouts would be of interest to anyone.

The technician, Carlos, came to the front of the security office looking more like a biker than a nerd. Alexa noticed he had a sleeve tattoo, a stud in the side of his nose, and slicked-back hair that could have used a wash. With his well-defined features and lean form, not a bad looking guy, just someone you might not bring home to Mother.

"Mind if I take this to the back?" he asked.

"Not as long as you return it."

"Gotcha!" he said as he whisked away Alexa's phone.

She and Jared talked in low whispers. "Wonder if this has something to do with your getting jumped," Alexa finally said. "Maybe someone's after both of us."

"But why?" Jared asked. They ran through a series of possibilities, but none seemed likely.

Before they came up with an answer, Carlos returned. "Got it. FlexiSpy," he said, handing the device back to Alexa. "No more sharing, right? And you'll keep your phone locked?" Alexa assured him that she'd be more careful and thanked him profusely.

"It really galls me when these guys get away with stuff like this," Carlos said as he closed out the job ticket. "Man, someday I'm gonna outsmart them."

Alexa smiled and thanked him again. "Like your tats, by the way," she said as they left the office. Carlos stood behind the desk, beaming.

"I can't believe I was so stupid," Alexa said to Jared as they walked to English class. "I had no idea...." Her sentence trailed off as she caught a glimpse of someone in a red and white baseball jacket rounding the corner to a side street. "Did you see that?" she asked Jared as she broke into a run.

"Wait up!" he called, racing after her. "What are you doing?"

"I could swear that's the guy, who borrowed my phone," Alexa said as she looked up and down the street. No one was there. "Maybe he ducked into one of these buildings."

Jared protectively pulled her back. "You should stay away from here. I'll check him out as soon as I have time. There's no telling who this guy is or what he wants."

After English class, Jared and Alexa hung around the lecture hall, talking about anything but stalking. Not wanting to be alone, they ended up at the Student Union, happy to see a career fair underway. They walked around the tables and found a quiet spot to sit down, obscured by the throng of students.

"Now how would Red and Lydia act in a situation like this?" Jared mused out loud. "They seem to be tough and resilient." His eyes were playful as they looked at Alexa. She leaned over and whispered something in his ear. He turned beet red.

"You think they would do that?" he asked in mock disbelief.

"Well, Lydia would do that for sure," Alexa replied, puckering her lips and batting her eye lashes.

"Then let's not wait," Jared said, getting comfortable in his chair. They put their backpacks on the floor and set their phone alarms for two hours later. Jared took the small silver buckle out of his pocket and held it in the palm of his hand. Alexa reached over, her fingertips cool as they covered his. There was an immediate electrical charge, but they couldn't tell if it was from their connection to the buckle or their growing attraction to each other. A moment later, Lydia and Red were standing in line at the general store.

✦✦✦

"What do you mean eggs cost $2.50 a dozen? That's the acre price of a placer claim," Red said to the store keeper.

"Sorry, buddy, but food's scarce. No better in Denver."

"That's gouging, if you ask me," Red retaliated.

"We could skip the eggs," Lydia suggested, knowing they should cost a fraction of that.

Red glanced at Lydia, wanting only the best for her. "We'll take a half dozen," he stated as he reached into his pocket for the money. Two days later, he showed up at her cabin with four young chickens, a bag of feed, some boards and a roll of wire. "Better investment," he said, bending over to kiss her on the back of her neck. "I'll build a coop tomorrow."

"Guess that makes me a farmer," she smiled, happy. She twirled around in a dance move and he reeled her in.

"Once the chicks start laying, I can take the extra eggs to church," she said, excited at the possibility of donating them to the needy. "I've wanted to bring something down there for ages, but I haven't had much to give."

Red closed his eyes and thanked his lucky stars for having Lydia in his life. "Beautiful inside and out," he thought to himself. He also figured this was a good time to broach a subject that had been on his mind. "So how long do you plan on dancing?" he asked as he kept his arms around her.

"Long as I can, I guess," Lydia said, not really thinking about the implications of his question. "Why do you ask?"

"I was just hoping to book you up for a while," he said, pulling her closer, not quite mustering the courage to ask for a long-term commitment.

She laughed—that light, lilting laughter that had attracted him many weeks before. "You're at the top of my dance card," she assured.

"Then dance with me," he said.

"Now?"

He nodded yes.

"But there's no music."

"I'll sing," he said.

"That could be scary," she teased, as they began the box step.

"Only if you listen," he joked back. And with that, he burst into a respectable rendition of *Gentle Maiden*.

"I love thee gentle maiden,
For thy merry, merry gladsome face,

Thy cheek with blushes laden,
Thy soft and winning grace.
Thine eyes so full of joyance,
Thy rosy laughing lip.
Such lips are an annoyance
When one can't take a sip."

Lydia circled the floor, feet hardly touching ground, as Red lifted her and spun her in the air, easing her down against his body as he sang the last line. "Time for a sip," he said, melting his lips into hers.

Red was a tough man to resist and Lydia didn't try too hard. There was something about him that made her feel sacred and safe. Something that felt right. Clean and wholesome. Soon they were a tangle of arms and legs, wants and needs, bodies synchronized until the final collapse.

For Lydia, meeting Red was the best thing that had ever happened to her. Since her youth, she had been fiercely independent. She had left Missouri at a tender age after her mother passed away. It was then that Lydia learned to parlay her beauty and her voice into a profession. She was never sure whether her father had been killed or whether he had simply deserted them, but she always felt a void by not having a male presence in her life.

Most of the men she encountered wanted nothing more than a roll in the hay. One tried to steal her money, another attempted to marry her, so she could mother his kids. She had been conned, lied to, threatened, and coerced, but had never been treated properly. Red was an exception to the rule and she wondered if he were too good to be true.

Lydia liked that Red had standards…ethics…expectations… and he respected her like no other. That's not to say he didn't have his moods and his quirks, but he was solid in character, humble in demeanor, and generous in spirit.

Sometimes he talked wistfully about working on a ranch as a boy, riding through the open spaces of Texas, marveling at the miracle of birthing calves. The best Lydia could tell is that Red had two older brothers, their whereabouts unknown. His family had split up when his father went looking for work, taking Red's brothers with him in hopes that they could find jobs, too. Red, the youngest, was just 15 when he was left to care for his mother. That was the last Red ever saw of his siblings or his Dad. While growing up, he had heard rumors about Indian raids, gunfights, droughts, and blizzards—all of which supposedly took their lives—but it was the not knowing that ate at him.

✦✦✦

That afternoon, Red said he was going to help his friend, Sam, burn brush around a lode claim. Setting miner fires was common practice as they cleared the land fast. The only problem is—they were dangerous. "Be careful," Lydia said as he headed out the door to saddle up his horse.

"Don't worry, I will," he called back, adjusting his hat to better shield his eyes. Lydia leaned against the door frame watching him mount the muscular steed and ride out across the flats. She liked what she saw and knew she wouldn't mind seeing it for a long time.

When Red reached the claim site, Sam was already pouring kerosene on the dense undergrowth. A moment later, with the flick of a friction match, the ground cover was ablaze. The flames raced in both directions, gobbling up dry weeds and tough grasses, engulfing small trees and low brambles, circling a few stray cacti that were green enough to resist the fire. That's when they heard a call in the distance.

"Hey, what do you think you're doing?" the old man yelled. Red and Sam strained to see through the smoke until they spotted a white-bearded miner standing next to his burro.

"Get away from there," the young men hollered, gesturing to the geezer to move. "Back up. The fire's tearing through there."

"Whaddayuhsay?" the old man called, hand cupping his ear, trying to improve his hearing.

"Fire's gonna blow back against the cliff," Sam shouted. "You need to move."

"Sally doesn't move unless she wants to," he said, patting his burro.

"Well, she's gonna have to," Red hollered, "Or you'll both get fried."

"Not sure it matters much," the old man said. "Been striking out these days."

"Go over the hill and get out of range," Sam thundered, pointing repeatedly in that direction. "You don't have much time."

With that, Red dug his heels into the flanks of his horse and bolted forward toward the old man. Red lifted the frail fellow onto his saddle, moving forward to make room for him, and reached out to smack the burro on the backside. The burro brayed loudly and sauntered over the rise, oblivious to the firestorm coming at them.

"Put me down, I'll be fine," the old man insisted, kicking his legs, trying to dismount, but Red kept the reins tight in his right hand and used his left hand to reach behind and hold onto the old man's belt. Once a safe distance away and back at Sam's side, Red dismounted and helped the old man off the horse.

"What were you doing up there?" Sam asked, walking over to the man. "This claim is staked."

"Yeah, I know. I was just passing through. I've been looking for a deserted mine supposedly somewhere around here. Got a funny name like Minnie Who or Many Cow...." The old man paused and extended his leathery hand. "I'm Asa, by the way and you already met my mule, Sal."

"Glad to meet you," Red said, nodding his head. Sam, who stood closer, offered his hand. What Red didn't reveal is that the mentioned mine sounded a lot like the one he had claimed years before in his mother's maiden name: Matilda Howe—Mattie to friends.

"What makes you think that mine's deserted?" Red asked.

"Ain't seen any action there in years. You know, miners talk."

"Maybe the owner's just away or signed up with the army."

"Dunno. But I found a nugget downstream the other day, so there may still be some gold around here."

"Probably just a fluke. Most of the placer finds are dried up in these parts," Red commented.

"It's the lode that interests me."

"Well, good luck to you," Sam said, as he watched the fire die out against the cliff wall. He started to drag his shovel around the edges of the burn area to make sure no live embers remained.

The old miner walked off and waved without looking back. "Salleeee," he called and followed that with a whistle. Red could see the ears of a burro sticking out above a hillock beyond the fire zone.

"Maybe some of that treasure is sitting right here," Red said as he picked up a shovel and went to help Sam.

"Hope so," Sam said, as he wiped the sweat from his brow. "Lotta land to carve up," he said as he gazed across his claim. "Thanks for the hand."

Red was just about to say 'my pleasure' but was interrupted by a friendly female voice. "Jared, is that you?"

+++

Jared blinked his eyes, looked up and noticed a beautiful blond woman smiling at him. The conversation brought Alexa back to the present as well.

"Bobbie?" he said, standing up to greet the newcomer. He grabbed the buckle and stashed it in his pocket. "What are you doing here?"

"Grad school," she said., "Fine arts…drama." She certainly did appear polished. Alexa wondered how Jared knew this attractive older woman.

"Oh, Lexa, this is Bobbie…err, Roberta…I'm embarrassed to say she used to babysit me and my sister when we lived up here."

Alexa immediately felt a sense of relief knowing that Bobbie wasn't going to be competition. She extended her hand and introduced herself.

"I really wanted to go back to school and be in the city," Bobbie continued. "More live stage and a bigger arts community than out in the boonies."

"I hear you," Jared said, fondly remembering the days when he and his sister would play hide and seek in a corn field. "Do you want to join us?" he asked, motioning to an empty chair. "I can get some coffee."

"Thanks…but no, I need to be going. But let me give you my email and number, so we can stay in touch."

As Jared was about to hand Bobbie his phone, he felt Alexa pull back his arm. "OK. Just tell me what they are," Jared said as he palmed his phone. He entered the information and smiled at Alexa. Already they had each other's back.

As Bobbie disappeared down an escalator, Jared and Alexa turned off their phone alarms, their thoughts still back in their Buckskin Joe cabin. "Thanks for the dance," she said, winking at him. "Not a bad voice."

"And not a bad body," Jared whispered back.

This time it was Alexa who blushed. "Small world, meeting Bobbie," she said, quickly changing the subject.

"Guess so," Jared said, glad to have another friend in the city.

4
STRANGERS

Messages from the mysterious Will stopped as soon as the stalker app was removed from Alexa's phone. She now had a brighter outlook on life, despite her heavy academic load. Thanksgiving was on the horizon and soon she'd be flying home to be with family as would Jared.

Jared was consumed with class projects, too. He'd hurry through his required subjects, so he could spend time researching the Gardner Museum heist, focusing on the missing art and the reported leads that didn't pan out. When he had time, he'd hang around parts of the city linked to the crime—trying to get a feel for the setting and talking to people who lived there. He really didn't know why he was so drawn to this mystery, but he just couldn't let it go. The crime had occurred well before he was born, yet he felt a civic—maybe even, moral—obligation to help solve it.

When Friday evening rolled around, he and Alexa both needed a break. Jared had agreed to meet at her dorm and texted her from the lobby. While she finished drying her hair, he settled into an armchair and checked his Facebook feed, carefully smoothing the dark brown leather jacket he wore when he wanted to look cool.

Out of the corner of his eye, he saw jeans and a red and white sleeve, but didn't put it together until he heard the guy ask at the desk, "Well, can you at least tell me if she lives here? About 5'4", long dark hair, pretty face, first name is Alexa."

"That would describe a lot of students. Besides, I can't give out personal information," the woman at the desk replied. Jared strained to hear. He didn't want to stare, so he stood up and walked closer, pretending to stop and read one of the free newspapers in a nearby rack.

The fellow he saw was in his early thirties, reddish hair, freckled, otherwise nondescript. One might think it odd that someone his age would be hanging around a college dorm, but the guy had a boyish grin and upturned nose that made him look a lot younger and innocent, like the kid next door.

Jared could hear the young man persisting. "I met her at Dunkin' this morning and she said to swing by. Maybe I could just leave her a note then?"

"Sure," the receptionist said, handing him a pad of paper. "I'll check our roster and see if anyone by that name matches your description."

Just as the visitor turned to leave, Alexa appeared at the elevator door. "Hey, Jared," she called across the room. The visitor turned to see the source of the voice, but Jared ran into his line of sight, obscuring Alexa the best he could. Jared grabbed her elbow and steered her into the vending machine room.

"What are you doing?" she protested.

"Stay here. I want to make sure it's all clear."

"What's clear?" she started to ask, but he was out of earshot.

The fellow in the baseball jacket was just leaving as Jared got back to the lobby. He grabbed his phone and took a picture. It was blurry, but he thought there might be some small detail a trained eye could discern. Jared went over to the desk. "That guy who was just here…the one in the Red Sox jacket…looking for Alexa… have you seen him before?"

"Nope. First time. Why?"

"He seems to be overly interested in my girlfriend, that's all," Jared said. It felt odd saying 'girlfriend', but that was the best word he could find. "Can you keep an eye out for him and let me know if he comes snooping around again. If so, I'll talk to Security." Jared showed his student ID and the receptionist took the information.

"Any chance I could see the note he left?" Jared asked.

"Threw it away," the receptionist said, pointing to a sealed trash container with a narrow slit in it. "I didn't like the looks of that guy."

"Me neither," Jared agreed and returned to Alexa. Together they walked outside into the brisk night.

"What was that all about?" she asked, buttoning up her short coat. Jared's first instinct was to lie to protect her, but that wasn't the kind of relationship he wanted.

"There was a guy in a red and white baseball jacket looking for a girl with long dark hair. I asked the receptionist to let me know if he comes back."

"Do you think he meant me?" Alexa asked eyes wide.

"Could be, but there are a lot of students who match that description," Jared said, borrowing the receptionist's line. He did not tell Alexa that the fellow knew her name. "Just be careful. Do you have a safety app on your phone?"

Alexa nodded yes. "It puts out a GPS alert that responders can follow."

"Good. Keep it handy," Jared said.

"I will," she promised, then paused. "But I really don't want to think about that right now. I'm so beat, I just want to relax." Alexa groaned.

"Fair enough." Jared paused to kiss her cheek. "Movie?"

"Yes, something mindless," Alexa said. "My brain is toast."

Rather than go to a new release, they decided on a small out-of-the-way theater that was hosting a comedy fest. They bought a vat of popcorn, splurged on two overpriced sodas, ducked into the darkened room, and slid down into their seats. The 3-day program included vintage Charlie Chaplin shorts and Woody Allen films, along with modern classics like "When Harry Met Sally," "Something About Mary," and "Ace Ventura: Pet Detective." Interspersed were cuts from stand-up comedy clubs, late night talk shows, and Saturday Night Live. All light and lively fodder to make tired students forget about math and science.

As Jared and Alexa were about to stand up for intermission, they overheard two men talking a few rows back. What Alexa discerned was conversation about home renovation—wanting an armoire, guaranteed delivery, and needing to call the Gentle Giant moving company. But what Jared heard was something entirely different—names that rang a familiar bell: Amore—the Security Director at the Gardner Museum; Guarente—one of the since-dead suspects in the art heist; and Gentile—an alleged mobster, whose Connecticut home had been searched multiple times in connection with the missing art.

Jared grabbed Alexa's arm and put his forefinger to his lips, signaling her to be quiet and stay down. Just as the men said something about "time for them to see the light"—or, as Alexa heard— "time for them to see the lights," plural—a group of loud teenage girls, talking in exaggerated Valley Girl dialect, sat in the row between. A moment later, the room dimmed, the audience hushed, and the heavy maroon velvet curtain parted. When the last film ended, the men were gone.

"Did you hear that?" Jared spouted with excitement. "They were talking about the Gardner heist! I think they know where the paintings are."

"No, they weren't," Alexa said, scrunching her nose as she reached for her coat. "They were just talking about interior design. It sounds like they bought a house."

Jared continued, undeterred, hoping he had stumbled on the lead of a lifetime. "I wonder who they are and if they live around here."

"You're getting obsessed with this," she said.

"Maybe I'm just hearing something you can't."

A stilted silence followed. Alexa didn't hide her irritation. "Let's make this a no-work night," she pleaded. "You can go back to your sleuthing tomorrow."

"You're right," he admitted as they left the theater. "This is *our* time. Schoolwork can wait. Besides, if no one has found the paintings in 30 years, they're not going to surface in the next ten minutes."

Alexa's gentle laugh reminded him of Lydia's. He flashed back on the sensual moments Red and Lydia had shared, and he longed for the same with Alexa. "Go slow?" echoed in his head as he recalled Alexa's request. Jared paused under a street lamp. "What's wrong?" Alexa asked.

"Absolutely nothing," Jared said as he looked at the aura of light around her hair. He moved closer and kissed her deeply. The night air smelled of snow, sea, and a hint of shampoo. He positioned Alexa against the lamp post, unbuttoned her coat and slipped his hands beneath the fabric. He cupped her contours and greedily absorbed her warmth, using her coat to ward off the chill that surrounded them. She in turn unzipped his jacket and slid her arms under the lining, reaching around his fitted waffle-weave shirt that reminded her of the one Red wore. She relished the heady scent of leather—a pheromone that conjured up all things manly— and she pressed against Jared, welcoming his heat. Her pulse quickened as one kiss led to another.

"Hey, get a room," a group of passersby yelled before heading to the bar across the street. Jared and Alex pulled away and laughed. "We probably should go back," Alexa said as she smoothed her hair and buttoned her coat.

"Or get that room," Jared muttered under his breath. He zipped up his jacket and took a halting breath before they continued walking toward the nearest T station.

Alexa, with eyes elevated, was preoccupied reading the destination headers on the trolleys, and Jared, with eyes down, was focused on putting away his Charlie Card. Neither of them noticed the man in a tweed coat approaching from the other direction.

"Sorry," the man said, as he grazed Jared's right shoulder.

"No problem," Jared said, not looking up.

✦✦✦

That night, in their separate dorm rooms, Jared and Alexa had trouble sleeping. They both dreamed of each other—and of being chased by the men who had sat behind them. When Alexa woke up talking in her sleep, her roommate Gail mumbled, “You OK?” and when Jared sent his covers flying across the room onto Doug’s bed, he heard a disgruntled, “Dude. Watchit.” Neither Alexa nor Jared were rested the following morning.

To say their exams were not grueling would be a disservice to the efforts they put forth. When their tests were completed, and papers handed in, Alexa and Jared went out to celebrate at a friend’s apartment. If you asked them, they’d probably claim they didn’t know the punch was spiked, but they ended up giddy, uninhibited, and sneaking off to a room where coats were piled on a bed. They eked out some space, fell back on the plush covers, and Jared rolled on top of her.

In their romp, the buckle slipped out of his pocket and landed in the hollow beneath Alexa’s back. The charge that ran through her and up into him was unlike previous jolts. Energy coursed through her veins and sparked off his synapses.

✦✦✦

Within seconds they were transported into the dimly lit corridor at Bill Buck’s dance hall. Lydia was standing against the wall, Red leaning into her. “I have to go,” he said, bending down to kiss her. “Night shift, you know.”

“I know,” Lydia said, hating to tear away. She suspected by now that the miners knew she and Red had ‘a thing,’ but she continued her ruse of being unattached for the sake of the clientele. That night, she sauntered up to a wizened loner sitting in the first row, having no idea he was the old prospector that Red had met. “What do you say, big guy. Dance with a girl?”

The wrinkled man with missing teeth cackled and declared that he might be old, but he wasn’t dead. He plunked a few coins into her hand and wobbled to his feet. Lydia took the lead and steered the old man across the floor. She glanced at Lou and cued him to play something slow, not wanting the decrepit fellow to collapse.

“So, what brings you out here?” she asked, making small talk.

The old man moved in to hear better—or to be closer. That’s

still up for debate. “I’m onto something hot,” he said with a mischievous look in his eye.

“Hotter than me?” Lydia quipped.

“Nothing could be hotter than you, missy,” the old man replied, playing along. “Naw, I’m talking about something that’s gonna melt down nice and fine at the assayer’s office.”

Lydia was wise to miner talk. “You’re not a pennyweighter, are you?” she said, thinking he might be pocketing someone else’s gold while on the job.

“Nope. Found this nugget fair and square. Just sitting in a stream way out in a place nobody goes.” He went on to describe the area near Red’s claim.

“Interesting,” Lydia replied but didn’t say much else until she thanked him for the dance. That night she told Red what she had heard.

“I bet it’s Asa, the old guy I met at Sam’s,” Red said, leaning back in a chair, stretching out his legs and rocking on the heels of his boots. “He’s been poking around the backcountry.” Red paused to run his hand over the stubble on his chin. “Maybe there *is* some gold breaking loose from a lode upstream. Probably should go out there anyway. Government says I need to put in at least $100 worth of work a year to keep my claim alive. Want to come?”

“I’ve never done any mining before,” Lydia said, “but I’d love to go. I can see if Bill will let me off for a night or two. Sadie might be able to cover.”

“Sounds good,” Red said. “I need to get you set up with a horse.” He looked at her petite and lady-like silhouette as she stood in front of an oil lamp. “Do you mind roughing it?”

“I grew up on a cow farm, remember?” she reminded him. “Everything was rough.” She smiled at Red, happy that he was looking out for her.

“Good. I’ll teach you a few things about mining when we get there,” he said, walking over to her.

“You already have,” she said, stepping on her tip toes to kiss his cheek. “You taught me that I really like miners—especially one in particular.”

5
DIGGING DEEPER

That weekend, they saddled up and rode out toward Red's claim. The rainy season had passed, so they worried less about floods and more about early mountain snows. The cabin was as they had left it, dark and deserted, but surprisingly warm. They unloaded some food supplies and several canteens of water. Red thought the spring behind the cliff was still producing, but he didn't want to take any chances.

This time Red brought Lydia into the mine through a door at the back of the cabin. He lit a lantern and led the way as she tried to ignore the claustrophobia that was making her lungs feel tight. She had heard about Fool's Gold—pyrite—and there was plenty of it, sparkling on the walls and in the crevices, taunting them with false hope.

Unsure of her footing, Lydia clung to an outcropping of rock, moving hand over hand as she followed Red along the narrow passage. Suddenly something gave way and a chunk of wall fell to her feet.

"Breaking up the place?" Red teased, yelling back over his shoulder, mostly wanting to make sure she was all right.

"Sorry," Lydia called out. "But us short girls have to grab onto something, you know."

Red retraced his steps and walked back to her. "I forgot," he said, playfully pointing out their differences in height. "You can grab onto me any time."

"Very funny," she sassed, as she bent over to move away the debris. Red was already walking ahead when she spotted it. "Red, what's this?"

Red, who was usually patient, was getting exasperated. He was not accustomed to having inexperienced female companionship in the mine. "Lydia, stop calling me back. We'll never get anywhere."

"But I think you should see this."

Reluctantly, Red returned and looked at her. "What's so important?"

"This," she said, pointing to the piece of rock at her feet.

Red bent down and noticed a thick line of crystal in it. After running his finger along the pattern, he looked up at the wall where the rock had separated. As he moved his lantern closer to the chasm, he suddenly stopped. There, along the ragged break, was a large vein of quartz. He could see flakes of gold suspended in it and small chunks of yellow embedded in rock where the vein met the ledge. Lydia could feel her heart thumping as she stood slack-jawed, staring at their find. "I'll be damned," Red said in voice that couldn't quite contain his excitement.

Lydia was no miner, but she knew gold when she saw it and she had heard enough stories about mother lodes to know it could happen.

"Hold the lantern," Red said, handing her the light. He took the pickaxe he was carrying and chipped away at the crystal in the wall.

"Take this," he said, giving her a small block of clear points. Lydia set the lantern on a ledge, so she could free up her hands. She held the sample up to the light and gasped at the reflection. Flecks of gold, as brilliant as the leaf on the dance hall mirror frame, floated in the quartz. The piece of attached rock was also laced with yellow. She put the facet into her bodice and took the lantern again, holding it high to illuminate the space.

Red kept tapping away at the now-deep recess in the wall, muttering, "This is amazing." Lydia stared, incredulous, at the streak of quartz edged in gold, appearing as a wide smile in the otherwise serious stone. "Oh, boy. Oh, boy," Red repeated as he struck the quartz, releasing nuggets onto the ledge below. "Big vein here. Big vein."

Lydia held both hands out as Red filled them with yellow-studded crystal. He swept up the nuggets in one smooth move and put them into his pocket. "Let's not take too much until we can tackle this properly," he said, grabbing the lantern and encouraging her to return to the entrance. "We need to get some value on this." When they got back to the cabin, they emptied their bounty onto the table, too scared to say anything that might jinx their luck.

"What are you going to do with this?" Lydia asked in a voice just above a whisper.

"Take it to Denver to be tested. Don't want to do it in town. Too many eyes."

"I can't breathe," Lydia said, tapping her chest.

"Me neither," Red said, inhaling slowly until a "Wahoo!" escaped from his lips—at which point he swooped Lydia off her feet and spun her around. "Do you know what this means, woman?" Lydia was too stunned to say anything as he put her down. "This means we can buy land. Have babies. Eat well." By this time Lydia was laughing to the point of tears, unable to stem the joy she was sharing with this remarkable man. Red pulled a whiskey flask from a chink in the wall and held it up in a toast. "To us!" he said, taking a swig and passing it to Lydia.

"To us!" she said, accepting it and swallowing twice. She toasted back. "I'm still shaking," Lydia said, trying to steady her hands.

"I'm shaking, too. You just don't see it," Red said, grasping her hands between his. She looked up at Red, trying to comprehend the enormity of their find.

"I guess this means we won't have to answer to other people—or go to work every day," he announced in slow realization as he sat back in the chair and took another belt. Red was grinning from ear to ear. He motioned Lydia to his knee and she sat down, spreading her skirt across his leg. She threw her arms around his neck and nuzzled his ear. His fingers threaded through her hair.

"God, woman. You're gorgeous!" he said, standing up and lifting her as she clung to his shoulders. What followed was a combination of lust, love, strong alcohol, and the unfathomable feeling of financial freedom. Shortly after, they lay spent on the small cot, daring to speak their dreams and innermost wishes. They eventually got dressed and warmed a can of stew over a small fire outside the cabin. Despite the discovery that lay hidden in the rocks behind them, they used one bowl and two spoons. No need to be extravagant.

✦✦✦

A loud knocking on the door brought Jared and Alexa into the present. "Hey, you two, in there. You alive?" It was their hostess, Kim, needing to get someone's coat. Alexa and Jared sat up as he scooped the buckle off the bed and pocketed it. "Do I need to close my eyes?" she joked.

"No, come on in," Jared called. "Lexa was just feeling a little light- headed, so she stretched out," he lied.

Alexa stared at him as if to say, "Why make me the wimp?" but thought better about protesting.

"Do you want some tea?" Kim offered, assuming her guest had consumed too much punch. Kim was a college Junior, set on getting an MBA. Alexa was never sure whether it was Kim's Asian ancestry or the fact that she had taken dance for so many years, but she was tall, lithe, and graceful – all qualities that Alexa envied.

"That would be great," Alexa answered, feeling coarse and clumsy as she followed Kim into the hallway. Alexa motioned Jared to fall in step. As she sat in the kitchen chatting with her friend, Jared mingled with the others.

"Tough time of year," he heard someone say. "Yeah, Charlie's on his own. His parents just split up a month ago and neither is doing Thanksgiving."

"That's too bad. Where does he live?" Jared asked.

"Maryland, I think. He's going to his Mom's house, but that will be depressing."

"I'll send him a note. He can join my family if he wants."

"You're a good guy, Sutherland," one of the guests said, punctuating his compliment with a punch on the arm. Jared enjoyed being one of the guys and not the odd man out.

+++

Saying good-bye for the holiday was painful. Jared and Alexa were just getting to know each other and didn't want to spend time apart. "Think of it this way," Jared said, hoping to make her feel better. "I'll be hanging out with a buddy, so I can't get in trouble, and you'll be chowing down on so much gravy and shoofly pie that you won't be able to move." Alexa laughed at his jab about life in rural Pennsylvania. She looked forward to relaxing with family and eating something that wasn't cafeteria food.

They packed lightly and went to the airport together a few days before the holiday. Jared waited with her while her plane landed and then killed a couple of hours until his taxied in. They were ahead of the travel crush and praised each other for being so smart.

6
HOME GROWN

Jared had almost forgotten how safe and familiar his family's home felt. Although this wasn't the place where he had learned to walk, this had become home during the past seven years. His sister, Abby, was growing up. Gone were her geeky little girl traits and in their place was an emerging sense of confidence. His dad, Carter, was as philosophical as ever, enjoying the mental stimulation of working in a think tank while his Mom, Sarah, unable to say too much about her government job, was clearly happy to be solving crimes rather than selling houses.

"Sweetheart, you look taller," his mother said, reaching up to kiss his cheek, before going back to chopping celery.

"Just my boots, I think," Jared replied, giving her a hug. He was still their humble, matter-of-fact son.

His father quickly whisked Jared away to look at a project in the garage, and Abby joined her Mom in the kitchen.

"We'll need another setting for tomorrow," Sarah told Abby. "Jared's invited a friend from school."

"A guy friend or a girl friend?"

"Guy friend." Abby looked pleased.

Later that night, Jared and his mother stood talking in the kitchen. Carter and Abby had retired to the den and were watching a bad movie on TV.

"So, about this girl…." Sarah started, aware that Jared had mentioned Alexa several times.

A wistful look crossed Jared's face. "She's different, Mom. We have a connection."

"Sounds like you like her a lot," Sarah said, keeping the conversation light, not wanting to pry.

"Yeah, but it's more than that," Jared finally said. "We share something special." He scowled a bit as he said this.

Sarah dried her hands and pulled out a chair. "What's on your mind?" she asked, sitting down, sensing that something was troubling her son.

Jared sat down opposite his mother and told her about his first encounter with Alexa, the accidental pairing of the buckle and the cup, their extraordinary ability to slip back in time, and the lives of Red and Lydia that were infiltrating their own. He knew his mother wouldn't laugh, because she had experienced something similar. He was right; she listened intently.

"The problem is we're out of sync," he continued. "In the past, we're ten years older, more mature, sure of ourselves, ready to be together…but in the present, we're just beginning. We're like voyeurs—novices—watching something we shouldn't see. Makes it awkward, but it's too intriguing to stop."

Sarah reached over and put a knowing hand on his knee. "Believe me, I understand what you mean. When Terrence and I were together—that is, when I was transported back before the Revolution—I found it very difficult to reconcile the past and present. I was 19 years old there, but clearly much older in real time. We had a strong physical attraction that I tried to spare your father." A faint look of longing crossed Sarah's eyes. "But I couldn't deny it."

"I think I finally understand what you were going through," Jared said, seeing his mother in a new light.

"The one thing I did learn," she continued, "is that there aren't answers for everything. If you try to figure it all out, it will make you crazy. Sometimes you just have to go with the flow and enjoy it." Jared sat there a moment, soaking in his mother's comforting words.

When Carter and Abby staggered out of the den, bleary-eyed and craving something sweet, Sarah brought out a small apple pie she had made with left-over filling. Gathering around their square kitchen table—the one that rocked if someone leaned too hard on one side—she cut the warm pastry into four gigantic portions. The crust was buttery, and the fruit, perfectly flavored with cinnamon and nutmeg. Sitting around the small table, they reminisced about past holidays, caught up on family gossip, and relaxed in each other's company. Jared thought this simple moment was better than the most lavish Thanksgiving feast.

The next afternoon, when Charlie Thompson arrived at the door carrying flowers and home-made cookies, his brown curly hair controlled with a generous helping of gel, Jared could tell that Abby was smitten by this smart 'older man.' Charlie was majoring in science and minoring in math, most likely on a path to biology or statistics. Jared had no doubt this guy would excel in life. He was nice, smart, and affable.

Abby alternated between saying nothing and saying too much about her high school projects. Charlie listened politely, pausing occasionally to slide his eyeglasses back up the bridge of his nose and to ask knowledgeable questions. Abby loved being taken seriously and appreciated the attention.

After Charlie went home, Jared called Alexa to compare notes. Her father was recovering nicely, her mother had prepared a fabulous dinner, and Will was "tolerable" as she put it. When her parents weren't around, she let Will know that someone had been trying to impersonate him online and made him promise to tell her of any suspicious activity on his accounts. Even though Will replied with a typical "Whatever," she knew he was paying attention.

Alexa headed back to Boston on Friday night, but Jared planned to enjoy a few more days in D.C. That evening she called him to say her flight had been cancelled. "Apparently incoming flights are backed up due to a blizzard out West. Looks like I'm going to be stuck at BWI overnight or I'll have to make my way home again."

"Don't do that," Jared told her. "We live close to the airport. You can stay at our house. I'll pick you up." There was a weighted silence on the phone. "No strings attached. Promise. Separate rooms," he added.

He sensed some relief in the dead air. "Are you sure it's OK with your family?"

"Absolutely. We have space. Tell me where you'll be waiting, and I'll be there in a half hour."

+++

"Well, isn't this a pleasant surprise," Sarah said as she greeted Alexa, combining a hand shake with a hug. Sarah felt an immediate liking for this girl. She sensed a sharp mind, gentle spirit and kind heart. Carter was equally gracious. Abby was nowhere in sight.

"You can stay in the guest room down the hall," Sarah said, apologizing for the sewing machine in the corner and her pile of patchwork yet to be stitched.

"Not a problem. Thank you so much," Alexa said, looking at Jared with appreciation.

Once settled in, she booked a ticket on Jared's flight and called her family to let them know about the change in plans. "Now, who is this boy?" her mother asked, although Alexa had already told her about Jared.

"Just make sure he's a gentleman," she could hear her father say in the background.

The next two days were ideal according to Jared. Having Alexa join his family felt right; they all got along splendidly. He wasn't sure if his mother had said something about their unique ability to sense the past or whether Alexa was relieved by the normalcy, but he thought she seemed more comfortable than she had in ages.

He showed her around town, gave her the grand tour of his high school, and they stopped at his favorite hangout for a pizza.

Before Carter dropped them at the airport on Sunday night, Sarah took Jared aside. “She’s lovely.” Sarah said with a twinkle in her eye. “And I know she can dance.”

+++

On the plane, Alexa managed to sweet talk a passenger into swapping places, so she could sit next to Jared. Once settled, he maneuvered the buckle out of his pocket, set his phone alarm, reached across the seat, and took Alexa’s hand with the buckle nestled between their palms. “We might as well take a little trip on our trip,” he word-played. She smiled easily and let herself go back to Buckskin Joe.

+++

Lydia was waiting in line at the bank, planning to deposit her earnings, when she felt a cold breeze blow in and heard a voice boom out at the open door. “Everyone, down on the floor. This is a hold-up.” She saw a nervous gunman and his greasy sidekick with Colts drawn. The customers dropped to the ground as instructed and the tellers froze in place. “Hands where we can see them.”

Lydia knew it was payday at the mine and suspected the bank vault was full. She was also aware that monetary incentives from the government arrived regularly to persuade local mining companies to send their gold North instead of South.

She quickly concealed her small fold of Demand Notes in her bodice and hid her gold poke in her pocket before putting her hands in the air. While her pouch didn’t hold any nuggets this time, it did contain several vials of gold flakes and a few cylinders of dust she had gotten as tips—hard earned tips—and she wasn’t about to hand them over.

“Who’s in charge here?” the older robber barked. He was a coarse-looking man maybe about forty, with graying hair, a hooked nose, and malicious eyes. A black kerchief was pulled over the lower part of his face. The bank manager—a meek and accommodating fellow in a vested suit—stepped forward.

“I am,” the manager said, trying to embolden his voice by repeating his answer.

"Point me to today's drop," the gunman said, referring to the stagecoach delivery. "I hear there's some big, Federal money in it, too." Using his gun, he gestured the manager toward the safe.

"Don't know about that," the manager said, "but here's what came in for the Phillips payroll." He slowly opened the door to the vault. "This belongs to a bunch of hard-working men, you know," the manager continued, reluctant to see their salary taken. Without warning, the sidekick—a skinny kid in a stained gray shirt, a crumpled hat low over his eyes—spun around and pistol-whipped the manager. The manager fell to the ground with a thud. The tellers gasped, and customers screamed.

Lydia watched from her low vantage point, scanning the walls and ceiling around her. She noticed a fly buzzing noisily in the window frame, batting itself repeatedly against the pane, trying to get out. She felt a lot like that fly and knew that she had to do something.

That's when she spotted Tim Shaw at the teller's station, his young face ashen, hands trembling as he held them above his shoulders. Tim was Tom's kid brother—that is, Tom from faro and gunshot fame. She saw a frosted pitcher inside Tim's window, and suspected he knew his brother's trick of stashing a gun within reach.

"If only I could get to that pitcher," Lydia thought, but realized that if she just created a diversion, Tim could easily access it.

Lydia watched the gunman in the vault as he tossed handfuls of new banded greenbacks into a sack. The sidekick kept guard. "That's more like it," she heard the first robber say as he pulled the string tight. He flung the bag over his left shoulder and carried it out to lobby. With his right hand, he kept his weapon trained on the room.

"And now, we'll take what *you* have," the sidekick said to the customers, spinning on his heel and sweeping the area with his pistol. He held open a small bag for incidentals. Lydia could hear Sadie sniffling. A young boy clung to his mother's hand asking, "What's going on?"

"I do believe I'm going to faint," Lydia said in a loud voice, sitting up slightly, pressing the back of her left wrist against her forehead. “Could I trouble you for a glass of water?” she asked, looking at Tim and pointing to the pitcher at his station.

“I’ll get it, ma’am,” Tim said glancing at the gunmen for permission. Lydia had a feeling that Tim didn’t need to be coached.

“Go ahead,” the leader grunted, using his gun to gesture. It was hard to resist a damsel in distress. Lydia stayed low, knowing what would happen next. Tim reached for the pitcher, grabbed his Colt, and shot the gunman’s weapon out of his hand. The gunman dropped the bag of bills and clutched his bloodied knuckles. His sidekick wasted no time in taking the sack and bolting out the back door, running smack into a group of miners walking through town at the end of their morning shift.

“Not so fast, young fellow,” said Red’s friend, Sam, holding the kid by the scruff of the neck. “Looks like you might have our payroll there, unless of course you’re planning to deliver it personally.” The men laughed as they circled the sidekick, who, by this time, was whimpering and apologizing.

“If you want to see the sun rise tomorrow, I suggest you hand that over,” one of the miners said, stepping closer, taking a pistol of his own out of his waistband and aiming it at the thief. The kid dropped the bag and Sam kicked it aside.

By this time, the Sheriff was in the bank, standing over the wounded robber with a gun aimed at the robber’s head. “Everyone OK?” the Sheriff asked as customers got to their feet and dusted themselves off. Tellers pulled themselves together and pretended to tidy their work areas.

Lydia went over to Tim Shaw. “That was a brave thing you did, young man,” she said, extending her gloved hand to shake his. He awkwardly returned the handshake, staring at her beautiful face.

“My pleasure, ma’am,” he said, finally looking down. “After what you did for my brother and all, this was the least I could do.”

Lydia remembered the night she had stayed with Tom Shaw at the edge of the street, hoping he wouldn’t bleed out, praying he wouldn’t die from his wound. She had done it without expectation of repayment, but it made her feel good that someone remembered.

Lydia retrieved the hidden bills from her bosom to the wide-eyed stare of the young man behind the teller bars—and she reached into her pocket to pull out the poke. "I'd like to deposit these," she said, lining up her collection of currency. By this time, Tim Shaw was all business. "And this is for you," she said, giving him one of the vials of flakes.

"Oh, I couldn't accept that!" he deferred, as he took out a scale to weigh the other gold particles.

"But you must," said Lydia. "You deserve it." After which, she turned and walked out.

Lydia wanted to tell Red about her adventures in the bank, but that would have to wait. He was traveling to Denver under the pretense of seeing family—in reality, taking his crystal and ore samples to an assayer. After that, he would go to Clark, Gruber and Company, a bank and mint on the corner of McGaa and G Street, to have his metal turned into something more portable.

+++

Red held his breath as the assayer set out three crucibles and added the ore and gold-bearing quartz to a mixture of sodium bicarbonate, potassium carbonate, borax, lead oxide, and flour. The assayer then heated the flux to cause a reaction. Red watched as the man poured off the molten glass that floated to the top, directing the liquid metals into molds.

The men talked about the weather and the escalating Civil War as they watched the metals cool. Once removed from the molds, the assayer placed the blocks on a container of bone ash to absorb the lead oxide. Red's pulse was going rapid fire as the assayer extracted the resulting pieces and put them into a solution of nitric acid, dissolving away the silver and lead and leaving behind hefty lumps of pure gold. Red watched anxiously as the assayer put them into a green felt, draw-string bag. To Red, nothing looked better.

He paid the assayer, sold the silver back to him, and walked to Clark, Gruber and Company where—as allowed by law at the time—they would mint private coins for his personal use. Entering between the pillars at the front of the building, Red wasn't sure he belonged among the suited, vested, pocket-watched men. But he held his own, strolled up to the window and placed his order, accepting a receipt in exchange for his weighed gold. What resulted were $5, $10, and $20 coins, the latter two denominations imprinted on the front with an eagle clutching a sheath of arrows and impressed on the back with an image of Pike's Peak. He also asked them to craft a special $2.50 coin drilled with a small hole, which he would put into a pocket closest to his heart.

With the coins safely hidden on his person—in boots, pants, and pouch—he made his way to a branch of the General Land Office to check on his claim. The clerk was a neatly clad fellow, young and accommodating, his hair slicked over from a left side part. He pulled out a ledger bearing entries from 1851, the year Red had staked the claim in his mother's name, and he laid the book on the counter.

"Mattie Howe Mine, filed for Matilda Howe Suter by James Suter," the clerk confirmed after riffling through the pages.

"Yes, that's me," Red said. "Mattie was my mother."

"Should I assume she is deceased?"

"Yes, I was 18 at the time. She passed when I was 20," Red said, trying to forget the time he came home from the fields to find his mother dead in bed. Diphtheria, they said.

"Sorry to hear that," the clerk replied. "I see you've paid the annual fees, so the claim is current, but I am not seeing the paperwork needed to verify your $100-a-year investment in working it."

Red thought back. Had he forgotten to submit the papers? He was sure he had…Maybe the papers were misfiled. Maybe the express rider never made it to Denver. Truth is, he hadn't thought too much about the mine during the past ten years, but each year he did check on it and make small improvements. He had excavated new tunnels, built scaffolding in the shaft, piped the spring that flowed behind it, and of course, built a cabin at the entrance. He just didn't have much to show for it.

"Well, here's a statement of work for this year, along with receipts," Red said, handing the man an itemized list of what he had done most recently. He purposely didn't mention the strike, but he listed things like, "Reinforced walls in main corridor," "Cleared debris from excavation sites." "Replaced beams."

"And if I send someone out to look at it today, they'd see that this work was done?" the clerk asked.

"Absolutely," Red said, not flinching at the threat of an on-site inspection. "I have a witness if you need a statement," he said, thinking of Lydia.

"Not now. Everything seems to be intact," said the clerk, "except for those missing papers."

"Should I be concerned about that?" Red asked.

"Not unless you're claim-jumped. We have your affidavits, just not the supporting documents. Might be hard to prove ongoing maintenance if you were challenged."

Red scowled at the possibility and said he would check his records. He bid the clerk good day, put on his hat, and caught the next stage back to Buckskin Joe, comforted by the feel of gold in his pocket.

+++

Jared must have been smiling on the plane when his phone alarm rang, because Alexa, who had already returned from the past, was sipping a soda and watching him intently.

"Did you have a good trip?" she asked just as the pilot announced they were preparing to land.

"Superb," he said, not wanting to elaborate in public. "But I missed you. How was Buckskin Joe?"

"Adventurous," Alexa replied. "I'll tell you more when...."

Just then, with a thud and a whoosh, the wing flaps dropped, and the wheels touched down, propelling the twosome forward before pushing them back against their seats.

"Welcome to Boston," the pilot said in a cheery, practiced voice. "The temperature is a balmy 23 degrees, with a threat of snow." The passengers laughed, groaned, and applauded simultaneously.

"It was a nice Thanksgiving, wasn't it?" Jared said to Alexa as he stood up and retrieved her backpack from the overhead bin.

"I've got a lot to be thankful for," she said, looking over in a way that included him.

They maneuvered through the narrow aisle, thanked the crew, and clomped down the ramp onto the concourse, walking toward an escalator that went to the ground level. Picking up their luggage and rolling it through the stanchions, they waited outside near a shuttle stop, trying to ignore the bitter cold and uptick of wind. A few yards away behind a pillar, a young man in a red and white leather baseball jacket waited, too, smoking a cigarette with his head down and his collar up.

Rejuvenated by the holiday break, Alexa and Jared renewed their commitments to schoolwork. Alexa met with her counselor to solidify courses for the next semester, and Jared consulted with his advisor about doing an independent study. "If I could just devote more time to the Gardner Museum heist, I would learn so much," Jared pitched. "The best thing is that this is not a hypothetical case. It's very real and it's still open."

Peter, Jared's long-haired advisor, rocked back in his swivel chair, resting his pointed boots on the desk. He had a reputation for being an upstart—cool among kids, annoying among academic peers. He had always taken great delight in challenging authority and would help students jigger their courses to get the ones they wanted, or he felt, needed. He was outspoken and opinionated, known for bending the rules and going through hoops for students who showed gumption. He liked Jared and admired his spunk.

"It's not typical for a freshman to be granted an independent study," Peter said, looking up through his eyebrows, "and you would have to cover the disciplines taught in comparable classes—that is, interview method, archival research, first-hand observation, and use of the Freedom of Information Act. I will expect an in-depth article at the end—something worthy of publication—not just a classroom paper. That means—original thinking, at least three substantiated theories, evidence where possible and first-hand accounts. This cannot be a rehash of what was done before. You'd have to bring something new to the party."

Jared sat on the edge of his chair, tapping his foot subconsciously and shaking his head vigorously. "Yes, I would do all those things to get the information I need. But don't forget, I know the basics of investigative journalism. I interned at a newspaper last summer."

"True," Peter said, "but you won't have the support of an editorial team or media company behind you. It can get pretty scary out there alone." Jared weighed the negatives, but said he was determined to try. Peter reminded him that there would be tight deadlines for deliverables and that the two of them would meet regularly to discuss progress and next steps. He would be held accountable. Jared indicated that he would expect nothing less and after confirming the credit value, he asked Peter to make it happen.

"I'll email you an outline once I structure the requirements," Peter said, bringing his feet to the floor and reaching for his now-cold coffee. "Tell me one more thing," he pressed, leaning forward before letting Jared leave. "Why are you doing this?"

Jared thought for a moment. "Two reasons I guess," he started. "To help recover the artwork for the city and to establish a career."

Peter glared at Jared for a moment, wanting to see if he would squirm. Jared didn't. "Good answer, kid," Peter said, motioning Jared to the door. "And good luck."

When Jared got back to his dorm, he immediately texted Alexa. "Got it!" he wrote, adding a string of applauding emoticons. Then he sat down and started writing a list of things to do.

Alexa smiled as she texted back "Congrats! Way to go!" and noted, "Still working on my own little victories."

+++

In the following days, Jared was consumed by his mission. He immediately reviewed existing information about the heist, starting with a *New York Times* article from February 26, 2015, written by Tom Mashberg, recounting his days as a *Boston Herald* reporter, back in August of 1997. Mashberg had followed a hot, though possibly bogus, tip that led him to a Brooklyn warehouse in hopes of recovering the stolen art. In the process, he had received paint chips and turned them over to the FBI, who deemed them unrelated to Rembrandt's *Christ in the Storm on the Sea of Galilee*, the biggest and most commanding canvas of the lost lot. Yet years later, upon reexamination by a Vermeer expert, the chips were said to have contained the same Red Lake pigment used by Dutch masters in the 17th century and the crackled pattern was in keeping with the age of the stolen masterpieces. But all this led nowhere.

Jared then went to a bookstore and lucked into a signed copy of Stephen Kurkjian's book, *Master Thieves—The Boston Gangsters Who Pulled Off the World's Greatest Art Heist.* Here the veteran *Boston Globe* reporter, who had covered the story for decades, not only aggregated his findings, but now, as a free agent entitled to his own opinion, put forth some strong hypotheses about the case. Jared looked at the seven pages of character profiles at the beginning and knew this was going to be a massive undertaking… not so much in trying to confirm or refute what had previously been reported—the crime itself was of less interest—but in proposing a "What If" scenario that might actually lead to recovery of the art. Jared thumbed through the book, resisting the urge to start with the 'Afterword'. Instead, he stared at the heavy black inscription on the cover page. "Thanks for reading," the message seemed to say, but upon closer inspection, he was convinced it said, "Thanks for caring."

7
CLAIMS

"I've missed you like crazy," Jared said as he cornered Alexa outside the lecture hall, kissing her and playfully poking his tongue into her mouth. He had just come back from a run, had showered, and smelled like sandalwood. His hair was wet and as shiny as hers.

"I would say so," she said, returning the gesture.

"Yeah, this schoolwork keeps interfering with my other life," Jared joked. He surely felt buoyant now that he could devote more time to his investigation. "Want to join me tonight?"

"For what?"

"I'm going to a program called 'Art Heists of the Ages'. Figure I could learn something new—or at least, old." Alexa enjoyed Jared's ability to turn just about any phrase into a pun or play on words.

"You're certainly getting sucked into this thing, aren't you?"

Jared nuzzled her neck and worked his way up to her ear. She squirmed but didn't try to get away. "Can't help it. Just like I can't help doing this when I'm around you." He pinned her arms against the wall, pressed against her and continued to kiss her. She willingly kissed him back.

So much had changed since their first awkward encounter, she kept thinking. Now they were so comfortable with each other, aware of each other's moods, and in tune with each other's thoughts—sometimes to the point of not having to say much at all.

"I'll make a deal," she said. "I'll go with you to the program tonight if you come with me to Buckskin Joe tomorrow. I want to see what's happening there."

"You got it, Lydia, ma'am," Jared said, in his best Red impression.

✦✦✦

That night, the wind chill factor hovered below zero as Alexa and Jared made their way to the library where the art heist program was being held. "Man, I'm freezing," Jared said as he pulled his watch cap lower over his ears and zipped his parka up to meet it.

"You should wear a scarf," Alexa said, talking into the wool fabric that wound around her neck, across her mouth and up to her nose. The fringe danced wildly behind her head.

Leaning into the gusts, they finally found the building and pushed the door open, taking seats in the back row. The room was filled with golden oak book cases and smelled of elementary schools, grange halls, and country post offices. Jared noticed a carafe of coffee sitting on a side table and brought back two steaming, white disposable cups.

Alexa peeled off her gloves and stuffed them into her knit hat. She forced the entire wad into the sleeve of her coat, which she draped around the back of her chair. She kept her scarf on for warmth. Looking at the interlocked seats, having hoped to sit on something more accommodating, she snarked, "The finest orange plastic money can buy." Alexa knew this wasn't going to be her favorite night out, but she had agreed to attend this lecture and here she was.

Jared took out a small spiral pad, unbothered by the physical discomfort of the seating. He preferred this low-tech method of note taking to typing on a tablet. A radiator hissed at his side.

The speaker stepped to the front of the room and introduced himself as an art historian and author. He adjusted the microphone clipped to the neck of his gray Shetland wool sweater and cued his AV assistant to crank up the presentation, which began with stunning photos of paintings, sculptures, and jewels, followed by the words, "Stolen. Stolen. Stolen." A long list of recent thefts followed. Except for recovery of da Vinci's *Madonna of Yarwinder,* taken from Scotland's Drumlanrig Castle in 2003, most of the pilfered goods had not been recovered. Jared was glued to his seat as he imagined the wealth of artifacts just waiting to be found.

The presenter continued by showing pictures of museums, war zones, and sunken ships—all settings of wrong-doing where art and antiquities were misappropriated and where human greed had flourished. But it wasn't until the presenter zoomed in on the dial of a home safe that Alexa sat up and paid attention. Somehow the idea of hiding public art for personal gain resonated—or reminded her of the bank holdup in Buckskin Joe.

After an informative introduction, the speaker became more animated, arguing for greater government support and public outcry. He pointed out that in some countries, such as France, art heists were considered a national crisis, but America had grown complacent. "We must pool our intelligence and technology to locate these treasures," he argued, citing the Isabella Stewart Gardner Museum heist as an example of a crime that had dragged on too long.

Jared made note of links to additional information, while Alexa considered how she might use this topic for a paper on public policy. As they stood in line waiting to thank the speaker, Jared noticed the sleeve of a tweed coat at his side. He glanced up at a middle-aged man with tortoise shell glasses and a tan plaid Burberry scarf.

"Excuse me, have we met?" Jared ventured to ask, offering his hand and introducing himself. "I think I've seen you before."

The man extended his hand in return. "Bob Camelion, like the lizard, just spelled differently," he said with a smile that lifted his peppered moustache. "Yes, we seem to move in similar circles."

"You were at the Mayor's press conference on public safety, weren't you?" Jared asked.

"Sure was. I saw you there," said Bob. "I try to cover events like that in hopes of selling my work to the highest bidder. Unofficial stringer you might say." He shrugged. "Most papers can't afford to send paid staffers anymore."

Jared looked at the laminated card clipped to the man's pocket. "The *Independent Press*…I'm sorry, I don't know it."

The man chuckled. "You wouldn't. It doesn't exist, but I always keep a bunch of these handy." He patted his badge. "Great way to get into places. With security these days, everyone is more concerned about backpacks and concealed weapons than the authenticity of credentials."

"I'll have to remember that," Jared said, smiling, explaining he was a journalism student, already interned, hoping to go pro.

"I actually remember your name," Bob said. "I've got a thing for bylines. You worked on that report last summer about the Gardner heist… something like "Still Missing After All These Years."

"Wow, I'm floored," Jared said. "Thank you for remembering. It really was a team effort."

"Good work," Bob said, turning to greet the speaker.

Jared noticed Alexa standing silently, observing. He turned to her. "I'm so sorry I didn't introduce you; I wasn't thinking," he apologized.

"Not a problem," Alexa said, prompting Jared to move forward. "I know you were getting some high praise there."

Jared was beaming as he watched Bob prepare to leave. "It was nice meeting you," Jared called after the tweed coat. "I'll look for your articles." Without turning around, the man nodded.

+++

The next day over cups of hot cocoa, in the comfort of Alexa's dorm lobby, they let the little buckle take them back to Colorado.

Red and Lydia were saddled up, ready to head out to the Mattie Howe mine.

"Got everything?" Red called over his shoulder.

"Food, blankets, water, shovel…and buckets to carry our bounty," she joked. "And you?"

"Yup. Guns. Ammo. Pick. Lanterns."

Without saying much to each other, they rode out to the place where two boulders rose in front of sun-etched cliffs, beyond the agaves, yucca, and ocotillo, not far from a stream bed, but far enough to be removed from civilization. When they got there, Red led the way up the arroyo to the ledge in front of the cabin, but before proceeding, he stopped his horse and put his forefinger up to his lips in a signal for Lydia to be quiet. She steadied her horse and remained in the saddle. "What is it?" she mouthed.

"Not sure," Red mouthed back. "Something doesn't feel right."

As is often the case on a windswept bluff in Colorado, they could hear little more than the rustle of dry weeds rubbing against each other and the occasional howl of air currents catching in a rock formation. Lydia could discern the warble and high-pitched trill of a lark bunting. "Wheet! Wheet! Wheet!" it seemed to say before going off in a shrill whistle at an octave even she couldn't reach.

"Did you hear that?" Red whispered.

"You mean the bird?"

"No, the voices. Seem to be coming from behind the cliff." As Lydia strained to listen, she could detect the faint callings of one man to another.

"Wait here," Red instructed, but Lydia being Lydia, she immediately followed.

"I'm going with you."

As Red and Lydia rounded the back side of the mountain, not far from the natural spring, they saw an older man and two younger ones moving a pile of rocks.

"Excuse me," Red said as he rode closer, Lydia just a few horse lengths behind. "This land is claimed."

"I don't see any signs," the older man said keeping his eyes to the ground.

"Trust me, it is," said Red. "I claimed it over 10 years ago."

The older fellow finally looked up. "Asa?" Red asked, surprised to see the prospector he had previously met.

"Well, if it ain't the guy who gave me a ride on his horse!" the old man commented.

Red couldn't tell whether Asa was happy to see him or annoyed—although he suspected the latter. The two young men—less weathered versions of Asa—stopped to wipe their brows, squinting against the sun to better see Red and Lydia.

"What do you want?" the old man asked.

"I'd like you to kindly remove yourself from my land," Red answered, tempering his displeasure. He knew these things could be a simple misunderstanding. Mining regulations were lax and often unenforced.

Asa shifted his weight but didn't budge. "Now why would I want to leave?" Asa retorted. "My sons here and I finally found the Mad Cow mine we've been looking for."

"That's Mattie Howe," Red corrected. "Named for my mother, Matilda Howe Suter—Mattie for short."

"Well, ye haven't been workin' it as far as I can see," Asa accused. "And it's a miner's duty to keep his claim 'live."

"It *is* alive. You're just poking at the wrong side of the hill," Red said, not really wanting to draw attention to his cabin, but trying to reason with the old man.

"Don't see any markers or tools," one of the sons challenged. "We've ridden around this whole area. You should have a central stake and posts on each corner with your paperwork up on the pole in a tin can."

"I do," Red said, pointing in the general vicinity, only to realize that the flash flood had wiped them out. "Who do you think piped this spring?" Red asked, pointing to the spigot that channeled fresh water from the source.

"Beats me," said Asa, ignoring what he didn't want to know.

The group seemed to be at an impasse at which point Lydia said, "I remember you, mister. We danced at Bill Buck's not long ago."

"Thought I recognized you, pretty lady—but you look a whole lot different than you did all dolled up as a dance girl."

"That's 'cause I'm not working."

"So, what are you doing out here?"

"Red's a friend and I'm helping him…tidy up his cabin."

"Well, unless you can prove he owns this claim, we ain't movin'."

"I've got paperwork right here that says it's my claim," Red asserted, reaching into his pocket.

"Lemme see that," the wizened prospector asked, moving closer. Red showed him the paper. The old man turned his eyes into slits. "All this says is that you paid some permit fee. My boys were in the city and said there's no proof of you workin' this spot."

"Look, gentlemen, I don't want any trouble." Red's fingers inched down toward his gun. "But if you don't get off my property, I'm going to bring back the law."

"Law. Shmaw," the prospector said. "Everyone knows we make our own law."

"Well, I guess I'm going to have to make some law of my own then," Red said, drawing his pistol on the men. Lydia knew he carried but never saw him use a weapon. She wasn't sure how she felt about the rougher side of this mild-mannered man.

The old prospector and his sons looked Red up and down and slowly gathered their tools. "We'll be back a week from today," they warned, "with help."

Lydia exhaled as the men rode off. Red put away his pistol. "We'll need to line up some help, too," Red said, not really wanting to get embroiled in an altercation, "unless we can prove I've been working this mine all along."

Lydia starting thinking. Between herself and Red, they had a lot of friends in Buckskin Joe. It would be easy to round up a group of men, but it would be asking a serious favor for them to ride all the way out here.

With the claim jumpers gone, Lydia and Red dismounted, watered the horses and refilled the canteens before riding around the ledge to the cabin. When they got there, Red pried off the wooden slat that held the door shut and walked in. "Almost starting to look like home," he said as he set his rucksack on the small table.

"We'll need this," Lydia said, unrolling an extra blanket from the bundle she carried and smoothing it out on the bed. "Nights are getting cold."

After she and Red had organized their supplies, they walked along the ridge, looking over the vast grasslands and small hills. Thoughts of an Indian attack ran through her head, but Lydia knew the Arapaho and Cheyenne were preoccupied with negotiations at Fort Wise.

She had mixed feelings about the idea of Indian reservations. It seemed wrong to force people off their rightful land, but if a designated area could preserve some of it, maybe that was better than losing it all. “Interesting that the Natives never bothered with gold mining,” she mused.

“Maybe that’s because they already felt rich,” Red replied, reveling in a sense of contentment as he looked across his acreage and at the woman beside him.

That night, with several lanterns glowing, Red shuffled through a metal box of papers he had stuffed under the cot, hoping to find a bill of sale for supplies. Lydia had brought the September 9th edition of the *Rocky Mountain News* with her and set about reading it. She loved looking at the ads that touted fancy goods and perfumes. She noticed that someone was seeking to employ a woman who could sew. “I could do that,” she decided. One ad announced a service to track down stray livestock. Another ad sought $1,000 in bricks or lumber in exchange for Denver lots.

“Maybe someday we could go to Denver together,” she said to Red, causing him to glance up from the pickaxe he was cleaning. “I see there’s a tightrope walking show at the National Theater, and The City Hotel on Larimer Street sounds divine.”

“Maybe we should get married there,” Red said, as if discussing nothing more than the weather.

Lydia stared at him until he looked up again. “Are you serious?” she asked. “You would marry someone like me?”

“I would if you’d have me,” Red said, not for a minute thinking Lydia was anything less than ideal.

“Have you?” Lydia exclaimed. “I’d have you anytime, night or day.” She put down the newspaper and walked over to him.

Red was still sitting. He set the pickaxe on the floor and welcomed her into his arms, resting his head on her waist as she stood before him. Bending over to kiss his head, Lydia said, "If that was a serious proposal, Mr. Suter, I say yes."

Red stood up and embraced her. "I have something for you," he said, reaching into his left shirt pocket. "It's just a token, and I promise I'll do right by you later, but I thought you might like this." He took Lydia's hand and slipped a small warm disk into her palm. When she looked at it, she saw a flat gold coin impressed with LC on one side and JS on the other. Red pulled a thin gold chain from his other pocket and strung it through the hole.

"Is this from your gold?" Lydia asked, clearly moved by the gesture.

"Our gold," Red corrected. "But do you know what it represents?"

"I'm not sure," Lydia said. "That you love me?" she asked, almost doubtful.

"That goes without saying," Red said. "This is a $2.50 piece… the inflated price of eggs. I just wanted you know that I will always be here to buy you eggs, to take care of you and to protect you."

Lydia was speechless and overcome with emotion. She asked Red to help her fasten the simple necklace around her throat and smiled as it settled right over her heart. That night, their love making was special. Torrid, of course, but tender, too, with a sense of leisure that suggested they had all the time in the world. The next day they worked side-by-side inside the mine to clear rock away from their find.

The following week Red confided in his friend, Sam, telling him about the Mattie Howe claim and how it might be in jeopardy. "I need to round up some guys to go back with me on Saturday and I hoped you could come."

"I'll not only come," Sam said, "but I'll bring my crew—and they'll get their brothers, fathers, and uncles, too."

"I think it will just be a stand-off," Red said, "but it could be dangerous."

"What we do every day is dangerous," Sam reminded, and then with a slap on the back, Sam assured, "Don't worry. We've got you covered."

That Saturday, before daybreak, Red and 19 other miners rode out to the Mattie Howe and were in position when Asa and a handful of others arrived. Red's friends had helped him re-stake the property and put claim papers into cans on each post. They also carefully placed tools at the mine entrance near the cabin and at the back of the cliff—miner's code for "Hands off. We're working here."

Lydia stayed behind this time, needing to perform a show that night. She worried about Red and tried to divert her thoughts elsewhere. After a late breakfast, she wrote a long entry in her diary, then took a basket and walked out toward the woods where the aspens were turning gold and the air hinted at the chill to come. "I hope he'll be OK," she thought as she gathered pine cones and small branches for tinder.

After bringing them home, she stoked her wood stove and put water on to boil. She brought her tea caddy down from a shelf near the window and reached for her mother's delicate china cup, one of the few tangible memories she possessed. As she spooned out a serving of loose tea, she thought about the practical impact Red had made on her life.

He had installed a pipe to vent the stove at the side of the cabin. He had bought her a heavy iron pan that perfectly fit the flat-lidded burners. He had even talked about getting one of those new, mechanical refrigerators once the claim started producing.

All was not perfect, of course, she admitted with affection. He had hung shelves at heights she couldn't possibly reach and had moved her chairs to illogical locations. His shaving razor sat on her dresser when not in use, and his miner's jacket seemed perpetually affixed to the hook where she previously kept her bonnet.

She smiled at the mild inconvenience as she glanced at the tintype of local miners, suspended by wire from a nail on her kitchen wall. Studying the men standing near Buckskin Gulch, she couldn't help but admire them. They led such tough lives, yet they never complained.

She remembered the day that itinerant photographer had walked into Bill Buck's saloon for a shot of whiskey. He had started talking with her and, soon, she found herself bartering a dance for a picture. She didn't mind losing the money, because what she gained was a piece of history—preserved in silver particles, frozen in time.

Maybe that's why she didn't think it strange when that very night, out of the blue, just before she went on stage, the same photographer wandered up to the bar carrying a thick album with a fancy metal plaque on the cover.

"What do you have there?" Lydia asked as she poured him a drink.

"Photographs," he replied, tipping his hat. "I believe we talked before."

Lydia was pleased that he remembered her. "Yes, we did. I have one of your pictures on my wall."

"I'm flattered," said the young man, reaching for his drink. "You'll keep a tab for me?"

Lydia nodded. "Sure. Hard night or celebration?"

"A little of both, I guess," the photographer said. "Business has been slow, but I've completed something I've been working on for years."

"And what would that be?" Lydia asked, wiping off a spill on the bar, hoping the conversation would lead to another drink and a dance.

"An artistic endeavor," the photographer said. "Doesn't pay the rent, but it feeds the soul."

"I know what you mean," Lydia replied. "Sometimes I need to dance, even if I don't charge for it."

The young fellow knew he had found a friend. "Can I buy you a drink?" he asked.

"I would love a glass of sweet tea," she said, not wanting to impose the cost of liquor on him.

As the photographer went to the bar to get it, Lydia couldn't resist peeking at his album. His work was stunning, capturing a mix of haunting faces and dramatic landscapes. He had caught sunrises over mountain peaks and close-ups of snow-laden branches…pristine alpine lakes and rows of spiny cactus. Then she came upon a series of images that recorded a single place throughout the seasons.

"I see you found my masterpiece," the photographer joked as he handed Lydia her tea. "This is my five-year project."

Lydia studied the photos. The agaves, ocotillo, and yucca spikes in the foreground looked strikingly familiar and she felt as if she had walked this landscape before. She knew the path that wound through the grasslands and up into the arroyo, the dry stream bed that cut into the hills like a jagged scar. She recognized the cliffs rising above a ledge where a lone figure was shown pulling a cart of wood. In another picture, she saw a lanky young man leaning on a shovel near a mine entrance, a shock of dark hair obscuring his right eye. Smoke curled from a small cabin in a different picture—a winter setting—and in its summer counterpart, she saw a horse transporting a man with a pickaxe toward two large boulders.

"Where is this?" Lydia asked, trying to contain her excitement.

"Oh, it's way out beyond town. Backcountry, you might say," the photographer explained, smacking his lips after downing his shot.

"Let me get you another," Lydia said. "My treat." She reached into her gold poke.

"Are you sure?" the photographer asked.

"Absolutely," Lydia said. "I want to learn more about your work and whether it's for sale."

The photographer's eyes lit up at the thought of business. When Lydia returned with his second shot, she explained that these pictures could help a friend keep his mine because they proved he had been working his claim.

"They're for sale, sure thing," the photographer said, "and they're dated, too." He selected one and flipped it over in his palm, proud that he had kept such meticulous records. "Look," he said, pointing to the back.

"How much do you want for them?" Lydia asked.

"Let's see…how 'bout 25 cents for a quarter plate." He pulled out a sturdy 3 ¼ x 4 ¼" image stamped 'Neff's Melainotype Pat

19 Feb 56.' Then he extracted a newer one that felt lighter. He proceeded to take out a few smaller images as well. "What do we say 15 cents for a sixth-plate and 10 cents for a ninth." Lydia carefully stacked up the 3 smaller pictures and set aside a tiny 2" one for her personal enjoyment. That one showed Red smiling, leaning on his claim post.

"So that would be fifty, forty-five, and ten," Lydia said, doing the math in her head. She reached into her pouch and took out $1.05 in coins and dust. "I think you'll find enough in dust to cover the last five cents and then some," Lydia said, knowing that she had given him more than was expected.

"I'm mighty glad I came in for a drink," the photographer said as he thanked her and slipped the 6 images into a paper sleeve he kept in the back of his album. "I hope your friend will be able to keep his claim."

"He will now," Lydia said, all smiles, as she set the packet behind the bar. "Care for a dance before you go?" she offered.

The young photographer started to reach for one of the coins she had given him.

"Put that away," she said, taking his arm and leading him onto the dance floor. "Sometimes a girl's just gotta dance!"

8
TRANSITIONS

Alexa was grinning when her phone alarm rang, which brought Jared back to the present. “Hey big guy, I think I’m going to save the day,” she said, jostling his shoulder.

“You are?” Jared asked, dazed and bleary-eyed. “I sure could use some help ‘cause I’m out there facing a bunch of claim jumpers.”

“Not to worry. I’ll rescue you tomorrow,” she said, patting his forearm.

Just as they pulled their things together and tossed their cocoa cups, Jared noticed the stalker in the red and white baseball jacket standing at the receptionist’s desk again.

“I left a note a few weeks ago,” the fellow said. “Trying to reach a girl named Alexa, about 5’4”, long dark hair. Did she leave any information for me?” Alexa heard her name and looked up at Jared who was blocking her view

“Let me handle this,” he whispered, quickly steering her into the vending machine room where she had taken refuge before. “Wait here.”

Not one to shy away, Alexa resisted initially but reluctantly agreed to stay behind.

"Hey, buddy, I overheard your conversation and I think you're looking for my girlfriend. Can I help you?" Jared was more brazen than usual.

The red-headed fellow spun around, surprised to have anyone address him. "I doubt you can. I'm looking for the lady."

"Well, I might know where she is. What do you want?"

"I don't need to tell you. It's between her and me," the guy said, an edge rising in his voice.

"I don't think she knows you and I doubt she wants to," Jared said, looking up through the hair that cut across his right eye. "Why don't you just be on your way and leave her alone."

"I need to deliver a message, that's all."

"Maybe I can deliver it for you," Jared said, working his jaw in displeasure.

"Sure, buddy. Tell her we know that she and some guy are poking around where they don't belong, and if they don't stop, it's not gonna be pretty."

Jared thought there was something familiar in that voice. Was this one of the guys who had jumped him?

"Poking around where?" Jared asked, leading the guy on.

"Gardner Museum, that's where," the fellow replied. Not being the brightest bulb in the circuit, he stepped back and sized up Jared. "You wouldn't be that fellow, would you? The one who's been writing about the missing art?" he asked.

"That depends," Jared said. "What's this guy doing that's got you so riled up?"

"It's not me; it's my friends. Let's just say there's a big deal going down and this guy stands a good chance of messin' it up. He's asking too many questions and getting people talking again."

"What kind of deal?" Jared asked.

"A deal worth millions of dollars."

"So, someone's going to buy the stolen art?"

"Could be. You know, some people don't care about that sort of thing. Stolen or not. They just want the goods."

Jared wasn't sure how he had become so bold, but he heard himself say, "Well, you're not the only one with potential buyers."

"What do you mean by that?" the freckled fellow asked.

"All I'm saying is—I know some people who might be interested, too—maybe at an even higher price."

Alexa overhead the conversation from within the vending room and mouthed a "WTF?" not believing how far Jared was going with this bluff.

"Do you now?" the guy challenged.

"Yup. Maybe my people should check out the stuff for themselves. They can put money on the table," Jared continued.

By this time, Alexa was rolling her eyes, palm planted firmly on her forehead. "What the hell is he doing?" she said half-aloud.

"Of course, they'll need proof of authenticity," Jared added, trying to assume an air of nonchalance.

The red headed guy backpedaled, losing some of his bravado. "Well, I don't know where the stuff is personally…." Jared noticed the fellow kept looking over his shoulder. "All I'm saying is that it's my job is to make sure this meeting happens without interference from some cub reporter and his girlfriend."

Jared stepped back, hands raised. "Whoa. I have no intention of interfering with your deal. The last thing I want to do is get in the middle of it." Then he lobbed out some bait to see just how gullible this guy was. "But I *am* working on a story about the heist—actually, about the hunt for the paintings—so, if you could provide any information that leads to the discovery, I could make you famous."

"And then I'd be dead," the baseball jacket guy said with no hint of humor. With that, he turned around and pushed his way out through the revolving doors. When Alexa heard Jared say, "All clear," she peeled herself off the wall of the vending room and walked toward the doorway.

"Are you crazy?" she asked him once she stopped shaking. "You're gonna get yourself killed!"

Jared seemed remarkably calm. "Naw," he said, "I'm just gonna get myself some information. Want to help?"

Alexa knew she was in deeper than she had planned, but she liked Jared a lot and this mystery appealed to her sense of adventure. She nodded OK.

"He'll get back in touch, I'm sure," Jared declared. "Just don't freak out if he corners you. Call me before you say anything, because I have an idea."

"What is it?" Alexa asked.

"I'll tell you as soon as I know more."

Jared watched the elevator doors close in front of Alexa, whisking her away to a safer floor above. He was so immersed in formulating a plan that he didn't even remember walking across campus to his dorm.

Classes dragged the next day and, no matter how frequently Jared checked his phone, the digital minutes didn't seem to advance. Alexa was equally distracted, eager to return to a place where life was raw, rowdy, and romantic. They decided to meet mid-campus at the little coffee shop where they had first talked. This time, with two coffees set before them, they leaned over the table, hands touching. Jared held the silver buckle between his teeth, taunting Alexa with a "Come and get it"—and she did. Just as she grasped the exposed edge of the small rectangle with her teeth—split seconds before their lips touched—she was galloping into the back country, her dark hair flying, cape billowing in the breeze, a sleeve of tintypes tucked tightly into her saddlebag.

✦✦✦

"Red, Red!" she called as she neared the mine. Sam and several others were mounted on horses, standing guard. They looked down at her from the ledge and started to raise their weapons. Red came out and signaled them to lower their rifles. "She's with me," he said, thinking how nice that sounded.

Lydia was out of breath as she tied her horse to a scrubby tree and ran the rest of the way up the incline. "I've got proof! I've got proof you've been working the mine." Red looked puzzled as she pushed the packet of tintypes into his hand.

Red reached into the sleeve and slid out the pieces of flat metal, turning them over and back. "Why, that's me during the past years," he said, smiling, letting the words ease out as he looked at the images. Lydia stood there, her eyes shining.

"Where did you get these?" Red asked.

"I know the photographer," she explained. "And they're dated, too, so they'll be official when you file them in Denver."

Red had no words. This woman continued to amaze him. "Hey, Sam," he called to his buddy. "Let's round up the men and deliver these to the other side of the mountain," referencing the claim jumpers who were trying to eke out a back entrance.

"You got it," Sam said, and with a 'Gee-Hah,' he put his horse in motion. Soon twenty miners had circled Asa and his men.

"Hey, old man," Sam said. "We've got evidence that Red's been working this mine longer than you've been thinking about stealing it." He dismounted, took the packet of tintypes from Red, and fanned them out in front of the old prospector. "Look. 1857, standing by the claim post. 1858, excavating the entrance. 1859, bringing in lumber. 1860, building the cabin. And just this year, piping the spring."

Asa stood his ground, but his oldest son, thumbs hooked into suspenders, moved closer to look at the pictures. He walked away shaking his head. "It's no use, Pop. These make it damn clear this claim is not abandoned. We'll be charged with invading if we don't leave." Asa wasn't happy, but he was realistic.

"Well, it ain't no use beatin' the devil around the stump," Asa grumbled. "Guess we gotta go." He gathered his equipment, tied it into a bundle, and called for his mule, who didn't respond until he went over and got her. By this time, his sons were mounted on their horses, ready to be gone. "Be seein' you around," Asa said to the group as he sidled off, Sallie in tow and noisily braying.

"Don't hurry back," Red called after him. Red's miners let out a cheer.

"Anyone hungry?" Lydia asked.

"We're always hungry," one of the men said, "but there ain't much food out here 'cept for some scrawny rabbits."

"You bring me a few of those and I'll take care of the rest," Lydia said as she retraced her steps and went to her saddle bag. Upon hearing Red's predicament, Bill Buck had offered what provisions he could spare. From one side of the leather pouch

Lydia unloaded a bag of potatoes, three large cans of beans, a round of cheese, two loaves of bread, and some slabs of salted meat. From the other side, she pulled out a bottle of whiskey, a jar of pickles, a handful of wild onions, a cabbage, and a carefully lined box that contained two dozen of her homegrown eggs.

"How did you fit that all in there?" Red asked, taken with her thoughtfulness and Bill's generosity.

"I pack well," she said, pulling her hair back and tying it with a cord in an "I mean business" way.

While she set up the kitchen, Red carried the small table outside and laid a couple boards across two stumps. The men scurried down the path to the open land in search of game.

Within the hour, there were three fire pits going and six rabbits roasting over them, a can of beans set into the ashes of each fire. On the small cabin stove, she cut onions, cabbage, and potatoes and then put them on to boil. She sliced the salted meat, pickles, cheese, and bread on a plank, using a hunting knife that would never be accepted in refined social circles. The eggs she tossed, eight at a time, into a cast iron frying pan, watching them sizzle in some pork fat that Red kept in a can. He didn't have much for plates, but she had brought extra utensils, so she set out the meal in random pots, bowls and cooking containers and let everyone dive in. The rabbits were served on a sheet of metal, courtesy of Sam, steaming and smelling of smoke.

Ravenous would be an understatement, as the men pulled off pieces of roasted rabbit and rolled up slices of dry meat, licking their fingers with gusto. They spooned warm beans directly into their mouths, grunting with delight, then lapped up eggs with thick slices of bread. They speared chunks of potatoes, wedges of cabbage, and rings of onion and went back for more. They gobbled up squares of sharp cheese and rounds of pickles, toasting each other with tin cups filled with cold spring water. They passed the whiskey bottle around and someone took out a harmonica. Soon, a party was in full swing. As the facing mountain cast a shadow across the cliffs, candles were lit and lanterns, set between rocks. Red and Lydia watched from the perimeter, holding hands and smiling. "It's good to have friends," he said, looking out across the amicable gathering of men.

"And lovers," she added, looking up at him.

Once the food was consumed and the partying done, the men rolled up around the fires, leaving the cabin to Lydia and Red. By morning, the men were gone and the fires, extinguished.

In the following days, Red and Lydia worked the mine hard, chipping out quartz, exposing new rock, and filling a cart to take back with them. For safe-keeping, they would store it at Lydia's place since few people knew exactly where she lived, and Red would bring the ore to Denver soon after.

✦✦✦

Hearing their phone alarms ring, Jared and Alexa bolted into the present and finished their coffee. The buckle was sitting on the table. "Glad we didn't swallow this," Jared joked as he pocketed it.

"Want refills?" the waitress asked as she walked by with a spouted glass pot in hand.

"No thanks," Alexa said, apologizing for sitting there so long. "We've gotta go." The waitress returned with the bill and slid it under a salt shaker.

They split the cost and stepped outside, still contemplating the events at the mine. December darkness had dropped over the city like a shroud, descending all too early on what should have been a bright afternoon. "You didn't tell me your grand plan for finding the museum art," Alexa reminded.

"Still working on it," Jared answered, taking her gloved hand as they maneuvered through the crowds.

✦✦✦

The next time they saw each other was a week later, on a frosty Saturday night, planning to stroll through the Commons. Trees were strung with Christmas lights, couples were carrying shopping bags, and children, energized by the magic of the season, were skating on the duck pond, way past their bedtimes. A group of music students dressed in red and green elf hats, caroled on the corner, attracting an audience who joined in the chorus.

The smell of fruitwood, burning in someone's fireplace, mingled with the scent of fresh pine coming from a wreath vendor's kiosk. In the deep recesses of Jared's mind, he remembered this same intoxicating fragrance from long ago…from a time when homes were simple, and forests were dense with old growth.

He and Alexa continued to walk until they reached a hole-in-the-wall restaurant in the North End that offered a half-price student special. Good conversation and a filling meal were just what they needed.

They eventually retraced their steps and caught a trolley back to campus. Alexa detoured at Jared's stop and walked with him to his dorm. Before he opened the door, she impulsively stood on her tip-toes and pressed a kiss onto his cheek. He encircled her in a bear hug. "What am I going to do about you?" he said, shaking his head as if in wonderment.

She wasn't sure how to take that remark until he continued. "You came into my life when least expected and now I can't seem to live without you." She was beginning to feel the same way. "Will you visit me over the holidays?" he asked.

"If you invite me." She flashed him a coy smile.

"You're invited," he said. "And by then, I might know how I'm going to find those missing masterpieces."

"Count me in, detective," she teased. And with that, she said good night.

✦✦✦

The following days were consumed with taking final exams, finishing semester projects, and buying Boston mementos for family and friends. A few days before Christmas, Alexa took a cab to the airport and texted Jared from the terminal. "I'll have something special for you when I see you."

"Me, too," Jared replied, appreciating the time to think about a gift. "Wish your family a happy holiday for me," he wrote before signing off.

"Yours as well."

9
ENCOUNTERS

As much as they railed against the commercialism, both Alexa and Jared got caught up in the spirit of the season. There was something about being with family that rekindled childhood memories and traditions. Alexa and Will went with their Dad to cut a tree at a nearby evergreen farm. They had gone there for years, ever since Alexa learned that even Santa needed helpers. Truth is, half the fun was coming home to hot cocoa, afloat with little marshmallows that melted into sweet foam.

Jared helped his mother bring down vintage ornaments from the attic. "Aren't these toxic?" he asked as he reached into a green hatbox, rummaged between layers of tissue paper, and extracted a delicate glass fruit.

"The original ones were," his mother said. "They contained lead and mercury to make them shine—but these were made later. These have silver nitrate and sugar in them instead. A lot safer."

"How old are they?" Jared asked.

"Civil War era. Late 1860s."

"Wow," he said. "So Red and Lydia could have seen something just like these." He imagined an old-fashioned Christmas tree festooned with bows and small glass fruits standing in the corner of a tall Victorian sitting room.

"Absolutely," Sarah said. "That's the joy of antiques. They bring you back in time."

Jared thought a while, then broached a different subject with his Mom—locating the missing art from the Gardner Museum heist. Sarah listened carefully as she laid out the ornaments on a table, but when he mentioned the stalker in the baseball jacket and maybe meeting with some questionable art dealers, she stopped what she was doing and motioned him to sit next to her.

"You've probably heard that the mob is likely tangled up with this thing," she confided in a low voice, a darkness passing over her hazel eyes. "Stolen art can be leveraged to get friends out of jail."

"I know," Jared said, shaking his head to affirm. "I've read that, too."

"This is big time stuff—not petty theft," she went on. "These are people who kill people."

Jared ran his hands across his face until they rested in a peak over his mouth. He reminded her that all he would be doing is brokering the deal. "I'm not looking to get anyone arrested. I'm not interested in the money. All I want is a good story. And to see the art found."

"Even then, you'll need safeguards," his mother cautioned. "This is dangerous. You'll have to deliver on your promises and you'll want a smart exit strategy. I don't really like you getting involved.

"I realize that," Jared agreed. "But I have an idea I want to run by you. If it goes anything like planned, it could help find the art and launch my career."

Sarah leaned forward, elbows on knees, chin in hands. "So, what are you thinking?" she asked, glancing up at the clock on their mantel. An hour later, they were still talking.

+++

The next day Jared went downtown to buy a gift for Alexa. He wanted it to be meaningful, but not too large; classy, but not excessive. He walked into a small jewelry store where the windows were sprayed with fake snow and where holiday music was amplified through loudspeakers facing the street. There he saw a selection of sterling silver charms carefully arranged in a locked case. The one that stood out was a tiny pair of shoes resembling the ruby slippers in *Wizard of Oz*, much like the dancing shoes he imagined Lydia wore. He selected a thin silver chain and had the jeweler affix the charm, but rather than purchase a small box which Alexa might misconstrue as a ring, he asked for a larger box that could accommodate a note. He thought Alexa might like a poem from his heart, rather than a card from Hallmark. That night, he set about writing it.

Simultaneously, Alexa wandered into a consignment shop in a small strip mall near her home. The shelves were decorated for the season, draped with garlands and sprigs of holly. On a mahogany side table, surrounding a punchbowl of eggnog, sat small paper cups with reindeer designs. A sign in front of them said, "Happy Holidays. Help yourself." To the side was a platter of perfectly shaped Christmas cookies adorned with glass-like sprinkles in red and green. A deep wicker basket, containing small balsam pillows, perfumed the air from below.

Alexa couldn't help but smile as she strolled around the store, sipping the cold creamy liquid that tasted of nutmeg and clove. She took her time, savoring a cookie, enjoying the old English ballads that played on a CD. Then she spotted it. Sitting on the seat of a stenciled Hitchcock chair was a small book containing excerpts from *The Miners' Record*, an imprint of the *Rocky Mountain News*. Alexa, as Lydia, had read about this new publication to debut in June of 1862. It was to be "devoted to the interests of the great mining region of Tarryall and South Park," "Union in sentiment," and regarded as "a miner's friend." Although the price of the newspaper would have been $5 a year, she would pay considerably more for the excerpts now, but it was the perfect gift for Jared.

+++

When she and Jared finally saw each other on December 28th, they snuck off to a quiet corner of Jared's house. Their feelings for each other had not lessened during the holiday break and, in fact, had only grown stronger. They steamed up the windows in the small alcove off the guest room until they heard his father call.

"What do you want, Dad?" Jared asked, tucking in his shirt and smoothing his hair as he stood at the top of the stairs in his stocking feet.

"Just wondered where you were, that's all," his father, Carter, said.

"Alexa and I were exchanging gifts. Did you need us?"

"Nope. Maybe later."

Jared and Alexa looked at each other as if they should make that statement true. "I do have something for you," Jared said, reaching into the inside pocket of his black fleece vest as they walked back to the alcove. He pulled out a small square box wrapped in gold paper.

"And I have something for you," Alexa said, going to her backpack and taking out a flat rectangular item covered in red foil.

"Trade?" Jared said, waiting to open his gift until she opened hers.

When she saw the tiny silver shoes, Alexa had to swallow back her emotions. Not only were they beautiful, but they signified something special that she and Jared shared. It wasn't until she read his poem, however, that she felt warm tears spill over the rim of her eyes.

"She danced out of the past
and into my heart when
the West was rugged and wild.
There's something to be said for being
old and new at the same time,
for exploring the unknown together.
Happy Holidays from Red."

Alexa wasn't quite sure what to say. Here was the guy, who initially stumbled over his words, now pouring out deep feelings and baring his soul. She looked up into his dark eyes and uttered a very faint "Thank you," not sure she could even find her voice.

He tucked her hair behind her left ear and sealed the moment with a kiss.

"Your turn," she finally said. Jared carefully ran his fingernail under the tape that sealed his present.

"I like the red color," he said, trying to lighten the mood, "Fits my name."

When he saw the small book with the vintage cover, he immediately thumbed through the pages. Upon noticing the origin, he realized that Alexa understood him better than most. "I'm so glad you didn't get me a tie," he joked, then more seriously added, "This is the most original gift I've ever received. Thank you so much." He brought Alexa close and held her against his chest as he gazed out over her head to where snow was turning the trees white. They eventually went downstairs together, hand in hand.

+++

"Hey, Mom, how much time do we have before dinner?" Jared asked as he snitched a cucumber from the salad she was making.

"And do you need any help?" Alexa offered.

"About an hour and a half…and no, I'm fine for now. But maybe later I'll ask you to set the table. You guys go off and catch up on things."

With that, they headed into the den, put their phone alarms on, placed the silver buckle between their palms, and were effortlessly transported across time.

+++

October was encroaching in Buckskin Joe, and the fields were losing color. Katydids had grown silent and flocks of birds were heading south. The town was bustling in preparation for winter, running, as before, on a timeline three months behind Jared's and Alexa's reality. So much had happened in this small mining town since Joseph Higgenbottom—a local eccentric—had set foot in the area a few years back. He had planned to name the town "Laurette" for his sweetheart, but he lost the moniker to his own buckskin-clad persona.

There were now two hotels, fourteen stores, a mill, a bank, an assaying office, and of course, numerous saloons. A courthouse was under construction and local politicians were lobbying for Buckskin Joe to become the Park County seat. The Beery Irrigation Ditch was bringing water into South Park, making life viable for the nearly 2,000 people, who lived there. Horace and Augusta Tabor had moved into town that August and had opened a well-stocked general store, setting their sights on managing the post office, too.

Father John Dyer, a Methodist preacher from Ohio, could be seen standing on a box in the middle of the street, shouting fire and brimstone. A group of merchants, gathered in front of the bank, complained about an income tax being levied to help pay for the Civil War. Several young men—hardly more than tall boys—stood in front of a Union recruiting office that had opened on the corner.

There was new currency in circulation now—greenbacks officially issued by the government as $1 and $2 United States Notes. The time for minting private coinage was coming to an end. The region had finally shaken its schizophrenic identity as Kansas, New Mexico, Utah, and Nebraska territories—and was now proudly known as the Colorado Territory. Voluntary infantry regiments organized under the territory's new Governor, William Gilpin, were being funded by unauthorized drafts on the federal treasury. Their mission: to intercept gold shipments going to the South. Just this past spring, Confederate troops had seized the Charlotte Mint and turned it into a base of operations.

The Pony Express was still running, but with the telegraph gaining popularity, the need was becoming less critical. Six months earlier, President Lincoln's inaugural address had been delivered by Pony Express to Placerville, California, and from there, telegraphed along the west coast. Here, it had simply been telegraphed direct to Fort Kearney.

Red and Lydia walked through town holding hands, catching up on the news of the day. Buckskin Joe was becoming a crossroads, a destination for ranchers, miners, and entertainers who hoped to gather audiences there.

Lydia noticed a finely dressed woman approaching, her lacy purple parasol matched exactly to her carefully tailored dress, most likely colored with those new mauveine aniline dyes from Europe. The woman wore a checkered shawl folded on the diagonal that picked up the purple in her dress. Her hair was parted in the middle and swept back in twisted plaits secured behind her head. Her waist was cinched by a fancy fitted Swiss belt that rose in a peak below her breasts. Twin bracelets were clasped around her wrists and small orbs dangled from her ears. Lydia couldn't help but think the woman out of place in this rough-and-tumble town.

As the woman came closer, Red tipped his hat in a cordial greeting and Lydia nodded with a smile. That's when the woman stopped in her tracks and stood directly in front of them. She looked at Red and then Lydia and back at Red again, squinting at them, her eyes narrowing with suspicion. Without warning, she took her right gloved hand and smacked it across Lydia's left cheek. Lydia lost her balance and fell backward. "How dare you steal my sister's beau!" the woman accused. "You hussy! You home wrecker!"

Lydia dusted herself off, brushed the sting off her cheek, stood to her full height, and stared the woman down. "I don't know who you think I am, but I don't know you or your sister—and I certainly don't know her boyfriend, whoever he is."

"Well, he's standing right next to you!" the woman said, looking at Red.

Red was visibly confused.

"George Smith, from Coloma, California."

"I'm afraid you have me mixed up with someone else," Red said. "Besides, I've never even been to Coloma."

"Well, if you're not George Smith, then you have a twin brother out there."

"Sorry to disappoint. But my brothers are most likely dead, and neither is named George."

Lydia stood with her jaw jutted out, arms folded, foot tapping. The woman retreated as she began to realize her error. "Maybe I'm mistaken," she muttered, embarrassed. "I could have you confused with someone else. I'm so sorry, ma'am. Are you feeling all right?" she sputtered, looking at Lydia, horrified. "I don't know what came over me—but my sister has been so distraught, and I thought for certain you were walking down the street with her man."

Lydia was surprisingly gracious considering the circumstances. "I'll be fine," she said, ignoring the welt that was rising on her cheek. "Where is your sister now?"

"Back in California. Her beau ran off with some dark-haired gal from Colorado, so I guess my imagination got away from me. I don't rightly know what she looks like, but this fellow here is a dead-ringer for George."

"I don't even know a George," Red said, matter-of-fact, but trying to be conversant, asked, "Are you just passing through or planning to stay in Buckskin Joe?"

"I'm here visiting family for a while, but then I'm going to Denver to spend some time with my cousin."

"Well, do have a good stay, ma'am," Red said as he tipped his hat and started to leave. Boy, could he be charming!

"Gosh, you even sound like him," the woman couldn't resist adding. "George, that is…."

"Well, you're going to have to find your George elsewhere," Lydia clarified. "This is Jim Suter. We call him Red." The woman processed the new information as Lydia added, "I work over at Bill Buck's dance hall, if you need anything while you're here. I'll certainly remember you if you swing by," she said, holding her cheek.

The woman apologized again and scurried off, hiding her face with her parasol. Red and Lydia continued down the street discussing the strange encounter.

"Wish I did have a brother George, who was alive and well, but mine were named Roger and Paul. There isn't a day that goes by that I don't think about them and my father. I wonder where they ended up—and what ever happened to them. My mother was never the same after they left." Red grew quiet as he said this, his thoughts drifting miles away. Lydia ran her hand across his back to comfort him.

10
PLANS

The electronic sound of their phone alarms brought Jared and Alexa to attention. The television was on, so it appeared that they had been watching a movie. “I could use that hand now,” Jared’s Mom, Sarah, called from the kitchen.

“Be right there,” he replied, shutting off the TV. He ran his fingertips over his eyelids and out to his temples, trying to focus. Alexa was at his side.

“If you could take those placemats from the sideboard and lay them out on the table, that would be great,” Sarah said to Alexa. “There’s silverware in that drawer, too.”

Alexa noticed that Sarah was looking at her peculiarly. “You must have been leaning on your cheek,” Sarah said, pointing to the rosy area on the left side of Alexa’s face.

“Oh, yeah. I dozed off on Jared’s shoulder,” she lied, her hand immediately going to the warm spot where the woman in purple had hit her. Alexa wondered if that bruise was visible to everyone or just someone with exceptional perception.

+++

On New Year's Eve, Jared and Alexa bundled up and drove into town where the Chamber of Commerce was sponsoring a First Night. The scene was festive and the mood, expectant. Lamp posts were wound with small white bee lights that turned Main Street into a corridor of enchantment. A local rock band played from a gazebo on the green and vendors lined the sidewalks selling pastries, hot cider and coffee. Actors in bright costumes entertained the crowd—jugglers, minstrels, and mimes. Other performers on stilts sported large paper maché heads, reminiscent of the statues on Easter Island. Artisans armed with chisels and small brushes were putting finishing touches on their ice sculptures in hopes of winning a blue ribbon. Stores and restaurants stayed open late, giving away free samples, encouraging visitors to continue their trek to the waterfront for a fireworks display.

As Jared and Alexa waited for the show to begin, they watched a barge strung with large, old-fashioned bulbs, maneuver in the water, creating loops of color against the blackness. Their breath rose in small puffs as they talked. "Do you ever wonder why we were brought together?" Jared asked. "I mean, why us, why Red and Lydia, why a dancer and a miner?"

"Part of life's master plan, maybe?" she suggested, then added, "But I think there's also something important in it for you."

"You said that before. Why do you think so?"

"Just a feeling. Otherwise, it would be too random."

Their conversation didn't go further, because suddenly the sky lit up with plumes of light—canopies of reds and greens that cascaded downward. There was a bang and a pop. Two golden domes formed then collapsed into tiny stars that gravity pulled to earth. The crowd "Ooohed" and "Ahhhed." The next display changed color mid-air, triggering another round of appreciation from the audience. Whistling Roman candles, set off in a line, spiraled high. Spinning rainbows danced across the water. Blue, purple, and silver streaks shot across the horizon, followed by a laser projection of an angel. Clouds of acrid sulfur and smoke drifted in off the water. Jared and Alexa could feel the sting in their eyes and the choke in their throats. A loudspeaker transmitted a broadcast from Times Square, letting residents experience the countdown of the famous ball dropping.

"Five, four, three, two, one," the emcee on the loudspeaker announced in a crackly voice as a tremendous roar of celebration arose—there in the sound system and here on the waterfront. In a grand finale, the night sky exploded with rapid bursts of color, each replaced by grander, faster, and more spectacular themes. Jared and Alexa looked at each other and kissed slow and long, knowing the year ahead would be special.

✦✦✦

January arrived with attitude. Alexa and Jared both tackled their rigorous academic schedules with a renewed sense of purpose. As promised weeks before, Jared revisited the street where they had seen the fellow in the red and white baseball jacket. Jared talked to several women waiting for a bus and asked if they knew anyone who fit the description. They did not.

He stopped at a couple of bodegas and spoke to the cashiers, but nothing rang a bell. His luck improved when he finally cornered a few kids hitting a hockey puck in an alley way. One of them said he had seen the guy before. "Sean somebody," the husky kid offered, red-faced, blotchy, and out of breath. "Lives down the street," he said, pointing to a brownstone with window shades half-drawn.

Jared thanked him and walked toward the building, taking a few photos with his phone so he could remember the location. During the next few days, Jared made sure to stroll that way again, hoping to spot the stalker on his home turf. Pausing at a bus bench to check his phone, Jared felt a tap on the shoulder.

"Didn't know you hung around these parts," the freckle-faced guy said.

Jared looked up to see familiar red hair and a baseball jacket. "It's a cut-through to class," he lied.

"Been giving some thought to what you said the other day," the older fellow began. "About having buyers, I mean. Would they want to meet up?"

Jared tried his best to remain cool. "I think I can arrange that," he said and added tongue-in-cheek, "Down by the docks, I presume?"

The red-headed guy didn't get the cliché. "No, I'll tell you when and where."

"How will you reach me?" Jared asked, not wanting to give out his personal contact information.

"Meet you over there on Saturday morning at 10:00 to discuss," the guy said, pointing to a small coffee shop with a partially-lit neon sign that read 'Coff'. The ee's were missing.

"You got it," Jared said. "And we'll need some proof."

"You worry about bringing your buyers. I'll take care of the rest." Before Jared could say anything else, the fellow flagged down a cab and took off.

That night, Jared made some phone calls and told Alexa what was happening, figuring if anything went wrong, she could notify the police. On Saturday morning, he squeezed behind a greasy table at 'Coff' and ordered a cup of coffee, black. He took a sip just before Sean came through the door, rubbing his hands together for warmth.

"Man, it's colder than a witch's tit out there," Sean said, nodding to the waitress and pointing his finger at the coffee to signal another of the same. The waitress brought the second cup over to Sean and dropped three small creamers next to the saucer, winking at him in a suggestive way. "Thanks, Rosy," Sean called after her. He slid a note across the table bearing the name and address of an automotive parts place outside the city. Jared assumed it was a chop shop but didn't ask questions.

"Noon next Saturday—and my people want to see money. $100K in cash just for talking. They need to know your buyers are serious."

Jared tried to ignore the adrenalin pumping through his veins and nodded as if this were routine conversation. "And you're going to show us something concrete?" Jared questioned.

"Hey, I ain't saying we have the goods on the premises—my guys are just negotiators—but they'll show you some stuff that's pretty convincing and we'll get what you need when the time is right. Let's just call this a good-faith fishing expedition."

"Fair enough," Jared said, leaving a couple dollars on the table. "This coming Saturday at noon." He put the note into his pocket and, for safe keeping, entered the address into his phone."

✦✦✦

The following weekend, Jared rented a Zipcar and picked up his potential buyers. "Private investors" is how they described themselves. "Collectors' Consortium" is what their business cards said.

Alexa stayed behind as backup—and for her own safety.

When Jared pulled his rental into the rutted lot, he noticed a row of cars, in various states of repair, parked against a chain link fence. The sign above the shop door was non-descript, saying simply "Body Work" in big block letters. The place was quiet except for a Crown Vic idling across the street.

As Svetlana stepped out of the passenger side of the car, lowering her 4-inch boot heels into the slush, she had a tough time keeping her skirt from riding up to her crotch. She pulled down the tight leopard skin cloth, over her black stockings, and adjusted herself in the cream-colored sweater that stretched across her chest. Her fur coat was open just enough to reveal her narrow waist and rounded hips. Her v-neckline was enhanced with a gold chain thick enough to anchor a boat. She called to the swarthy man in the back seat. "Rudi, be a dear and put down some footprints."

Rudi was in his early 30s, with dark, slicked-back hair, piercing eyes, a thin moustache, and goatee. He sported a diamond stud in his left ear that sparkled when the light caught it. He got out from the other side of the car and walked around to help Svetlana. There wasn't an ounce of fat on his body. He was dressed in black from top to toe, wearing a jet-black mohair car coat with a high collar and deep pockets. He had his tightly fitted collared sweater tucked into quality wool gabardine pants with a front pleat that hung from his hips and broke just right at the instep of his fine Italian leather boots. His belt was snakeskin, which only added to his slippery appearance.

"Hate to get these wet," Rudi said, looking down at his own boots, "but for you, sweetheart—anything." Rudi kept a slim leather briefcase in his left hand and reached for Svetlana with his right.

By this time, Jared, in comparatively casual attire, got out of the driver's side and walked around in front of them. "I'll lead the way."

Jared's other back seat passenger, who stepped out last, went by the name of Chaz. He wore a trench coat and khakis appropriate for an accountant, lawyer, or business consultant. With a slight build, glasses, and wiry hair, he presented a decidedly recessive personality. In fact, he looked rather nerdy carrying a laptop case in one hand and a wad of tissues in the other. He followed the entourage to the side door, pausing to blot his nose.

The shop didn't appear to be open, but Jared noticed several guys coming and going from a side entrance and a few men standing on the loading dock, smoking. He thought he saw someone looking down from the window of an adjacent building, but they shut the blinds as soon as they caught him looking up.

When Jared knocked on the door, Sean opened it, a cigarette dangling from his mouth. "Glad you could make it. Stand here, please." The foursome waited as they were frisked. "Sorry about that," Sean said. "Policy, you know." Sean took their phones and put them into a metal cash box.

He pointed the group to a lunch table, where crumbs had been swept to one side. The smell of gasoline, rubber, and hot solder was thick in the air. In addition to Sean, there were two other men already seated. Introductions were made to Frankie and Joe.

"I hear you're interested in purchasing some automotive parts," Frankie said, steepling the fingers of his beefy hands. Jared noticed that a wedding ring cut into the guy's porky flesh and despite the cold weather, the fellow had a sweaty look that made his forehead shine.

"Yes. We're interested in learning about your rare automotive parts," Svetlana said, a hint of a Russian accent creeping into her words. The men looked at Rudi who remained silent and ominous.

"Do you know what we have?" Joe asked.

"We've heard rumors. We're collectors," Svetlana clarified, laying her card on the table. She eyed Sean's cigarette and deftly changed the subject. "Do you have an extra one of those?" Sean fumbled in his pocket and handed Svetlana a smoke, moving in with his lighter.

Svetlana sat back in her chair, blew a smoke ring and used her left pinky tip to remove a speck of tobacco from her tongue. "I think we should start small and work our way up," she said, subconsciously tossing her bleached hair as she talked.

"What do you think, Igor?" Frankie asked as he looked at Rudi.

"It's Rudolph. Rudi for short." He was not amused. "And I think whatever the lady wants is what we should do." He rocked back in his chair, clasping his hands behind his head so his elbows stuck out like wings. Jared noticed a tattoo of a shark inside each wrist.

Chaz sat quietly with his laptop case closed, sniffling into a tissue and trying to be as inconspicuous as possible. Jared watched as Svetlana steered the conversation.

"So, what are you selling that's small and portable?" she asked, looking between Frankie and Joe. Joe was a scrawny, nervous, rodent-of-a-guy, who fidgeted with anything within reach: pens, paperclips, the paper wrapper from a straw. After he had turned the last item into a thin white accordion, extending it to full length and collapsing it again, he looked up and said, "We have something the size of a postage stamp."

"I'm not sure I was thinking that small," Svetlana replied, adding in a more seductive voice, "Sometimes, sweetheart, size really does matter." She glanced appreciatively at Rudi, who reached out and massaged her neck.

"Keep that in the bedroom," Joe said. "We're all business here. I'm just saying we can't show you the big stuff until we have a deal on the table, but maybe this will whet your appetite." He reached for his wallet.

Jared strained to see and even Chaz looked up. Sean appeared bored, as if he had witnessed this scene a hundred times before.

Svetlana continued smoking, cool and controlled, as Joe took out a small glassine envelope, the kind the U.S. Post Office provides for stamps. It contained a tiny black and white etching of a soft-featured young man wearing a floppy cap affixed at a rakish angle. Ringlets of hair escaped from the right side of the hat where the brim dipped marginally over his eye, allowing uncontrolled curls to cascade down his left cheek. Svetlana noticed the shadows on his face were created by intersecting lines which seemed to fly off his forehead and get tangled in his hair. His moustache followed a similar path, upturned at the left side more so than his right, where it got lost in the crosshatching. His nose was doughy and wide at the base but pleasant enough at a glance. There was not much detail from the neck down.

"What are you showing me?" Svetlana asked.

Rembrandt's Self Portrait—*Portrait of the Artist as a Young Man*.

"I thought it was bigger."

"He did many self-portraits. Some are large." Frankie clarified. "This just happens to be the one that was on the side of an oak cabinet in the Dutch Room at the Gardner."

"How do we know that?" Rudi asked, tilting his head to look at the small etching.

"You don't," Frankie laughed. "That's the beauty of this arrangement. But if you'd like to show us a hundred thou to continue the conversation, we might be able to convince you."

Jared looked at Chaz who unzipped his laptop case and set out ten bundles of crisp hundred-dollar bills banded in lots of 100 each—$10,000 to a stack. Joe glanced over at the Ben Franklin design with the pale quill imprint and blue security strip. "These real?"

"Should be. I was at the bank when Svetlana and Rudi got them," Chaz answered, then zipped his empty case shut and sneezed into his tissues.

"Gentlemen, I can assure you there's more where this came from," Svetlana added, reaching across the table to extinguish her cigarette in a gray plastic ashtray. "We just need to know if you're as reliable as we are."

Frankie looked at Joe as if to give him the go-ahead. “I’m not handing you paint chips, if that’s what you mean,” Joe said.

“Yeah, someone already tried that,” Sean piped in, perhaps referencing that incident with the Herald reporter. “And it didn’t prove anything.”

Joe took the tiniest vial from his pocket. He held it up but didn’t let it leave his hand. It looked like a pipette used to draw blood. “These are trims from the Degas. I think if you test them, you’ll find they come from the mid-to-late 1800s.

“That’s not so long ago,” Rudi commented. “Could be fake.”

“Could be, I suppose,” Frankie said as he slipped the glass tube back into his pocket. “But I’m going to show you something else, too.”

Frankie reached into a cubby on the wall and removed a manila envelope. He opened the clasp and pulled out 13 photos. Each photo showed a corner of an art object held against a newspaper from March 1990. “Yeah, I know…could be Photoshopped, but I don’t think people were doing that back then.” Svetlana leaned over to look more closely. Sean stood behind her, more interested in her cleavage.

“Intriguing, gentleman,” she said. She noticed that the hand holding the artwork looked a lot like Frankie’s, especially the thumb with its black nail. He saw her staring at the image and then at his hand.

“Car door,” he said, “When I was a kid.”

“So, you have these pieces in your possession?” Svetlana asked, glancing down her nose just a tad as she spoke.

“No, no, no,” said Frankie, wanting to clear things up immediately. “We don’t have them at all, we don’t own them, and we didn’t steal them. We’re just representing the sellers.”

“Then why are you so eager to deal?” Rudi asked. Jared was thinking the same thing.

“Because we get a piece of the action. Simple as that. That’s why if you’re willing to pay more than someone else, we’re all ears,” said Joe.

“But you’ve seen the art?” Rudi asked, trying to confirm its existence.

"We've seen these pieces," Frankie said, pointing to the photos. "Looked real to us, but we're no experts."

"I'd like to get a picture of that little etching, so I can show someone who is," Rudi said. "Since you have my phone, can I use yours?" Rudi asked.

Frankie slid Rudi his phone and Joe took out his wallet again, laying the stamp-sized graphic on the table.

"Just want to make sure I get this right," Rudi muttered. "You have a lot of settings here." Rudi pressed a few buttons and slid the selection from panorama to video to square and back to normal again. "Not sure if I should take this vertically or horizontally."

"Oh, for cryin' out loud," Frankie said. "Give it to me. I'll take it." Frankie clicked off a couple shots. "Now where do you want these sent?"

"I'll put my email into your Contacts. It will be under Rudi. My last name's too hard to spell."

Frankie slid his phone back to Rudi, who entered his information. "I'll send these to you from an unrelated address. Probably will say 'Car Parts,' so check your spam filter."

"Not sure what this will prove," Joe interjected. "There are a ton of copies out there. You're either gonna have to trust us or not."

"I know," said Rudi. "It just makes me feel better."

"Suit yourself," Frankie said.

"You do know, by the way, that if you say anything to the authorities about us, this location or our little chit-chat, we'll deny everything, and you will find yourself at the bottom of the Charles," Joe said, in the same forced, civilized tone he had used throughout the meeting. The chill in his voice cut through the room. A prolonged and uncomfortable silence followed.

"Understood," Jared finally said, looking at his counterparts for consensus. "Then what's the next step?"

"We need to check out your friends here and come up with some pricing. You realize the total legitimate value is over $500 million dollars, right?" Jared nodded yes; he had read the FBI reports.

"And there will be additional handling fees." Frankie shot a knowing glance at Joe.

"As I said, let's start small and work our way up," Svetlana commented. "But I can tell you right now, a postage stamp doesn't cut it for me," she said, shaking her head as if offended by the small artifact. "I'm thinking bigger, like *The Concert*…just about 2 feet square. Easy to slip under an arm." With that, Svetlana stretched her arm out, did a game show host move from wrist to armpit with her other hand and reached simultaneously for her coat. Rudi jumped to his feet to assist.

Svetlana stood up and shook each man's hand, leaving a trace of perfume on their palms. Rudi and Chaz followed her to the door as Jared brought up the rear. Sean handed them their phones and Jared confirmed, "Meet at the 'Coff' next Saturday, 10 a.m. to discuss?"

"Yup. Unless I find you sooner. In the meantime, don't you or your lady friend go mucking around the Museum. Got it? We don't want any more attention on this than we already have. But if we *do* find you're meddling, we're done talking and you're toast."

"Got it," Jared said, raising his hand in a semi-salute. He nodded a good-bye to the men at the table.

"Not so fast, kid," Frankie called after him. Jared stopped and turned around, his heart thumping.

"I just want to know how a clean-cut college kid like you knows people like them," Frankie asked, gesturing his double chin toward the buyers who had stepped outside.

"I don't. I ran into them doing a story. They're sources, that's all—but that's good for you. No matter what happens here, I can't reveal their identity—or yours."

"You're gonna write about this?" Frankie asked—incredulous and worried about exposure. Jared watched the veins in Frankie's forehead bulge.

"Not about the theft. Not about you. Just about the search for the missing art," Jared assured. "How it could have remained hidden all these years."

"That better be the extent of it," Frankie muttered. "Not that I like it."

"Well, the statute of limitations ran out on this crime years ago, so no one can be prosecuted," Jared noted.

"Yeah, that does make things easier," Frankie laughed, lightening up, familiar with the legalities.

"So, what's in it for you?" Joe asked, repeatedly clicking the tip of a ballpoint pen, his beady ferret eyes zeroing in on Jared.

"A few things. First, my deal with the buyers is that they return one piece to the city. After all, the art is magnificent. Second, they are to give me the reward offered by the Museum; that will pay for college. Third, I will get an exclusive story to sell to the media, which will lock in my credentials and career. You see, I don't care what you do, or they do. This is just a means to an end for me." He purposely lied about the money—as a journalist, he couldn't accept it anyway—but he needed to make this sound good.

Frankie and Joe found Jared's explanation greedy enough to be plausible but not so greedy as to suggest he had experience. Jared stood in place, clammy hands in pockets. "Anything else?" he asked, wanting nothing more than to bolt.

"That's it for now. We'll talk through Sean."

11
HINTS

The group stood shivering next to the car, wishing for warmth, as they waited for Jared to return. When he arrived and unlocked the car, they hurried to get inside. He turned on the engine, blasted the heat, and backed onto the wet street. No one dared talk until they were a mile away.

Jared noticed a black car with tinted windows pull out of an alley and sit on their tail for a while, but it turned off with no further fanfare. His accelerated heartbeat gradually slowed, and his hands steadied. He dropped off his passengers, returned the rental, and walked back to campus.

That evening, Jared went to Alexa's dorm, planning to fill her in on his adventure. This was one of those dank mid-winter nights with bone-chilling cold coming off the river, hinting at snow that never materialized. He sat on her bed and ran his fingers through his hair. "We're going to have to be careful," he said, looking up at her, trying to relax his tight shoulders. He took a large gulp of air, as if he had forgotten to breathe for a while.

Alexa watched from across the room, worried about what had taken place. As Jared started to relay his conversation with Frankie, she noticed he had removed the small buckle from his pocket and was subconsciously running his thumb over it.

"Maybe I should hold that for you before you take off the finish," she teased, reaching out to grab it. Without thinking, they had set up a connection to the past. Unplanned and not ready for it, they felt themselves being propelled into Buckskin Joe on a similarly bitter night.

+++

Lou, the piano player, was setting out a jar for tips and Bill Buck was behind the bar wiping it with a cloth. "Don't know where everyone is," he grumbled. "Been quiet all day."

Lydia stopped choreographing a dance move to listen. "It does seem that way. Maybe folks are just busy putting in firewood and stocking up before it snows. It's brutal out there for so early in the season."

"Nah, there's usually a bunch of hearty souls who want a shot before heading home," Bill replied.

Just then the door swung open, bringing with it a blast of frigid air and shards of tumbleweed.

"What would you like, gents?" Bill called out from the behind the bar as two ranchers sidled up to the other end.

"Something for a sore throat," one of them said. "Musta picked up a bug in town last week." He ran his dirty fingers across his Adam's apple and massaged it.

"How 'bout some nice bourbon straight up?" Bill said, taking a bottle down from the shelf. "I save the good stuff for special occasions."

"Guess this would be special," the other man said. "We made a killing on some lamb we sold. Had a bunch of fine mutton chops in there."

"Sheepherders," Bill thought, wanting to retract his offer of good liquor. Most of his friends raised cattle, and those damn sheep ate the grass right down to the ground. But the saloon was near empty, and business was business. Besides, this was mining country more than anything else.

The first man coughed into his sleeve and took out a bandana to wipe his nose. He swallowed the bourbon in a single gulp, savoring the fire in his throat. "That's better," the man said. "Know any place where we can sleep? Too cold to camp outside tonight." He shivered.

"There should be some room down the street," Lydia said, edging toward the men. "Not many visitors at the inn this time of year." He gave it some thought.

"Hey pretty lady," the second man said to her. "You dancin' tonight?"

"Sure thing, mister. Dance most every night."

The man slipped a coin into her hand and steered her onto the dance floor as the piano player began a lively tune.

"Are you sure you're doing all right?" Lydia asked as they moved to the music. "You feel like you're burning up." She recoiled slightly.

The man used his sleeve to wipe his brow. "As I said, we picked up a bit of ague, that's all. A couple days off and we should be fine."

Lydia thanked the man for the dance and went to the back room. Something didn't seem right with these guys. She plunged her hands into the bucket of water Bill kept near the dry sink and splashed some of it on her face.

The next day she saw Sadie at the Tabor's general store, looking for lemon drops and spices to put in tea. "My Mother's got a nasty cold and her back is aching like crazy," Sadie said, as she put a few items into a basket. "Told her I'd bring her some things to make her feel better. Too bad, because we all had such a nice lamb dinner over there after Father Dyer's sermon last Sunday."

"You're a good daughter," Lydia said, patting her friend's arm. "Must be something going around. There were two fellows in last night, who were barely holding it together. If they're not flat out today with fever, I'd be surprised."

Lydia went home early that evening, and Lou put away his tip jar well before midnight. Red showed up at Lydia's place after his shift and announced that he was taking some time off work. "I need to get that ore up to Denver before we get socked in," he said, referring to the cartload he and Lydia had gathered. "I want to see if it's as pure as the stuff we already assayed, plus I need to line up some labor to help me get the rest of it out of the lode. Hopefully after that, I won't have to work at the Philips mine—and you can say good-bye to dancing for gold dust."

"I like dancing," Lydia said, setting out a beer for Red. "But, sure, I could use a break." She smiled at him, pausing to study his face. Although Denver was less than 100 miles away, travel was treacherous, especially during this time of year. "How long do you think you'll be gone?" she asked.

"A month or so. Aside from dealing with the ore, I need to square away my claim, buy some equipment, meet with a few people and make reservations for a wedding, right?" Red winked at Lydia, who was busy folding a shirt. She glanced up just in time to catch his intent. "I'll be back before Christmas," he said, reaching for her hand as she went by. Lydia was quiet.

"You seem deep in thought," Red said.

"Oh, sorry. Guess I am. I feel like something weird is going on here. It's been strangely quiet at Bill Buck's lately. Sadie's mother is sick, and two guys came in the other night, burning up with fever."

"Sounds like something's going around," Red said. "Make sure you stay warm and eat right," he said, assuming his protective role. He tossed a few logs into the stove.

Lydia walked over to him and kissed his cheek. "I'll miss you," she said, as she put away her plate and cup.

"I'll miss you, too," he said. "But just think—this is the beginning of our future."

Lydia smiled. "That's true. I can't believe it's really happening, the wedding I mean. I'll need to find something to wear."

"I'll look while I'm up there," Red promised, "and if I see anything as beautiful as you are, I'll bring it back with me." Lydia still wasn't used to these kinds of compliments and thoughtful gestures. "Or maybe you can come up with me next time, so you can shop for yourself." She liked that idea even better.

"How did I ever get so lucky as to meet you, Mr. Suter?" Lydia asked. By this time, she had put down her dishtowel and was undoing her hair. "Beats me, Miss Calhoon," Red said, coming up behind her, and kissing her neck, deftly moving her hair away, and working his hands down her back to unfasten her dress and bodice. With each undone button, he planted a kiss on her smooth skin, causing her to squirm until he got to the base of her spine. At that point, he reached around to the front of her hips and with a swift motion, pushed her dress and crinoline to the floor. He watched as she stepped out of them and bent over to unlace her boots.

"Brrr, cold." Lydia shivered as she stood in her unmentionables.

"Then let me warm you up," Red said, bringing her into his arms. He lifted her up and set her small feet down on top of his boots. She laughed as he duck-walked her over to the bed, where she jumped under the covers. He sat on the edge of the mattress to remove his boots, but she playfully pulled him back to set him off balance. He landed on the covers next to her.

A flurry of garments followed, tossed up from the bed like a geyser. Soon Red and Lydia were a tangle of softness and muscle, gentle words and naughty suggestions. Their lovemaking was long and sweet as the wind howled around Lydia's cabin and rattled the pail that hung from a hook outside the door. Just as sleep was taking hold, a tree limb crashed to the ground, hitting the stove pipe on its way down.

✦✦✦

Jared and Alexa both jumped at the sound of clanging metal. They squinted as their eyes adjusted to the dorm lighting. "Too bad I can't stay," Jared said, looking around the room, longing be with her for the night.

"House rules," she said, "but maybe soon." Both she and Jared were becoming envious of what Lydia and Red shared.

Jared said good night, made sure the silver buckle was back in his pocket, and walked across campus, trying to ignore the gusts of wind that pummeled his back and the ache that worked at his groin. He was asleep as soon as his head hit the pillow.

The next Saturday, when he met Sean at the 'Coff', Jared was uneasy. "What did you learn about my buddies?" he asked.

"They seem to have a nicely checkered past," Sean said as he flagged Rosy for a cup of coffee. "Implicated in handling stolen property…most likely involved in an art heist in the Netherlands. Of course, Frankie and Joe would feel better if they had some mutual friends."

"Not sure if *they* do, but I had an uncle who did some work in Connecticut—Manchester, to be exact," Jared bluffed, remembering the house that had been searched three times by the FBI. "Seems that he and Mr. Gentile went to school together. Does that help?"

"It might," Sean allowed.

"Well, my buyers should be good for the money," Jared continued. "I hear they own a building in New York. Use the penthouse as a private gallery, if you know what I mean."

"Frankie and Joe will be checking that out, I'm sure. If your buyers can pay more than ours, this will most likely get a green light."

"So, Frankie and Joe will see the art before they broker the deal?" Jared asked.

"If they can get down to it," Sean said as he slurped his coffee.

Jared's eyes widened. "Get down," he thought, immediately seizing on the language. Maybe this was just Sean's way of saying 'get to it,' but this could be a telling slip of the tongue.

Jared's mind raced wildly as he tried to decipher Sean's casual remark. Maybe "down" meant points South, as the FBI originally suspected. Down in Connecticut or Philadelphia. Then again, "down" could be colloquial for "Down East" as in Maine or "Down Under" as in Australia.

"Let's say this thing comes to pass," Jared finally continued. "What kind of timeline are we looking at?"

"That depends how fast your Ruskies can get the money."

"I don't think that's a problem," Jared said, taking a sip of coffee, which this time had the questionable benefit of synthetic cream. "They know how to move cash."

"Do you know how these things play out?" Sean asked.

"Nope. Haven't a clue. Never did this before." Jared was being honest.

"Well, we'll probably bring your guys to another place for a look-see and deposit. If the proof checks out, we'll lock in the deal, then meet up again for the balance and hand-off. Frankie and Joe will have some home boys around, of course."

"Of course," Jared said, resigned to the muscle that followed these men. "Do you know if everything's still intact? I mean, it's been like 30 years…." He could almost taste the article he was going to write.

"Far as I know, everything's in good shape," Sean said. "Preserved, packed up and moved around a lot, I gather."

Jared nodded, trying to imagine where the art could be stashed. "So, do I wait to hear more from you or do we just meet up?" Jared asked.

"I'll leave you a note at your girl's desk. That is, in her dorm lobby," Sean said. "What name should I use?"

"Leave it for Red," Jared said, wanting to conceal his identity as much as possible.

"Red, clever…Ruskies," Sean said, feeling proud for catching on.

"Hardly," Jared thought, but he just smiled. Sean paid for the coffee this time and they both walked off in different directions.

+++

The following week, in a cramped school office, Jared met with his advisor, Peter, to discuss the progress on his independent study. "I just want to make sure you go beyond what has already been researched and written," Peter pushed. "Get out there and do some legwork. Ask questions that haven't been asked. Look at things with fresh eyes." Jared didn't tell him that he was already hot on the trail of something big.

"Remember, no idea is too crazy, as long as you can support it. The feds have already exhausted the logical explanations. You need to be original. Dare to imagine. Find the 'what ifs.' Dig and dig deeper."

Jared left this meeting feeling pumped and ready to take on the world. First, however, he had to finish some assigned reading, so he headed to the library to avoid distraction. When he got to there, he noticed that Eric, his summer camping buddy, was holed up in a corner, eyes glued to a monitor.

"Whatchadoin'?" Jared asked as he walked by, tapping Eric's shoulder.

Eric jumped and removed his headphones to talk. "You scared the crap out me," he said, giving Jared a grin. "You shouldn't sneak up on people like that."

"Sorry," Jared said. "Just wanted to say hi."

"How you been? You look a lot better than the last time I saw you," Eric said, referring to the time Jared had been assaulted. "Ever figure out who did it?"

"Nope. Still investigating. But I think it has to do with the museum story I worked on last summer. Just got an independent study to do more on it."

"Cool. Still seeing that girl?"

"Alexa. Yeah." Jared could hardly think of her without smiling.

"No need to say more, buddy," Eric teased. "I recognize that faraway look in your eyes. Got it bad, huh?"

"You know, she's not like anyone else," Jared said.

They shot the breeze a while longer and then Jared found a seat near a window. He opened his laptop and tried to read, but his mind kept drifting back to Sean and the shady guys known as Frankie and Joe.

"If they can get *down* to it," Jared thought, replaying the phrase that Sean had let slip. "Get down, get funky." The old Teddy Pendergrass lyrics that Jared had heard on his father's music mix rattled around his brain. "Maybe Sean just meant 'get down' as in 'get serious about it', but then again, maybe he was referring to a nearby location like down town or down the street." Jared was stymied. He fingered the silver buckle in his pocket as his eyes glazed over the screen in front of him. He took the buckle out and absent-mindedly tossed it from palm to palm. He couldn't concentrate.

Just then he became aware of a ringing in his ears. The screen brightened and began to pulse. His surroundings blurred. He felt disoriented and short of breath. His head throbbed. His throat was dry. Cold beads of sweat began to form on his brow. Myriad smells engulfed him—dust, smoke, sagebrush, liquor…oil paint, turpentine, cheese, and poffertjes. His realities were colliding. He heard bursts of laughter, whispers, conversations, and cries for help. He was dizzy. Nauseous. As his stomach churned, he recognized the signs of an extrasensory experience much as a migraine sufferer can predict an impending headache. He tried to stop it, but his efforts failed.

✦✦✦

Jared found himself swept up in what could only be described as a wind tunnel, drawn in and hurled through space. Objects whizzed by at a remarkable speed. Details bombarded him and confused him. He saw a top hat roll across the floor and knew it was significant, but it could have represented Abraham Lincoln as easily as the missing Manet painting, *Chez Tortoni*. A piece of sheet music fluttered just out of reach. Was it from Lou's dance hall piano or Vermeer's *The Concert*? He spotted a woman's glove. It could have belonged to Lydia or, as easily, to Rembrandt's *Lady and Gentleman in Black*. Too much was happening at once. Time seemed to stretch and morph. He heard horses whinny and gallop away. Were they from a corral in Buckskin Joe or from Degas' *Three Mounted Jockeys*?

The information overload frightened him. His heart beat erratically. He clutched the table top to steady himself. As soon as the room stopped spinning, he called Alexa. "I'm at the library. Something crazy is happening to me. I'm drifting…seeing things…losing touch… I can't breathe."

"I'll be right over," she said. "Wait there." When she found him, he was pale, sitting with his laptop open but his screen dark. He had a distant look that worried her, and she saw in him a vulnerability he had not previously displayed.

She put her hand on his shoulder and gently jostled him. "Jared, I'm here. It's Alexa." He turned to her, trying to process her features. Finally, he spoke.

"I don't know what to do about this," he said, putting his face into his hands. He seemed near tears. "I thought I had this under control, but apparently not. I'm seeing things from different time frames…vivid impressions. Smells. Textures. Sounds. I don't know where they're coming from or what they mean."

Alexa reached over and took his hand. "Maybe you're trying too hard to resist what is natural for you. Maybe you're meant to see these things, to figure them out, and use them for the greater good."

Her voice was calming. Her smile, warm. Maybe she had a point, he thought. Instead of denying his abilities and considering them forbidden, what if he embraced them just like a singer celebrates her voice or a math whiz utilizes his genius? What if he opened himself up to this anomaly and welcomed his gift as a tool that was rightfully his to enjoy? Or maybe even, his *responsibility* to use and not waste?

"I'll sit with you if you want to try again," Alexa said, pulling a chair next to Jared, coaxing him to relax. "Can you pick up where you left off?"

Jared shrugged, not knowing the extent of his skills, but this time, with Alexa at his side, he approached the transition with intrigue, rather than disdain. He closed his eyes and heard a buzzing in his ears as if this were a cue for him to be elsewhere. The library faded away and once again, he found himself in the wind tunnel. When the vortex subsided, he saw Red standing there.

Red looked over and tipped his cap. "I'm so glad you finally confided in me. We have a lot in common, you know." A shimmer of luminescence followed Red's hand as it moved in slow motion, leaving a trail of particles behind. Jared gawked. This time he was an observer, not a participant. Was he watching someone else or just an older, wiser incarnation of himself?

"There are treasures underground, you know," Red said. "Most are not visible to the average person." He chipped away at a piece of rock, sending sparks into the air with each strike. Jared looked around, but all he could see was a dimly-lit corridor in a mine. Red exuded a soft glow as he moved closer, as if to share ancient wisdom. Jared could almost touch him. "Sometimes riches are right in front of our eyes or under our feet," Red counseled. He stepped back and removed a chunk of quartz, holding it up to a lantern. "A gold mine is usually closer than we think."

"Are you trying to tell me something?" Jared demanded, feeling foolish talking to his alter-ego.

"I think I already have," Red said and just as effortlessly as he had appeared, he vanished. With that, the room returned to normal.

+++

"Are you OK?" Alexa asked, staring at her dazed boyfriend.

Jared nodded yes, but he sounded as if he were in a trance. "Answers about the missing art are in the mine," he said as he looked at Alexa. "Clues to the present are in the past."

"How do you know this?"

"Red told me."

"He did?"

"Well, he inferred it. This time we weren't the same person. It was as if he were a guide from long ago."

"Then maybe that's why you were destined to meet him—so you could gain insight from his experience."

"Who knows? This is all so weird, but I'm starting to connect the dots. I think Red meant that the missing art—*our* treasure—never left Boston at all but is buried right here, beneath our feet—underground."

Alexa sat there wide-eyed. "But where?"

"Ahah, that is the question." Jared said, parroting Shakespeare and regaining his composure. "Sean said the artwork moved around a lot, so we should think about places where art could be stashed that would allow for easy transport."

"Maybe there's a clue in the gold itself," Alexa said. "Maybe the art is in a gold-colored building or at a storage company with a name like Goldfarb or Goldstein."

"Or maybe it's under the golden dome of the State House," Jared added, arching his eyebrows, intrigued by the idea.

"Maybe the answer has something to do with rock," Alexa suggested. "Like hidden in the side of mountain."

"Or between a rock and hard place," Jared joked. Alexa rolled her eyes.

"Maybe there's significance in the tools that Red used in the mine…like a pickaxe or ice pick. What if the art is frozen in ice and preserved like a Woolly Mammoth?" Alexa tossed out.

"OK, that's pretty far-fetched," Jared remarked. Alexa shrugged, but his comment didn't deter her. She liked brainstorming.

"What else then?" she continued. "Mines have a shaft. Maybe the art's in an elevator and just rides up and down all day. It could be in plain sight in a high rise."

"Or in a silo," Jared said.

"What else?" she asked aloud. "Mines have tunnels. Maybe the art is in the Callahan Tunnel or Ted Williams Tunnel," she hypothesized. Jared watched Alexa purse her lips as she thought. She looked up and caught him staring at her. "What?" she said.

"Just watching you think," Jared said with affection. "I like the way your wheels turn—and your lips work." He bent over and kissed her.

"Seriously, the art could be in a tunnel somewhere."

"Just like it could be on a space station somewhere." His enthusiasm was turning to sarcasm as he considered the vast possibilities.

"Maybe not a space station, but a subway station," Alexa continued, bent on establishing a premise. "There's a huge transit system under Boston."

"That would be like looking for a needle in a haystack," Jared groused.

"Not if you had a clue."

"Apparently, I'm missing a few of those."

"Maybe you need to tap your intuition again. I mean, consciously summon your ability to see what others don't. You know—patterns, paths, links, lines, double meanings."

"Some other time," Jared said. "My brain's running on empty and I'm exhausted. Hungry, too. Want to grab some food?" He gathered up his things, put on his coat, and reached for Alexa. She slipped her hand into his.

As they walked out into the January chill, their minds raced with ways to locate the missing art. "Bad food cheap?" Jared asked, approaching a store front with a yellowed menu taped to the window.

"It's actually pretty good here," Alexa said as she pulled open the door. A rush of warm air and the smell of home cooking greeted them.

"Super," Jared said. "We can sit down for a while, I can refuel, and if we want, we can visit the old haunts." They were shown a booth in the corner and served water.

"I'm not sure I want to rush back there," Alexa said as she opened the menu. "I got a bad vibe the last time I was in Buckskin Joe."

"Well, we don't have to go, you know. I like being with you in the here and now, too," Jared assured. Under the table, he put his hand on her thigh.

"You're sweet," she said, sending him an endearing look. "It's not that I never want to go back. I like it there. It's fascinating. And we know each other so well." Jared could read between the lines. "It's just that I have an uneasy feeling."

They ordered their meals and, in minutes, two plates of steaming comfort food arrived. "This is so good," Jared said with a mouth full of meatloaf interspersed with a scoop of mac and cheese.

"I know," Alexa agreed, spearing part of a hot turkey sandwich and topping it off with a sliver of jellied cranberry sauce.

Once satiated, Buckskin Joe didn't seem so off-putting. Fact is, it was hard to resist. The restaurant was quiet, and they knew they wouldn't be disturbed. They set their phone alarms and laid the buckle on the table. "One, two, three," Jared teased, letting his hand hover over the sparkling rectangle. Alexa was fast and slapped her palm over it first. Jared cupped his hand over hers. The transmission shot through Alexa and into Jared like a lightning bolt.

✦✦✦

"Do you have everything you need?" Lydia asked as Red hooked the cart to the horses. God, he looked appealing in his long duster, western boots, and wide-brimmed hat.

"Think so. Food. Water. Clothes. Supplies. Ore's loaded in and covered. I'll try to get word to you once I arrive in Denver." Red walked over to her and lifted her off her feet for a kiss that didn't last long enough.

"I know you probably think I'm crazy, hauling all this up there, but I just don't want the locals to know. People talk. They'll assume I'm a wealthy man and will treat me differently. I'm not ready for that."

Lydia admired his humility and didn't try to persuade him to stay. "Take care of yourself," she said, clutching his arm.

"You, too," he replied, keeping her in his gaze.

She reluctantly let go and watched Red climb up onto the seat of the buckboard and snap the reins. A cold wind was blowing, and she pulled her shawl tighter, staring at her feet to avoid seeing him ride away. By the time she looked up, he was gone.

12
DISCOVERIES

Arriving at the dance hall, Lydia saw Sadie adjusting her garter. "How's your mother doing?" Lydia asked, knowing a week had passed since she had run into Sadie at the store.

"Not so good. She can't keep food down and her fever is raging."

"Maybe she should see Doc Jones."

"I'm not sure she has the strength to do that," Sadie said, concerned.

"I'll be out and about tomorrow, especially with Red gone. I can swing by Doc's to see if he can look in on her."

"That would be great. I'd do it myself, but I'm feeling a little under the weather, too."

"Are you up for tonight's show?"

"Not really, but I'll be fine. Besides, you've got all the dancing parts. I just have to stand there and sing." Sadie smiled at her friend, more with affection than with jealousy.

Bill Buck's was quiet that night, as it had been for the past two weeks. Lydia didn't like it at all. The lack of customers made her nervous and she took it out by pacing the room. The show went on as usual but was attended by only a small audience that produced a few distinct claps rather than a roar of applause. After her dance routine was over, Lydia stepped aside, and Sadie moved to center stage for her vocal. Sadie's voice, which usually was clear as a bell, sounded thick and muffled. "I don't know what's wrong with me," she apologized to Bill, once she left the stage, at which point she collapsed onto his shoulder. He was quick to catch her and move her to a couch in the back room. Lydia rushed over to loosen Sadie's bodice and to fan her flushed cheeks. It was not unusual for women to be laced so tight that they fainted.

"I'll cover for her," Lydia said, glancing at Bill.

"Not to worry. There's hardly anyone here for dancing."

Lydia looked out to the main room and, sure enough, it was eerily vacant. Tables were set with overturned glasses waiting to be filled. Bowls of bar crackers were left untouched. Decks of cards were stacked, but not shuffled. Even the cash drawer remained closed.

Lou seemed forlorn as he sat at the piano, hands idle. "What's the matter?" Lydia asked, suspecting he might be sensing the same thing.

"I had a strange dream last night," Lou said, looking somewhat shaken. "I dreamt that we were carrying people down the street in coffins. Young and old… rich and poor…men and women…I woke up thrashing around and couldn't get back to sleep. Guess I'm tired."

"Odd you say that, because a few months back when Red and I were walking around the cemetery, a similar picture popped into my head. People trudging through the snow carrying loved ones. Lots of crying and cold."

Bill Buck piped in. "OK, you two, you're spookin' me. I think we need a couple drinks on the house. He poured them each a shot of whiskey and poured one for himself. Lydia took a swig and then went to check on Sadie.

"I'm so thirsty," Sadie mumbled as Lydia approached. Lydia left to get a glass of water. When she returned, she noticed red blotches on Sadie's face.

"You look overheated. Let me get a cold cloth for your head."

"That's funny, I'm freezing," Sadie said, curling into herself for warmth.

Lydia dampened one of Bill's bar rags and folded it in thirds. She brought that and a blanket from the storage chest back to Sadie. "I'm not waiting for tomorrow," Lydia decided. "I'm getting Doc Jones now."

She threw on her cape and hurried toward Doc's small office just off Main Street. Pounding on the door, she knew she'd wake the doctor, who tended to go to sleep early. "Sorry to do this, Doc, but Sadie just collapsed at the saloon. Can you come see her and bring the buggy to help get her home?"

"Lydia? Is that you?" The doctor called, slowly processing her voice as he lit a lamp. He came to the door wearing a rumpled shirt over long johns.

"Yes, it's me. I was going to wait until tomorrow, but I'm getting worried. Sadie's mother is ill, too."

"I'll be right there," he said as he went into the back room to change. Lydia thumbed through a copy of the *Louisville Medical Journal* that was sitting in a pile of books on his table. "You know, a few of the men from the mine also came in this morning," he called out. "Didn't see any symptoms other than a cold, but I want to keep an eye on them. Seems like a lot of people are getting sick at the same time."

When he reappeared, he noticed that Lydia was looking at the *Boston Medical and Surgical Journal*. "You can borrow any of those if you'd like," he said, pointing to his reading material. "I always have my trusty *Medical Repository* for reference," he said, nodding at a vintage book on his shelf. "Just bring them back the next time you see me." Lydia thanked him and slid one of the journals under her arm.

"Sadie's blotchy," she said, cutting to the chase. "On her face."

"Anywhere else?" the doctor asked as he organized his supplies.

"Couldn't tell," Lydia answered, lifting the doctor's bag to help him along.

"Well, I'll see when I get there, I guess."

Lydia and Doc Jones climbed into his carriage and rode down the street, entering Bill Buck's dance hall through the side door. By this time Sadie was sitting up but looking drawn. "How long have you been feeling poorly?" the doctor asked as he checked Sadie's tongue and peered into her eyes. He requested that she roll up her sleeves and roll down her stockings.

"About a week. Shortly after my mom took ill."

He discreetly examined her chest and back. "Well, whatever it is, she seems to have shared it with you. Let's get you back home, and I'll check your mother, too." Sadie nodded a thank you.

Lydia bundled Sadie up in the blanket and helped her into the buggy. "I'll talk to you tomorrow," the doctor said to Lydia as he climbed on board.

Lydia was exhausted by the time she got back to her cabin. It certainly wasn't the same without Red there. She put some wood into the stove, slipped into a sleeping gown, extinguished her flat wick lamp, and slid under the covers. She slept restlessly and woke early the next day. Having a hankering for a sweet roll, she walked down to the hotel where they served a light breakfast. "Is Penelope around?" she asked at the desk.

The concierge nodded no. "Been out sick all week. Our handyman is sick, too, and so is that Chinese guy who does our laundry."

Lydia was starting to get alarmed. She took a seat in the alcove that doubled as a dining area and ordered a cinnamon bun and coffee. This was a treat she savored. She picked up a copy of the city newspaper that was sitting on a sideboard and thought about Red en route to Denver.

Not wanting to go home quite yet, she detoured by the general store. There were always a few miners down there willing to shoot the breeze. Before Lydia got to the wooden steps, she heard one of the local dogs barking. These mutts didn't belong to anyone special, but to anyone who would feed them. Lydia stepped inside and came out with a piece of jerky. "There you go, Champ," she said as she put the dried meat into her palm and let the dog take it. She paused for a moment to pat his head and ruffle his thick neck fur, figuring he would go away, but he kept circling her feet and whining.

"What is it, buddy?" she asked as she looked down at him. He barked a few times, bobbed his head and pointed his nose toward the corrals behind the store. She took a few steps in that direction and stopped. The dog continued yipping and whimpering. "OK, you take the lead. What do you want to show me?" she said, following the agitated mongrel.

Lydia walked around the building and heard a low moan. "Who's there?" she called but got no answer. She looked at the dog as if he had misled her, but the mutt persisted. Lydia walked closer to the stalls and heard the moan again. She peered over the side and that's when she saw it—the two sheepherders collapsed in a heap, their faces covered with crusty bumps—so many in some places that it looked as if a layer of leather had formed over their skin. Where their shirts were open, and their cuffs rolled up, Lydia could see that the rash covered their bodies, some lesions just erupting, others filled with pus. A stench arose from human waste and the smell of death. A few hardy horse flies buzzed around them. The men's eyes were sunken and their breathing, raspy.

Lydia turned her head and retched, unable to quell the bile coming up into her throat. She doubled over to expel the sharp liquid and found a handkerchief to wipe her mouth. She went to a trough and scooped fresh water into her hand, drinking heartily to replace the taste of her own repulsion.

+++

Jared returned to the present first and noticed Alexa was coughing. "Are you OK?" he asked, shaking her arm. When she opened her eyes, glassy and unfocused, her face was ashen.

"Lexa, what's wrong?" Jared asked, staring at her.

She reached for her water as if the acid were still in her throat. She couldn't speak for a moment.

"It's there," she said dead serious.

"What's there? Where?"

"Smallpox in Buckskin Joe."

"How do you know? I mean, it's been eradicated for years."

"I studied it when I did a summer abroad. Humanitarian project. We were sent to a village where diseases were rampant. I was inoculated—hasn't been done since 1972. Only the CDC has the vaccine." She glanced at her upper left arm. Jared had wondered about the little, round scar.

"Wow. You never told me!" he said, impressed and surprised to learn about Alexa's colorful past. "So, what are you going to do now?"

"I need to go back to Buckskin Joe and help. People are afraid and starting to leave town, so there's no one to care for the sick."

Jared listened as Alexa thought out loud. "I wonder if I can go without you. That way you can tend to business here and I can tend to business there. I'm not seeing Red anyway, because he's away."

"I'm not sure that's smart," Jared said as he helped Alexa on with her coat. "I don't like the idea of you being alone." He paid at the front register and they stepped out into the darkness.

"I won't be alone. I just won't have present-day you with me."

Jared shook his head. "I have a feeling I'm not going to win this argument."

Alexa smiled. "The fresh air feels good," she said, filling her lungs as if to dispel the sickness she had inhaled. She was still pale and swayed slightly as she stood there.

"I'm walking you back. You don't look too steady."

"Hate to make you go out of your way, but thanks."

In the dorm lobby, they quickly kissed good-bye and Alexa rode up to her room. Jared swung by the desk out of habit and asked if there might be something for Red. "Sure is," the receptionist said as she reached for a crinkled envelope. "Guy just came in and dropped this off."

"Thanks," Jared muttered as he used his thumb to open the sealed flap. The note was brief. "Same place. Same time. Saturday. All of you." Jared knew what this meant. Now they were getting down to business.

+++

When Jared got back to his dorm, he made some calls. "$200 million for one painting? Incredible!" he exclaimed in learning the estimated value of Vermeer's *The Concert*. It turns out that this price was modest compared to a Gauguin that had sold for $300 million in 2015. "Boy am I in the wrong business," he joked as the voice at the other end chewed his ear about escalating art prices and black-market undercutting. "I hate to say it, but Frankie and Joe mentioned handling fees, too. Are you sure you can cover it?" he added. The voice continued to talk.

Jared was having a tough time imagining anyone owning a private collection of world masterpieces, let alone *stolen* ones. "I'll rent a car and pick everyone up," he confirmed. "Guess we'll have to transfer some money." The person on the other end of the phone must have offered some assurance because Jared nodded and nodded again, ending the call with an, "OK. OK. Got it."

Jared paced the room, worried that he was in over his head, but the idea of landing an exclusive story, getting published, and launching a career, motivated him. "Just be cool," he told himself as he rounded up his acquaintances on Saturday. "You can do this."

+++

When Jared picked up Chaz, he was still sniffling. He was dressed plainly—as before—his laptop case in tow. Svetlana, however, was coiffed and perfectly put together in a long, black, rhinestone-studded sweater that topped tight black leggings. Her ankle-high black suede boots had tufts of fur around the edges, which accented her well-toned calves. Rudi was wearing black as usual, but Jared noticed that his diamond stud had been replaced by a turquoise earring that matched the aqua cabochon in his belt buckle.

As he approached the destination, he saw Frankie and Joe standing in front of the door and Sean pacing the parking lot, taking a smoke.

"You're late," Frankie said as the group got out of his car. Jared looked at his watch. 12:01. He suspected the accusation was just a tactic to put him on edge.

"We were here. I just had to wait for one of your customers to pull out, so we could drive in," Jared said, showing no emotion.

"Whatever," Joe replied, turning around to go inside. He signaled for the others to follow. Sean frisked them, took their phones, and gave the all-clear.

This time another fellow was at the table. "This is Jack," Frankie said, pointing to a muscular man in a tight black tee shirt. "He's a Jack-of-All-Trades." Frankie laughed at his own joke.

Jared nodded hello. He wasn't sure if the guy was a head honcho, a security guard, or a hired gun, but the fellow's expression didn't change.

"Let's get to the point," Frankie said, as Svetlana settled into her seat, tapping Sean for a cigarette. Rudi leaned back, and Chaz rolled his damp tissues into thin snakes.

"I've seen the piece you want," Frankie said. "It looks fine. No damage. No mold. Might have lost a flake or two.

"Not a problem," Rudi said. "We have restorers, who keep their mouths shut."

"Good," said Joe, as he reached across the table for a discarded paperclip. He pried it apart and opened it into an "L" before bending it into a straight line with hooked ends. "We need to talk pricing and logistics."

"And proof," Jared added.

"That, too." Frankie looked at Jack as if the guy could deliver.

"Well, *The Concert* is valued at $250 mil," Frankie said.

"That's 50 more than I hear," Svetlana countered, letting a long puff of smoke escape from her ruby lips. "Or does that number include your 'handling fees'? There was a touch of sarcasm in her voice.

"It's a baseline. We're looking for 10% of that, black market rate."

"So, $25 mil?" Svetlana calculated. Her eyes didn't waiver.

Frankie nodded.

"I'd say half that is more like it." Rudi interjected. "5%. That's 12.5."

Joe huffed. "You'll need to do better than that if you want to beat out our other buyers." Svetlana guessed they had come in at 15.

"What do you say we meet closer to the middle at 18." She looked at Chaz for consensus.

"We'd consider that," Joe said. "Of course, it's not up to us."

"That includes everything, right?" Chaz confirmed, resting his chin on his hand. "Fees, delivery, anonymity."

"Yup."

Chaz pondered the amount. "So, $18 million for *The Concert*, if your guys accept the offer…" He sighed heavily. "That will require some fiscal acrobatics." He turned his face away to blow his nose. "Pardon me."

"Not too healthy there," Joe commented, pulling his chair back in disgust.

"Just allergies," Chaz mumbled.

"Why don't we say 3 installments, 6 mil each, assuming the art proves authentic," Svetlana suggested, clearly the money manager of the group.

"Sounds reasonable," Frankie replied. "I'll get back to you."

"Do you have the art?" Jared asked, still more interested in the paintings than the purchase.

"Not on me, doofus," Frankie said. "But I can have the piece brought out for inspection."

"Now you're talking," Svetlana said, pausing to push back a strand of hair.

"We'll want to bring in our own art expert," Rudi said, not breaking eye contact with Frankie.

"No problem, as long as he shows up with money for the first installment and takes a vow of silence. I'm thinking $6 mil to see it and get paint chips for testing, $6 mil to seal the deal if everything checks out, and $6 mil to take the thing with you."

"And what if it doesn't check out?" Svetlana asked. "You'll give us our money back?" She knew that was unlikely but wanted to see Frankie's reaction.

"Might be gone by then, but I'll put up $6 mil in collateral. I've got some property you might like." Svetlana nodded and said that could work. “And where do you come in, Jack?” she purred, practically salivating at the brawny man.

“Pretty much anywhere,” Jack replied. “As Frankie said, I’m a Jack-of-All-Trades.” He uttered a throaty “Heh-Heh.”

Joe piped in. “That means anything from collection to security to transportation—and gentle persuasion, of course,” Joe added with a knowing look.

“I hear you,” said Rudi. “So how do you want to do this?”

“Through Sean,” Frankie said, nodding to the young guy in the baseball jacket. Sean was snapping a piece of gum but stopped when his name was mentioned.

“Yeah, we’re still checking your credentials,” he said, “but if we get the go-ahead, I’ll set up a meeting—not here.”

“Sounds like a plan,” Jared agreed, looking at the rest of the group.

“And you’ve been keeping quiet?” Frankie asked Jared.

“Quiet as a mouse. Who am I gonna tell? If I tell anyone, I’ll blow my exclusive.”

Joe leaned over the table, shaking his head from side to side. “You’re crazy, kid. Here we’re talking millions of dollars in priceless art and all you’re worried about is writing a story.”

“Hey, what can I say?” Jared deflected.

Svetlana stood up. “I say we get ready to move some money.” She glanced around the room. “Gentlemen, it’s been a pleasure,” she said as she stepped forward to shake their hands. “Nice to meet you, Jack.” He grunted in response but didn’t return the gesture.

With phones returned and pocketed, Jared and his buyers walked out together. Chaz was preoccupied with financing. The others didn’t say much.

That afternoon, after everyone was dropped off, Jared called Alexa. “We’re done for the day. We’re going to see something very soon.”

“I’m glad you’re back in one piece,” Alexa said, a sense of relief punctuating her words. “Where are you now?”

“Returning the car,” Jared said. “You around?”

"Yeah, just working. They're piling on assignments this semester."

"Do you have time for a visit?"

"Not really. How 'bout tomorrow? Then maybe we can figure out how I can get to Buckskin Joe by myself." He agreed to come over in the morning.

+++

The next day Jared arrived with fresh bagels and cream cheese. "Just what I need!" Alexa said, grabbing the bag out of his hand, then kissing him hello. "I totally missed breakfast." She sat down at the edge of the bed and spread out the tissue wrappers, handing him a sesame seed bagel and keeping an 'everything' for herself. They chomped happily and made small talk.

"This waxed paper gives me an idea," Alexa said, holding up the translucent square. "Light can pass through it, right, but not everything can." Jared nodded. "I wonder if we could set up a barrier with the buckle, so I could feel your energy, but not absorb all of it. That way, we might not have to travel together."

"I'm not sure there's any scientific basis for it, but we could try."

Alexa finished eating, crumpled the bag, and tossed it into her wastebasket. Jared flattened out a sheet of waxed paper. "OK, let's layer it on and see what happens," he said, putting the buckle into his hand and setting the tissue paper on top of it. Alexa placed her hand over the tissue where she could feel Jared's warmth, but not his skin. She thought of Buckskin Joe and willed herself to leave, while Jared willed himself to stay.

After she transitioned, Jared slipped his hand out from under hers and took his backpack into the lounge. He removed a large sheet of folded easel paper and a permanent marker. This would become his wall chart or 'logic tree' as his professors called it. He would use it to try to find meaning of his other-worldly experience. He started by putting a line down the middle, then began writing random words on each side.

On the left side, he wrote:	**On the right side, he wrote:**
Big bucks	Tunnels
Dig deeper	Jack
Mining	Frankie
Art	Joe
Shafts	Sean
Gold	Chaz
Heist	Svetlana

He continued to do this until the page was filled with thoughts. "There must be patterns here," he said out loud. "There have to be clues!" Jared stared at the page until the words swam together.

+++

Meanwhile, Lydia found herself in Buckskin Joe at Sadie's bedside, trying to comfort her. Sadie's mother slipped in and out of consciousness and now had small flat bumps on her face, chest, and arms. These didn't look exactly like what the sheepherders had, but Lydia knew this was just the beginning. Doc Jones knocked on the cabin door and Lydia poked her head out. "Sadie's holding her own, but her mother's not so good."

"Rashes?"

"Yes. Both," Lydia said. "All over."

"Damn," said the doctor. "I had hoped this was something else."

"Don't think so," Lydia said without articulating further. "Some folks from the hotel are sick, too, and more miners have taken ill."

"I know. I've telegraphed Denver for help and supposedly some nurses, who already had smallpox, are on their way. But with the weather so bad, I'm not sure they'll make it, at least not for a while."

Lydia immediately thought of Red, who should be in Denver by now. He had probably been riding in snow all the way.

"Would you have time to swing by the mine office?" Doc Jones asked. "A bunch of men are hunkered down in there. I'm trying to keep them quarantined and have told them not to go home. That means we'll need to get food to them."

Lydia knew she could obtain food from Bill Buck and the Tabors, and she was happy to donate some of her own boiled eggs. A couple hours later, she loaded up her saddle bags and rode out to the arrastra, where she had been terrorized only months before. She called to one of the foremen, who came out to talk to her. "Keep your distance," she said, putting up her hand, explaining that either of them could be contagious. "I just want to get food to the men who are sick."

"We've got about a dozen in here. Not sure if they'll eat much, but I can bring out their lunch pails, if you want to pack them up," the foreman offered.

"That would be great. How are you feeling?" she asked as she started to apportion her supplies.

"Fine so far, but my wife's taken ill and so have her parents. Just heard about our neighbors and their kids down the road, too." The foreman looked tired having been up with his crew most of the night. He returned in two trips with twelve metal lunch boxes.

Lydia carefully divided the provisions and watched as the foreman carried the lunch pails back inside. "I don't know how we're going to keep this up," she thought to herself as she rode back toward Doc Jones' office. "There are just too many people getting sick and the number is growing."

No sooner had she left the mine did Tom Shaw come running out to her. "It's my brother, Tim. He's got a gun and he's threatening to kill himself. He's covered with pox and says he doesn't want to live like that."

"I'll follow you," Lydia said, forgetting her fatigue. "I'm not sure what I can do, but maybe we can talk him out of it."

Tom opened the door to the cabin that he shared with his brother. Tim was standing there leaning on a chair for support. His skin looked like a topographical map, rife with mountains and craters. His eyes were sunken. He was delirious from fever. The stench was horrific.

Lydia covered her nose with a scented hanky, then calmly talked to him in a soft voice. "Tim, it's Lydia. Remember the day you saved my life?" she said, slowly walking toward him. He trembled and shook his head yes. "Well, maybe today I can save yours." She reached out to support his weight, but he pushed her away.

"I don't want to be saved. I don't want to live lookin' like a monster. And I don't want to go through weeks of suffering only to die." He waved the gun in the air.

"Chances are you won't die," she said, recalling what she had read in Doc Jones' medical journal. "7 out of 10 people with smallpox live," she said, cleverly turning the thirty percent mortality rate into a positive. "You're young and strong. You can fight this."

"I don't have any fight left in me," he said, teetering, as he attempted to stand straight. "I just want to be out of this misery." He put the gun to his temple.

"Think of the people who love you. Your brother, your mother, and that young lady you have yet to meet." Lydia thought she saw a flicker of hope in his eyes.

"We'll keep your blisters clean to reduce infection. That will minimize the scarring. Besides, I've heard that plenty of women prefer rugged men with a few scars to those with baby faces." Tim tried to smile, but the vesicles on his cheeks cracked and oozed. "Give me the gun," Lydia requested, extending her hand.

"Please, Tim," Tom appealed. "I need my kid brother around. Who else am I going to harass?" Tim listened, but didn't drop the gun. Tom edged closer. Just as he was within reach of the weapon, Tim whipped it around and let a bullet fly into his own chest. Lydia screamed, and Tom cried out, both running over to Tim, who lay bleeding on the floor. Lydia cushioned his head in her lap as her skirt turned dark with his blood. She gently rocked him and smoothed his hair.

"That was a good day in the bank, wasn't it" he said, struggling to breathe, wistfully looking up at Lydia.

"It was a very good day," she placated. "You were very brave."

The color drained from his face. "Too bad I couldn't be so

brave this time," he said, stopping to look at something no one else could see. There were no further signs of life.

Tom let out a sob as he bent over his brother. Lydia brought her thumb and forefinger down over Tim's eyes to close them for eternal sleep. His lids were covered with bumps and pustules that extended to his cheeks and forehead. Lydia sat there, silent, then broke into in tears.

"I can't save them! I just can't save them fast enough!" Lydia anguished, berating herself, overcome with emotion. She covered her face with her bloodied hand and wept, her shoulders convulsing, as she remained on the ground holding Tim's corroded body.

Tom walked over, eased Tim away, and helped her up. "I know Red's out of town. Otherwise I would take you to him. Let's just sit here a while, we'll clean you up, and then I'll ride with you to Doc Jones."

Lydia used the back of her wrist to wipe her tears. Tom's mouth contorted as he tried to control his own. He brought her a bowl of water, and she washed her hands, drying them on a cloth that Tom provided. He left the room for a moment and returned with a clean filled bowl. "This is for your pretty face," he said, hoping it would be spared the cruel disease that was ravaging the town. Lydia turned the cloth inside out, wet it, and pressed it against her eyes, trying to remove the image of Tim that was imprinted on her retinas.

"Here, let me get that," Tom said, dabbing off blood that had splattered onto her chin and ear. His kindness reminded her so much of Red, she ached for him.

Tom escorted Lydia back to her horse, guiding her elbow with one hand. "Are you all right to ride?" he asked before going back for his own horse. Lydia nodded, "The air will do me good."

When the doctor opened the door, Lydia and Tom stood there, silent and shaken. They shared their story and the doctor embraced them both, praising Tim as a fine young man. Tom thanked the doctor for his kind words and said good night, preferring to be alone with his sorrow.

"We're losing the battle and it's just begun," Doc Jones said to Lydia as he warmed up some water for tea. "First there were two, then there were twenty, now there are probably forty. There's no telling how fast or far this thing will spread." Lydia already knew that. "The disease takes two weeks to incubate, four days for lesions to appear, another week for blisters, and then a few days to crust," he explained. "We're looking at a full month for each victim. That means we can have people in any stage of the disease at any time. And until the scabs fall off, they're all contagious."

"So, what can we can do?"

"Just isolate and inoculate. That's it."

"I saw something about that in your journal, but I'm not sure what it means," Lydia said.

"It means introducing them to a mild form of the disease," the doctor replied.

Lydia was puzzled and listened closely as he continued.

"Physicians found years ago that if people were exposed to a tiny bit of smallpox—inhaled as scab dust or as pus scratched into the skin—they'd get a harmless form of the disease. This was called 'variolation'. About sixty years ago, a doctor named Jenner started experimenting with cowpox, because he noticed that milkmaids, who at one time had cowpox, did not get smallpox. He was so convinced of this connection that he injected his own son with cowpox and the child didn't get smallpox at all. Jenner called this process 'vaccination'—from the Spanish word, *vacca*, for cow."

"That's amazing! So why doesn't everyone get this vaccination?" Lydia asked, carefully enunciating the word.

"Fear. Cost. Availability. Stubbornness. Some people don't even know about it."

"Can we get some?"

"It would be too late for most people here," the doctor said. "They've already been exposed. Plus, it's not like there's a bucket of the stuff sitting at the edge of the road. Besides, have you looked outside?" Lydia opened the door and was blown back by a blast of wind and sheets of biting snow.

"In fact, I think you should stay here tonight. Are your chickens in the coop?"

"Yup, I left them inside. Was too cold this morning for them to be running around."

"Good," Doc Jones said. "There's room for your horse in the stall and you can sleep out here on the couch. I'll find some more medical books for you to look at. I have a feeling I'm going to need all the help I can get."

The next day, armed with new information and rudimentary medical supplies, Lydia rode through the snow to the row of cabins just beyond the mine. Once-strong men lay there in various states of decline. Some were feverish. Others were moaning. Lydia went to the first cabin and helped an old timer roll over. His back ached and his open sores were sticking to the bedding. Lydia laid out a new sheet and tossed the old one into the fire. The man was tearfully appreciative. In the next cabin, she found a fellow she didn't know tended by a frail wife, who was in no better shape. Lydia poured a jar of Bill Buck's soup into a pot, warmed it, and fed them both. The woman took Lydia's hands in hers and said a prayer of thanks. Lydia continued to knock on doors and administer relief. Sometimes she just sat with the stricken and talked, answering questions, and sharing news from town. Other times she sang to them while wrapping their arms and legs in clean bandages.

Between cabins, she exhaled ferociously, trying to expel the sickness she felt sitting in her lungs. She thrust her hands into the snow in hopes of cleaning them, only to find them becoming raw and chapped. By the time her rounds were done, her energy was as depleted as her supplies. She rode back to Doc Jones' office and crumpled onto his couch. "Have you eaten anything?" he asked.

"No. Not hungry after seeing what I did," Lydia said, trying to suppress her nausea.

"I'll make you something light," the doctor said. "You need to keep up your strength."

"Any word from Denver?" Lydia asked as she took off her wet boots.

"Just that they're snowed in. Big blizzard up there."

"Then we're on our own?"

"Seems so. At least for a while."

Doc Jones laid out a jelly sandwich and some broth. Lydia devoured them both but didn't linger long. She put some supplies—food, cloths, soap, herb tea, and a small tin of balm that Doc had prepared—into a basket and walked down Main Street to the living quarters above and behind the store fronts. Careful not to expose customers to the disease she might be carrying, she avoided main entrances and instead knocked lightly on the obscured residence doors.

"Come in," a distraught shopkeeper said, as he pointed to a small girl lying in bed. The child was covered in bumps that ran along her hairline and seeped into her eyes. Lydia figured that even if the little girl recovered, she would most likely be blind. Lydia offered the man some encouragement and left him a meat pie, knowing he would not leave his daughter's side. Three days later, she saw him hunched over, weeping with grief, as he carried a small box down the road to where he had buried his wife.

The casket maker's shop was the only business in town that was thriving. Lydia stood at the front door and called to Caleb, using one hand to keep him at bay. "Anything I can get you?" she asked.

"Just more wood," he said, grim and drawn, looking at her with a numbness she assumed was a means of self-preservation. His eyes were red, and the dry salt stain of tears streaked his cheeks. "I'm burying my friends here," he said as he fitted the lid on yet another coffin.

"I know," Lydia consoled. "My friend, Sadie, just lost her mom and she, herself, is clinging to life."

The casket maker offered an empathetic nod as he laid another plank across a sawhorse. His small frame was stooped, and his head was topped by a disheveled mass of wispy white hair. He wore a stretched-out, brown wool sweater with holes at the elbows and badly patched pants that, even when tightly belted, tended to slide below his waist. His hands were covered with gray knit gloves that had the finger tips cut off, so he could better grasp the nails he was driving into the freshly cut pine.

"I'm leaving you some bread in case you get hungry. There's butter in this crock." Lydia said, setting a loaf on the corner of a table and a small pottery jar next to it. "I'll check in again." He thanked her as he leaned another box against the wall.

Lydia made her way to the dance hall, deserted except for Lou, who was trying to look busy. "I'm surprised you're here," Lydia said. "Show doesn't go on for a while."

"I can't stand it out there," he said. "I can hear the moaning through my walls. Every place is depressing except this one."

"Let's try to keep it that way," said Bill, who seemed to be resisting the disease. "What do you need, Lydia?" he asked, pointing to his pantry shelves.

"Anything easy to eat like crackers and preserves, soup and soft stuff. The men can't keep much down."

"I can help you with that," Bill said, his blue eyes sad. "I'll pull some things together."

"Thanks, Bill," Lydia said as she put her arm around him. Lou leaned over the keyboard and let his fingers briefly dance across the ivories.

"My brother and father have it," Lou suddenly said, stopping and looking grim. "But don't worry. I haven't been to see them. Got word from a neighbor."

"I'm so sorry to hear that," Lydia replied, reminding him, "You stay clear of them, and I'll check on them tomorrow." He thanked her and watched as she filled a basket with provisions.

Days turned into weeks and weeks turned into mid-November. The skies were blustery, and the nights were bitter. Mining operations slowed to a crawl and food started running out. There would be no harvest celebration this year. Lydia received a telegram from Red saying he had arrived safely in Denver. He said he had heard of the sickness in Buckskin Joe and cautioned Lydia to take care.

"Take care?" Lydia thought almost cynically. "How about 'give care'. There's no one here to help me!" People were leaving

Buckskin Joe as fast as they could pack. Doc Jones tried to examine them first, but many filled their wagons in the dark of night, saddled up, and simply disappeared. Between the snow and the warnings, no one else was coming in.

During this time, the stage stopped running. Shelves at the general store became depleted and people started raiding the pantries of those who had died. Lydia worked at Doc's side, learning as much as she could. At least now she could recognize the stages of the disease and could tell whether someone was going to make it or not. She encouraged those who survived to allow their scabs to drop off naturally, and she taught those with retinal scarring, to 'see' with their hands.

The exhaustion was oppressive. Day after day, Doc Jones rode out beyond Main Street to check on farmers and those too old to travel, while Lydia covered the mine, the miners' cabins, and the small dwellings in town. When both parents were ill, she'd feed the children, hug them, and wash their clothes. When the children were sick, she'd care for them, so the parents could get some rest. But mostly it was the men who needed help. Many had worked alone in the mines and had no family to comfort them, so Lydia became their family and their friend.

At night, she'd fall into bed drained, staying at Doc's office when the weather was bad or the hour too late to go back to her cabin. Red sent word that he had updated the paperwork on his claim and had met some good men, who would help him mine it. He didn't say anything about the value of the ore or the gold in his possession, but that was to be expected.

By late November, Lydia had given up dancing. There was no one around to see her show and she knew she could be more useful tending the sick. Bill provided her with a stipend, so she could buy food and, at least, feed the chickens. She missed Red terribly. After one especially grueling day, she put her face into her pillow and cried. The sobs came in waves—for her sheer fatigue, for those who had died, for the unrelenting demand of it all. There was no end in sight. The sick kept coming. Coming and dying.

Lydia cried for Sadie's mother and for Lou's brother, who had succumbed, and for the brave young man, who shot himself rather than live a life of disfigurement. She cried for the coffins left above ground when the soil was too frozen to shovel or when there were no healthy men to lower them. She cursed the sheepherders for coming to Buckskin Joe and, just as quickly, asked for forgiveness as she prayed for their souls. She railed against the snow and the obstacles to better medical care. She sobbed at the futility of it all.

+++

"Lexa. Lexa. You need to come back now," Jared said, as he stepped into her room. "You're crying, you're upset," he persisted as he put his arm around her.

Alexa's eyelids fluttered, and she looked at Jared as if to process his features, finally grabbing onto him and burrowing her head into his shoulder. "It was awful. Horrible. People dying all around." There was a tremor in her voice as she described the scene.

Jared did his best to console her, smoothing her hair, and holding her close. "Take a minute to catch your breath," he said. "None of that is here. You're safe with me, healthy and well."

Alexa calmed down and put her hand over her mouth, blinking back tears. "I don't know how she did it," Alexa finally said, referring to Lydia. "She was so brave, so devoted, up against such odds."

"These were strong people," Jared said. "Think how privileged we are to know them."

Alexa looked at Jared's warm brown eyes. She tried to smile and pull herself together. "It's February, isn't it?" she asked, realizing that November in Buckskin Joe meant it was three months later in real time.

Jared nodded yes. "Guess I'll have to ask you to be my Valentine," he said, running his hand up and down Alexa's back. She felt herself relax.

"Guess you'll have to be mine," she said.

A short while later, Jared retraced his steps and returned to his dorm. He taped his easel sheet of random words to the wall and stared at it, looking for clues and deeper meaning, trying to apply the message in the mine. The pressure was taking its toll.

He didn't see Alexa at all the following week, but on Friday night, he swung by her dorm to take her out for pizza. In checking at the desk, he learned that another envelope had been left for Red. When Jared opened it, he saw that the next meeting would take place the following Sunday at an obscure storage company in a part of the city he didn't know. Once again, everyone was to meet at noon.

Sitting in the pizza parlor, Jared mapped the location on his phone. The building was tucked under an overpass, not visible from the highway. He filled Alexa in on the details, but it was clear she didn't like what she was hearing. "It's too risky," she said. "You're playing with the big guns. This is not some classroom case study. It's dangerous!"

"I know. I know. But we're being careful," Jared answered. She shook her head. Jared overrode her concern with his enthusiasm. "Just think—I may actually get to see—even touch—the Vermeer! Can you imagine?"

"I can imagine you turning up dead in the Harbor," Alexa replied, not smiling.

"Not gonna happen," Jared assured. "Besides, all I have to do is help broker the deal. After that, it's out of my hands. I don't have to hang around for the logistics or the money transfer. Tomorrow, I'll get together with the group and make sure the funds are where they need to be."

"I'll be glad when this is over," Alexa said, sipping her soda. "I can't believe you're so calm."

"I'm not," Jared said. "My stomach's in knots."

+++

That Sunday, Jared slipped on a sweater and cords, making a valiant effort to look neat. This time he rented a van and picked up the art expert first, a pompous guy from the West Coast with a full-of-himself demeanor. The fellow wore faded jeans with a navy blazer, white dress shirt, open at the neck, loafers, and no socks despite the temperature. Enriqué, as he introduced himself, sported a Fitbit on his left wrist and had his long blond hair pulled back in a ponytail. He looked tan, even though it was mid-winter. Surfer boy, Jared thought, making polite conversation as he picked up the others.

Svetlana, Rudi, and Chaz said very little as Jared followed his GPS down the Interstate. Enriqué seemed distracted. "Kind of deserted here," Svetlana muttered, looking out from her passenger seat at the landscape of warehouses. Rudi craned to see from the middle row. Chaz sat in the far back, polishing his glasses with his ever-present tissues.

"I wouldn't want to be stranded here at night," Rudi said, pointing out that there wasn't a person in sight.

"Well, it *is* Sunday," Jared reminded.

"Let's just hope we don't break down," said Svetlana, looking in the visor mirror, touching up her lipstick and running her tongue over her teeth.

Jared put on the radio to ease the tension. Just as a catchy pop tune came on, the program was interrupted for a breaking news alert: an eighteen-wheeler had jackknifed across the Southeast Expressway and careened through the guardrails, hanging precariously over the surface road below.

"Turn that up," Chaz demanded. Rudi and Enriqué were already checking their phones to see if they could determine the location. Svetlana rolled down her window to better hear the sirens that were whizzing by. Jared noticed traffic building up ahead of him, creating a wall of red tail lights. His travel app instructed him to exit right at the next off-ramp.

As Jared veered right, the radio voice continued. "This just in on that jackknifed truck. The Highway Department and first responders are on the scene. It appears that the truck and several vehicles skidded on ice from last night's freezing rain. We don't know the status of the truck driver or any other drivers involved. Let's go to Barry Bright for a first-hand report."

Rudi and Enriqué leaned forward to listen.

"This is Barry Bright on the Southeast Expressway just below Boston where an eighteen-wheeler headed southbound has breached the guardrails. The truck is now suspended dangerously above a surface road as highway workers attempt to reinforce the railing. It does not look good. I can hear creaking now. Police are trying to clear both upper and lower levels, but time is not on their side. These big rigs can weigh 80,000 pounds, so you can imagine the pressure being exerted on this structure." The reporter paused and gasped as screams were heard in the background. "Oh, no, this is terrible. The guardrail has given way and the truck has gone over the edge. Repeat: plummeted to the street below."

Svetlana looked horrified as she stared at Jared. "Do you see what I'm seeing?"

"Blue strobes, red fire engine lights?" Jared brought the van to a crawl as he turned onto a surface road.

Just then a police officer in a yellow slicker stepped into the line of traffic and vigorously motioned Jared to detour through a side alley. His colleague was setting up cones and stretching 'Caution' tape across the pavement. Jared watched in his rearview mirror as the cop's white gloves continued to divert traffic away from the scene. The whomping sound of helicopter blades could be heard overhead.

"I think that was our corner, guys," Jared said, a note of resignation hanging in his voice, "and if our friends were out there waiting for us, they may be kaput."

"How could that be?" Svetlana said. "I mean, what are the odds?"

Chaz was on his phone Googling information. "Actually, it says here that death by road debris is fairly common. Happens at least 800 times a year in the United States." He continued reading and sharing the information. "Not long ago, a woman was killed near here by a flying manhole cover."

"That's crazy," Enriqué said. "Talk about being in the wrong place at the wrong time...."

"It's gotta be fate." Rudi lamented. "But why us? Why now?"

"Just when we were getting so close," Svetlana whined. Jared saw his Pulitzer Prize winning story going up in smoke.

He parked the car, so he could think. He noticed an old Grand Marquis pull over, too. "I really want to go back there and find out what happened, but I don't dare. The place will be crawling with cops and reporters, and we can't exactly ask about our guys by name."

"Personally, I've had enough for today," Svetlana remarked, sounding shaken. "Can we follow up tomorrow? I'd like to be as far away from this as possible."

"Me, too," Chaz echoed.

Enriqué looked annoyed. "What a waste of time."

"I wonder if the artwork was actually ever there and if it was the real deal," Jared pondered out loud. "Or were they conning us all along?"

"We may never know," Rudi said, sounding disappointed. "But we did learn a few things."

Jared cut him off. "Yeah, we learned there are a lot of disreputable people in this world," Jared said, not hiding his sarcasm. "And now we're no closer to finding the missing art than before."

Svetlana was quietly picking at a chipped nail. "Well, maybe our guys survived…." But Jared sensed that wasn't the case. He dropped off his associates and called Alexa.

"Check the news," he said. "You won't believe it. We're at a dead end—literally." He could hear her pump up the sound on her computer."

"Oh, my God. Are you're OK?"

"We're all fine. We never got there. Had we been a few minutes earlier, we would have been standing right under that highway. We still don't know what happened to our guys, but I doubt they made it."

"That's awful. What a close call," she said, obviously distraught. "Someone must have been watching over you."

Jared shrugged, crediting the timing to sheer luck. "But now I'm back to square one on the story," he grumbled.

13
RETHINKING

That night, Jared was at his desk doing homework, staring at his wall chart again, hoping for an epiphany. The 11:00 news confirmed the first names of the crash victims as Franklin, Joseph, Sean and John—pronounced dead on the scene. Memorial services would be held later that week.

Jared shook his head in disbelief. He was saddened by the loss of life, but truthfully, more miffed that the hook for his article was gone. Now what was he going to do so late in the semester? He had invested a lot of time chasing this angle, hoping it would lead to the missing art, but if he couldn't deliver, he would need at least three strong theories about where the art might be hidden.

+++

Valentine's Day rolled around, and Jared went overboard in wooing Alexa. He made reservations at a fine restaurant and showed up at her dorm room in a sports coat. As he handed her a bouquet of red roses, he noticed she was wearing the necklace with the tiny silver shoes that he had given her. She buried her nose in the soft petals of the flowers, inhaled deeply, then put the long stems into a clear vase. She stepped out to the shower room for water, while he waited.

"These are beautiful," she said to Jared, when she returned. "Thank you so much." Her gaze went through him like an X-ray, revealing he was sure, his innermost feelings.

"You look amazing," he said, coming up behind her and nuzzling her ear as he reached across her collarbone to touch the necklace. "This looks great on you." He continued to kiss her neck. "And you smell good, too."

"If you don't stop that, we'll never leave," she said, slipping out of his grasp to put on her heels and grab her coat.

Jared felt like a goofy high school kid throughout most of dinner. He couldn't take his eyes of her. In between bites, he stared at the low-cut neckline of her strappy black dress that contrasted vividly with her pale skin, just like Lydia's gowns did at the dance hall. He drowned in those dark eyes time and again, tonight luring him with a hint of taupe shadow. She didn't need mascara. Her lashes nearly swept her cheeks.

Alexa looked at Jared with a stirring she had not felt before. She imagined him ten years older, as mature and confident as the man she loved so long ago, ruggedly handsome, proud, and protective. Jared was buff these days, lean and toned, and she thought how nicely those muscles would fill out with a bit of age and experience.

They toasted each other with Perrier and allowed themselves to order lobster and steak. Jared knew this would blow his food budget for the rest of the month, but he didn't care. They walked along the waterfront, taking in the skyline and admiring the twinkle of lights, before summoning a ride back to campus. Someday, Jared thought, school would be behind them, and they would go home together.

✦✦✦

"My mother's coming into town," Jared texted Alexa the following week. "Want to meet at her hotel? She's up here with her FBI colleague, Nora."

"Sure, if it's on the weekend."

"Yes, Saturday. Say 11 a.m.? I'll send you the address."

+++

When Jared's mother saw Alexa, Sarah embraced her as she would a daughter and introduced Nora as her friend. Jared hugged his mom and gave Nora a warm handshake.

"I've booked a room," Sarah said. "I think it will be easier to talk that way."

"Sounds good," Jared said. "Anyone want coffee?"

"There's some coffee in there, along with pastries and fruit."

"Yum," Jared said. He was still her hungry kid.

When Jared and Alexa walked into the small room, Bobbie, Carlos, Charlie, and Eric were already there, ready for a debriefing.

"So how are my favorite partners in crime?" Jared asked, trying to break the ice. The image of Frankie and Joe sitting at the chop shop table was still clear in his head.

"Well, regrettably, I no longer have Svetlana's sexy wardrobe," Bobbie said, "but I do have her lovely blond hair." She fluffed her long tresses in a familiar way. Bobbie was now a semester into her Fine Arts Masters and had just given the performance of a lifetime.

"You were outstanding," Jared said, complimenting his former babysitter. "And that accent was incredible. Not too much Russian, but just enough."

"Good dialog coach," Bobbie said, flashing her pearly whites.

"And Carlos, I hear you were a star," Alexa commented.

"I don't know about that," the IT guy said, "but Rudi was a cool dude. Played to my natural attributes," he joked. The group laughed—one of those laughs used to relieve stress. Jared was glad he had thought of Carlos from the Security office. Carlos had the technical knowledge and right attitude for revenge. "With all that back and forth about taking a photo, I had plenty of time to install a stalker app on Frankie's phone," Carlos continued, pausing to look at Nora. "I assume you got the data feed?" Nora nodded yes.

"I'm surprised Frankie handed over his phone so readily," Alexa said, patting Carlos on the shoulder, "but I guess turnabout is fair play."

Sarah realized this group of young people had undertaken considerable risks and wanted to give them time to unwind and ask questions. She poured herself a cup of coffee and sat down next to Charlie. "And Chaz, my man," she said, "your character was nothing less than stellar. We especially appreciated your coughs and sneezes to punctuate the mention of money. You're not sick, are you?"

"Not in the slightest," he said, grinning broadly and looking extremely well. "It's wild how microphones can be so small, they can fit anywhere," he remarked as he ran his hand through his curly hair. "I just regret that I didn't get to do any lab work on the art evidence." He also regretted that Jared's kid sister, Abby, wasn't a bit older, but he figured he'd check back in a few years.

Nora addressed Eric, who had posed as the art expert. "Sorry we weren't able to use your art history expertise, 'Enriqué,' but maybe another time," she said, emphasizing his exotic name.

"Not a problem," he answered. "I'm honored to have been asked." He was certainly humbler than guy he had portrayed.

Nora walked to the front of the room and picked up a remote, dimmed the lights, and turned on her presentation. "First I want to thank all of you for your help and share some of the results. I also want to assure you that you can still have protection if you want it." Jared thought back to the car with the tinted windows that had tailed them upon leaving their first rendezvous and to the old Grand Marquis that had pulled over with him at the last. He asked for a few more weeks of security until the news story of the truck accident died down. Nora said that she would work with campus police to put necessary patrols and safeguards in place.

"Before we go further, I also wanted to say how much we appreciate your time, Alexa, in coaching the team on negotiation technique. Role playing is hard to do long distance, so it was very helpful that you could get together on campus." Alexa beamed at the compliment.

Nora proceeded to explain that through the stalker app, which Carlos had been authorized to install, they were able to monitor Frankie for several months. This provided far more intelligence than stakeouts typically did and had kept their agents out of harm's way.

"While the picture of the Rembrandt is small and certainly not conclusive," she continued, "we have experts looking at it. If it is real, it will be the first sighting since the theft and will lend credence to the belief that the art is safe." Jared could feel his pulse quicken.

Nora added, "Your GPS tracking to the automotive shop will also assist in future investigation. We suspect they are dealing in stolen parts, and anything else we find will be a bonus. Thanks to you, we'll be able to get a search warrant. And even though the second location didn't pan out for your story," she said, looking at Jared, "we'll put that place under surveillance, too."

Alexa raised her hand. "What's going to happen to the $100K that was paid initially?

"Well, we're going to lose some of that, but the bills are marked, so they will leave a valuable trail. It will be interesting to see where it leads."

"But how did you manage to establish our identities so quickly and connect us to past crimes?" Bobbie asked.

Nora smiled. "That would be classified, but let's just say we know people in the right places. It is actually quite easy to create false personas when you have access to databases." Nora was appropriately vague and assured them that all traces of criminal behavior would be erased and stricken from their records.

Sarah was glad to see the kids talking about their experience and sharing their concerns. "Any other questions?" she prompted.

"If we really had to pay the first 6 million, how was that going to happen? That's such a huge amount," Charlie asked. "My hands are still shaking at the thought of transferring that kind of money."

"We were never going to put that money into their account. We were just going to make it look that way," Nora clarified. "I really can't go into specifics, but trust me, we're smarter than they are." Jared and Alexa looked at each other, sharing a sense of relief. "Is there anything else we can answer?" Nora asked. No one had further questions. Jared glanced at his mom and mouthed a thank you to his friends who were getting ready to leave.

"I'm proud of you," Sarah said, as she rested her hand on her son's arm. "Someday you're going to be a brilliant investigative reporter." Jared was outwardly embarrassed, but inwardly, he relished the compliment.

"The only problem is, we still don't know where the artwork is stashed, and in a few weeks, I have to turn in a publish-worthy article," Jared complained.

As Jared said this, Alexa noticed a slight shift in Sarah's posture, an adjustment not unlike the change she had detected in Jared when they were standing at Long Wharf on their way to Salem. Not too different from his demeanor as he sat entranced by his laptop in the Library. "There are clues all around you," Sarah said to Jared in a tone that seemed to convey sacred knowledge. "You just need to find them. Use your natural talent, and they will appear to you. Connections will be made. You just have to be receptive to them." Sarah snapped back to her usual self and Alexa could sense Jared analyzing his mother's words.

"Let us know if you discover anything else, and we'll keep you apprised as well," Nora said, shaking hands as the group parted ways. "Now we're going over to ask the police about those fine gentlemen, who met such an untimely death."

Jared hugged his mother good-bye, as did Alexa. "Stay in touch," Jared called to his friends. Carlos gave him a thumbs-up, revealing the shark tattoos inside his wrists.

14
PERSISTENCE

The predictions for snowfall changed every few hours. What had started as 6-12" evolved into 18-24," and by the time night rolled around, the city was in for a Nor'easter about to drop 3 feet. People in coastal communities were shoring up cottages and sandbagging low-lying beach roads in anticipation of tidal surge. Doors and windows of summer business were boarded shut. Electricity was intentionally disconnected in strategic places to control potential fires. Newscasters were stationed at Chatham Light to monitor Cape Cod wind speeds and erosion.

Inland, plows lumbered to and from road salt storage stations. A driving ban was put into place and only a few telltale headlights could be seen crawling West on the Pike. MEMA was broadcasting shelter locations and emergency numbers from a bunker in Framingham where the governor, looking casual in a cream-colored V-neck sweater, advised residents to stay inside. Typical February in Boston.

Both Jared and Alexa were hunkered down in their respective dorms. From her tenth-floor vantage point, Alexa could see snowflakes swirling in the streetlight, obliquely descending only to be carried away by updrafts before spiraling down again. A layer of white was already covering parked cars likely to be buried for days. Trees and road signs were being plastered with a coating of sleet that seemed to freeze in place.

Alexa was comfortable in her sweatpants and slippers. Wanting a change of scenery, she wandered down to the lobby with a magazine tucked under her arm, ready to watch the Weather on the TV. Holding a cup of hot cocoa from the vending machine—watery but, chocolaty and sweet—she settled into an armchair. Wind was whipping around the building, moaning in corridors, rattling unused bike racks, and battering flimsy bus stop signs.

The Charles River, framing its picturesque Cambridge side, was for the most part, obscured by blinding snow. Alexa texted Jared to make sure he was all right. He assured her that he and his roommate, Doug, were having a grand old time. Popcorn, poker, movies, and video games…not a bad way to ride out the storm.

Blizzard advisories were already scrolling on screen when Alexa looked up: no classes the next day and limited transportation throughout the city. The newscast showed skeleton crews attempting to clear runways at the airport. A rookie reporter, stationed alone at a deserted terminal, seemed desperate for someone to interview.

"Maybe there's something good about blizzards after all," Alexa thought as the storm raged. "They force you to slow down and think…to realize your insignificance in the world." Eventually she went upstairs and climbed under her down quilt, happy to get some extra sleep.

Jared, on the other hand, sat up with Doug, talking. They had both been so busy this semester, they hadn't had time to socialize. Jared told Doug about his independent study on the Gardner Museum heist and his quest for the lost art. Doug told Jared about his decision to pursue civil engineering.

While Jared didn't mention his journeys back to 1861—nobody wants a crazy roommate—he did take Doug into his confidence.

"I'm really stuck on where the paintings could be," Jared agonized. "I thought I had a lead, but it fizzled out. Now I'm grasping at straws. Unfortunately, I need to come up with three strong theories about the missing art, and time is running out." Doug listened intently.

"This probably sounds nuts," Jared continued, "but for some reason, I think that clues to the present lie in the past."

To Jared's relief, Doug didn't laugh. "There may be something to that. They say history repeats itself."

Jared liked that reasoning. He glanced at the wall chart. "I thought so, too, so I started writing down names, places and random words from my research and experiences, hoping they would tie together. Only problem is, I'm not seeing any connections."

Doug's eyes ran down the left column of the wall chart starting with Big Bucks and Dig Deeper and then went to the right column, topped with Tunnels and Jack. "Seems pretty clear to me," he said as he turned to Jared. "Tunnel jacking under the Big Dig."

Jared was dumbfounded. "I know what the Big Dig is," he said, referring to Boston's 25-year $24 billion Central Artery renovation, "but what's tunnel jacking?"

Doug offered a scholarly explanation. "Tunnel jacking uses structural boxes to form tunnels underneath active roadways or railways, so they're not disturbed. Soil is removed ahead of the boxes and the boxes are pulled or 'jacked' forward into place."

Jared's brain was reeling.

"The boxes are enormous—as big as baseball fields—and can weigh thirty million tons," Doug continued. "They're basically the framework for the tunnels themselves. When the ground is too soft to remove, the soil is frozen and then excavated, so the box can slide into place."

Jared remembered Alexa's far-fetched theory about ice picks and woolly mammoths—and thought that maybe, as a clue, it wasn't so off-base after all. He pumped Doug for more information. Doug explained that tunnel jacking is common in Europe and Japan, but not so much in America. The Boston installation under Fort Point Channel is one of the largest, if not *the* largest, uses of tunnel jacking in the states.

"That could mean something!" Jared agreed, excited. The idea was certainly in keeping with Red's hint about treasure being right under our feet. With this information, it might even be possible to pinpoint a location.

"I know what you're going to ask next," Doug went on "and the answer is yes. Yes, there was plenty of open space under the city during construction and yes, a lot of people had access to it."

"So, as unlikely as it seems," Jared calculated out loud, "this priceless art could be walled up underground right here on home turf." The concept was extraordinary, but plausible.

"Yup. With jacked tunnels, stolen paintings could be quickly hidden, safely stored, and easily relocated," Doug added. "They would be a moving target."

"And that could be one reason why the FBI has come up empty," Jared offered.

He and Doug talked into the wee hours of the morning, developing theories and dismantling them. By the time they turned in, snow had blanketed the city. Beyond the window, only the tops of parking meters were visible as drifts built up around the bases. Jared closed his eyes but was too excited to sleep. Doug was out like a light.

Snowfall had subsided by the time sun broke over the Citgo sign. Road crews were beginning their daunting task of clearing the streets. Apartment dwellers were starting to shovel paths from their doorways, mostly to walk their dogs it seemed. From different ends of the campus, Jared and Alexa each bundled up and joined their classmates for a spontaneous snowball fight along Comm Ave. When they finally met up, their coats were wet, their noses red, and their cheeks were flecked with droplets of water where snow had melted.

The experience left them invigorated, and they ducked into a clothing store to dry off and catch up. Spring break was quickly approaching, and they hastily made plans for Jared to visit Alexa in Pennsylvania. Two weeks later, he was on a plane, ready to meet her family.

✦✦✦

Alexa's family was easy to like, and Jared could see in her, the qualities of both her parents. Her sense of humor came from her Dad, Ray, and her inherent sweetness from her Mom, Nancy.

Ray had been in the computer business prior to his heart attack but had purposely slowed down to regain his health. He had become a barbeque master, a respectable poker player, and a hobbyist handyman, who took great delight in renovating their house.

Nancy was a librarian for the local school district and spent her time traveling between locations. She sang in the church choir, cheered for their local sports teams, and loved animals.

Will, Alexa's kid brother, despite her biased portrayal, was surprisingly cool for his age. Like his Dad, he was a whiz at computers and a darn good guitar player. Although a bit rusty, Jared picked up the old acoustic that was in Will's room and they jammed together for an hour.

"I didn't know you could play," Alexa said, poking her head into the room between sets.

"There are still a few things you don't know about me," Jared said, giving her a sly smile. He was convinced that Will liked having 'a big brother' around.

Spending time together, away from campus, helped Jared and Alexa see each other in a different light. They talked about things they hadn't previously shared and relaxed in each other's company. The quiet, rural setting provided a wholesome atmosphere in which to unwind.

The sweeping countryside, with its rolling hills and open fields, reminded Jared of those near the old Tory house that had lured his mother into the past. The following day, he and Alexa walked along a back road with the luxury of knowing they had nowhere else to be. They stopped at a footbridge and watched a stream that ran under it, following the current around fallen branches and slippery rocks. They said very little as they leaned on the railing, listening to the gurgle of water, waiting for ice to break from the banks and float downstream until it disappeared.

"I need to go back, while I have time," Alexa finally said, reminding Jared that she had unfinished business in Buckskin Joe. "Lydia has more to do."

"I know. I think I should go, too," Jared said. "I want to find out what happens to Red in Denver—and even more than that, be there when he comes back to you." Jared squeezed her hand.

That afternoon, they retreated to the living room, set their phone alarms for two hours later and, holding the buckle between them, traveled to the snowy slopes of Colorado.

+++

Buckskin Joe was a mere cluster of buildings set in miles of whiteness. The town was deserted, and the vitality, gone. Lydia had lost weight during recent weeks and her blush of beauty had faded. She found herself struggling to carry pails of water and fresh blankets to a row of cabins near the mine. Several of the miners, previously quarantined, had insisted on going home and brought the disease with them.

Every day, friends and families transported loved ones to their final resting place at the edge of town. When the weather allowed, crosses were hammered into the hard cemetery ground. Otherwise, names were painted on rocks in remembrance of those who had died.

Those who survived bore the scars of infection. Some were so pock-marked that their lips, noses, and ears merged into misshapen blobs of tissue. Young girls, once pretty and pursued, put ribbons in their hair to defy the markings on their faces, but knew in their heart-of-hearts, that they would likely never marry. Men, who had managed to pull through the worst of it, were emaciated and disheartened. Mine production was in a steep decline and the few business owners, who had stayed in town, were barely eking out a living.

Christmas was approaching, and still there was no sign of Red. Lydia was dividing her time between her cabin, Doc Jones, and the dance hall. More nights than not, Bill Buck told her to go home early and get some rest, advice she willingly accepted. Too exhausted to undress, she would often collapse on her bed, boots and all.

Then one day, just as Alexa and Jared had awoken to a pristine morning after the blizzard in Boston, Lydia opened her cabin door to a sparkling expanse of fresh snow.

As she stood in her doorway watching the aspens whip the sky, she noticed a blur of movement in the distance. The glare made it hard to see, but she could detect a buckboard and horses making their way across the flats where she had laid tracks the day before.

She went inside for a cape and bonnet and, when she returned, the moving shape was closer. She could see a man driving the horses hard, leaning forward, his shoulders hunched under a long dark coat. "Red!" she cried running toward him, ignoring the snow that dropped into her boots and caught in her skirts. "Red!" she called again as the horses picked up speed. He barely pulled them to a stop when he was out of the cart and running toward her. She fell into his arms.

"Oh, Lydia, I've been so worried about you. We knew there was smallpox in Buckskin Joe and were warned to stay away. But as soon as the weather broke, I had to come back," Red said, not hiding the desperation in his voice. "Are you all right? You look tired. Beautiful, but tired."

"I *am* tired, but I'm fine. I've just been caring for people around the clock. Mostly miners and their families, if any are left. We have some survivors, but the disease is still in full force, and the cemetery is filling up fast. I spend half my time helping Doc Jones these days."

"But you haven't gotten sick?" Red tried to confirm, bewildered and relieved at the same time.

"No, I've been lucky," Lydia said. "Or maybe it's more than luck. Come in and I'll tell you."

Red dropped his gear on the floor and hung his frozen duster and hat on a hook, stopping to warm his hands near the stove. Lydia set the morning coffee on to heat as she recounted her experience over the past few months. She could not hold back tears when she described the children who had died so innocently, their faces flushed with fever, their eyes looking heavenward. As she mentioned the names of friends, who had lost their battles with the disease, Red grew grim.

He sat with her, knee to knee, holding her hands as she talked. She told him that Doc Jones had let her read his medical journals and, while she couldn't understand everything, she had seen something that explains why she was resisting the disease. Just as Dr. Jenner had observed in the milkmaids sixty years before, Lydia too, had gotten cowpox as a girl. She held up her fingers to show Red a few faint scars. "I never noticed those before," he said, kissing her palms. "They are truly the most beautiful things I've ever seen."

They both laughed—the kind of nervous laugh bordering on tears—at which point Red added to the story. "Come to think of it, I also had cowpox. Remember, I told you how we used to birth calves on the ranch? I was always around cows. I hardly remember getting it, but I know I did, because my mother told me it was a good thing. I never understood why, but now I do."

Lydia's lips were trembling as she realized that she and Red would survive the epidemic. "Now I can help you," he said with a catch in his voice. "Together we can heal this town." Lydia threw herself against him and he didn't let go.

"You're the best Christmas present a girl could get," she said, kissing him deeply.

"And I can't wait to unwrap you," Red replied, tugging at her skirts.

The next morning Lydia looked radiant as she watched Red from across the table. His face was wind-burnt, and his hands were cut, but they had surely felt fine on her body the night before. How she had missed his strength and ardor, pleasuring him and receiving his pleasure in return.

"It's so good to be back with the two things I missed most: you and real food," he said, reaching for a biscuit and plateful of eggs. "I'll ride down to Doc Jones' with you in a little while, but first, I thought you might like these." Red pulled from his pocket a handful of small glass ornaments that looked like fruits and nuts. The burgundy ones were molded into apples, grapes, and berries. The amber ones glowed like oranges and acorns. Each was tied with a thin wire and swung ever so slightly when held. "I got these from a German fellow who brought them here from his home country," Red said, placing them into Lydia's hands.

"They're beautiful," she said, holding one up to catch the light. "Now all we need is a tree to decorate." She had seen Christmas trees in *Godey's Lady's Book* when she read about Queen Victoria's latest social trend.

"We'll take care of that after we make our rounds. The woods are filled with young pine."

Lydia felt as if a weight had been lifted from her shoulders. With Red back home, she was renewed, restored, and at peace. Maybe this was love in its most practical form.

15
SMALL MIRACLES

Doc Jones moved slowly as Red helped him load supplies into the buggy. There were powders for pain and vials of liquid for fevers, but nothing that could cure smallpox. Red and Lydia followed the doctor as he made house calls and assisted where they could. Sometimes their efforts were as simple as fluffing a pillow or filling a hot water bottle for cold feet; other times, they physically lifted patients to change their clothes or walk them to the outhouse.

"How are you doing, Fred?" Lydia asked one miner who was seriously stricken. "Much better now that you're here," Fred said, lifting his chin and sharing a toothless grin. She brought him tea and gently washed his face. The next day he died.

Although the epidemic still raged, Lydia noticed a subtle change. Sadie, who had battled the disease, was now past the point of contagion and had been minimally scarred. More importantly, she was regaining her strength and was now immune. Lydia enlisted her services.

Later that afternoon, while there was still light, Red and Lydia walked to the woods and cut a small, feathery pine, which they put into a barrel to take home. Once inside, they filled the barrel bottom with water and propped the tree upright between strips of wood, which they nailed to the rim.

They took turns hanging the ornaments on the delicate branches and smiled as the molded glass fruit glowed in the candlelight. Moments later, there was a knock at the door. Sadie and 'Father' Dyer were outside, songbooks in hand. They greeted Red and Lydia with holiday wishes and started singing. Sadie's clarion voice rang out in the still, cold, night, evoking a sense of calm and a feeling of joy. Red and Lydia got their wraps and followed Sadie and the preacher to the next cabin, where those, who were recovered and now immune, joined the procession. Soon there was a parade of well-wishers calling on others who had little else but hope.

When their tour was done, they made their way to Bill Buck's for warmth and libation where, to their surprise, tables were set with thick slices of ham and roasted potatoes. Red looked at Bill and thanked him for cooking up the feast. Bill looked at Red with a "You're Welcome," surprised that a humble miner could afford to underwrite the cost. Bill did not know that Red, thanks to his claim, was now a man of means.

+++

Alexa and Jared, jarred by their phone alarms, rallied to attention. Despite the struggles in Buckskin Joe, they had seen human kindness at its best and had witnessed man's capacity for resilience. They savored their last days of vacation with Alexa's family and returned to Boston, refreshed. They brought with them the optimism and fortitude they had seen in Buckskin Joe and tackled their school work with renewed enthusiasm.

College demands hit hard, but their commitment didn't falter. They had less than two months to complete their papers, wrap up their projects, and take final exams. Jared told his advisor, Peter, that his best lead for the Museum story had fizzled and that he wasn't sure how to proceed, but Peter just reiterated what he had said before. "Dig deeper."

Jared spent hours online searching through newspaper archives and watching videos of FBI interviews. He listened to the "Last

Seen" podcasts produced by WBUR and the *Boston Globe.* He went back to the museum multiple times, hoping to notice something new, something that would lend credence to Doug's tunnel jacking theory. He strolled through the corridors, trying to pick up a vibe, but to no avail. "So much for ESP," he groused.

Disheartened, he'd walk a few blocks away and observe the setting from afar, trying to visualize the paintings being removed in the dark of night. There was no epiphany. He returned to the movie theater where he and Alexa had overheard the two men talking, but nothing seemed out of the ordinary and no one looked particularly suspicious.

With Frankie, Joe, Sean, and Jack gone, he was back to the beginning. He thought for a while, and he hoped, that the people who possessed the paintings might reach out directly, but they did not. Probably too risky. He wondered if the artwork had been sold to the other bidders. Maybe the sellers had changed their minds. Maybe the artwork never existed at all.

Nora and his mother sent occasional updates, but little arrived that Jared could use in his article. He felt as if he were hitting a wall.

Jared found himself turning to Alexa for consolation and encouragement. Her compassion and intelligence continued to amaze him, and he knew their relationship was becoming something neither had planned. When they were together, there was a lightness about them, quirky humor, and easy banter.

One day, while sitting on a campus bench, Alexa looked up at the trees and mentioned that chickadee calls were changing from the cold weather 'chickadee-dee-dee' to the distinctive springtime 'fee-bee' of the mating male. Jared wasted no time in 'fee-beeing' her, only to receive an audible groan and exaggerated eye roll in return.

The following Saturday, rewarding themselves for a week of hard work, they took the T out to the waterfront. People were milling around as if let out of winter's cage. Children flew kites in open spaces and young couples strolled among the early daffodils. Dads tossed Frisbees with their kids and Moms talked to each other on playgrounds, subconsciously rocking strollers that contained infants asleep in the warm breezes. Older folks leisurely walked arm in arm as they had likely done for decades.

The mild weather also brought out street people and panhandlers. Jared and Alexa tried to keep walking but were intercepted by a homeless man shaking a cup with a coin in it. "Spare change for coffee?" the scruffy man asked. Jared glanced down at the fellow wearing multiple layers of stained, gray clothing, and dropped a couple quarters into the cup. Suddenly Jared felt Alexa grab his arm. He looked over at her and she was nodding in the man's direction.

"That's my cup," she stage-whispered. "The cup from the miner's lunch pail." Jared looked more closely and sure enough, it appeared to be the same.

"I like your cup," Jared said to the man. "Where did you get it?"

The weathered man gestured toward downtown. "Behind some school, in a dumpster. Cool, isn't it?"

"Would you consider selling it, for a good price I mean?" Jared asked. "I'm kind of a collector," he lied.

"That depends," the man said. "What's a good price?"

"Twenty bucks?" Jared offered. "That's all I have on me."

"Maybe," the homeless man said, trying to negotiate.

"How 'bout we throw in a meal?" Alexa suggested. "I have a few dollars."

The man's eyes lit up at the thought of food. He rose slowly, unfolding his stiff limbs, and reached for his shopping cart that was stuffed with trash bags and assorted household items. "There's a diner near here," he said, starting to walk in that direction, left pinky toe poking out of his worn black sneakers.

"At least he has socks," Alexa thought as she glanced down at the bright red fabric protruding from the hole. "Socks, and rainbow suspenders."

Before they ordered, Jared introduced himself and slipped the man a $20 bill. The man ignored the introduction, took the money, and slid the tin cup across the table. "Guess I can find another one of these."

Alexa reached for the cup thinking, "Not really," and tucked it into her backpack. She offered her name also but got nothing in return.

Jared was intrigued by the man and suspected the fellow had stories to tell. Alexa, compelled by empathy, encouraged the man to choose anything on the menu. She even read parts of it out loud, not entirely sure of his eyesight or literacy skills. Not surprising, he selected steak and eggs.

The waitress came over with glasses of water and took their orders. She returned with 3 steaming cups of coffee, which they eagerly sampled. Jared and Alexa kept their distance; the man was a little ripe.

"Do you mostly hang around these parts?" Jared asked.

"I hang all over the city. Sometimes I ride the T to stay warm."

Alexa studied the man's face. His beard was uneven, his skin was coarse, and his hair was stringy, but his eyes were clear blue. She wondered how he had come to this plight. "How did you end up…doing what you do?" She was going to ask 'how did you end up like this' but thought it sounded rude.

"You mean, being on the street?" the man replied, pulling no punches.

"Yeah," Alexa answered, uncomfortable saying more.

"Well, I used to be a writer, but that's a hard way to make a living. I lost my job, my wife got sick, the kids left home, and I just couldn't get back on my feet."

"Couldn't you get some help?" Jared asked. "I mean, from the city or state?"

"I got a few dollars, but that ran out. After my wife died, I was evicted. I lived in my car for a while, but I had to sell that for food. I tried heading south where it was warmer, but the stories are up here."

"So, you still write?" Jared asked.

"When I can, when I have paper, when I have a quiet place to work. Of course, I have no credibility now, so I can't really sell anything, but I do it for myself."

"It's nice you have that passion," Alexa said, pausing as the food arrived.

The weathered man greedily dove into his meal, cutting big chunks of meat and dipping them into the runny yolks of the fried eggs. He scooped up hash browns as if his fork were a shovel, chomped on his toast, and gulped down the coffee. Alexa and Jared nursed their drinks, having spent their money on the man's meal.

"Tell you what *is* crazy, though," the homeless man said between bites, looking up, eager to share what was on his mind. "It's the ineptitude of law enforcement in this city." Jared glanced at Alexa, not wanting to get into a heated discussion. "They protect the streets all right; they've saved me from a few beatings, but when it comes to solving crime, they know nothing."

"I doubt that's true," Alexa said, trying to diffuse the man's ire.

"It is *absolutely* true," the man said, swallowing a swig of water. "Take that museum heist ages ago. They think they know the guys who did it," he said with sing-song sarcasm, "but they never recovered the art. How long has it been? Thirty years?

Jared but dropped his cup. This had to be more than a coincidence. He heard his mother's words echo in his head, "There are clues all around you. You just have to see them."

Jared stared at the man. "You follow that case?" Jared asked, incredulous.

"Oh, yeah, been following it forever. Turns out I was near the building the night it happened, when that red hatchback pulled up with the crooks in it. I could have told that guard those guys were phonies. Their tin badges looked like they were bought at a costume shop."

"Did anyone ever question you?" Jared asked. "I mean, the cops or the feds."

"You kidding? When you're homeless, you're invisible."

This encounter was the closest Jared had ever come to an eye-witness account. "Did you see anything else?" he asked, adrenalin pumping. "I'm writing a story on it for school. Hope to publish it someday."

"Oh yeah, I saw a lot of stuff. I saw that dude come in to the museum the night before. He seemed to be casing the joint. Nobody paid any attention back then, but now they're saying it was a test run."

"You saw the recent video?" Jared asked, finding it hard to believe.

"Sure. I just go to a big box store and stand in the TV department until they kick me out. You can catch all the news you want on those giant screens."

"That's clever," Alexa said, off-handed.

"Don't think that because we're out on the street, we're stupid. We need to be smarter than the average guy just to survive," the man retorted, throwing her a stern look.

"I wasn't implying…" Alexa backpedaled. The last thing she wanted to do was insult the man.

"Yup, I've seen a lot. I take notes. Write down my theories about where the art's hidden," the man said as he used his bread crust to sop up the last of the egg yolk. Jared stared at the yellow streaks left on the plate, wanting the conversation to continue, but the man seemed eager to leave.

"Well, if you ever care to tell us more about it, we'd love to hear. I have a few ideas of my own about the missing art," Jared said as Alexa rummaged for the emergency cash she kept in her wallet.

"Come around next weekend, same time, same place, and I'll show you what I've got. You'll have to buy me some food to get at it, but that seems like a fair deal." With that, the man stood up and walked out to his cart, leaving behind a whiff that wasn't exactly pleasant.

Jared and Alexa waited for the bill and went to the register to pay. "Strange guy," the waitress said as she rang up the payment. "See him around a lot. Always in some crazy get-up. Never looks the same way twice."

"Guess you have to wear what you can find when you're homeless," Jared said, trying to be tolerant.

"Guess so."

As Jared and Alexa retraced their steps, they were deep in thought. Other than for his lifestyle, Alexa liked the man. "It must be incredibly difficult to be alone and out on the street," she sighed. "I wonder what he was like when he had a job and a family." One of the things Jared admired most about Alexa was her affinity for small children, lost animals, and wayward souls. A lot like Lydia.

✦✦✦

Pressure was mounting as academic deadlines neared. Alexa was working on the format for her Voter Apathy forum. Jared was spending endless hours scrutinizing maps of the Big Dig. The following weekend, just as they had done before, they rode across town and walked to the corner where the homeless man had been sitting. Not entirely convinced he would show up and not seeing him there, they poked their heads into the diner. "Howdy," Jared said to the waitress. "We were in last weekend with that fellow who hangs around here," Jared said, not quite sure how to reference the man.

"I remember you. You brought him a meal. That was nice," she said. "He's in the back corner waiting for you." Jared and Alexa noticed the man sitting there, wearing a frayed rep tie over a loose green sweater with a large moth hole in the front.

They made their way to the table where the man was sipping coffee. He would drink some, add cream from a chrome dispenser, drink more, then add more cream, until his cup was filled with a pale liquid that resembled Rhode Island coffee milk. Alexa suspected the waitress had purposely brought him an extra-large pitcher.

"Greetings," said Jared. "Can we sit down?" The man gestured with an upturned palm as Alexa and Jared slid across the bench seat facing him.

"What can we get you?" Alexa asked, knowing the deal.

"Burger, fries and a large Coke," the man said. "I don't want to break the bank."

Jared couldn't tell if the guy was being sincere or snarky, or maybe even trying to be funny, so he ignored the comment entirely. "You said you would show us your notes about the Gardner Museum heist," Jared reminded.

"Got 'em right here," the scruffy man said, patting a grungy manila envelope at his side.

Alexa strained to see the package beyond the table edge. When the waitress came over, they ordered three sodas and the one meal, hoping she would take her time bringing it out.

"We've been thinking a lot about you," Jared said, trying to prompt conversation. "And what you might have seen."

"I can tell you this: I don't miss much," the man confirmed. "I remember that rainy Saturday night like it was yesterday."

He laid the tan envelope on the table and gave it a little push. "Take a look." Jared lifted the flap and tentatively reached in.

"Pull something out. Anything. I'll tell you what it means," the man insisted.

Jared felt around and extracted a piece of white lined paper, ragged at the top as if it had been ripped off a pad in haste.

"Go ahead. Read it," the man urged.

"It says 'St. Patty's Day, 4th of July, Marathon Monday, playoffs at Fenway Park.'"

"Okay. Those are the craziest days here. That's when the crowds come in, the cops are preoccupied, the T is packed with people, and no one is paying attention. Think about it. On the evening of March 17, 1990, St. Patty's Day was winding down. Parents had gone home with their tired kids and were busy washing painted shamrocks off their little faces. Singles were still out celebrating, hoping to get laid. Police were off their regular beats, assigned to patrol the pubs in Southie. Businesses were closed for the weekend. What a great time to steal a bundle of art and move it across town. Wouldn't even have to leave the city."

"Funny you say that," Jared volunteered. "I think the art is still here, too, and my roommate is convinced it's buried under the Big Dig."

"Might be. There's a lot of room down there—and a steady stream of people comin' and goin'," the man said, pausing when his burger arrived. He attacked the meat like a hungry dog. "Take something else out." He grunted toward the envelope.

Jared reached in and extracted a folded napkin. "*The Concert* by Vermeer contains a hidden painting called *The Procuress*, which also appears in his other work."

"Oh, yeah, that's a good one," the homeless man said, proud to be so clever, "but I'm not sure where it fits. You see, there's a painting in the background of that stolen Vermeer, which the artist has also used in his other work. That hidden image was done by a different Dutch painter named Dirck van Baburen. What makes this interesting is that the Vermeer is very prim and proper, but the incorporated painting is bawdy—it shows a guy giving a hooker some cash. *Bordeeltjes*."

"Excuse me?" Jared said, not catching that last word.

"Brothel scenes," the homeless man said. Alexa was surprised at the fellow's depth of knowledge and immediately thought of the working girls in Buckskin Joe. Maybe there was a connection.

By this time, the man was dipping fries into pools of ketchup. "Try me again," he said, stuffing his mouth full.

Jared pulled out a business card from an insurance company. "Life insurance?" Jared asked.

"No, other side, you fool," the man growled.

Jared saw "Hayden House" scribbled in blue ink. "What's Hayden House?"

"Ah, one of my better ideas!" the man said. "That was a safe house on the Underground Railroad, where runaway slaves from the South hid prior to the Civil War. There are 23 locations in New England, making a ready route for transport."

"Where are these places?" Alexa asked.

"All over," the homeless man said. "Ross Farm in Northampton, Liberty Farm in Worcester, Wayside Inn in Concord, Bowditch House in Brookline, Jackson House in Newton…."

"You certainly are well-informed," Alexa remarked, surprised.

"I have plenty of time to read," the man quipped, and went back to his food.

"Then you're suggesting, a natural circuit already exists," Jared reiterated, "meaning the art would never have to stay in one place for any length of time."

"Exactly. I'm not saying anyone affiliated with these places knows about the art—but this established network provides points where paintings could be stored and rotated, without a lot of conversation. I figure if 100,000 slaves could escape this way before the Civil War, so could 13 masterpieces."

"Wow! So where is this Hayden House?" Alexa asked, looking at the card.

"Up behind Beacon Hill. Sixty-six Phillips Street."

A puzzled expression crossed Jared's face.

"Why are you lookin' at me like that?" the scruffy man asked. "I've got a photographic memory, that's all."

"It's not that. It's the street name."

"What about it? Phillips with two 'l's'…."

"I had a feeling." Jared uttered a little laugh. "That's the name of an old mine in Colorado that I've been learning about." Alexa's eyes widened as she made the mental leap to the Phillips Mine.

"So?" the man asked as he slurped down the rest of his Coke.

"So, Jared is convinced that clues to the present lie in the past," Alexa explained.

"Not a bad way of thinking," the man said, as he reclaimed his envelope. "They say everything old is new again." He slowly got to his feet and adjusted his tie as if he were wearing a finely tailored suit. "Thanks for the meal."

"Are you leaving already?" Jared asked, hoping to see more notes.

"Even a homeless guy has places to go and people to meet." The man headed for the door.

"How do I reach you?" Jared asked, quickly standing and hurrying to follow him outside.

"Not sure you can."

"But I have more questions to ask," Jared sputtered as he stood on the street corner. He got no response.

Jared came back to the restaurant and paid for the meal. "I wish we had more time with him," Jared said as he and Alexa walked toward the trolley station. "He's got me thinking, though. As far-fetched as it sounds, use of the Underground Railroad is as good a theory as any. I just need some reason to believe it."

"Not sure I can help you much there," Alexa said, as they slid into a seat on the T. "I'm up to my eyeballs preparing for this forum."

"Good luck with that, by the way. I'll see you there."

They rode in silence, deep in thought, until Jared got off at his stop.

✦✦✦

Three days later, Jared texted Alexa. "Sorry to bother you. I want to go back to Buckskin Joe. Need some answers, but you don't have to come with me."

"It's probably still pretty grim back there."

"I'll be fine. Maybe if I'm not distracted by a beautiful woman, I'll be able to focus," he teased.

"Very funny, but thanks for the compliment," Alexa said. "Swing by tonight and we can sit in the lounge. If you put the buckle directly into the cup without my touching it, you might be able to travel alone." Jared agreed, then headed to his next class. He finally felt he was onto something.

16
CONNECTIONS

When Jared landed in Buckskin Joe that evening, the streets were muddy from an early winter thaw. He wandered over to Bill Buck's out of habit, but Lydia wasn't there. He noticed a new 1862 calendar, featuring an illustration of a voluptuous woman, tacked to the wall. Bill Buck was smiling from behind the bar, happy to see his customers starting return. Most of them looked weak and pale, but at least they were buying liquor.

"Hey, Red," Bill called when he noticed the tall miner standing there. "Too bad you weren't here a week ago. Buckskin Joe became the official County Seat. All the mucky-mucks from Tarryall City came in to introduce themselves, and they bought booze for everyone." Bill looked dapper, wearing a blue shirt that matched his eyes, and a black string tie threaded through a disk of silver.

"We were out in the back country, getting some fresh air, trying to stay healthy," Red said, concealing the fact that he and Lydia had been working the mine. "Figured we'd take advantage of the warm spell."

"Yeah, a lot of guys here are still sick—especially the ones who didn't get it right away. Cryin' shame. Strapping young men cut down in their prime." Bill shook his head in dismay.

"Lydia thought things were getting better. Maybe by spring it will be gone," Red said as he ordered a whiskey and sat down at a table to drink it. He was tired from helping Lydia care for the stricken, tired from working his claim, tired from putting in time at the Phillips mine, and tired from his recent travels to Denver.

"Anyone sitting here?" a voice asked over Red's shoulder.

"Nope," Red said without looking up. He didn't mind company; he just didn't want to talk.

"George," the friendly man said, putting out his hand. His dark hair was cut to the ear. He had a neatly trimmed beard and a moustache that accented his upturned mouth. He was a few years older than Red.

Red looked up from his drink and introduced himself by his first name. "You from around here?" he asked the stranger, feeling obligated to be civil.

"Naw," the fellow said. "California." There was something in the way he leaned back in his chair that reminded Red of himself.

"What brings you here?" Red asked as he took another swallow of whiskey, letting it roll around on his tongue.

"Lady out in Fairplay," George said, getting a softer look around his eyes. He was well-dressed compared to local folk, wearing a shawl-collared jacket and buttoned vest over wool twill pants.

"And you?" he asked.

"Mining mostly. Got a lady here, too. Used to do ranching, though."

George kept staring at Red. "You wouldn't know the Suter ranch down in Texas, would you?"

Red set his glass aside and leaned across the table, eyes drilling into George. "Why do you ask?" His hands inched toward the small pistol he kept in his pocket. After the claim-jumping incident, Red was wary of people he didn't know. Especially those who seemed to know him.

"I once knew some folks there," George said. Those soft eyes clouded over ever so slightly.

"My family actually owned that ranch, but my Dad and brothers left when I was a kid," Red said, swirling the remaining whiskey around in the glass. "They went off to find work and never came back. Figure them for dead." Red looked down at the table as if he couldn't bear the intrusion of eye contact. George, however, didn't break his gaze.

Silence hung in the air until the newcomer leaned forward and put his elbows on the table. "Jim?" George asked in a tenuous voice.

Red looked up, skeptically eying the man with features like his own. "Roger?" he dared to ask.

George nodded yes. "I shuffled the letters in my name and became George Smith a few years back. Figured Smith was close enough to Suter that I'd remember it." He flashed a smile that resembled Red's.

For a moment Red was immobilized. "Are you really my brother?" Red asked, finding it hard to get the words out. He hadn't seen the guy for thirteen years. "Tell me something only I would know."

Roger thought a moment. "Our Mother's name is 'Matilda,' but she goes by 'Mattie.'"

"You could have heard that somewhere," Red challenged. "Tell me something else."

"Father gave you a red Lisk lunchbox."

"More."

"I'll do you one better," Roger said. He reached into his vest pocket and pulled out a tintype of himself, their father, and Paul, standing by an old mill. "Always carry this close to my heart," Roger said.

Red stared at the picture and slowly smiled at the faces he recognized. He paused a long moment. "Guess I've got myself a brother again."

"Seems so," Roger said. He got up and clasped Red around the back. "You've sure grown up, kid."

Red stepped back and braced Roger at arm's length. "Look at you! Last time I saw you, you couldn't even grow a beard!" The men laughed, hugged again, and ordered more drinks.

"Father and Paul?" Red asked, hopeful.

"Lost them in an accident. They were together when some scaffolding collapsed. Pains me to even think of it. Paul was so young, and Father was so happy, having found a job in Coloma."

Red sat silent at the confirmation of what he had suspected.

"And Mother?" Roger asked.

"Gone, too," Red said. "Diphtheria. About 8 years back."

Both men were quiet, deep in thought, but the serendipity of the moment soon returned. "I can't believe this! What have you been doing all these years?" Red asked. "How did you end up in California? Why did you need to change your name?"

Roger polished off his whiskey. "Long story. Got time?"

The two brothers ordered some food and talked late into the night. Roger told Red about their journey westward and how they had struggled to find work.

Red told Roger about his time on the ranch.

"How did you and Mother survive?" Roger asked, knowing it took more than two people to run the operation.

"Wasn't easy. We turned the unused fields into grazing pasture and rented that out. We had a few cows, so we sold milk. A family moved in across the road, so we hired them to help. We raised cattle and traded meat for supplies. We even gave riding lessons to any greenhorn with a horse."

Roger chuckled at the last remark, and Red sat back, relishing the familiar sound.

"But the hardest part for Mother was not knowing where all of you were," Red continued as he chewed on a ragged fingernail.

"We kept moving, that's why. We landed in California just before the Gold Rush," Roger said, "so we never thought of ourselves as Forty-Niners. We were just handymen. We worked mostly for a fellow who had a saw mill. But once gold was found on his property, things went wild. Most of his crew left to prospect for themselves. Poachers came in. They ruined his land, stole his crops, took his livestock, and made a mess of his waterways. Within a year, he had to sell the property. He eventually moved his family to Yuba City."

Red tried to envision the turmoil.

“Father saved every penny he earned in hopes of bringing Mother and you out to us, but, of course, he didn’t make it. Sometimes we didn’t get paid at all, so we worked for provisions. When food was scarce, they’d give us a piece of land or a share of the business. There was never enough money to live well.”

“After the boss left, I tried to keep things going, but I got hounded by his creditors. That’s when I changed my named to George Smith and hit the road. Too bad, ‘cause I had met a nice woman. But she wanted security, and I couldn’t offer that. Then, along the way, out of the blue, a gal from Fairplay caught my eye—and stole my heart.” Roger leaned back and smiled.

“What have you been up to since then?” Red asked.

“Little of this, little of that. Cleaned up my act and worked in a clothing store in Denver for a while,” Roger said as if to justify his wardrobe. “I went back to the old ranch, but, of course, you and Mother weren’t there, and the land was carved up. I tried to find you, but people I knew had either left or died and, of course, I had no way to describe you as a grown man.”

Red sat there trying to absorb this new information. He told Roger about the woman in purple who had come into town, mistaking him for a guy in California named George and walloping Lydia for supposedly stealing him away from her sister. Roger grimaced. “Sorry, that would be me. Guess we do look alike.”

“Bad news for both of us,” Red joked. He had longed for a brother more than he cared to admit. Not wanting the conversation to end, Red invited Roger to stay at his place in town. There, the men talked until the first rays of sun crept over the mountains, at which point Roger fell asleep on the couch and Red crawled into bed, missing Lydia at his side. When Red awoke it was to Alexa’s prompting and he was Jared once again.

+++

Alexa’s political forum attracted a sizeable crowd, mostly because of the prestigious panel she had assembled. She had been able to land a news anchor, a strategist, a well-known professor, and the founder of an activist group to provide perspectives on voter apathy. The discussion was lively and the audience, attentive. During intermission, Alexa kept busy, making sure the table top signs were lined up straight for the cameras and that water glasses were refilled.

"Good job, young lady," Alexa heard behind her. She turned and saw the man in the tweed coat—the unofficial stringer—who Jared had met at the heist history program, the same fellow who had been watching him at the Mayor's press conference. Sure enough, the guy had a laminated badge clipped to his lapel, this time for the *Action News* rather than the *Independent Press*. Alexa assumed it was also a fake. "Bob Camelion," the man said, extending his hand.

"Alexa St. Clair," she replied, reaching out in return. "You look familiar. I'm a friend of Jared Sutherland's." She expressed regrets that they had not been properly introduced before.

"I recognized you. How's that guy of yours?" he asked, knowing that Jared was an aspiring reporter, not unlike himself.

"Doing well. He should be here, but I don't see him yet. He's probably preoccupied following a lead on his favorite subject."

Bob was standing in the window light, his adaptive lenses darkening up. "Ah, I know the topic well. We talked about it, last time. Many mysteries." His spiral notepad was in his left hand, a pen jabbed into the curl of wire.

"There sure are," Alexa acknowledged. "He has some theories about the missing art, but he needs proof."

"Well, as they say, a picture's worth a thousand words," Bob replied as he turned toward an empty seat. A trail of aftershave followed him as his polished shoes slapped the floor.

"It was nice seeing you again. I'll let him know we connected," Alexa called after him.

"Sounds like a plan."

Alexa flicked the lights on and off to signal the audience to return. She kept the discussion fluid and at the end, asked how voter participation might be improved. Several students raised their hands as did faculty members. Bob stood up and suggested using online registration and email or text reminders. That seemed like the most constructive idea. With no further input, Alexa summarized the session, thanked the panel, and circulated feedback forms.

As the crowd dispersed, she collected the evaluation sheets and unused pens, then unfastened and folded the banner that was draped across the front of the table.

"I'm so sorry I'm late," Jared said, out of breath and rushing toward her. "I got here just in time for the second half. Don't ask. But this was super. Congrats." He planted a kiss on her cheek. "I see Mr. Camelion was here, too. We talked for a minute." Alexa nodded as she tossed the table toppers into the trash.

"He came over and asked about you," she said.

"Really? That's great. Maybe someday we'll work together," Jared replied, appreciating the importance of having contacts. He walked Alexa back to her dorm and followed her up to her room. "I've missed you so much," he said, cornering her against the desk and coming on strong. He took the tote out of her hand and set it on the floor. "All this school work is making me crazy—almost as crazy as being away from you." She responded readily as his lips found hers. His hands moved quickly.

"Not here. Not now," she said as she reluctantly pulled away. They were both out of breath.

"I think we're just going to have to live together," Jared said, surprised that those words flew out of his mouth. "Or at least live off-campus next year," he modified.

"That works for me," Alexa said, turning to brush her hair—sleek, black and wild. In her mind, it was a foregone conclusion. They took a moment and looked at each other as if sealing a pact.

"Well, I'd better go back and stare at the wall," Jared finally said, knowing they both had school work to do. Like it or not, I have to start writing this article." He lingered in the doorway for another kiss, which Alexa gladly provided. After he left, she sat on her bed and thought to herself, "That guy's a thoroughbred."

Jared locked himself away for twenty-four hours, stopping only for a few hours of sleep. During this time, he outlined his premise regarding the missing art—basically, that it was still in

Boston, hidden below the streets in jacked tunnels, or constantly moved along the historic Underground Railroad. He chronicled the steps he had taken to formulate his theories. He explained the research he had done, people he had interviewed, and resources he had used. He omitted his interaction with the past.

He described in detail the logistics that would be required to locate the concealed art and argued at the end, why finding it was so important to the city and to a civilized society. He knew he was one hypothesis shy of his goal, but he felt the article was solid. Solid, but unfortunately, not award-winning. He went back to edit.

Hours later, Jared emerged bleary-eyed, desperate to clear his head. April days were longer now and, even at 6:00 p.m., the sky was light. He grabbed his leather jacket and headed toward the Fens, a fresh water greenway that had been an ancient salt marsh before it was engineered at the turn of the century. This untamed land mass became part of Olmstead's 'Emerald Necklace,' and was home to Victory Gardens during World War II.

As Jared inhaled the earthiness around him, he could hear the distant voices of war widows as they tilled the soil and planted rows of seed, hoping for a harvest that could supplement their rations. He spotted a Spitfire streaking through the clouds and noticed a "Loose Lips Sink Ships" sign tacked to a wooden fence. He heard a crackling radio and paused to listen. FDR was giving a fireside chat. Jared stood fixed on the spot, until a chorus of peepers brought him back to reality.

Unencumbered by winter clothing, he felt buoyant as he cut his way through a side street, humming to himself and freely swinging his arms. The last time he had worn this jacket was in the fall, when he and Alexa went to the movies and kissed under the street lamp. He remembered it vividly.

As he walked along, he noticed children playing catch with a pink rubber ball, ignoring the descending darkness and calls from their mothers. He found a hole-in-the-wall restaurant, a noodle shop, and ordered a hefty bowl topped with stir fried vegies.

On his way back to the dorm, he walked purposefully, hands thrust into his jacket pockets, deep in thought about his assignment.

That's when he felt it – a USB stick sitting in his right pocket. Strange, he thought. He hadn't put it there. It certainly wasn't there the night of the movies, because that's where he had stashed his ticket before tossing it out. The flash drive must have been in his pocket all winter long.

When Jared got back to his room, he booted up his desktop and popped the drive into a slot on his tower, running a scan to make sure it was clean. When the menu opened, all he could see was a list of JPEGS, no Word docs or text files.

When he clicked on the first image, it was dark and blurry, but it distinctly showed two men carrying a large crate about 5 feet x 4 feet through what looked like an underground chamber. Jared could make out water pipes bracketed to a concrete wall behind them. The second image showed the same two men carrying a cardboard box, a bit smaller, about 4 x 3. Jared noticed the partial lettering of a wall sign at the edge of the photo, bearing some sort of utility company logo.

He continued clicking through the list, eyes glued to the screen. The following picture revealed a man carrying foam boards, about 2 x 2, secured with strapping tape. There was an Exit arrow above their heads.

Next was a photo of someone with manila envelopes fanned out under his arm. The person's face was hidden, but Jared could see the envelopes clearly. They seemed to be of standard size: one 10 x 13, two 9 x 12s, and one, 6 x 8. In the background, Jared could see the words 'Low Clearance' stenciled in yellow spray paint.

Next was a guy in a hoodie carrying 2 stacked corrugated boxes, maybe a foot high each. Lastly, there was the shadowy form of a squat man holding an extremely small box in front of himself, cupped in both hands, as if it might explode. Jared wondered if he might be Frankie.

It took Jared a moment to process this gallery of photos, but he knew he had just hit a bonanza. Before anything else, he downloaded a copy of each file to his computer and backed it up to his external hard drive. He then zipped up a set of images and emailed them to himself. Thirteen items couldn't be a fluke, since thirteen pieces of art were stolen from the Gardner Museum. Jared immediately located his notes on the artwork sizes, which he had converted from metrics to inches. Sure enough, there seemed to be a correlation.

Object	**Dimensions**
The Storm on the Sea of Galilee	Just over 5 x 4 feet
A Lady and A Gentleman in Black	Close to 4 x 3 feet
The Concert	About 2 x 2 feet
Landscape with an Obelisk	Similarly, square
Chez Tortoni	10 x 13 inches
Program for an Artistic Soirée	9 x 12 inches
Three Mounted Jockeys	12 x 9 inches horizontal
Courtège Aux Environs de Florence	About 6 x 8 inches
Chinese Bronze Beaker	10 ½ inches tall
Eagle finial from a Napoleonic flag	10 inches tall
Rembrandt's Self-Portrait	1 ¾" x 2 inches small

Jared sat stunned as he stared at the treasure trove of images. Who had taken these photos and how did they end up in his pocket? His emotions careened between confusion and jubilation. He immediately called Alexa. "You'll never believe what I found!" he said, then quickly filled in her in. She said would be right over.

When Alexa arrived, Jared had the files open on his screen. She stood behind him, eyes darting from one to another, immediately grasping the significance of what she was seeing. "I think you just got the proof you were looking for," she said, resting a hand on Jared's shoulder, "especially if someone can identify the backgrounds."

Jared got out of his seat, picked her up, and swung her around. "Wahoo!" he said, not concealing his excitement. "I think we should celebrate, but first I've gotta make a call." He reached for his cell and phoned his mother. "I have something you guys need to see. I'll use your Secure File Transfer."

After sending the files to his Mom, Jared and Alexa went out for a decadent dessert. "This is so amazing," Jared kept saying after they placed their order two molten brownies. "It's like a gift fell out of the sky and landed in my lap."

"Here's to modern miracles!" Alexa toasted with her water.

"But really, how did this happen? Who put the flash drive in my pocket? The last time I wore this jacket was in the fall with you and, then, I hung it up for the season."

"Let's reconstruct the scene," Alexa said. "What did we do? We went to the movies, heard those guys talking, we kissy-faced under the street lamp—that was nice." Her eyes danced at the thought. "Then those partygoers told us to get a room—embarrassing." Those same eyes rolled. "Then we came home on the T, right?"

"Yeah. I don't think we talked to anyone."

"Maybe it happened when we were walking down the street or on the subway platform. Did you bump into anyone?"

"I don't think so," Jared said, though he vaguely remembered someone brushing against him. "These photos make such a huge difference. They validate my thinking," he said, pausing to check his cell. "You know what they say about a picture being worth a thousand words."

Alexa chuckled. "That's funny. That's exactly what Bob Camelion said the other day. But I guess these are going to be worth a lot more."

Their brownies arrived topped with whipped cream. They both dug in, savoring the sweetness. "He's an interesting guy, isn't he?" Jared commented between bites. "Seems to turn up wherever I do." Jared noticed a trace of chocolate on Alexa's lip and pointed to the area on his own face. She reached for a napkin to dab it off her lips. "I could get that for you for if you'd like," Jared offered, his dark eyes glinting.

"Oh, I would like," Alexa replied, coy and teasing, "but you need to go back and write."

"I know," Jared said. "Just hold that thought."

"I will," Alexa said. "I actually may need a trip to Denver soon. A bride has to shop, you know."

+++

That weekend, they went into downtown Boston for a change of scenery. They wandered through a hotel lobby looking for a place to sit. The ferns and chrome ambiance made them feel as if they were adults on a mini-vacation. They set their backpacks on the floor, sank into two plush armchairs, and turned on their phone alarms. Jared rested his hand on Alexa's, the buckle underneath his palm. Within seconds, they were standing at the stage coach stop in Buckskin Joe. The weather had mellowed, and nurses were arriving from Denver, much to the delight of Doc Jones and Lydia.

When the Dan McLaughlin stage pulled in and rattled to a stop, three neatly attired women disembarked, wearing simple brown cotton dresses, no frills, no bows. No jewelry or crinolines either. They looked remarkably clean considering their journey. Their hair was uniformly pulled back, parted at the center and discretely affixed behind their heads. Each carried a satchel and a small box of medical supplies. They arrived ready to work. Red and Lydia greeted them and walked them to the inn where rooms had been scrubbed clean and bedding replaced.

"How lovely this is, out in the country," the first one said, looking across the open landscape. Lydia noticed the woman had fair hair, green eyes, a touch of freckles and a slight row of scars along her jaw line that did not detract from her natural beauty. She exuded a sense of calm and grace. Red figured she had already battled the disease and was now immune. Lydia immediately wanted to match her up with Bill Buck.

The second nurse, perhaps the prankster of the bunch, looked across at the mine. "Bet there are some eligible bachelors in there," she giggled. "By the way, you can call us A, B, C. That's Amanda," she said, nodding at the nurse with the green eyes. "I'm Beulah—B for bountiful," she joked, pointing to her generous bosom and hips, "and that's Caroline. She's not as mean-spirited as she seems."

Caroline smiled weakly, said hello, and tried to relax her stern expression. She was all business. "We worked with Dr. John F. Hamilton in Denver," Caroline said, a look of pride crossing her face. "He was the city's first official physician. As you may know, we had our own smallpox scare not long ago."

"We've heard," Lydia said.

"We'll need to get a briefing from your doctor once we're settled," Caroline continued. "Number of active cases, recoveries, and fatalities. We'll also need a sense of who hasn't been stricken, so we can protect them with good sanitary measures. We follow the strictest guidelines of the Nightingale Training School for Nurses in London." Caroline straightened her shoulders and lifted her head, causing her chin to jut out a bit. Lydia detected a kind inner quality under that brusque exterior.

Just then, Doc Jones came scurrying toward the inn. Red took the nurses' luggage inside, while Lydia made introductions. It was obvious the doctor was taken with Caroline's professionalism and maybe her trim figure. "Very nice to meet all of you," he said, graciously extending his hand and opening the door for them. "Thank you so much for coming to our rescue. Perhaps we can talk later over tea. I heard you worked with Hamilton. I've heard he's a promising young physician, fresh out of Connecticut by way of Chicago." He looked directly at Caroline. Lydia thought she could detect a slight blush on those otherwise restrained cheeks as Caroline nodded yes. Within moments, Beulah was talking to the concierge and inquiring about his health.

"Ladies, we'll let you relax for a while," Red said as he took Lydia's arm to escort her out of the lobby. "We'll come by tonight around 7:00 to make sure you have had a good meal and meet some of the folks. It may be a little rowdy at Bill Buck's dance hall, but we'll try to keep the men under control." Red smiled as he pushed back his hair and returned his hat to his head. Amanda was ready to go with the flow. Beulah was excited. Caroline seemed skeptical.

"Don't worry. I work there," Lydia smiled. "I've got some influence." Caroline shot her a pious look. "Just dancing, Caroline," Lydia clarified. "I don't work on the line."

Caroline seemed flustered, when she realized that Lydia had read her mind. "Oh, I wasn't suggesting…." Caroline sputtered.

"That's okay," Lydia said. "Lots of people confuse the two." Lydia patted Caroline's arm and turned to leave.

Red returned to his room in town, and Lydia, to her cabin. Once home, Lydia felt a sense of relief. She heated pots of water and poured the contents into her clawfoot tub, relishing the warmth and peacefulness that surrounded her. She washed her hair with floral soap and took ample time to dry it in front of the stove.

When Red came by that evening, she felt tranquil and clean, as if purged of the disease that had dominated her recent life, as if the grief and sadness had washed away with the grime. She put on a dress she had been saving for a special occasion—navy blue with white piping— and together, they went to pick up the nurses.

Bill Buck's was noisy and boisterous as the group made their way to a table, he had saved for them. Although this was her night off, at Bill's cue, Lydia took to the stage and welcomed the crowd. Cheers and applause followed. "Gentlemen—and gentlewomen," she said, looking over at the nurses. "We have some honored guests here night, so I'm going to ask you men to keep it clean and tone it down." A few good-natured groans arose. "I'd like you to meet three brave, lovely ladies from Denver, who are going to help nurse this town back to health." There was a round of clapping and a loud "Amen."

Doc Jones put his arm protectively around the back of Caroline's seat as she sat demurely observing the scene. Beulah was shamelessly flirting with Sam, who made it clear that he liked bountiful women. And Bill Buck came over to Amanda to ask if she wanted a drink. When her clear green eyes met his blue ones, that was it. Lydia, observing from the stage and being an instigator at heart, requested that Lou play a waltz and embarrassed Bill into asking Amanda to dance. "I also want to thank Bill Buck for his unwavering support in helping the ill—and for being so kind to me, personally," Lydia said, a hint of emotion creeping into her voice. "Let's toast to his generosity and good nature as he welcomes Amanda with a spin on the floor."

Bill squirmed and shot Lydia a daggered look, flustered as he tried to wiggle out of the obligation, but Amanda stood up, graceful and elegant, moving into position. "Mr. Buck?" she said, waiting for him to encircle her waist and take her hand. She was a tad taller than he, but neither of them seemed to mind. Bill's eyes were twinkling that night.

Later, Red and Lydia walked the women back to the inn and Red returned to Lydia's cabin. "Don't you just love when two people are meant for each other?" Lydia said, thinking of Bill and Amanda, as she unlaced her boots.

"I do, especially when it's us," Red said, moving closer. His arms fit around her like a custom-made coat, and she slipped easily into them. She could feel his heart beating rapidly in tandem with hers, accelerating as they touched. Lydia relished the anticipation of their lovemaking, maybe even more than the act itself. For a man inherently shy, Red did not disappoint. Later that night, after his eyes closed, she watched his chest rise and fall as she placed her palm over the tuft of hair where his heart now beat calmly.

That morning, before she stirred, he slipped his hand over the eyelet part of her gown that covered her breasts and watched her sleep like a small songbird in a nest.

The sun woke her up and she stumbled to the stove to make coffee. Mug in hand, she lingered in the doorway, looking over the peaceful countryside. The nurses were already out on their morning rounds, and they waved to her as they rode by in Doc Jones' buggy. Red was busy chopping up the limb that had come down in the winter storm, his horse grazing lazily behind the cabin. A flash of black and white in the trees—a lark bunting ditching its dull winter plumage for the regal tuxedo that signaled spring—caught her eye. Red came over and gave her a peck on the cheek. "Got any more of that?" he asked, nodding toward her drink.

"Take this one. I'll pour another for myself," Lydia said as she went back inside. She returned to the doorway with her mother's china cup. "Sometimes I miss Missouri. It seemed so civilized there," Lydia said to Red, as she looked at the delicate floral pattern and recalled the advantages of growing up near a city.

"Then maybe it's time for us to go to Denver and buy that wedding dress," Red said. "I've already talked to a pastor and the hotel on Larimer Street can accommodate us with just a three-day notice."

"Really?" Lydia said. "I'm so excited!" She finished her coffee and looked out at the snow-capped mountain in the distance. "As beautiful as it is here, I need to get away."

"That's understandable," Red said, putting his arm around her shoulder. "You've seen more suffering in a few months than most of us see in a lifetime."

Red had already reduced his schedule at the Phillips mine to accommodate his work at the Mattie Howe. The three men he had hired in Denver were due to arrive shortly. "Now that I've found Roger—or rather, he found me—he could be our best man," Red suggested. Lydia couldn't help but notice how happy he was. "I can even pay for his ticket," Red said, reminded that he didn't have to pinch pennies anymore. "What do you say we go up there next week, once my men get settled? That will give you time to brief the nurses and finalize things with Bill before we leave."

"That sounds great." Lydia said, immediately sitting down to make a list of things to do. "Maybe Sadie can care for the horses and feed the chicks," she suggested, but Red was already out the door. She saw him standing at the edge of the lot, hands on hips, looking down the road, watching his future gallop in on a glorious steed.

17
GIFTS

"Would you care for something to drink?" the hostess asked, holding a round tray with glasses on it. Jared and Alex looked up to see an attractive dark-skinned woman dressed in tailored black pants and a black blouse with a white collar, the hotel logo on her pocket.

"I'm sorry, what did you say?" Jared asked, trying to shake off the past.

"Just wanted to know if you two would like anything to drink."

"A cranberry juice would be great," Alexa said, blinking Buckskin Joe out of her eyes.

"Make that two, please," Jared added.

After the server walked away, Alexa said to Jared, "I feel a happy ending coming on," thinking of Lydia's upcoming wedding and the excitement of going to Denver.

"It will be nice for them to finally be together," Jared agreed, mixing his past and present thinking.

They sipped their drinks, letting the ice dilute the claret color until nothing was left but rose-colored water. Jared stood up and headed for the men's room while Alexa walked through the door with the scrolled 'W' on it. On her way out, she looked in the mirror and saw not only a pretty girl from the present, but deep in her eyes, a strong woman from long ago.

That week, Jared worked steadily on his article, applying his theories to the images he now had in his possession. Unfortunately, any help from his mother and Nora would not arrive in time for his deadline, that is, if they could even identify the locations of the photos. When Alexa read his article, she was supportive but not effusive. "This is a great start," she told him. But she couldn't lie. Details, emotion, and a third scenario were still missing. "Too bad our street person didn't share more," she commented.

"I know," Jared said. "That's the one big gap in this whole thing. I need more first-hand input. I need a third idea. It could go right here," he said, pointing to a place between paragraphs.

"You know what we need to do then," Alexa said. If nothing else, she was decisive.

Jared nodded. "Yup. Go back to the waterfront and see if we can find our guy."

+++

That weekend, with brisk breezes blowing, they walked along the waterfront to the familiar diner on the street corner. The waitress recognized them and, without saying anything, motioned with her chin to where the homeless man sat. "Sometimes I pay for his coffee," she whispered. "He thinks it's free." Alexa marveled at how kind people could be.

"Greetings stranger," Jared said, still not knowing his name.

The scruffy man looked up. This time he wore a reddish corduroy jacket with too-short sleeves over plaid flannel pants. He had a woman's frilly blue scarf at his throat, covering the stretched neck of a faded black tee-shirt. "Well, if it isn't the ace reporter and his gal," he said in a way that neither confirmed nor denied he cared.

"I was hoping we could ask you more questions," Jared said. Before the man could answer, Jared added, "Do you want some pie to go with that coffee?"

"That would be nice," the man said. "Apple with vanilla ice cream."

"You got it," Jared said, as he summoned the waitress. "We'll have three apple pies à la mode, please," he said, looking at Alexa for consensus. She gave him a thumbs-up.

"So, what do you want to know?" the street man asked.

"Anything you can tell me. What you saw. What you suspect. What the authorities don't know. I really need an inside scoop." The man thought a while but didn't respond. "I've written a decent draft," Jared continued. "Even stumbled onto some photos that support my theories—but I need to make the story come to life… you know, make it feel human."

"Human is good," the man said, scratching the whiskers on his cheek. The pies arrived, looking like three small snow-capped mountains. "These hot?" the man asked the waitress.

"You bet," she said, winking at Jared. "Gotta have hot apples to fully enjoy the cold ice cream."

"That's right," the man said, shoveling a forkful of both into his mouth. He turned to Jared, contemplating the young fellow's quandary. "Then you need emotion. Not just facts."

"I agree," Jared said. "But I wasn't there. You were."

"True," the man said, savoring the confluence of cinnamon and vanilla that pooled on his plate.

"Would you ever consider sharing some of what you've written?" Alexa asked, figuring it didn't hurt to try.

"I'll do you one better. You guys can have it."

"Oh, I don't want to take your work," Jared said, "and I can't really afford to buy it from you. I just thought that if I could read some of it, I might be inspired or learn something new."

"I want you to take it," the man insisted. "I've got it all up here anyway," he said, pointing to his own head. "Besides, you remind me of myself back in the day. And you could use a break."

"Are you sure?" Jared asked.

"What am I going to do with this stuff?" the man huffed. "It's not like anyone knows me anymore and I certainly don't have an agent." The street dweller laughed at his own sarcasm. "I'll be right back."

Alexa looked at Jared as the man toddled off to his cart. Through the window, they could see him rummaging around in

the trash bags that stored his prized possessions. "Guess the apple pie put him in a good mood."

A few moments later the man returned with the dirty manila envelope he had surfaced before. "Here you go," he said to Jared, sliding it across the table. "I added some stuff."

"I don't know what to say. This is very generous of you," Jared remarked, appreciating the value of the resource that had just been put into his hands.

"Well, someone might as well benefit. You're a promising young man with your life ahead of you. I'm on the downside." Alexa sensed a tone of finality in the man.

"I'll get this back to you as soon as I'm done, I promise. If you're not here, I'll leave it with the waitress."

"Whatever," the man said as he used the side of his fork to corral the last few crumbs and melted ice cream. He took one more swig of coffee and stood up to leave.

"Would you like to give me your name, so I can credit you properly? Jared asked.

"Not important," the man muttered as he pushed down on the door handle and walked into the sunlight. Jared and Alexa paid for the food and left the waitress a large tip. Jared clutched the envelope all the way home, but it wasn't until they were in his dorm room that he opened it and dumped the contents on his bed.

"Probably not the cleanest thing to do," Alexa said, eying the mix of grease-stained yellow sheets, crumpled napkins and inside-out gum wrappers. Jared picked up a sheaf of typed pages, most likely written and printed at a library. As he started to read, his eyes grew wide.

"Some say that cities have no heart, that they're an impersonal mix of concrete and congestion. But for those of us who live on the street, we know that heart exists. We are that heart, and our energy helps drive the pulse of the community. We see things that others miss. We watch people come and go…young lovers, old friends, children at play. But the public at large doesn't see us. We are transparent, invisible, and, like parts of a mobile, constantly in flux."

Jared flipped to another page. “This guy can write,” he said out loud.

“Twenty-four hours after the paintings were stolen, the museum staffers went into mourning, numb and elusive, talking reluctantly to the press only when pushed. Their demeanor was somewhere between apologetic and defensive. Local police and federal agents huddled together, conferring amongst themselves, trying to be civil…but each faction wanted the jurisdiction; each wanted the collar. In the confusion, no one saw the stranger lingering across the street, nursing a cut on his left forefinger. No one noticed the knife in his back pocket—a knife that could have cut canvas. No one saw what I saw. No one asked.” A chill ran up Jared’s back.

By this time Alexa was flipping through a small note pad much like the kind reporters use. “Listen to this,” she said.

“A young guy is coming around here, asking questions. Determined, dark-haired dude just like myself when I was a kid. Museum mucky-mucks are giving him the brush-off. Luckily, he’s persistent. Too bad they don’t understand that new eyes on old things are important.”

“I think that’s you,” she said to Jared. He put down his packet of writing to look at her, unsettled at the thought he had been watched.

She picked up an envelope on which was written a short, but eloquent, note. “I used to stare at the painting—*Christ in The Storm on the Sea of Galilee*—grand and imposing, turbulent in theme and spirit—that is, before it was ripped from its frame like a fetus from the womb, leaving a trail of pain that no civilized society should endure.”

“Wow,” Alexa said. “Heavy.”

Hours later, Jared and Alexa were still reading. “This is incredible. I can’t believe he’s letting me use this stuff,” Jared commented, eyes glued to the mound of papers. Alexa was exhausted. She said goodnight and went back to her dorm, knowing Jared would work into the wee hours of the morning.

+++

Later that week, Jared met with his advisor and turned in his article.

"Good enough to be published?" Peter asked.

"Not quite," Jared said. "It's solid, but it needs one more theory. Could I work on it this summer?"

"We'll see. You might have to accept an Incomplete," Peter said, not wanting to promise anything. "Let me take a read. I'll get back to you after finals."

Classes wound down with the arrival of May. Alexa was flat out studying, so Jared stayed away, except to deliver cookies and caffeine, before disappearing down the hall. Alexa gladly accepted these 'anonymous' gifts, knowing that she and Jared would reconnect once exams were done.

+++

By the next weekend, they were home free. Assignments had been completed, papers turned in, and, for better or worse, tests taken. Some students were already clearing out their rooms. Others were hanging around for graduation. Traffic in the city had become visibly lighter as the student population thinned. Their respective roommates, Doug and Gail, were almost packed. Doug was heading off to a summer job at a civil engineering firm and Gail was planning to travel. Eric was going back to LA to work at a small art gallery. Bobbie had landed a gig in summer stock. Carlos was still working in the Security office.

Alexa and Jared sat on the bed in his room, wanting to roll around in the joy of each other, but they knew that RAs were patrolling the floors. Instead, Jared reached into his pocket and took out the buckle. "One for the road?"

+++

Alexa set the tin cup on his desk and stepped back. They stood over it, holding hands, as they let the buckle drop. With a whoosh, they were riding in a crowded Concord coach, knees uncomfortably pressed against each other, as they headed north to Denver. Lydia looked radiant in her long, navy dress, her dark hair swept up in a silver barrette, and Red was dashing in a vested suit his brother had loaned him.

"Roger will meet us there in a few days," Red said as Lydia gazed out on the moving landscape. She could hear rifle pings overhead as a passenger on the roof aimed at prairie dogs for sport. Red reached over and took her gloved hand in his. "I never gave you a proper engagement ring," he said, watching the reflection of sky and trees pass across her dark eyes.

"Not to worry," Lydia said. "I don't need a ring to prove anything."

"But would you wear one?" Red asked, reaching inside his coat pocket for a small box. "After all, it *is* Valentine's Day."

Lydia bit her lip, not sure what to say. She had always thought herself too clever to fall for surprises. "Of course, I would," she finally answered, realizing Red had gone to lengths to acquire this gift, in time for their trip.

"Then I will ask you officially to be my wife."

With that, Red removed her left kidskin glove and opened the box, facing it toward her so she could see the delicate gold band inset with garnets. She spread her fingers and he slipped it on in a remarkably accurate fit. "Measured your finger while you were asleep," he said, winking at her.

"Aren't you the crafty one," she said, reaching across to give him a quick kiss. The other passengers applauded and Red blushed.

"It's beautiful," the woman sitting next to Lydia said. "May I see?"

Lydia slipped the ring off and held it up to the light. It was then that she noticed the inscription inside: "For eternity. JS." Lydia felt a lump rise in her throat. She didn't like to cry or to be seen crying, so she stared out the window, blinking hard. She put the ring back on and let her hand rest in her lap, glancing down at her finger to admire the promise of engagement. She caught Red watching her and knew that she couldn't keep her feelings from him. She slipped on her glove, and he covered her hand with his.

+++

Denver was bustling when they finally arrived. The thin cold air made it difficult to breathe and the frozen ground, hard to walk. "We don't have to rush," Red reminded her as they looked for The City Hotel on Larimer Street. Lydia clutched a clipping from the *Rocky Mountain News*, which contained a line drawing of the façade. "Best of accommodations can always be found and the table is furnished with the best the market affords. Proprietors W.T. Shortridge and L.J. Winchester," the ad read.

The hotel was easy to recognize, luxurious by Buckskin Joe standards. The handsome brick front and arched windows were in keeping with the developing urban landscape. Upon entering the lobby, Red and Lydia were greeted by a concierge, who showed them to a desk where a large brass bell awaited the call for service. The décor was impressive, anchored by forest green carpets, gold-hued wallpaper, and cream-colored drapes that spilled abundantly onto the floor. Parlor ferns, set into large ceramic planters, stood on stone pedestals where they gracefully spread out and bowed to the window light. Embroidered tapestries hung from dowels. Portraits of local dignitaries were framed and suspended by wire, giving the lobby a museum-like quality.

They summoned the bellhop and anxiously waited. He placed their bags on a rolling cart and pushed it into one of those new steam-driven Otis elevators. They rode to the third floor, effortlessly. Lydia's room was pleasantly warm both in temperature and hue—a combination of soft rose and peach tones, complete with the canopy bed Red had imagined. A large fireplace was stoked with logs and additional wood, placed to the side in a circular rack. A pitcher of water and wash bowl sat on a chest of drawers. A chamber pot was in the corner beside a closet where it would be discreetly hidden after use.

The bellhop showed Red to his adjacent room, but after giving the man a generous tip, Red quickly returned to hers.

Lydia took off her hat and gloves and folded her cape over the chair. She looked out the window onto the street where horse-and-buggies were lining up to accommodate the brisk foot traffic.

Red removed his suit jacket and stood behind her. He looked trim in his tailored vest and crisp white shirt. "What do you think, soon-to-be Mrs. Suter?" he asked, nibbling her ear.

"Why Mr. Suter, aren't you feisty," she teased.

"Not as feisty as I'm going to be later tonight," he promised. He took off his boots and stretched out on the bed, welcoming the length that let his legs straighten out after their cramped carriage ride. Lydia climbed up next to him, settling onto her back, careful not to crease her dress. She gazed at the salmon-colored brocade that edged the canopy above her head. What an elegant and romantic setting; she felt like royalty.

Within moments their eyes closed, and they awoke a few hours later, just as the day's light was fading. Street lamps were being lit and candles were aglow in windows across the street. Red and Lydia freshened up and walked to the dining room arm in arm. The aroma of rich onion soup and a savory roast greeted them. The maître'd led them to a table near the window and pulled out a chair for Lydia.

Contrary to life in Buckskin Joe, the accommodations were genteel—from the small silver forks, designated for desserts, to the cut crystal goblets, set out for water. Denver was by no means New York City, but after a faltering start when the original settlers left to prospect for gold, many had returned. Now the area was booming. New businesses were opening, visitors were arriving, and word was spreading about the exciting Mile-High City. The view of the Rockies was exquisite.

As Red sized up the guests, Lydia kept thinking about her wedding dress. She had read that a Mrs. A.R. Palmer was operating a Millinery & Fancy Store on Fourth Street near Front, offering a large assortment of ladies' and children's apparel. Mrs. Palmer had an experienced dressmaker on the premises, versed in New York styles and able to 'execute with promptness.' Lydia has also seen an advertisement for Mrs. G.W. Bacon, Fashionable Dress & Cloak Maker, on F Street, within walking distance between Larimer and Lawrence. Either would surely do.

As they perused the menu and waited for orders to be taken, Lydia and Red enjoyed a basket of warm rolls served beneath a linen napkin. A waiter came over with two flutes of Heidsieck champagne and a pitcher of water which he poured with a flourish. Red stretched out his legs under the table while Lydia kept hers tucked beneath her chair, ankles crossed, knees pressed tight, but that didn't stop him from playfully finding her calf with the tip of his boot. She shot him a look to reprimand his bad boy behavior, but she secretly relished his attention.

The onion soup was delicious as was the rest of the meal—slices of lamb, scalloped potatoes, green beans, apple fritters, and Charlotte Russe for dessert. Lydia felt like quite the lady, being served by a man in a suit. Red kept looking at her with pride and admiration.

"I want to add your name to the claim," he finally said, glancing up from his dinner. "Then we should talk about where to live after we're married."

"I hadn't really thought about that," Lydia said, assuming they would just return to Buckskin Joe and hole up in her cabin.

"Well, you should," Red prompted. "Now that we have some assets and the promise of more, we can begin to think about the future. Besides, I want to give you everything I can. You've worked hard enough already." Lydia was accustomed to hard work and didn't mind it, but the thought of time to spare and expendable cash was tantalizing. She watched silently as Red polished off his meal and ordered coffee, pouring a large helping of cream into his cup. "Slightly better than heating up yesterday's grounds in the old pot at the mine," he joked.

"I like that old pot," Lydia said, "and the guy who goes with it." Red knew she wasn't in this for the money.

The next day they set off toward the Land Management Office only to find that it wasn't there. A hand-lettered sign nailed to a pole directed them to a tent across the street. Red held the flap door open for Lydia and ducked in after her. He noticed the same clerk who had helped him before, now kneeling over a box of records. "Why, Mr. Suter, I remember you," the young fellow said, standing to shake Red's hand. "How do you like this?" the clerk asked with irony, gesturing at the flimsy canvas walls. "Fire in the record room."

Red looked alarmed. "I hope my records are intact," he said, taking off his hat and moving closer to the young man. He introduced Lydia, and the clerk greeted her.

"Well, there's good news and there's bad news. Your records were, in fact, burned—except for the tintypes—but I've restored your claim information from federal files. Unfortunately, in doing that, I discovered a dispute about your land – as to whether it was leased or purchased."

"It was patented; I bought it outright," Red said, "and, as you know, I built a cabin on it."

"Well, that's part of the problem. The question is not whether you paid for it, but whether the agent who sold it to you was authorized to do so—and whether he was honest. If he sold you unpatented land and pocketed most of your money, the assumption would be that you were leasing it. In that case, a permanent structure is illegal. Your cabin would have to come down. So, if you want to keep your cabin and your claim, you'll either need to prove the transaction was legal or maybe even buy the land again."

"I bought that land ten years ago. Not gonna buy it a second time," Red said, in no uncertain terms. "It's not my fault if the government can't keep their records straight or if they hire disreputable people."

"I know," the clerk soothed. "No one doubts your integrity, sir, but if the land was never officially sold to you, there could be other claims on it. There could be liens against it or plans for its use. Do you happen to have any documents with co-signatures that could prove your deal was legitimate?

"I doubt it, but I'll look. Maybe there's some correspondence...." By this time the color had drained from Red's face.

"Well, I've filed an appeal on your behalf," the clerk informed, "but the original agent and his supervisors are long gone, nowhere to be found. This could take a while to sort out. The federal office will have to re-construct the original intent and decide whether the terms of sale were in keeping with their mandate."

"That puts me between a rock and hard place, doesn't it?" Red replied, running his hand through his hair and exhaling loudly. "What would I need to pay if I have to buy the land again?"

"At least $5 an acre," I suspect. "As you know, placer claims have been going for $2.50, but farm land is at a premium. Land that was $1.25 a few years ago, is now four times that. A nice fifty-acre spread like yours with a mix of fields and rock ledge, plus access to water, could bring a pretty penny—and there might be legal fees on top of that."

Red sat down in a chair, deflated. He leaned his elbows on his thighs, resting his chin in his hands. "I just hired three men to start tunneling," he muttered, thinking of the commitment he had made to his Mattie Howe crew. I can't very well let them go."

The clerk empathized. "That's too bad, because you might not be able to sell your ore until your claim is verified. Otherwise, what you take out of the ground could be considered stolen."

"This just keeps getting better," Red sighed, not tempering his sarcasm. Lydia put her hand on his shoulder.

"Is there anything we can do in the meantime?" she asked as she watched their hopes being dashed.

"Just wait it out, ma'am. I promise I'll stay on top of this and will be back in touch in a couple months. I'm sorry I can't do more for you right now." Red and Lydia thanked the clerk and stepped outside, numb.

"Under the circumstances, I don't feel like I should buy a dress," Lydia said. "I can wear my blue one just fine."

Red looked crestfallen. "No, I want you to get yourself one of those new fancy white numbers that are all the rage. Sadie showed me one in a magazine. We still have money from the first strike, so we can cover it, and if we live carefully over the next few months, we'll have enough to pay the men and buy food. Besides, I can go back to working more hours at the Phillips mine.

"And I don't mind dancing. We can live at my place until we figure this out," Lydia added, taking Red's hand at they walked down the street. She seemed to rise above life's disappointments with more grace than most.

"I'm so sorry, Lydia. I would never have asked you to marry me, if I knew this was going to happen."

Lydia stared at Red, defiant. "I'm marrying the man, not the mine," she said, setting her jaw. He pulled her close and let her words comfort him.

A few days later, Roger arrived, disheveled from his journey. "How's my favorite brother?" Roger asked, grasping Red by the upper arms.

"Could be better," Red admitted, telling Roger about the claim. "After working so hard for other people, so long, so many hours, we finally thought we had something to call our own."

"Try not to worry. You'll get this fixed and will be back on your feet in no time," Roger encouraged. "Besides, I have money saved from my last job if you need some," He offered, patting his brother on the shoulder.

"No, we'll be fine for a while," Red said. "We know what's important in life."

The next day, Lydia picked out a dress at Mrs. Palmer's shop. The white satin fabric was elegant and edged in lace at the neckline and cuffs. The full skirt, supported by crinolines, created the illusion of clouds. Lydia chose a simple white headband to match, knowing their funds were limited.

While waiting for a fitting, she admired a more elaborate headpiece adorned with orange blossoms made of wax. According to Queen Victoria, orange blossoms were the 'must have' for modern weddings, signifying innocence, commitment, eternal love and fruitfulness.

"Do you know what real orange blossoms smell like?" the seamstress asked, as she helped Lydia step into the gown.

"No, I've never seen any," Lydia said, "but if they smell like earth and sunshine, they must be grand."

"Even better. They're like the most exotic perfume you could imagine," a woman behind her chimed in. "Sweet as the fruit itself. Delicious. Devine."

Lydia turned around and to her surprise, she saw the woman in purple—this time in mauve—who had smacked her in Buckskin Joe. The two women stared at each other, stunned at first, then amused by the awkward encounter.

"What are you doing here?" the woman in mauve asked.

"We came to the city to get married and to honeymoon," Lydia answered, "And you?"

"Visiting."

"I have a story to tell you about that man named George," Lydia said.

"I'm so embarrassed about that whole incident. I acted horribly. Please forgive me," the other woman said, covering her face with her hands.

"I don't hold grudges," Lydia stated. "We all make mistakes."

"In which case, I'd love to hear that story," the woman replied. "Care to talk over tea?"

In that moment, Lydia was no longer a dance hall girl. She was a lady who socialized. She waited patiently for the seamstress to complete her pinning, thanked her graciously, then slipped back into her dress. She arranged for delivery of the gown, and shaking hands with the shop owner, expressed her gratitude for the quality of service. Confidently, she strolled with the other woman, down the street, to a small parlor that sold and served tea.

"It's high time I properly introduced myself," the woman said. "My name is Ophelia Winchester. My cousin is one of the proprietors of The City Hotel."

"Why, that's where we're staying," Lydia said, marveling at the coincidence. "It's very lovely. We're going to have our wedding there. Perhaps you could join."

"It *is* lovely, but I don't think I should impose," Ophelia said, scanning the small deckle-edged menu that was written in calligraphy. "I mean, we got off to such a rocky start and we hardly know each other."

Aside from being flamboyant, Lydia liked the woman. "No need to worry about that. Besides, I don't know anyone else here who could be my maid of honor. It would mean a lot to me."

Ophelia paused to give it some thought. "In that case, I'm flattered and would love to attend," she said. She ordered a cup of Darjeeling and a watercress sandwich. Lydia did the same, not being versed in the selection of teas or tea etiquette. She noticed a footnote on the menu that boasted, "Watercress harvested year-round from a pure, local stream."

"So, tell me about George," Ophelia prompted.

Lydia relayed the story of George being Roger and Roger being Red's brother and, despite the confusion, the happiness that ensued. Ophelia was astounded and charmed by the story. "What ever happened to your sister?" Lydia asked, knowing that George, aka Roger, had left her behind.

"Well, sometimes things happen for a reason, I guess," Ophelia confided. "My sister finally noticed the apothecary owner, who has been sweet on her for years. He invited her to a dance, she accepted, and now they are engaged."

"That's wonderful," Lydia said as she took out her string purse to pay for her tea, but Ophelia's hand stopped her.

"My treat. I insist."

Lydia thanked her and confirmed the wedding date and time—Saturday morning, 10:00 a.m., in the ballroom. Ophelia mentioned that getting there would be easy as she had a suite at the hotel, courtesy of her generous cousin. Lydia could hardly imagine living in that kind of luxury for any length of time. Ophelia described her room as having a large east-facing window that caught the morning light and provided a steady stream of warmth all day—a stark contrast to Lydia's cabin where wind whistled through the logs and rattled the chinking.

Both women walked back to the hotel together and said good-bye in the lobby just as Red and Roger were heading out to pay the pastor in advance. Introductions were made, and plans put in place, that on the day of the wedding Roger would join Red to help him get ready and Ophelia would assist Lydia.

That Saturday, when the bellhop knocked, Lydia unlocked the door, eagerly accepting the oversized package and the small, square container that accompanied it. She laid both on her bed, untying the ribbon around the long box, carefully lifting the lid and examining her gown. The tailoring was perfect and masterfully done. When she opened the small box, she immediately knew something was different. An intoxicating sweetness greeted her and permeated the air. Lydia had never inhaled anything so fragrant. She brought her nose close to the contents and saw that real orange blossoms had been stitched among the wax ones on the elaborate headpiece she had admired. "There must be some mistake," Lydia said out loud. "We can't possibly afford this one."

"There is no mistake. Do you like it?" Ophelia asked, standing in the doorway. "It's my gift to you. I know your seamstress quite well and asked her to do me a favor."

"Like it? I love it! But how did you ever find real orange blossoms in February?"

Ophelia smiled, adjusting her pale pink dress ever so slightly. "I told you my room was warm. It's like a greenhouse. I once brought back a miniature orange tree from California and, every year in late winter, it blooms. I pollinate the flowers with a brush, so the plant will bear fruit, but I have more flowers than the plant can support."

Lydia gently touched the small white petals that looked like stars and smelled like heaven. "I don't know what to say," She replied, holding the headpiece to her hair. The contrast of white against black was stunning. She carefully set the headpiece aside and hugged Ophelia.

Ophelia had arranged for a hot bath to be brought up, and Lydia gratefully sank into the tub. She emerged clean and relaxed, ready to be corseted and have her hair fashioned to frame her face. She slipped on her gown, which accentuated her small waist, and affixed the sweet orange blossom tiara to her head. Ophelia dabbed Lydia's neck with a touch of Hunt's Bridal Wreath Perfume, promoted as "a double extract of orange blossoms with cologne from The Perfumers to the Queen." Ophelia also gave Lydia a good-luck token—a pearl on a pale blue ribbon—to wear at her neck.

Meanwhile, in the room next door, the Suter brothers were nothing less than debonair—bathed and shaven. They sported fresh haircuts and new shoes—a gift from Roger. They wore trim gray frock coats, starched white shirts, and fine woolen trousers—Roger in subdued charcoal gray, Red in pinstripes. An orange blossom boutonniere, the handiwork of Ophelia, was fastened to Red's lapel and, despite his hair being slicked back with Macassar oil, a tell-tale shock fell over his right eye, hinting at mischief.

As previously agreed, Red and his best man, Roger, went to the ballroom first to superstitiously avoid seeing the bride before the ceremony. Once Ophelia confirmed that the men had gone, she and Lydia followed.

Red handed Roger the gold wedding band that matched Lydia's engagement ring, nervously asking him three times if he had it. Each time, Roger patted his breast pocket, assuring Red it was safe. When Ophelia arrived with Lydia, the pastor cued the pianist to begin Mendelssohn's wedding processional. Red turned to Ophelia, offered his arm, and together they walked to the front of the room, through a corridor created by chairs.

Roger escorted Lydia, admiring his brother's good taste in women. She was radiant, floating, enveloped in white. The air around her was perfumed as if standing in an orange grove on a sunny day. As they proceeded down the aisle, Lydia noticed Bill Buck and Amanda sitting in the audience, along with an attractive woman she assumed was Roger's friend from Fairplay.

Lydia's hand went quickly to her mouth upon seeing the unexpected guests. She sent a look of love and appreciation to Red, who beamed from the front of the room. He had paid for their coach tickets and accommodations, proving once again, he was adept at surprises.

As Roger and Ophelia stepped back, all eyes were on Red—tall, rugged, and handsome—and Lydia—petite, pretty, and looking as if she had emerged from a Renoir painting.

After blessings were cast, vows exchanged, and the wedding band slipped onto Lydia's finger, Red bent over and kissed his wife. For Lydia, the moment froze in time. The previously sedate onlookers broke into hoots and hollers in finest western saloon tradition and the piano player switched to a lively tune. Chairs were reorganized, and tables moved in, laden with an elaborate spread for eight—the likes of which Lydia had never seen.

There were coddled and scrambled eggs; platters of ham, smoked fish, sliced meats, and joints of cold poultry. Baskets of bread and sourdough biscuits anchored the tables, along with sweet rolls and Johnny Cakes, to be enjoyed with butter, honey, and gravy. Delicate jelly sandwiches, cut on the diagonal, were fanned out on a silver tray next to pieces of cut fruit. Individual servings of Jaune Mange, a fine lemon custard, were set to the side in crystal goblets.

There were covered dishes of pearl onions in cream sauce, casseroles filled with baked beans, and bowls of roasted potatoes.

On a serving table to the side sat tureens of porridge and terrapin soup, which guests were encouraged to take for themselves.

The happy couple was toasted with sparkling wine from Nicholas Longworth's winery in Cincinnati. Madeira was poured throughout the meal. Coffee and tea stayed warm in sterling carafes. Pitchers of cream sat on trays of crushed ice.

For dessert, a rich wedding fruitcake, topped with scrolls of white icing, was cut into precise 2" squares and passed around. Lydia and Red enjoyed themselves immensely.

Ophelia entertained the pastor with tales of her travels, while Roger and Fannie from Fairplay, gazed into each other's eyes. Bill Buck and Amanda sat with Red and Lydia talking about business and expressing their hopes for the future. Later that afternoon, the guests boarded a coach to tour the city, while Red and Lydia retired to their room.

Knowing each other so well only added to their pleasure, as did the elegant surroundings. Soft sheets, the color of seashells, caressed them beneath their protective canopy. The scent of orange blossoms lingered.

As strains of *Lorena* drifted up from the lobby, Lydia felt mellow from the wine and fine dining. She couldn't help but smile as she thought of the friends who had made the long journey from Buckskin Joe. She still couldn't believe that Red was 'hers.' She rolled languorously into his arms, fitting into the contours of his body, and he welcomed her with slow, sanctioned love. The experience was both familiar and excitingly new. The culmination made her feel cherished.

Neither of them wanted to leave this plush retreat. Neither one mentioned the troubles at the mine.

The next day they met their guests at the stage coach line and wished them well on their return journey. Lydia and Red would spend a few more days in the city before going back to Buckskin Joe.

18
REALITY

Jared and Alex were jarred by their phone alarms, and they arrived in present time with mixed emotions. They were happy for Red and Lydia, having watched them fall in love and marry, but they were sad for themselves in that summer meant separation.

By the following week, they would return to their respective family homes, reprising their roles as children, surrounded by childish things. They would sleep in their old beds, amidst books, bulletin boards, and grade school trophies. They would contend with parents and siblings, house rules, and curfews, expected to be accountable for their whereabouts whenever asked. What a strange regression this experience would be after two semesters of freedom.

Within the hour, boxes were picked up for Ground delivery and remaining items, stuffed into oversized duffels for air travel.

"We're not going to let this summer apart break us up, right?" Jared asked, wanting to be sure.

"Not on your life," Alexa vowed. "I'm going to start working on my parents about living off-campus."

"And I'll start looking for an apartment."

The dorm was closing that afternoon, and all students had to be gone. Jared and Alexa shared a cab to the airport and, like so many couples do, they clung to each other, despondent, as they watched planes taxi in on the tarmac. Grades were to be available online later that week and registration for the next semester was already underway.

"I'll let you know if I get published," Jared said, as he fell into line to board.

"And I'll be the first to read it," Alexa said as she waved goodbye.

He carried with him the image of her dark eyes, silky hair, and soft skin as he slid into the window seat of the plane. High above the harbor, he could see the white dots of drifting sailboats and the plumes of speeding watercraft, all becoming smaller and smaller, until he rose above the clouds.

Alexa looked over the patchwork of brown and green beneath her—textures and colors defined by hedgerows and rock walls—as her plane left New England and headed south. If all went well, they'd meet in Boston in June and stay at Kim's place.

Jared began his summer job as an editorial assistant at a suburban newspaper. His position had no formal description, because he was expected to handle projects as needed. That meant on some days he would conduct research, other days he would clear permissions, and, in between, he would write, fact check, file, and proof copy, but more times than not, he'd respond to the demands of anyone with more seniority, which pretty much meant the entire staff.

Alexa started working at her local Town Hall, helping to manage summer recreational programs through the Parks Department. When things were quiet there, she'd assist in the Town Clerk's Office, dealing with business certificates and permits. This experience was not as challenging as she had hoped, but it gave her a practical sense of local government—the good, the bad, and the tedious.

Alexa's grades were in the upper percentile, but Jared received a B for his independent study. He wasn't thrilled, but he knew he had not met all the criteria. At least he didn't get an Incomplete. Just before Memorial Day, Peter called to talk. He said he thought Jared's article had merit, but felt it required more depth and polish. He would not submit it for publishing without additional work.

In his gut, Jared knew Peter was right. A third theory was needed to create balance, and, with three theories, they could pitch it as "Three Roads to Recovery…A Quest for the Lost Gardner Museum Art."

Peter offered an incentive—Jared could earn an A, if he continued the project on his own time. Jared appreciated the opportunity and promised to produce something better by the end of summer. Before concluding their call, Peter asked one more thing. "About those photos you referenced. Where did you get them?"

"I'd love to tell you, but I honestly don't know. They just showed up."

"Showed up? What do you mean?"

"I mean, I found a USB stick in my jacket pocket and I have no idea how it got there. I hadn't worn that jacket in months."

"That could be a story on its own. Maybe even a better one. I'd say someone is trying to help you—but you need to find out who and why?" Jared explained he was trying to figure that out.

✦✦✦

The following weeks dragged for both Jared and Alexa, as they counted the days until their weekend in Boston. "You guys are getting the couch and the futon," Kim said, when they finally arrived and dumped their backpacks on her brightly lit apartment floor. Alexa noticed a misshapen cactus growing in a festive Mexican pot on the window sill and a tower of magazines leaning against the wall.

Kim was one of those perky people, who could get away with wearing flowered sneakers and pigtails. She used her glasses as a fashion statement and had a selection that rivaled Elton John's—purple wire rims, flaming red heart-shaped frames, and sophisticated black rectangles. She was tall, lean, and constantly in motion—a good motivator for Jared and Alexa, who tended to be more laid back. Working in Boston at a financial institution for the summer, she had her eye on the prize, and had already lined up a better place to live for the fall. Jared admired her drive.

Happy to be back in the city, Jared and Alexa visited their favorite haunts—campus book store, taqueria, bench by the river. "I still have to work on my article," Jared sighed as they sat and watched the water, "though I'm not sure it will see the light of day. Peter says the whole thing needs to be more compelling. He wants to 'feel the humanity.'" Jared gestured expressively, with sweeping arms, then more matter-of-factly added, "He's also expecting a brilliant new idea that will solve the mystery."

"Maybe you should tap your talents again," Alexa suggested as they wandered over to 'Coff', the seedy diner where Jared had rendezvoused with Sean. "I know you don't like doing that, but if you're lucky enough to have a gift, I think you should use it," Alexa persisted. "In fact, it might be selfish not to…." Her sentence trailed off as they walked into the diner and found a booth furthest from the door. "I bet there are clues back in Buckskin Joe just waiting for you." Jared shrugged, still wrestling with the ethical dilemma.

"Do you mind if we sit here for a while?" he asked the waitress, Rosy, as they requested two English muffins and coffees.

"Not at all. Ain't busy this time of day." A few minutes later, she returned with their order. "I remember you. You met up with Sean here a couple times. Terrible what happened to him—truck going over the Expressway like that…him standing right underneath," she said, shuddering and pulling a "Tsk" in through her teeth.

"Terrible," Jared agreed as he blew the heat off his coffee. Rosy left for the cash register, and Jared and Alexa left for Buckskin Joe.

+++

A spring blizzard was raging when they walked into the dance hall, stamping their feet to dislodge the snow on their boots. Bill Buck was distraught, polishing the same spot on the bar repeatedly.

"I told Amanda not to go this morning. I just had a feeling in my knee…." Bill said, running his hand over his whiskers, brow furrowed with worry.

"How far away are they?" Red asked, figuring he might be able to ride out and escort the nurses back.

"Could be ten miles. Maybe more. Too dangerous to try. They're probably near those families out by the foothills. If so, the women could stay there 'til this thing blows over."

"Do they have food and blankets?" Lydia asked, trying to think how the nurses might survive without shelter.

"Yes, fortunately. They borrowed a wagon from Tom Shaw and he keeps it stocked with tools and supplies, plus they're loaded up with provisions for the families. But these storms can be tricky. A couple years back, we had someone get caught in a blizzard very close to home—but he got disoriented and his body didn't turn up 'til summer."

Lydia put her arm around Bill's shoulder. "Don't even think like that. These women are smart and resilient and, as soon as the storm subsides, Red and I will ride out to see if we can find them."

Just then, Doc Jones came into the building, his hat wet and low over his eyes. His collar was propped up, leaving a raw streak on his cheek where it rubbed. Small icicles hung from his nose and moustache. "Any word on the women?" he asked, hoping they might have turned around.

"No. Best I can figure is that they're too far out to risk riding back. My guess is that they'll just hunker down somewhere—maybe with one of the families."

"If they make far," Doc Jones muttered. "There's not much between here and there."

+++

The snow was blinding as the nurses pushed on. Affectionately known as "A, B, C", they were skilled at roughing it. Each had worked in a frontier hospital and had read just about everything written by Florence Nightingale—and she survived the Crimean War. There was little need for discussion.

Amanda was the first to spot the protected area beneath an overhang. Beulah, who carried more heft than the others, steered the horses toward the drift that had built up there. Caroline unhitched the team and tied the animals to a small grove of trees, which provided a natural windbreak. Removing a shovel from the cart, Amanda followed Caroline's footsteps and started digging a trench toward the drift. Beulah found a saw in Tom's tool box and cut pine boughs for insulation. When the saw was available, Caroline took it and carved out blocks of snow at the end of Amanda's trench, creating an entrance that could later be back-filled. They worked together to dig out a cave.

With every gale, the horses whinnied, and the women shivered. Beulah tramped through the snow to comfort the animals, putting blankets over their backs and speaking softly to them. She poured water from her canteen into Tom's mining pan and the horses drank greedily. She refilled the pan with oats from a sack they had brought with them, and she fed the animals one at a time.

Within the cave, Caroline and Amanda carved out three raised sleeping surfaces and smoothed the walls around them. Then, they went to work on the ceiling, forming it into a dome to minimize dripping at the center. Beulah returned and pushed the shovel handle through the roof to vent the space, then set about dragging their supplies into the hollow. After taking a bathroom break beyond the structure, the women moved inside, managing to seal the entrance with the blocks of snow they had removed. They reinforced the makeshift door with pine boughs, which added a refreshing scent.

Amanda and Caroline covered the sleeping surfaces with sheeting originally intended for the stricken and distributed the blankets they had brought with them. Using a candle from Tom's supply, Caroline lit it with flint she kept in her pocket. Amanda pried open a can of beans with a screwdriver and located some spoons among their provisions. Bread was unwrapped and pulled off in chunks A canteen of water was shared. Amanda discovered a sleeve of jerky that Bill had slipped into her pouch—what a guy! They broke that apart and ate it with gusto.

Once consumed, the women climbed up on the sleeping platforms, rolled into the blankets and stretched out, casually talking as the candle burned down. The wind howled fiercely, drowning out the calls of wolves and coyotes—perhaps a blessing in disguise.

"I wonder how long this will last," Amanda said, listening to the fury outside, worrying about Bill not knowing where she was.

"Well, we have enough supplies for a while," Caroline said, practical and optimistic. "Unless there's another storm on the heels of this one, we should be fine."

"I wish Sam were here to keep me warm," Beulah joked, longing for her new-found beau. "I could really use some body heat right now."

With nothing else to do, the women went to sleep, savoring the warmth and safety of their improvised shelter. When they awoke, the wind had lessened. Beulah went out to assess the damage and to shovel a path for bathroom needs. Amanda and Caroline quickly followed, flattening a trail to the horses. Amanda fed the horses from her hand and enjoyed the feel of their noses, warm and damp, against her skin. Beulah reached into the food tin and cut an apple into wedges. She distributed the treats to the animals, saving three pieces for herself and her colleagues. Caroline took inventory.

Miles of white surrounded them, silent and glistening. Rock formations that had previously been landmarks were now nondescript mounds of snow. Two hawks circled high above, whistling their "Tzee" into the clear air. The women squinted to see the road, but a good three feet of snow covered it. In hopes of continuing their journey, they shoveled the snow out of their cart and packed up their supplies. Still unable to get their bearings, they decided to wait for the sun to work its magic. They built a small fire in the trench, using bandages as tinder, and fueled it with wood that Tom had tossed into the cart for balance.

Caroline put handfuls of snow into the mining pan and melted it for the horses to drink. Amanda found a beat-up pot hooked on the inside of the wagon and did the same, refilling their canteens with snowmelt and adding corn meal to the rest. She opened the jar of strawberry jam intended for one of the families and scooped it liberally over the mush. Soon the women were enjoying sweet hot cereal in the most pristine of settings.

As the sun rose higher, the new-fallen snow compressed, revealing recognizable terrain below. The women immediately spotted the row of rocks they had seen before the storm struck, and in the distance, they could discern a faint curl of smoke coming from one of the cabins.

Loading up the rest of their gear and collapsing their cave, they climbed up into the wagon—two seated high on the front bench and one bouncing in the back with the supplies. Progress was slow as heavy hooves plodded through the drifts, but eventually, the nurses arrived at the first house where a ranching family lived. The parents had survived, but the children were sick. The nurses administered what care and comfort they could provide, advising the family about contagion and sanitation. They added some staples to the pantry, then moved on to the next house. And, so it went. When their supplies were depleted, they turned their cart around and prayed that they could make it back to Buckskin Joe.

When the returning nurses arrived at the outskirts of town, Red and Lydia were waiting for them, greeting them with a flask of whiskey and Bill's famous biscuits. The nurses looked rumpled, but no worse for wear. As the group rode down the main street, Doc Jones came rushing out from his office. "Is everyone all right? No frostbite, I hope." The nurses assured him that they were fine and praised the benefits of burrowing under the snow.

19
RECOVERY

"Burrowing under the snow," Jared thought as his phone alarm brought him back to present day. But, as Alexa watched him from across the table, she knew he hadn't made a complete transition. He sat there, breathing haltingly, eyes fixed in the distance.

Jared was caught an extrasensory interlude—a bizarre and disconcerting experience that turned him from an active participant into a wary observer, just as he had done while sitting in the Library at school.

Surrounded by a cyclone of impressions, he saw the nurses standing in a pool of light—flickering as if projected in an old silent movie. This time they spoke in unison, their voices distorted by an echo. "We're so glad you found us," they said, hovering just out of reach. "We have something important to tell you."

Jared remained motionless, staring at them, as his field of vision swirled with random artifacts from Buckskin Joe: a buggy whip, jar of jam, deck of cards, gold coins. An owl swooped in front of him as if to reveal what was previously hidden, its massive wings sounding like a muffled heartbeat.

Jared's own heart was pounding, and he couldn't slow it down. The smell of sage brush and gun smoke was overpowering. He coughed out road dust and took a deep breath. Jared saw the shadowy figure of Doc Jones bending over a patient, Caleb, the casket maker, hammering a lid. He heard Sam's hearty laugh rise above the dance hall din as the last notes of *John Brown's Body* rippled across the piano. Bill Buck's steady arm clasped his shoulder in a grip of encouragement.

"We're A, B, C, you know," Amanda said looking at Jared, her green eyes, clear as water, flowing into his brown ones.

"We're a big, beautiful, bountiful clue for you," Beulah teased. She stood back and put her hands on her hips, rotating her shoulders so her bosom swayed.

"It might be elementary, but it could be collegiate," Caroline winked, playing with words that encrypted a message.

Jared didn't know what to make of his heightened awareness. As he mentally stepped forward to ask for more information, the nurses' skirts caught in the wind and lifted them into the surrounding blur. When he regained his composure, the images were gone, and his mind was clear.

"I think I've got it," Jared said to Alexa as he completed his transition to present time. He reached into his backpack and extracted the grungy manila envelope the homeless man had given him. Lifting the rusty metal tabs of the clasp, Jared rummaged around. "I know it's here somewhere, because it was on a piece of bright orange paper."

"What was?" Alexa asked as she finished her English muffin and coffee.

"This," Jared said, flattening the edges of a small rectangle. On it was scribbled, "It's as easy as A, B, C."

"I'm not sure what you're getting at," Alexa said as she looked at the hasty writing.

"The nurses' names represent the alphabet, right? Somehow our street man was on the same wavelength."

Alexa listened, trying to follow Jared's thinking. "What do you mean?"

"The alphabet reminds me of education, and education reminds me of schools. The nurses burrowed under the snow, right? There's that tunnel theory again. Well, some colleges have pedestrian tunnels, so students and faculty don't have to walk outside in bad weather."

"They do?" Alexa asked.

"Sure. MIT has tunnels. Harvard has tunnels. Some campuses have steam tunnels, likely off-limits. There are probably a dozen more underground walkways in and around the city that we don't know about. Stolen artwork could be easily moved through any of these labyrinths, protected from the elements and hidden from public view."

"Wow. I suppose that's no crazier than anything else," Alexa allowed.

Jared was animated. "I'm going to work on this as soon as I get back home. Then I'll be able to propose three strong hypotheses: 1. tunnel jacking under the Big Dig, 2. following the Underground Railroad, and 3. using corridors beneath our colleges.

Their visit to Boston went all too fast, but against all odds, they found an apartment for fall, and using their summer earnings, put down a deposit. They texted Doug and Gail to see if they might like to resume their roles as roommates and share the rent.

+++

The next time they returned to Boston was in late July, at Kim's promise of driving to Cape Cod. They had always wanted to see those beautiful beaches, so they took 2 unpaid days off work and made it a mini-vacation. Friday was scorching from the start, dripping with the kind of humidity that only ocean breezes could cure. Even tall iced coffees from Dunkin Donuts couldn't cool them down as they slid across the back seat of Kim's car. "Sorry, no AC," she apologized, as she dropped the windows.

Sitting in traffic, the heat was oppressive, but once they got beyond the bottleneck at the Braintree split, they could feel a breeze. They cranked up the radio, broke out some granola bars, and enjoyed a sense of freedom they had sorely missed. By the time they got to the Sagamore Bridge, they were all singing loudly and badly, relishing the cool, briny air.

Jared draped his arm over Alexa's bare back, his fingers working a small circle on her skin. She nestled into his shoulder as if she belonged there.

Kim knew people in Hyannis, so she dropped her friends on Main Street, pointed them to the marina and planned to meet at Kalmus Beach later that day. Jared and Alexa were in no rush. They strolled through a bookstore and some shops, bought a box lunch, and started their trek down Ocean Street, stopping along the way to enjoy their wraps.

Once at the beach, they unrolled two towels, anchored them with their flip flops, and ran into the ocean, squealing with delight. They could practically hear themselves sizzle. Once refreshed, they returned to their spot and put on tee-shirts—pale lime and periwinkle colors they'd never wear anywhere else. They slipped the silver buckle between their palms and soared back to Buckskin Joe on the wings of a gull.

✦✦✦

Spring had finally arrived in that quiet corner of Colorado, forcing snow and sickness to recede. Lydia and Red walked through a field of columbine, holding hands, letting the sun warm their backs and relax their muscles. Hummingbirds hovered over the delicate flowers, piercing the blooms with needle-like beaks, gorging on the nectar. Lydia picked one of the blossoms and noticed a circle of white petals within the violet calyx. They really did resemble the doves for which the flowers were named. When she looked up again, she realized she was standing in a sea of purple surrounded by mountains that matched. She gasped at the beauty of it all.

Lydia intentionally burned the stained and bloodied dress she had worn all winter in caring for the sick. She aired out her cabin and washed the bedding in a vat of hot water to which she added chloride of lime. She scrubbed her walls with the strongest lye soap she could find, then splashed the soapy water onto the floor. The last case of smallpox had been documented more than a week ago and no new cases had erupted. Hope was palpable.

Wearing a simple day dress that Red had purchased as a surprise—tiny flowers imprinted on a tan background—Lydia felt rejuvenated as she puttered around the cabin. "Business was better last night," she told Red, jingling the coins in her gold poke.

"I still wish you didn't have to dance with other men," Red said, wanting the dispute over his mine to be done. There had been no word from the Land Office in Denver and he was getting anxious.

"Not to worry," Lydia said. "I like dancing and, besides, none of those men are you." She came up behind him and wrapped her arms around his torso, reminding him of that first time they made love. She rested her head against him, soaking up his strength.

"I know," Red said, tired and dusty from working the graveyard shift at the mine. "I just wanted to make our lives better and thought I had…." Disappointment coalesced on his face.

"My life *is* better—because you're in it," Lydia said. "Plus—there's still plenty of time for things to change. We're young, we're healthy, and I'm not giving up yet."

"That's what I like about you—always seeing the bright side," Red said, bending over to kiss her. "But in another few weeks, I won't have enough money to pay the men at the Mattie Howe, so we'll have to shut down operations…and I won't have anything left to buy the land if I have to do that again."

Lydia took Red's hand and made him stop talking. "Don't you dare get all depressed on me," she said, stern and determined. "We have so much to be thankful for—the first being that we didn't die in the epidemic."

"That's true," Red said, pausing to hug her. She folded neatly into his arms—a butterfly in a cocoon.

"I'm confident that things will work out. It just might take a while," she said, pulling back to look up into his dark eyes. "I have a good feeling."

Later that day, they walked into town and strolled into the telegraph office as they often did. This time, the telegraph operator told Red to wait right there. He came back with a message from Denver. "Word from D.C. on your land. Come in to discuss."

Red's heart was thumping in anticipation. "Why is the clerk being so vague?" Red complained. "You'd think he'd tell me the results."

"Seems like he wants to keep it private."

"Probably," Red said, shaking his head. "But time is not on our side. If I lose the mine, I lose our future. We may never find another lode or be able to afford this kind of land again. I'm going to head up there the day after next assuming I can get some days off work."

Lydia helped Red pack the following night. She was tired from dancing and her feet hurt. She set aside her silvery shoes and let her toes wiggle on the wooden floor. Red left early the next morning to catch the stage north. Other than pausing for a quick kiss at the door, he was deep in thought and said little to Lydia.

"How can I marry a woman on a miner's salary?" he worried as he bounced along the way. "How could we ever feed and clothe children?" When he got to the city, he found a cheap boarding room with an outhouse on a hill behind the building. He walked down to the Land Office tent, where the familiar clerk was sitting behind a small oak desk. "Mr. Suter," the young man greeted as he rose to his feet. "Have a seat." He motioned to a pressback chair with ornate carvings along the shoulder rest.

Red was somber as he sat down, spine against the wooden spindles, hands resting on the curved arms, hat in his lap. He just couldn't muster any pleasantries. The clerk positioned himself opposite Red. "I'm sorry to say your land is still in dispute," the young man began slowly, "but I do have more information." Red sat quietly, running his fingers around the brim of his hat. "Apparently there are conflicting records on file, but we can challenge them," the clerk continued as he leafed through a ledger. Red simply stared ahead, discouraged.

"What does that mean?"

"It means they have a memo stating that you were planning to buy the land—so that's good; it shows intent—but there's also a document that says this was an unpatented parcel." Red looked confused. "I think the unpatented description is old and predates your claim," the clerk went on. "It should have been discarded when the land status changed, but it was never removed from the file or marked void, and it's not dated. Additionally, while your payment was designated as 'Received,' there's no record of deposit, so suspicion is that the agent may have taken advantage of you—stolen your money—seeing that you were a kid. If he left with your cash, it will be hard to verify the legitimacy of the transaction."

Red sat there mute, working his jaw. "Well, I don't have funds for a lawyer and I sure as hell am not walking away from my property. The Mattie Howe means a lot to me, aside from the ore. It reminds me of my mother and was intended as security for our family."

"I know. I'm so sorry, Mr. Suter," the clerk sympathized. "I realize you were hanging your hopes on this land." Red nodded in resignation and started to reach for his hat.

"My advice is that you just focus on your other claim, while I request an in-depth review of this one," the clerk encouraged.

"What other claim?" Red asked.

"The claim in California."

"I have no idea what you're talking about," Red replied.

"Your given name is James R. Suter, right? Your father was Jakob Suter, formerly of Texas, correct?"

"Yes, but how do you know that?"

"It was on file when we cross-referenced your name and assets."

"I don't understand."

"I'm talking about the claim that was left by your father for you and your mother. Since she has passed, it's yours now."

"But my father and brother were killed in an accident at least twelve years ago."

"That sounds about right—just before Sutter's Mill went bust."

"What does this have to do with Sutter's Mill?"

The clerk looked at Red in disbelief. "Surely you know that the name Sutter is derived from Suter...and that your family is somehow connected to the place where the Gold Rush began, right?" the clerk asked. Red shrugged, palms up.

The clerk bent over and pulled a book out of a box that was sitting on the floor. "See…look here," he said, pointing to a bookmarked page. "John Sutter was born Johann August Suter, February 15, 1803, in Kandern, Baden (Germany), before coming to the United States, where he bought the Russian Fur Company at Fort Ross and went on to build Sutter's Fort in 1841."

"I've never heard that! My family has never talked about him," Red exclaimed.

"That's probably because John Sutter was…shall we say…of questionable character," the clerk continued. "Sutter left his wife and children in Switzerland and came to America escape his debt. But he fell quickly into debt again, lost his land, and was forced to sell his mill."

"Where is this mill exactly?"

"In Coloma—near Sacramento."

"I think that's where my brother worked, but he never identified it by name. I bet he doesn't even know about the family connection. Maybe that's why my father went out there in the first place, figuring if he couldn't find work along the way, he could always call on kin." Red's brow rippled as he tried to process this new information.

"Well, you should ask your brother. He'll probably tell you that it was common practice to receive land in lieu of salary, especially if the boss couldn't pay."

"He did mention that but didn't say much else." A smile began to play on Red's lips. "Then maybe Lydia and I have some hope yet—a couple acres out there where we could build a house and start a farm." He pictured Lydia and dark-eyed children, fruit trees, and livestock.

"You have more than that, sir. Looks like 125."

Red's jaw dropped. "A hundred and twenty-five acres? How could that be? That's a ranch! Or a mine. Or both."

The clerk grinned and continued. "Your father probably thought the land was worthless, because there was so much of it. But values have changed, and natural resources have been discovered thanks to new tools and machinery. It appears that your father's claim was subsumed by a larger one and is now being managed by a third party. Chances are, if you go out there and exert your ownership, you could find a considerable bankroll waiting for you, as well as the property."

"This is wild!" Red said, seeing his financial woes vanish into thin air, only to be deflated by the reality. "Unfortunately, I don't have any papers to prove that I own it."

"You do now," the clerk said, handing Red a packet of documents. "I had D.C. send a duplicate deed for California when they provided the status on the Mattie Howe. Just thought we should have all your records in one place." The young man rose and straightened his jacket, looking pleased at his forethought.

"I don't know how to thank you," Red said, standing and staring at the paper with the government seal. "You've saved the day. You've changed our lives. Guess we're going to California." Red vigorously pumped the young man's hand.

"Happy to help," the clerk said, shaking his fingers to recover from Red's grip. "I'll let you know the decision on the Mattie Howe as soon as I hear. If you need to re-buy the land, maybe we can work out a payment plan."

"That would be great," Red said, thinking of Roger, who would most likely stay near Fairplay to be with Fannie. Roger could share in the ownership and management the mine if he wanted. Red carefully folded the packet of papers and tucked them into the inside breast pocket of his jacket, patting the front twice to make sure they were secure. He bought a ticket for the next stage back to Buckskin Joe and waited for it to arrive.

Three days later, Red walked toward their cabin and saw Lydia outside feeding the chickens. Her sleeves were rolled up and she wore no bonnet. Her dark hair was loosely tied and cascaded down her back. He could tell from the pitchfork leaning against the wall and the patch of freshly turned earth, that she had begun to prepare a garden. His fingers fumbled in his pouch for the packets of seeds he had bought in Denver. He had heard that sugar beets fared well in Colorado and wanted to try a patch at the cabin and near the mine. Both locations had water for irrigation and plenty of sun.

In the distance, the nurses were passing by in Doc Jones' buggy. They could see Red lift Lydia and twirl her around. They heard gleeful squeals coming from the young couple and saw Red toss his hat up into the air. Not wanting to intrude, they clopped away, intent on catching the stage back to Denver. With Bill Buck, Sam, and Doc Jones living in Buckskin Joe, all three women had reasons to return.

+++

Jared and Alexa found themselves smiling, when they heard Kim call. Her voice brought them back to the beach in present time. "I love happy endings," Alexa whispered as she looked out over the ocean. "I do, too," Jared said, "Especially when they involve us."

He pocketed the buckle, then detoured to nuzzle Alexa's neck. She smelled of salt, sun, and coconut lotion. They could see Kim stepping gingerly across the hot sand and waved to her.

While Jared and Alexa waited, they watched the surf roll in and pull out, rhythmic and lulling, each wave leaving a smooth streak of wet sand in its wake. Bubbles from tiny clams burst among the threads of seaweed. Broken scallop shells floated in and settled into random designs. Smooth pebbles landed in the tide line—bright whites, pale yellows, greens and grays—all shaped, pummeled, and polished.

Jared wondered what brought those small stones here on this specific day, at this specific time. Their impermanence reminded him of the sand mandalas created by Tibetan monks. Those were built grain by grain, only to be intentionally swept away.

In considering the fluidity of nature, Jared started to gain perspective about his school project. Maybe it was the oxygenated ocean air or the comfort of having Alexa at his side, but suddenly, he understood that these temporal displays were just part of a grander scheme.

When he applied that thinking to the challenge of solving the Gardner Museum theft, he began to relax. He realized he might not have all the answers, but that was okay. He would do what he could. Someone else could take it from there. So, instead of berating himself and panicking at his lack of insight, he decided to accept his limitations and consider himself a contributor.

When Kim arrived, she took a quick dip in the water, then joined her friends on the sand. They spent the next hour catching up on gossip and comparing plans for the rest of the summer. Wanting to beat the crowds driving off the Cape, they left before the sun set and headed back to Boston. A few days later, both Alexa and Jared were home again, eagerly counting the weeks until their summer jobs would be done.

During this time, Jared worked diligently to expand his article, adding the third theory about pedestrian tunnels. He explained how he had been inspired by the writings of a homeless man who was an unappreciated witness and gifted observer of human nature. He said nothing about the insight gained from people he had met in other realms.

Jared analyzed the impact left by the loss of the artwork – both in monetary and cultural context. He suggested what steps authorities might take to test his theories and, in doing so, he employed the sound journalistic skills that were required.

Before filing the story with his advisor, Jared tracked down the waitress at the diner where the scruffy man panhandled and, through her, gathered more information about him. Finally, he hit "Send" and crossed his fingers.

✦✦✦

Several weeks later, summer jobs behind them, Jared and Alexa flew to Denver. They rented a car from one of those short-term student leasing companies and drove southwest toward a small campground near an alpine lake. Fir trees and lodgepole pines offered a canopy of coolness and dry pine needles provided a thick, fragrant mat below. Snow-tipped mountains rose in the distance, and just as the song says, they were purple and majestic.

As Jared and Alexa unpacked their belongings, fresh air filled their lungs, replacing the acrid fumes and artificial coolants of city living. They could feel tension exit their bodies. They could also sense the presence of Red and Lydia in the quiet countryside.

The young couple took a white blanket into a field of wildflowers and laid it out, creating a square sanctuary within the swaying mass of scarlet paintbrush, yellow cinquefoil, blue larkspur, and orange fire wheels. Alexa remembered Lydia's fantasy about making love in a meadow and now she understood the ideal. As she looked at Jared, she saw in him the same qualities that Lydia admired in Red—a strong, reliable, handsome man with conviction and confidence—someone who could share life's struggles and celebrations.

As Jared watched Alexa smoothing the blanket, her classic features caught in the brilliant light, he flashed on Lydia—a smart, selfless, beautiful woman from long ago. He saw in Alexa a meaningful future and the kind of possibilities that make young men mature quickly.

Neither of them had to say anything, because they both knew the outcome. There, under the open sky, near the place where Red and Lydia once lived, they gave themselves fully to each other. The moment was tender, urgent, and remarkably familiar. Afterward, they rolled onto their backs and watched clouds drift across the sky—one morphing from a turtle into a swan.

During the following days, they retraced the steps of Red and Lydia…hiking through Alma, Fairplay, Leadville, and the place that had once been Buckskin Joe.

For Jared, the proximity to the past was so intense, he had to cover his ears to block out the voices from days gone by. But for Alexa, she could hear the notes of Lou's piano and the din of applause in the old dance hall saloon. She heard a young woman named Sadie crying for her mother and three capable nurses discussing how they would stop an epidemic. She could smell cigar smoke and beer, and a hint of Hunt's Orange Blossom perfume.

Before they left, Jared and Alexa rode out to the backcountry and stopped at a bluff overlooking an arroyo. Standing side-by-side, they watched a tall miner in a faded shirt stroll toward a young woman in a crinoline dress. He put his arm around her and brought her close. In the distance, they could hear the bray of a burrow and the clink of a miner's pick.

Their Colorado visit felt inadequately short, but they brought the experience back to Boston, enriched by it. They moved into their apartment just when Red and Lydia were planning their move to California. A week later, with the buckle and cup between them, Jared and Alexa returned to Buckskin Joe to say good-bye.

✦✦✦

The summer of 1862 was in full swing, accompanied by hot days and only slightly cooler nights. The town had recovered from the smallpox scourge that ravaged it the prior winter. Shops were now restocked and reopened, much to the delight of returning residents. The Phillips mine was in full production again.

Red's brother, Roger, and his now-fiancé, Fannie, were spending more time in the backcountry to be closer to the Mattie Howe. Red was letting his crew use his place in town, keeping them busy at the mine. Sadie, from the saloon, and faro master Tom Shaw, decided they had a lot in common and were moving in together. When Lydia offered them her cabin, they gladly said yes, promising to care for the chickens and the small garden plot.

Red and Lydia looked solemnly at their wagon, stuffed to capacity with tools and household goods. Clothing, blankets, and boots were secured in a trunk. Lydia's prized tintype was wedged into a box of pots and pans.

"No guarantees," Red said as she carefully set her mother's china cup into a basket.

"Not expecting any," Lydia assured, knowing that this would be a bold adventure. The horses were eager to leave and repeatedly pawed the ground.

Red strolled out to Buckskin Creek for one last look, silently watching the stream rush along its narrow channel, snaking between rocks and grassy slopes. He said good-bye to his friends at the Phillips mine and bequeathed his red Lisk lunch pail to Sam.

Lydia hugged Doc Jones, Lou, and Bill Buck, blinking back tears while promising to see them again. She gave her silver dance hall shoes to Sadie and encouraged her to use them often.

Red's toughest farewell was with his brother, Roger, having just been reunited. But Red vowed to be back and knew his mine was in good hands. Lydia climbed up into the wagon as Red and Roger embraced. She couldn't watch.

Red joined her, paused for a moment, took a deep breath, then snapped the reins. The wagon pulled out to a chorus of good luck wishes and vigorous waves. Red swallowed hard and Lydia dabbed her nose with a hanky, pretending to be removing dust the horses had kicked up. Once they rounded the bend, they set their eyes on the horizon and didn't look back. Ahead of them lay the fertile valleys of Sacramento and a long life together.

With Red gone, Roger and Fannie harvested the sugar beets planted near the Mattie Howe and planned for a larger crop the following year. He and Fannie moved into the cabin at the entrance of the mine, while building a sizeable house on the sprawling acreage below.

Roger continued to mine the claim although the land remained in dispute. He kept faith that it would somehow all work out. When the Land Office clerk finally sent them a telegram, Roger and Fannie rode to Denver, not quite sure what to expect.

The clerk advised them that under Lincoln's Homestead Act, signed into law that past May, they might be able to secure the land after all. All they had to do was build a permanent home, improve the property, and pledge to farm it for at least five years. Roger and Fannie were already part-way there.

With the clerk's assistance, they rolled the Mattie Howe into a larger tract of property. By early 1863, once the Homestead Act went into effect, they sealed the deal with $10 for the land and a $2 commission for the agent. With the completion of a final form and a $6 processing fee, 160 acres of unspoiled countryside—including the Mattie Howe—became theirs. Roger made sure to list his brother on the deed.

In the months that followed, the three nurses came back to Buckskin Joe. Amanda and Bill married at the saloon, ready to enjoy, in later life, what they had missed early on. Caroline worked side-by-side with Doc Jones, finally admitting her feelings after he expressed his. Beulah and Sam tied the knot and had their first of many big, bouncing babies.

Red and Lydia settled in the rich Coloma-Lotus Valley of California near the South Fork of the American River. Rather than work in the mine, Red helped manage it as part of his agreement with the holding company. Soon he discovered that planting grapes and making wine could be just as lucrative and even more rewarding. He relished the early mornings, when he would walk out to their terraced hills, still cool and misty from the night. He would check the vines, staked and laden with fruit, and know their harvest would be good.

Lydia found a job with a performance troupe in Sacramento and started teaching dance near Lake Tahoe. Creative expression sprung from her like a fountain and she blossomed into a respected choreographer. Soon she and Red had a family of their own and watched them grow to appreciate the land and the people, who called it home.

On some days, she and Red would sit on their porch and simply count their blessings. The fields, ablaze with yellow coreopsis, were a gold mine of another sort—one to be walked, nurtured, and explored. In time, long after their steps began to slow, Red and Lydia became part of the fabric of history. Sadie and Tom brought them back to Buckskin Joe to rest beneath a mountain named for a woman who wore silver heels.

During this time, Sam passed Red's lunch pail onto his eldest son who took it into the Phillips mine just as others had done before—that is, until he left it on a rock one spring day. No one heard his cry of alarm, when he saw the creek cresting, taking the pail with it. Sadly, he watched as the box bobbed along, a square red boat afloat with memories, until it disappeared in the undergrowth.

No one saw Sadie's daughter remove the silver shoes her mother had tucked away in a satin bag, hoping a shoemaker could restore them to their former glory. She didn't know that one of the buckles had become loose and rolled beneath the floorboards of the shoemaker's shop. Replaced with a shiny replica, he handed the shoes back to her, leaving the original buckle in the soft soil below, only to be excavated years later.

Lydia's diary remained in a tin box tucked into the rafters of her Colorado cabin, unknown to Sadie, Tom, or the eventual tourists who passed it by. Some say a Park Ranger found the diary and gave it a new home, high in the rafters of another building. Others say it was placed deep into the recesses of the Phillips mine by the descendants of those who had worked there.

+++

When Jared and Alexa returned to present time, they felt a sense of loss, but also knew they no longer needed their surrogates from long ago. They now had a solid relationship and were committed to making it work. Classes would be starting soon. The leaves had begun to change. And the sweet recollections from Buckskin Joe continued to spark their romance.

Jared received an encouraging call from his advisor, Peter. He had shopped Jared's article around and had piqued the interest of a local newspaper chain. They would run the story next Sunday. Jared was ecstatic.

On Sunday, he went to the corner pharmacy and came back with a stack of newspapers. He and Alexa took an armful to the waterfront in hopes of seeing the homeless man. Not spotting him at his usual location, they walked into the local diner. The now-familiar waitress pointed them to the street. "Just left," she said. They handed her a paper and thanked her for her help.

"Hey, wait up," Jared called, chasing after the man with the shopping cart. "Our article was published! It's all over town. I have copies."

The scruffy man, today wearing a frayed blue pinstripe shirt, leopard vest and too-large khakis, stopped and looked at Jared. "I'm happy for you. You deserve it," he said with minimal emotion.

"But you should be happy for yourself, too. I gave you a credit," Jared said. The man seemed unimpressed.

Alexa was close behind as Jared returned the man's manila envelope and handed him a newspaper. The man pushed the envelope down into the side of his cart and started to thumb through the paper. "Page 12," Jared interrupted, too excited to wait. He watched as the man began to read.

"Good. Good. I see you included that bit about me being an eyewitness."

"Better than that. I included some of your writing, attributed to you, of course. It lends so much."

"Well, how 'bout that. Guess that makes me famous." As usual, the couple couldn't tell whether the man was being sarcastic or genuinely pleased. Alexa thought the latter.

She took two more newspapers from Jared and added them to the man's cart. "Here are a couple more in case you need them."

Just then, something caught her eye. Next the manila envelope, below a bag of mismatched clothing, was a tweed overcoat, much like the one Bob Camelion had worn. A pair of tortoise shell eyeglasses poked from the pocket, along with a narrow notepad. At the bottom of the cart, Alexa could see a highly polished pair of shoes. A small bottle of cologne was wedged into one of them.

Alexa tugged on Jared's arm, incredulous, pointing to her discovery. Jared peered over the collection of personal belongings. "Are you thinking what I'm thinking?" he whispered as the man fumbled with a fanny pack.

"That our homeless friend has been posing as a reporter to gain information about the heist?"

"That he and Bob Camelion are one and the same?"

"That he's the person who took the photos and slipped them to you, knowing you'd have a better chance of getting published?" Alexa stepped back and put her hand over her mouth.

The man looked up, oblivious to their conversation. "Well, time to mosey on," he said, buttoning his vest and hiking up his pants. "Thanks for the papers. See you around." Jared and Alexa stood speechless as they watched the man maneuver down the street.

That night over dinner, they couldn't stop talking about how clever he had been—pretending to be a reporter to get into places that interested him, able to hear about findings that weren't made public, gathering details to supplement what he had seen.

"He sure had me fooled," Alexa admitted. "Wonder how he cleaned up so well."

"Public restrooms probably," Jared suggested.

"It's so hard to believe. When he was Bob Camelion, you'd never know this guy was living on the street. He was so cultured, so refined."

"Guess that tells you not to take anything at face value," Jared said as he stood up to put their dishes into the sink.

Later that evening, when Jared and Alexa climbed into bed, they were still talking about the man. "That doesn't make his information less worthy," Jared reminded. "It just came from a variety of sources under false pretenses. Pretty ingenious if you ask me."

Alexa snuggled into Jared's shoulder, but she couldn't get comfortable. He, too, tossed and turned until, at 3 a.m., he bolted upright which of course, woke Alexa.

"What's the matter?" she asked, rubbing her eyes.

"I just had the craziest dream. Red was in it, wagging his finger as if to say, 'No. No. No.'"

By this time Alexa was wide awake. "What does that mean?"

"That I'm going down the wrong path?" Jared asked, half to himself. "That I overlooked something important?"

"Maybe it just means you've made a wrong assumption."

"About what?" Jared asked. "Are my theories about the art entirely off-base?"

"Obviously not. They were good enough to be published."

Alexa and Jared padded into the living room and sat on the couch. The city was still asleep. Street signs illuminated their apartment in a pale neon glow. A fire engine wailed in the distance. "Well, we must be wrong about something."

"Maybe, this has to do with our homeless friend," Alexa mused. "He's a rather complicated guy."

"That's for sure. He doesn't say much, but he's sharp. He thinks like a reporter."

Almost in slow motion, Alexa turned and stared at Jared. "Maybe that's it!" she said, sitting up straighter. "What if Bob

Camelion is the real deal—a working reporter—just posing as a homeless man to get closer to the truth? He would probably say that being invisible is the best thing since sliced bread."

Jared looked at Alexa with a sense of revelation. "Could be. It would be just as easy for him to dress down as it would be to dress up." Jared paused to think. "Imagine the stamina it would take to live on the street for the sake of a story."

"Imagine the dedication," Alexa added.

"Either way, I owe him one. His insight was worth its weight in gold."

The following weekend, Jared and Alexa set off for the waterfront, determined to get to the truth. When they cornered the homeless man again, the fellow turned his back and started to walk away. "Hey, there. Wait up! I want to talk to you," Jared demanded.

"I've told you everything I know," the scruffy man said, reluctantly stopping.

"Not quite. We want to know who you really are," Alexa insisted.

"Some things are better left unsaid," he muttered. The man paused to scratch his beard and rummage in his cart. He extracted a battered cowboy hat and set it on his head. Without saying anything else, he resumed his stroll.

"Well, whoever you are, you certainly helped Jared out," Alexa called after the man.

Jared got a peculiar look in his eyes and moved closer to Alexa. "Maybe he wanted to help you, too."

Alexa had no idea what Jared meant until they returned to the diner. That's when she saw the newspaper spread out on a table and noticed a sidebar she had originally missed.

The sidebar read, "Aspiring journalist and unlikely witness propose theories about missing Gardner Museum art." She stared at the byline: "By J. Red Sutherland and William Buck." Alexa shook her head in disbelief. "Bill Buck?" she asked. "What are the odds?"

"I know. When the waitress told me his name, I just about keeled over."

By this time, the scruffy man was out of sight, his frail form and overflowing cart swallowed up by the city. No one saw him adjust his string tie that was threaded through a disk of silver. No one heard him humming an old Civil War piano tune.

AFTERWORD and ATTRIBUTIONS

Although a work of historical fiction, *Silver Line* utilizes documented facts, timelines, and pages from newspapers like the *Rocky Mountain News,* circa 1860, to create a credible scenario for the story. While loosely built on the Silver Heels legend, the goal was not to retell the folklore but to use it as a springboard in developing characters who could anchor a plot.

Inspiration for this tale came years before writing it, while on a cross-country camping trip among the deserted mines and ghost towns of the Southwest – Tropeka Mine in the Mojave Desert; Bodie, east the Sierra Nevadas; Goldfield in Arizona and many locations off the beaten path. Upon returning to California where I was living at the time, I ordered a booklet called "Six Racy Madams of Colorado" by Caroline Bancroft, Copyright 1965, published by the Johnson Publishing Company, Boulder, Colorado. This eye-opening pamphlet, complete with photos and illustrations, brought to life an era that fascinated me. It wasn't until a few years ago, that I dove into writing *Silver Line*. I don't want to say, "the story wrote itself," but the opening certainly did, as I imagined what it would be like to be a dance hall girl living in a bawdy mining town.

To set the mood, I spent many hours reading through the comprehensive "Old West" series from Time-Life Books (©1973-1976). Each volume is bound in a cover that looks like hand-tooled leather: *Cowboys* (text by William H. Forbis), *Chroniclers* (text by Keith Wheeler), *Gunfighters* (text by Paul Trachtman), *Indians* (text by Benjamin Cappa), *Townsmen* (text by Keith Wheeler), and *Trailblazers* (text by Bil Gilbert)—all rich in dates, details, and photos.

Also intrigued by a more contemporary mystery—the unsolved 1990 art heist at the Isabella Stewart Gardner Museum in Boston—I wondered if I could combine the two. A stretch, maybe, but not impossible when you have an active imagination and the tool of time travel.

Perhaps this odd connection was meant to be, because by total coincidence, I found myself at the Boston Book Festival a couple years ago, sitting in a session hosted by Stephen Kurkjian, the accomplished *Boston Globe* Spotlight reporter (expert on the Gardner Museum heist) and author of *Master Thieves* (Copyright 2015, published in the United States by Public Affairs™, a Member of the Perseus Books Group). I bought the book and talked with him briefly. His writing led me to other resources, including the Gardner Museum website, videos of FBI interviews, and the more recent "Last Seen" podcast series produced by WBUR radio and the *Boston Globe*. I also drew on personal experience, having walked through the Fens to get to the Museum as Jared did.

HISTORIC TIMES

Locations: For the core of the book, I relied on online sources about Colorado prior to the Civil War. To learn about Buckskin Joe, I turned to Legends of America, Ghost Towns, and a site called Explore Old West Colorado, which provided photos of the town. I also relied on the National Park Service and local websites such as the Denver Public Library. I learned about Bill Buck from a May 2011 article by adamjamesjones.wordpress.com and in the process, discovered, although I did not read it, a book by

Tom Knebel called *The Road to Buckskin Joe*, a likely source for numerous posts.

Realtor.com provided information about the region in present time, as did Camp Colorado, Triple Blaze, Colorado Parks and Wildlife and Reserve America. Gold Bug Park offered insight into gold towns and frontier characters. I borrowed western slang from irongrizzly.com and rkcowles.wordpress.com and learned gold rush lingo from michaellamarr.com and the Gold Rush Trading Post. For Jared's early experience in envisioning Africa, I turned to Interesting Africa Facts. To determine the distance between Alma and Denver, I used Distance Between Cities. For plausible timing of stage coach travel, I drew from Outrun Change and mnn.com/green-tech, as well as several chat boards.

Mining: For specifics about Red's lunchbox, I turned to darylburkhard.com, Kittredge Mercantile, and Ruby Lane. To understand the tools and terms of mining, I referred to mindat.org, geology.com and the Clark Fork Education Program. The Smithsonian's National Museum of American History website provided excellent information about mining lamps and headgear. I learned about pickaxes from Sierra Nevada Geotourism, about gold pokes from the Yukon Museums in Canada, and about gold grades from Investing News Network. I discovered specifics about the minting company, Clark Gruber, and about coin styles from the philatelist, Richard Frajola. I was educated about Sutter's sawmill thanks to The Museum of the City of San Francisco, the City of Placerville, the town of Coloma, Voice of America, and an article based on the book, *John Sutter and A Wider West* by Howard R. Lamar and Albert L. Hurtado. Appreciation goes to Iris H.W. Engstrand, Richard W. White, and Patricia Nelson Limerick for bringing to light the original spelling of the Suter name as it relates to John Sutter's father, Johann Jakob Suter, in a book called *The Diary of John A. Sutte*r, edited by Kenneth N. Owens.

I was informed about gold dust by lornet.com and Gold Fever Prospecting; about scales and coins at gilia.com and Old West Gold; about staking claims and claim jumping at My Goldrush

Tales as well as The Prospector. Stanford University also posted an excellent paper on the subject. I read about assaying at the Idaho State Historical Society and about the Denver Mint at United States Mint.

To understand the differences between patented and unpatented mines, I turned to Mine Engineer and Gold Rush Expeditions. I learned about the early Bureau of Land Management and land ownership at the Environmental Working Group. I gained significant insight into the Homestead Act of 1862 from The National Archives and Colorado Preservation, Inc. In viewing "proof papers" required for acquiring land (May 20, 1862 and June 21, 1866), I got an acute sense of the past. The History Channel's website and The Bureau of Land Management (Department of the Interior), through a story by Mary Apple, was particularly helpful. The National Archives was also valuable in displaying an application to the Homestead Land Office in Brownville, Nebraska Territory, from Jan. 1, 1863. The University of Nebraska Lincoln, Great Plains Studies helped explain the role and rights of women.

Building and Construction: I looked at pictures of miners and mining shacks at Park County Local History Archives, Colorado History, Mining Artifacts and History and Western Mining History to get a sense of the community. The Mining Bureau (not to be confused with the U.S. Bureau of Mines) informed me about Horace Greeley, and resources like Grubstaker, provided details about the use of arrastras. The South Park National Heritage Area website covers the region where *Silver Line* takes place, and it offered an excellent chronology of mining events. From the University of Northern Colorado's Hewit Institute, I learned about Texas log cabins. I also gained visual cues by seeing photos of the Tabor's Store and Dance Hall through Legends of America. I deducted that Lydia could have lived in a structure such as those and described them accordingly. ThoughtCo and The Elevator Museum confirmed that elevator use would have been possible in Denver at the time.

People and Business: Although I initially made up the Doc Jones character, I later found, through Colorado Travel News, that a *real* Doc Jones lived in the area. I read about religion of the time at Hub Pages Network. To grasp the political climate, I turned to the Department of Political Science at Northwestern, the Columbine Genealogical and Historical Society, and the Pony Express National Museum. I became acquainted with women who lived during the Civil War through the Historical Society of Pennsylvania and the University of Vermont. I learned about local cemeteries from Colorado Gravestones, and to depict actual people who lived in the region, I researched obits in the Fairplay *Flume Newspaper* and drew details from Timothy Hughes Rare & Early Newspapers. Colorado: Come to Life gave me the name of Giles Ilett who I recreated as a living person. Intangibility was also helpful. The University of Colorado, Boulder, informed me about the Arapaho. To correctly describe banking and general store transactions, I reviewed images of paper money and 'demand notes' at Antique Money, the U.S. Currency Education Program, Old Currency Buyers, and the U.S. Department of the Treasury. I read about the impact of Lincoln's election on currency at U.S. Coin Values and Coin Community. The Digital Collections at the Denver Public Library and Colorado History provided images of stage coaches and details about the Dan McLaughlin Stage. The stagecoach photo-illustration used in marketing this book is my own work, adapted from a photo I took in Tombstone, AZ. For a sense of place, I checked antique maps at the Philadelphia Print Shop Ltd. I learned about crops grown in 1860 from the *New York Times* in an August, 2004, article and from Michigan State University. I discovered the importance of sugar beets at the AMBIFI Directory, Life on a Colorado Farm, and from Colorado Magazine which described the Great Western Sugar Beet Mill. Other helpful sources include the Greeley Chamber of Commerce and the Minnesota Historical Society which confirmed there was no leap year in 1862. I read about vintage cash registers at The Museum of American History.

Clothing and personal care: Exceptional detail about miner's clothing came from history.oldcolo.com and an article by Ruth Lang called "Clothing of the Gold Miners in the 1850s." From her, I learned about waders, oil cloth dusters, caps and canvas trousers. Stetson and Cowboy Hats in History provided valuable insight and substantiated the location context for my character, Red. Witness to Fashion was helpful in describing women's mining clothing. To learn about genteel attire, I turned to Recreating the 19th Century Ballroom, where I obtained information about slippers. Memorial Hall Museum Online from Deerfield, MA, informed me about undergarments. To properly convey men's hairstyles, I relied on University of Vermont, New Zealand History, and Badass Civil War Beards. Sara's Parasols informed me about Victorian parasols, Miller's Millinery illustrated multiple bonnet styles, and Basenotes provided general information about women's wear. I was able to identify the actual proprietors of Denver stores that existed in the 1860s from the Colorado Historic Newspaper Collection which named Mrs. A.R. Palmer and her Millinery & Fancy Store at Fourth and Front Streets in an ad in the *Rocky Mountain News*. I found Mrs. G.W. Bacon in the same newspaper, February 18, 1862, which listed her occupation as "Fashionable Dress & Cloak Maker." I read about soap at Soap History and about hair styling aids, razors, and Rowland's Macassar Oil on The History of the World of Hair. I also learned about soaps and perfumes through the International Wellness Directory, from the *Marshall Texas Republican,* February 2, 1861, from the *Savannah Republican* (Georgia), August 14, 1861 and from the *Daily Chronicle and Sentinel*, Augusta, Georgia, July 31, 1861, which specifically mentioned Hunt's Bridal Wreath Perfume.

Food, hearth, and home: To understand what people ate in the 1860s, I turned to The Food Timeline and Food Reference. Back in My Time: A Writer's Guide to the 19th Century and Legends of America: Saloons of the American West, aptly described saloon fare. Vintage Recipes and Your Aroma Therapy Guide provided actual recipes. Choosing Voluntary Simplicity detailed food prices, indicating that eggs would have typically cost 20-cents a dozen, but other sources, citing scarcity and gouging, put Denver pricing at ten times that. The Colfax Avenue Historical Society describes a dozen eggs being purchased at $2.50 by Schuyler Colfax's step-sister, Clara, to accommodate the future VP's favorite breakfast request. SF Gate and The Connexion for French News informed about potatoes. Forager Chef, Tulips in the Woods, and B & W Quality Growers described the joy of harvesting watercress in winter streams. Reprints of menus by the Boston Athenaeum provided a good sense of hotel fare. To describe an 1860s kitchen, I drew from Merrymeeting Archives, the Five Mile House, Antique Stoves and Old House Online. The TN Gen Web Project vividly portrayed one-room cabins. An article by Dallas Bogan, originally published in the *LaFollette Press,* and repurposed in the *Post*, discussed fireplace heating. I read about Victorian dining and the popularity of Jaune Mange pudding at Victorian Interiors and More and at The Oldie Foodie in a July, 2009, article. I verified that the can opener was invented in 1858. To correctly describe cooking appliances and supplies used on the Oregon Trail, I went to the Bureau of Land Management, The Smithsonian's National Museum of American History, and Appalachian Heritage.

Society and Décor: I learned about vintage Christmas ornaments from Old-Fashioned Holidays and Family Christmas Online, discovering that Hans Greiner introduced glass ornaments in the shapes of nuts and berries around 1847. I read about early street lighting at the Illuminating Engineering Society, ThoughtCo, and City of Boston Public Works, learning that the first patent for a gaslight was issued in 1810 to David Melville. Oil Lamp Antiques informed me about flat wick lamps and kerosene lighting. Deeds Design gave me insight into batwing doors. A blog at Victorian Interiors and More, by Gail Caskey Winkler and Roger Moss, ably described kerosene lamps, gardens, and popular color tones, referencing *Godey's Lady Book* of 1860 which cautioned against toxic, arsenic-infused green wallpaper. Here I also learned about floor cloths and drugget. I checked out pressback chairs at

Ancient Point and read about bedding at Strobel and The Better Sleep Council. Photo Tree provided in-depth information about tintypes and albumen prints; CO Gen Web detailed photographic plate sizes. Classical Works and United States Civil War taught me about 1860s music. I read about "The Battle Hymn of the Republic" and its origins as "John Brown's Body" at History Net. I listened to other timely tunes at OCLC World Cat and reviewed lyrics at Public Domain Music. I learned about player pianos from the Globe Gazette which offered a handsome image of a Civil War-era piano photographed by Jim Cross for the *Mitchell County Press News*. To confirm that Valentine's Day was recognized in the 1860s, I checked the History Channel website from A & E Networks.

Weddings: Details about wedding dresses came from Godey's Knits of 1860, Victoriana Magazine, All That Is Interesting (ATI), and Patches From the Past which mentioned the use of orange blossoms. One specific post by Sarah Begley from TIME magazine, 2015, called "The White Dress That Changed Everything," provided terrific context. Fact Retriever and The Ohio State University Historic Costumes and Textile Collection were also helpful. Susana Ives offered additional background about wedding traditions and the use of orange blossoms. I learned about vintage wedding clothes and the wedding breakfast at Tea Cakes and Teddy Bears, The Knot, and The Wedding Specialists. Yahoo provided a good overview of hotel bathing and indoor plumbing. National Public Radio confirmed Mendelssohn's "Midsummer's Night Dream" as an appropriate recessional, used by Queen Victoria in 1858. The Rare Wine Co., Eater, and Wine Searcher confirmed wines of the time, such as Madeira. Civil War Talk and the Pearl Wine Company also added important insight into beverages. A 2011 post in the *New York Times* reported on Civil War-era foods. I gained information about engagement and wedding rings from Wedding Zone and *Reader's Digest* which also addressed hair jewels popular in the 1800s. At 1stdibs I confirmed that garnets were appropriate for Victorian wedding rings.

Nature: I needed many specifics about birds, trees, and flowers. To verify what I know as "Mormon Tea" and other dry landscape plants, I turned to the United States Department of Agriculture, Web MD, and Mojave Desert. I learned about Colorado wildflowers, especially columbine, at The Flower Expert, Wildflowers of Colorado, and the National Park Service. Study Dot Com described the calyx in depth. I listened to the sound of the lark bunting at Larkwire and the chickadee at Annenberg Learner. The Cornell Lab of Ornithology, The Internet Bird Collection, and the National Audubon Society provided expansive information about birds in general. When I wanted to incorporate an owl into one of Jared's visions, I confirmed the symbolism at Spirit Animal Totems and Spirit Animal, relying on a post by their editor, Elan Harris. To accurately portray the life cycle of aspen trees and katydids, I turned to the Aspen Chamber, Insect Identification and Bug Guide. For a tutorial on growing citrus indoors, I relied on Martha Stewart and the Garden Geeks. I studied how to build a snow cave at Instructables and Enviro-Tech International, via a post by Randy Gerke.

Population: To get a sense of Western population in the 1860s, I went to Alter Net. The State of Texas provided a good overview of the region. Texas Escapes, Texas Almanac and Texas Rach Life were also helpful. History Colorado, Denver: The Mile High City and Genealogy Images of History taught me about stage coaches and politicians. CO Gen Web provided excellent details about Denver streets and life in the 1800s -- ranging from duels to fires. Through various sources, I confirmed that Denver was originally part of the Kansas Territory. Larimer Square, Indian Country Today, Denver Water, and Garden Park Dinos, which featured a 2012 post called "Historic Downtown Denver" by Dan Grenard, were very helpful. The History Channel's website documented some of the first stores in the city. Pictures from the Denver Public Library brought the area to life, showing the Blake Street Vault, bordellos, and noting that there were 17 opium shops in the city at one time. For information about Independence, Missouri, and the Oregon

Trail, I turned to History Globe and the City of Independence, Missouri. Information about the Santa Fe trail came from the National Frontier Trails Museum in Missouri. The Biographical Directory of the United States Congress and the Colfax Avenue Historical Society established a connection between Daniel Witter and Schuyler Colfax. To see actual articles and ads of the day, I visited the Library of Congress website, Genealogy Bank, the *Rocky Mountain News* (which first published April 23,1859) and Colorado Historic Newspapers Collection which alerted me to the *Miners' Record* for the Tarryall Region. Civil War Talk confirmed that the *Rocky Mountain News* was pro-North. For information about vintage weapons, I went to the NRA Museums, the Military Factory, and Wide Open Spaces.

Medicine: Many sources described the smallpox epidemics that befell America. The History of Vaccines and the College of Arts and Sciences at Case Western Reserve University in Ohio were particularly helpful. One interesting resource, "History of Smallpox in America," by Michele R. Berman, MD, published June 14, 2011, positioned immunity as a military advantage. CNN Interactive (October 2014), History Link, and Access Genealogy provided good timelines. I turned to numerous Colorado references to learn about early healthcare in the Denver area. I also found excellent information about nurses' uniforms, including Civil War era photos from: Female Nurses of the Civil War, the Dover, NJ Library, ThoughtCo on Women's History, and posts about Florence Nightingale at Biography. Methods for disease prevention and containment were thoughtfully discussed at Gettysburg, Pennsylvania: Historic Crossroads, and I confirmed the difference between a sprain and a strain at Very Well. On the Forgotten Books website, I saw a cover of the *Louisville Medical Journal* from February 1860, and through the Bernard Becker Medical Library, Washington University School of Medicine, I learned that the *Medical Repository* was the first medical journal in the United States, used during the 1797-1824 period, followed by the *Boston Medical and Surgical Journal* 1828-1928. Science Friday provided valuable information about vaccines.

MODERN TIMES

Isabella Stewart Gardner Museum: For information about the contemporary museum heist, I started at the Gardner Museum website and took the virtual tour. (It's been a while since I visited.) I read numerous articles published in the *Boston Herald* and the *Boston Globe* at the time of the incident and in years following it. A March 13, 2005, *Globe* story by Stephen Kurkjian was particularly helpful in recounting the events, as was the crime blotter from ABC News. The *New York Times* on 3/1/15 also provided an good recap. "Boston's Last Great Unsolved Mystery", an excellent video produced by the *Boston Globe*, and their March 18, 2017, update by Shelley Murphy and Stephen Kurkjian, called "Six Theories Behind the Stolen Gardner Museum Paintings," keep the story alive. More recently (in September 2018) WBUR (Boston's NPR News Station) collaborated with the *Boston Globe* and aired the first episode ("81 Minutes") of a series of podcasts called "Last Seen." From that broadcast, I learned things that I hadn't previously known: the names of both museum guards on duty that night and the fact that the paint was so thick on the canvas of Rembrandt's *Christ in the Storm on the Sea of Galilee*, that although the painting was cut from its stretcher, it could not be rolled. To hear first-hand accounts, I watched interviews with museum staff and law enforcement agents posted on YouTube. A site about Dutch master Rembrandt Van Rijn and Biography offered vivid details about the artist. Independent Bartending and Frommers provided a sense of life in Leiden. I learned that the recovery of stolen artwork continues to be newsworthy. For example, CBS News reported that two stolen Van Gogh's were returned to the Netherlands 14 years after they went missing. NBC News reported on a returned Rockwell 4/1/17. Radar Online ran a 5/2/16 item about "Bobby the Cook," whose home was raided twice in search of the Gardner art. To confirm the sizes of missing artwork, I visited The Federal Bureau of Investigation and then used Metric Conversions to calculate inch equivalents. CBC Radio - Canada and Essential Vermeer provided guidelines to pricing. The latter source also informed about "The Procuress," a painting by someone else, that appears within several Vermeer pieces. Business Insider, March 2016, published an article about the largest heists of all times, complete with an infographic noting values and status. A Reuters posting from June 4, 2018, headlined "Van Gogh Landscape Sells for 7 Million Euros at Auction," confirmed legitimate selling prices, and an October 16, 2012 *Forbes* article by Caleb Melby entitled "How to Sell Stolen Art, And Why You Shouldn't Bother," addressed black market pricing.

Trucks and Roadways: Answers and Truckers Report provided facts about 18-wheelers and their weight. Worried that the fate of the shady art dealers in *Silver Line* might be too preposterous, I checked Discover the Odds, the National Safety Council, and Brain of Brian to verify that accidents of this nature do happen. Research revealed many examples: Mike D. Smith at Al Com (Alabama news) reported on a similar accident, February 11, 2014. In May, 2015, CNN , New York Daily News, and many other news outlets, covered a Texas woman who fell from an overpass but managed to shield and save her baby. WBZ-TV Boston has shown a photo of a truck hanging over an overpass as did archives at Boston.com, in November 2013. The Massachusetts Department of Transportation was also helpful in documenting accidents related to road debris or guardrail failure.

Boston Basics: I learned about the Big Dig from WBUR 90.9 radio (7/12/12) in a comprehensive report by Nate Goldman and through the state of Massachusetts. Road Traffic Technology addressed tunnel jacking and graphics from Boston.com, in a *Boston Globe* article by Peter J. Howe 3/8/99, offered renderings of the technique. I confirmed a typical college class schedule at Boston University and turned to Trinity College of Arts and Sciences at Duke University for requirements of an independent study. I verified at the Department of Justice, Office of Information Policy, that anyone can request material under the Freedom of Information Act, as might a journalism student. I learned about the Underground Railroad at the Public Broadcasting Service,

National Park Service, History of Massachusetts blog and at *The Salem News* in a post by Muriel Hoffacker, February 13, 2010. The National Park Service offered extensive detail about the Lewis and Harriet Hayden House, but it wasn't until I visited the Travel pages at Boston.com did I realize the street name matched the name of the Phillips Mine in Buckskin Joe. The Museum of African American History was also helpful. I read about the Fens at the Emerald Necklace Conservancy and learned about WWII fighter planes at The Top Tens. American in WWII educated me about radios. I confirmed details about Halloween activities in Salem, MA, at the City Guide for Salem, New England Travel Planner & Guide, and Boston Harbor Cruises.

Campus tunnels: To include the possibility of transporting artwork via subterranean tunnels, I drew from first-hand experience having walked through the underground corridors beneath Harvard Business School. I learned more about these structures in a 1/27/15 post from the Huffington Post and from MIT News (2015), The Harvard Crimson (10/19/1978 and 12/4/1993), and BU Today (2012). The Boston Street Railway Association also provided insight into Boston tunnels as did Above Top Secret.

ABOUT THE AUTHOR

Jill C. Baker grew up in a small town in New York state where, as a teenager, she wrote a weekly newspaper column and reviewed summer stock theater. She pursued her interest in media and writing at Boston University's College of Communication. Upon graduation, she moved to Southern California to work in the film production. With a relocation to San Francisco and eventually back to Boston, she returned to her newspaper roots, serving as a copywriter and promotion manager for leading publishers such as Hearst and Harte-Hanks. Following a detour into the non-profit sector, she became Director of Marketing for a digital publishing provider in the magazine industry. Constantly facing deadlines and rigorous commutes, she often wondered what it would be like to simply disappear and do something else—thus the motivation for the Sutherland Series. She and her husband live in New England where they've raised two sons and several cats. The rich historic setting provides valuable inspiration.